In the Last Terrible Moments
of the Great War,
amid the Dead and Dying,
a New Hope, a New Life . . .

Lieutenant Ian Saxon rolled up his sleeves and prepared to deliver a baby . . .

The woman never spoke, although her lips moved silently in what appeared to be prayer. She was bathed in sweat as she strained downward, panting, every part of her body laboring to bring her child into the world. She gripped Ian's hands, holding on to him, using his strength as leverage for the last urgent heaving of her body.

There was one long violent contraction that brought a moan of pain to her lips, and her eyes rolled upward. Ian kneaded her hands, brushed her damp hair back from her face, afraid she was dying, willing her to live.

Then he looked down and saw the baby's head emerge, and his hands went instinctively to the tiny skull to guide its progress. He felt a surge of elation, a sudden euphoria that seemed to renew his flagging strength and communicate hope to the woman.

Suddenly he was holding a slippery baby girl, a shivering blue scrap of humanity that uttered a thin wail of outrage before Ian remembered he was supposed to slap the tiny bottom. He laid the baby down on her mother's breast . . .

And a Great Saga Begins . . .
ROSES IN WINTER

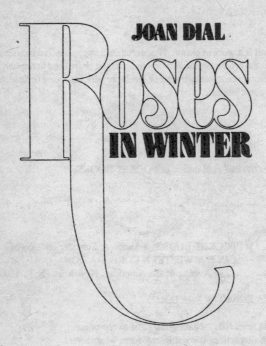

JOAN DIAL

Roses
IN WINTER

PUBLISHED BY POCKET BOOKS NEW YORK

Another *Original* publication of POCKET BOOKS

POCKET BOOKS, a Simon & Schuster division of
GULF & WESTERN CORPORATION
1230 Avenue of the Americas, New York, N.Y. 10020

ISBN: 0-671-41983-8

First Pocket Books printing September, 1982

10 9 8 7 6 5 4 3 2 1

POCKET and colophon are trademarks of Simon & Schuster.

Printed in the U.S.A.

For Missy

And to keep loyalties young, I'll write those names
Golden forever, eagles, crying flames
And set them as a banner, that men may know
To dare the generations, burn, and blow
Out on the wind of time, shining and streaming . . .

Mataiea, 1914
"The Great Lover"

Chapter 1

France,
November 11, 1918

HOSTILITIES WILL CEASE AT 1100 HOURS TODAY, NOVEM-
BER 11. TROOPS WILL STAND FAST ON THE LINE REACHED AT
THAT HOUR.

The message had gone out from Advanced GHQ at dawn,
and now, less than an hour until the end of the four years of
bloodletting that history would call the Great War, a British
patrol probing ahead of their battalion reached a small village
east of Valenciennes.

A German lieutenant, lying propped against a shell-
ravaged stone cottage, watched impassively as they approached. His right leg was soaked with fresh blood, and a
hastily applied bandage did not keep the shattered bones of
his thigh from protruding.

It seemed obvious to the young replacement officer leading
the British patrol that the German had been left for the better
medical attention the Allies could provide. Lieutenant Ian
Saxon told his corporal to give the German a cigarette. He
took it with a faintly derisive smile. Lieutenant Saxon then
began to explain in halting German that the stretcher bearers
would arrive shortly.

The German interrupted, "I shall be all right. There is no
hurry." His English was flawless, educated.

"Your name and rank?"

"Rauch, Wolfgang, Oberleutnant." He began to give his serial number in his own language, stopped, and gave it in English.

Ian Saxon said, "Are you the only one of your chaps here? The village appears to be deserted."

"The last of our rear guards left—perhaps two hours ago. The village is empty," Rauch answered, accepting a light for his cigarette.

"Good, good. Not much longer to go now. We don't want to precipitate anything." The English officer was silently battling a throbbing headache and the leaden limbs of fatigue. There was a gray pallor to his skin, and his eyes were unnaturally bright. He turned to the noncom at his side. "What time is it, Corporal?"

"Nearly half past, sir." The corporal was a reed-thin Cockney with the haggard look of a man who has seen too much suffering.

"Take a message back to the battalion that the village is deserted. They might as well come in."

The battalion arrived fifteen minutes later, a khaki column of weary men counting the minutes until the armistice freed them from the horror of killing or being killed. Halting, they formed ranks in the village square.

Instantly machine-gun fire opened from every vantage point, including the church tower. Ian and his patrol were still on the outskirts of the village, and the barrage of gunfire sent them racing toward the square. They arrived in time to see bullets screaming into the tightly packed lines, showering blood, torn flesh, and splintered bone on those who had not yet been hit, so that they spun in undecided circles, unsure whether to help fallen comrades or dive for cover. After a few seconds it was obvious that those still on their feet were unable to tell if the blood in their eyes was their own or that of the wounded men crumpling beside them.

Ian shook his head in disbelief. He grabbed the shoulders of the nearest moaning man and pulled him from the square, ran back to disentangle a blood-and-khaki confusion of arms and legs; aghast at the blind Teutonic dedication of the Germans, determined to die despite the eleventh hour of the war.

"Take cover! Take cover!" he yelled, crouching over a boy-soldier whose face was half shot away. Other shouted commands rose over the staccato crack of gunfire that sent the able-bodied sprinting for the buildings to root out the machine-gun nests. Ian's order died on his lips as he saw the enraged men storm into the buildings. He did not follow, but bent to pick up the wounded private. There were more than enough troops to take care of the machine gunners, who were cold-bloodedly using their last minutes to finish off the wounded men in the square.

He heard grenades silence a machine-gun crew even as men on the ground died from their last round of bullets. Looking up, he saw some of the English soldiers leap into the midst of a roof-based nest to slash wildly with bayonets and shoot at point-blank range. None of the Germans raised their hands in surrender; they went down still feeding clips of bullets into their guns.

The machine-gun crew in the church tower was the last to fall. They kept up rapid fire, aware that the other German guns had been silenced, aware of the superior force about to engulf them, *aware,* Ian thought, in numb horror, *of their own impending deaths . . .*

When the gunfire ended, Ian saw the corporal of his scouting party race back through the village. Ian realized his intent and followed. He was unsure if what he felt was blood lust or merely rage at the stupidity of it all.

The German lieutenant with the shattered thigh sat where they had left him, his expression now scornful, chin tilted, ice-blue eyes never blinking when the corporal's bayonet descended.

Steel ripped open his chest, driven into his heart again and again. The contemptuous expression froze on his face.

"He's dead, Corporal." Ian was sweating and his voice was hoarse. He had difficulty swallowing. He grabbed the corporal's shoulder to try to stop the butchery. The corporal wheeled around to face him, and Ian saw his eyes were filled with tears, making rivulets down his smoke-streaked face. For a split second Ian wondered if the man would slash his own officer in his frenzy of retribution, but at that precise moment they heard the woman's cry.

Startled, they stared at each other, then looked at the ruined cottage.

"Go around the back," Ian whispered. "I'll go in the front way. It could be another trap."

Most of the cottage roof had been blown away by shellfire, and the sunlight illuminated pitiful remnants of broken furniture, pots and pans lying about the littered floor. In a corner of the room lay a very young girl. She was covered by an army blanket that did not conceal her advanced pregnancy.

A delicate and piquant face, framed by tangled waves of dark hair, was dominated by eyes of smoky gray as iridescent as pearls. The compelling eyes were filled with pain and, oddly, defiance. Small white teeth came down over her sensually full lower lip, biting back another cry of pain.

"Parlez vous anglais?" Ian asked inadequately, more proficient in Latin than in French. Even if he had spoken her language, his embarrassment at her condition was more acute than his curiosity about her presence near the fighting.

She shook her head. Her eyes flickered in the direction of a tipped-over table near where she lay. Ian followed her glance and saw boots and khaki-clad legs lying on the floor.

"Corporal!" Ian shouted, approaching the body cautiously. The corporal appeared at the back door, rifle at the ready. Together they dragged the unconscious soldier into the middle of the room, turned him over to listen for a heartbeat. He was alive but bleeding profusely from a head wound.

"Blimey," the corporal said. "He's a doughboy. What's an American doing here? I didn't know there was any Americans near here, did you, sir?"

Ian turned the man face downward again and pulled an immaculate handkerchief from his pocket to press to the wound. "Go quickly and bring stretcher bearers, Corporal. A doctor would be better still. I believe the lady is about to give birth."

The corporal hurried away as Ian unhooked his canteen. He offered the water to the woman, who shook her head as a contraction gripped her body. She twisted convulsively, a scream held behind clenched teeth. Helplessly Ian picked up her hand, and her fingers bit into his. She turned her head and looked up at him. Meeting her pain-filled gaze, he felt his breath catch somewhere between his heart and his throat. Transfixed, he could only stare speechlessly. Something in the mute appeal of her eyes touched him in a way nothing before had ever touched him. He felt a wave of intense compassion. She was so vulnerable, helpless.

As the minutes ticked away Ian held her hands, mopped her brow, and felt her pain. He had seen men writhe in agony, suffering and dying inside broken shells of bodies. He had learned to accept that in war it was necessary for some to die. Now he was witnessing pain that had some meaning and hope and he was profoundly moved.

He ministered to the woman, murmuring to her in a language she surely did not understand, trying to convey his solicitude. Occasionally he left her side briefly to tighten the compress staunching the bleeding of the American's wound. Time was measured by the ever-increasing frequency of the young mother's labor, and Ian was beginning to suspect the corporal had been unable to persuade stretcher bearers or doctor to leave the wounded in the square.

Glancing at his watch again, he wondered what had taken place at the cottage before they arrived. The German outside had obviously been wounded by shellfire. Was the American a deserter, that he was so far from his own troops? It didn't seem likely, since he was in uniform. Had the German attacked him? That didn't seem likely either. The German would have killed him.

The woman then? She was perhaps on her way to a midwife, took shelter here, and was surprised by the American. She could have struck him from behind with a blunt instrument. But why? She was French, and the American would protect her from the German. What was she doing here, anyway, at such a time?

When her contractions became one long continuous pain and still the corporal had not returned, Ian rolled up his sleeves and prepared to deliver a baby. The American was still unconscious, the handkerchief-compress darkening ominously on his head wound.

The woman never spoke, although her lips moved silently in what appeared to be prayer. She was bathed in sweat as she strained downward, panting, every part of her body laboring to bring her child into the world. Her abdomen rose, grew rigid, fell. She gripped Ian's hands, holding on to him, using his strength as leverage for the last urgent heaving of her body.

There was one long violent contraction that brought a moan of pain to her lips and her eyes rolled upward. Ian kneaded her hands, brushed her damp hair back from her face, afraid she was dying; willing her to live.

Then he looked down and saw the baby's head emerge, and his hands went instinctively to the tiny skull to guide its progress. He felt a surge of elation, a sudden euphoria that seemed to renew his flagging strength and communicate hope to the woman.

Suddenly he was holding a slippery baby girl, a shivering blue scrap of humanity that uttered a thin wail of outrage before Ian remembered he was supposed to slap the tiny bottom. He laid the baby down on her mother's breast, wondering how he should sterilize his knife to cut the umbilical cord, when he heard voices outside. English voices; part of his battalion. Gratefully he called out to them, identifying himself.

Oddly, now that help was at hand, Ian felt a wave of dizziness. He looked up at the amazed circle of soldiers as though from deep inside a dark pit. Strangely, when he opened his mouth to speak, words would not come.

"I say, old boy, what *have* you stumbled into?" a voice asked. "Good lord—bring that stretcher in here."

Ian tried feebly to protest when he felt himself being eased down on the stretcher. Were they mad? There was a woman and a newborn infant, and a badly wounded, unconscious American. But everything rushed away and disappeared as Ian sank into oblivion.

He awakened in a bombed-out church that was being used as a field hospital, burning with fever, his teeth chattering. Every bone in his body ached, and it felt as though someone had rammed a brick down each side of his throat.

A doctor wearing a bloodstained surgical gown came slowly into focus. He met Ian's bewildered stare over the top of a chart he was studying. "Influenza," the doctor said. "Rotten luck. War's over. Eleventh hour of the eleventh day has passed. You've been delirious for the past two days, but we're going to pull you through."

Ian was in the ruined sacristy, in isolation. Through the half-open door behind the doctor stretched row upon row of wounded men, jammed side by side in every available inch of space. A low murmur of agony hung in the air, along with the stench of ether and blood and putrid flesh.

The others . . . in the cottage? Ian's question was a painful croak.

"Ah, yes. The American was treated and returned to his own company. Nasty head wound. They sent you a message yesterday, thanking you for helping him. He went to an aid station and then on to a forwarding camp. The Americans are sending their men home as solid divisions . . . I hope that poor devil lives long enough. They're hard hit by influenza too. I heard two hundred and fifty a day are dying of flu at Pontanezen. Let me see, I wrote down the message from the

American's company somewhere, along with his name. Here it is, *John M. Lauren.*"

And the woman and baby?

"Well . . ." The doctor's voice was guarded. "They were taken to a convent not far from here. All we could get out of the woman was the name of the convent. She was so agitated we decided to take them there rather than try to treat her ourselves. We sent word to French HQ to try to get a doctor over there. The woman was extremely weak."

Ian lay limply on his narrow pallet, thinking about the last hour of the war. Of death and life. Endings and beginnings. Above all, of the young mother. They had not exchanged words or thoughts, yet for a little while he had felt closer to her than to any other human being he had ever known. "How long until I can leave here?" he asked, feeling strength seep back and with it a sense of urgency.

"A fortnight, Lieutenant. At least."

He spent the next two weeks studying an English–French dictionary and daydreaming that the young mother was a war widow. On the day he was released to return to his company, Ian detoured to call at the Convent of the Sisters of Mary.

The convent was a Gothic structure, untouched by war, standing on a wooded hillside; a pastoral scene painted against the pale winter sky. Following a sweet-faced nun through the tranquil cloisters, he realized at last that the war was over. The aura of peace would soon be everywhere, not just in this sheltered spot.

The nun, who did not understand English or Ian's stumbling French, beckoned him into a small almost-bare room. An older nun was seated at a desk. She rose and greeted him, listening with growing concern as Ian explained why he had come.

"We are doing all we can, but, monsieur, I fear we are losing the battle," the mother superior said sadly. "She is still alive, but barely. She was weakened by the birth of her baby, you see, and contracted influenza."

Ian closed his eyes in mute sorrow. His fault, of course. Yet he meant only to help. He felt a wave of despair. Was there no end to the deadly irony of death and war?

Sympathetically the mother superior offered him a glass of wine. "We have been unable to learn who the mother is. She told us only her first name—Celine. We do not know where she comes from. Her accent is not common to these parts. We

have baptized the baby with the name Celine chose—
Geneva. The name seemed to have special significance to her.
Tell me, monsieur, have you known Celine long? Can you tell
us where to find her family?"

She was too polite to inquire if the baby was his, but Ian
saw the unspoken question in her eyes. He shook his head
wearily. Lying in the field hospital, he had allowed his mind
to weave a muted tapestry of hopes and dreams. Of perhaps
keeping in touch, helping in some way. And if the woman was
widowed. . . . Their shared ordeal and triumph of bringing a
new life into the world had helped him bear the anguish of
guilt he felt at taking the German lieutenant's word that the
village was empty.

"May I see her?" he asked.

"It would be better not to tire her. She is weak and we
think approaching the climax of her illness. But you may see
the baby."

At first he hesitated, but then, feeling obligated, went into
the nursery. He was surprised to find there were half a dozen
babies, side by side in handmade wooden cribs, and several
toddlers playing on the floor. "We run an orphanage here,"
the mother superior explained.

Celine's baby lay, pink and serene, swathed in a threadbare
blanket. She was awake, watching the golden specks of dust
float down a beam of sunlight near her crib. Her eyes had
already begun to glow like gray pearls, just like her mother's.
Tiny fingers closed around Ian's thumb as he touched the
small body wonderingly, thinking of the upheaval of birth.

Later he would wonder if that was the moment he knew he
would not be able to return to England and leave the child in
a French orphanage. Her mother died the following day,
victim of the virus Ian had given her, without telling anyone
who she was or where she came from.

Chapter 2

Saxon Hall,
Lancashire, England

A chauffeured Rolls-Royce passed through ornamental iron gates and proceeded sedately along a curving drive flanked by elms that had whispered a welcome for a hundred summers. Now they were winter-bare and silent.

Ian was tense, stiffly erect in his seat, gazing with unseeing eyes at the rolling lawns sweeping down to meet the trees. Had it been spring, there would have been daffodils and narcissus bordering the gravel of the drive. Rounding a curve, the house came into view. Originally a gabled Tudor manor, it had been restored many times over the years but retained a hint of its origins.

The car came smoothly to a halt, and Ian steeled himself for the confrontation with his mother. There had been a telephone call from London. His mother had told him of the memorial services for his father and brother, and Ian had promised to be there in time. His father and older brother had been killed on the Somme in 1916. A memorial service over two years later seemed to Ian a reminder that their sacrifice clouded his own homecoming.

He had hesitantly announced that he had fathered a child in France, having already decided that a blood connection was the only way to ensure the baby's acceptance. There had been a stunned pause, then his mother's strangled exclamation,

"Good God!" He had heard the long indrawn breath before she added, "We'd better wait until you get home to discuss the matter."

The chauffeur opened the car door, tipping his cap, and Ian stepped out, pausing for a moment to inhale deeply the chilled air. The land upon which the house stood had come to the Saxon family for service to their sovereign during the Wars of the Roses. Subsequent generations had been equally divided between prosperous merchants and loyal warriors. Ian had always felt like a changeling who had been substituted for a real Saxon, but this did not diminish his love for the gracious old house.

He walked slowly toward the front doors, which were flanked by a handsome pair of stone eagles reputed to have been a gift from Horace Walpole. Before he reached the eagles, the doors were flung open by a small plump woman, her face wreathed in smiles. She was dressed in black silk, a lacy jabot fastened to her ample bosom with a cameo brooch.

"Meredith!" Ian staggered under the onslaught of her hug. She had been governess to his father and was now taking up the reins for a third generation of Saxons.

Ian had always felt closer to Meredith than to his mother. It had been Meredith who bandaged grazed knees, applied hot poultices to congested chests, and listened sympathetically to a shy little boy's secret fears. Meredith, herself a childless spinster, had mothered all of them.

"Oh, you're far too thin," she lamented as the chauffeur brought in the luggage. "But we'll soon fatten you up. You'll find some changes, I'm afraid. We lost a number of the staff. We need a new butler badly—her ladyship thought you could see to it."

Ian looked around the entrance hall, where a combination of Grecian and Gothic styles blended harmoniously. There were a pair of marble busts at the foot of the staircase, and classic columns supported an upper gallery. Each generation of Saxons had made renovations and changes according to its own taste, with little regard for uniformity of period or design. That the effects were pleasing to the eye was a tribute to past Saxon respect for quality. A recent addition contributed the only jarring note. A massive grandfather clock, standing in an alcove that had formerly housed a statue, was monstrously ugly and, in a peculiar way, sinister.

"Where is Mother?" Ian asked.

"Up in the gallery." Meredith's face creased into a worried frown. Then she added brightly, "Terry is having his nap. He'll be down for tea."

The name jolted Ian for a second. His dead brother had also been called Terry, rather than Terence like their father. Terry's frail young wife had died delivering a second, stillborn son a few months after her husband was killed.

"I'll run up to the gallery then," he said, giving Meredith a fond smile that did not hide the trepidation in his eyes.

He went up the staircase, remembering the conversation he had with his mother the day he left to join the army. She had twirled in her pale fingers another white feather that had been delivered for Ian. The white feathers were sent to shirkers who had not rushed off to enlist in the army. The anonymous donors of that symbol of cowardice found a ready target in Lady Sybil Saxon, who felt personally affronted by Ian's reluctance to participate in the killing in France.

The wood of the balustrade was silken smooth; he trailed his hand, marveling at the simple pleasure of touch, the unexpected beauty of man's endeavors. For a moment he reveled in the pleasure of his senses, feeling both elated and guilty that he was alive when so many were not.

Opening the doors, he stepped into the gallery.

Lady Sybil Saxon was standing beneath two recently hung pictures, new to Ian. Full-length portraits of his father and brother, Terry, both in full dress uniforms. They joined all those other Saxon warriors, from the Boer War, the Crimea, the Indian Mutiny; opposite them were the naval heroes of Lady Saxon's family; a row of blue-uniformed, bearded seafarers, scowling behind sextants and ships' helms.

His mother was a tall, regal woman with light brown hair and hazel eyes, a commanding presence that dimmed lesser lights around her. Ian had inherited only her coloring. His heart sank when she turned and he saw the expression on her face.

Her greeting was cool. "Hello, Ian. How was the drive up from London?" She did not move toward him. He stood awkwardly, wanting to embrace her but held at bay by the accusation in her eyes. He murmured appropriate comments, knowing she was waiting for him to bring up the subject foremost on both of their minds.

At length her eyes flickered upward over the newly hung portraits. "How could you do this to them, Ian?"

"Mother, I know this has been a shock and I'm sorry. But the child is mine, I've acknowledged her and started the formalities necessary to get her out of France."

Her stare shriveled him. "You are a bachelor. What will people say? Why make a martyr of yourself because the mother died? Surely the family in France . . ." She waved a manicured hand, indicating the baby was their problem.

"There is no other family, Mother. Celine was an orphan. I can't have my daughter brought up in an orphanage."

"*Your* daughter." Lady Saxon's eyes deepened in anger. "What about Terry? Your brother died a hero. Why should his son share his home with your bastard?"

"That won't be necessary. I'll move out. I would still like to enter the Church—"

"That's out of the question now. God help us all, you are the only male member of the family to survive the war. You'll have to run the estate until Terry comes of age. There's been a great deal of trouble at the colliery; we shall have to involve ourselves more actively." She paced slowly up and down, still examining the portraits, and Ian was reminded of a galleon under sail.

"Then my daughter will live here with me," Ian said.

His mother sighed, unsure how to deal with her son's unexpected determination and needing him too much to cause a rift. If only Terry could have lived, taken his place as heir to the Saxon holdings. Then poor shy Ian could have been left to his own gentle pursuits.

"I expected a little peace in my old age, Ian. Instead I have a three-year-old grandson—and while Terry can be a delightful child when he chooses, he is also a handful." She had walked to the end of the gallery and was looking out of the window across the sculptured lawns, seeing the ghost of another charming little boy of chameleon moods, and remembering the scrapes her son Terry had got into as he grew to manhood. Yet it had been quiet and introverted Ian who produced the bastard.

"If you prefer, Mother, we could move into the guest house."

"Really, Ian. Now you're being ridiculous. The question is, if you're determined to do this, what shall we tell everyone? I suppose a secret marriage in France is the best thing?"

"There was no marriage—" Ian began, coloring as he remembered the embarrassment of Geneva's birth certificate and the suggestive grins of the French authorities.

The gallery doors burst open suddenly to admit a small boy with the face of a mischievous cherub, roguish amber eyes almost lost under a mop of golden curls and the force of sheer energy in every movement of his lithe body. He regarded them with solemn curiosity.

"Terry, darling—" Lady Saxon began, but her grandson darted across the gleaming oak floor to Ian, examining the uniform rather than the man wearing it.

Ian said, "Hello, young man. You don't remember me, do you? I'm your uncle Ian."

"Not Daddy?" Terry said, shaking his head sadly.

For an instant Lady Saxon's eyes, bright with tears, locked with Ian's. "No, darling. He's not your daddy." She choked on the word, swept Terry into her arms, and walked from the gallery.

Ian watched them go, then went to his room to remove the uniform. He did not wait for his valet to take care of it. As soon as he was dressed in civilian shirt and gray flannels, both hanging loosely on his gaunt frame, he took every reminder of his army service up to the attic.

As he stuffed the hated khaki tunic and trousers, Sam Browne belt, and swagger stick into the nearest steamer trunk, a kaleidoscopic picture of his military service lingered for a moment.

He no longer remembered the war as a sequence of events, but as sounds, images, single happenings. Mud that swallowed horses as well as men; arms and heads protruding from trench walls that had to be hacked off with shovels and buried; maggots squirming out of dried-mud cracks; mammoth rats gorged on human flesh; the stench of decomposing bodies, excrement, mustard gas, explosives. A pathetic line of soldiers with bandaged eyes, hands on the shoulders of the man in front, inching toward an aid station . . . the blind leading the blind. An embittered veteran officer telling him, "This war is being run by incompetents who consider it their duty never to see a wounded man, for fear it will impair their judgment. Remember that every time you're ordered over the top. The life expectancy here for a lieutenant is about seven weeks."

Ian slammed the lid of the steamer trunk, trying to stifle the memories. Emerging from the attic, he met Meredith, puffing up the stairs.

"There you are, Ian. I didn't know if they'd warned you about the dinner party tonight. I told your valet to lay out your evening clothes. Just a few friends and neighbors. They'll all bring their daughters, of course, so prepare yourself for the matchmaking."

Ian gave her a wry smile. "I doubt there'll be any match-making after I tell them about my daughter in France. I daresay fathers will warn their daughters to avoid me like the plague." The moment seemed appropriate, so he told her about Celine's baby.

Meredith hid her shocked surprise. What had the war done to the boy who had always been painfully shy with women? "Ian, you aren't really going to tell everyone the baby is illegitimate?" A woman with an illegitimate child was a pariah in their society, and Meredith could not imagine the reaction to a man raising a bastard.

"A secret marriage seems so . . . dishonest," he replied.

"Ian, dear, before you make any announcements you might regret later, stop and think about your daughter. Wouldn't it be better for her if everyone believed you had married her mother?"

Ian gazed at her wordlessly. Meredith had always cut to the heart of a matter, while his mother threw up smokescreens of unsupported demands that obscured any merits her suggestions might have had. "You're right, of course," he said at length. "I hadn't thought about how Geneva would feel. We'll make the announcement Mother wants."

The two chandeliers hung like twin ice palaces, glinting brightly in arctic sunlight, over the snowy linen cloth covering the eighteen-foot dining table. Serviettes sprang from silver rings like sculpted blossoms, while gold-rimmed plates were flanked by crested cutlery, in seven-course settings. The centerpiece of the table was a gigantic arrangement of hothouse roses, their subtle fragrance lost in the aroma of roast beef, poultry, and freshly baked bread waiting under silver-covered dishes on a pair of Chippendale sideboards of heroic proportions.

At the double doors to the dining room Ian paused, experiencing a wave of disorientation. For an instant the plaster ceiling with its scrolls and cherubs seemed to float downward. The murmur of conversation, the jewel hues of the women's gowns, the stiffly erect footmen moving to assist with chairs, all faded away.

In their place came a flickering image of the mud-walled maze of trenches, the rumble of distant gunfire, the stink of the disgusting slop served in billy cans that he dared not examine before eating.

"I said," his mother's voice jarred him back to reality, "that you may take your place at the head of the table." She wore a black chiffon gown with floating panels and the diamond brooch his father had given her on their last anniversary. Ian nodded, giving her an apologetic smile.

Dinner was being served by two inexperienced footmen badly in need of a butler's guidance. Taking his place at the end of the table opposite from his mother, Ian felt her eyes whisk from his ill-fitting dinner jacket to the inept manner in which the fish course was being served. He felt personally responsible, not only for his loss of weight, but also for the broken Dover sole being deposited on his neighbor's plate.

All of the older men present were veterans of other wars or service in the colonies. Of the few younger men present, only Ian was apparently unscathed by war. Beside Ian sat an ex-captain of the Guards, his right sleeve empty. He seemed to fix an unrelenting stare on Ian's right hand.

The sole mercifully gave way to pheasant, followed by roast beef. The women tried to keep the conversation directed toward cheerful topics, the resumption of parties, the London season, the rising stars of the theater, while the older men began a postmortem of the war.

Ian listened with half an ear while he toyed with a formidable serving of beef and Yorkshire pudding, swimming in rich gravy. Fragments of conversation floated, undigested, about his head.

". . . saw *London Calling* while I was in town. What? Yes—Noel Coward, a remarkable talent. Wrote the book, music, and lyrics *and* played the leading role."

". . . and I say Haig blundered and making him a field marshal doesn't change it. The idiot actually had the cavalry waiting to make a charge at the Somme—"

". . . our War Memorial Committee feels—"

". . . then I thought we'd resume our musical evenings."

". . . so Churchill's 'land battleship' had to be moved about secretly, and someone suggested they be passed off as water carriers for the Sinai desert, but one planner said he wasn't going to be on a W.C. committee—W.C.! Toilets, you see! So they used the synonym for water carrier—tanks. They were first used on the Somme, weren't they, Ian?"

Ian put down his fork with deliberate precision and sent his mother an apologetic glance, hoping she would not be upset

by the reference to the battle that had taken his father and
brother. He gave a deliberately vague smile and answered,
"The Somme? Ah, yes, a rather tranquil river. Flows through
Picardy. Poplars and rushes along the banks, marshes full of
blackbirds, heron . . ." He paused, eyes fixed on something
over their heads, thinking of the Somme running red with
blood.

There was an awkward pause. The captain with the missing
arm was remembering that as a boy Ian had always been
slightly out of step, introverted almost to the point of
mysticism, never as popular as his brother. One of Ian's
fellow officers had reported via a letter home from the front
that Ian's men had nicknamed him the Vicar, and they all
knew that despite two years in the army, Ian had progressed
only from second lieutenant to first lieutenant.

Ian said, "Forgive me for changing the subject, but I'd like
to explain why I shall be declining social invitations for a
time. You see, I'll be returning to France shortly. I have a
daughter . . . she was born during the last minutes of the
war. Her mother is dead."

Lady Saxon's voice broke the ensuing silence. "I'm sorry
there was no announcement of Ian's marriage. We kept it
secret because—the war—his father and brother being killed
. . . and, of course, his bride was French. Poor girl died in
childbirth, just like my other daughter-in-law." Her lips
clamped shut, and only Ian was aware that the stumbling
explanation and apparent verging on tears were actually
barely concealed anger.

Not knowing whether to congratulate Ian on the birth of
his child or commiserate on the loss of his wife, the guests
made noncommittal sounds and raised their glasses to their
lips uncertainly. At the end of the table Lady Saxon stared
straight ahead, her lips white.

Those first days back at Saxon Hall, Ian prowled nervously,
seeking the broken threads of his life, finding it difficult to
finish a task, often waking to what he imagined to be the
sound of gunfire. Once he opened his eyes to find Meredith
beside his bed, stroking his brow. "You're home, Ian dear.
It's all over. You don't have to go back to the trenches."

"I'm sorry, did I awaken you? I was dreaming . . . we were
all playing cricket, then all at once they started falling
down—blood on their white clothes."

Meredith wrapped her arms around him. "I know, dear.

None of your friends survived. Oh, dear heaven, we lost almost a whole generation of young men."

But the ghosts of fallen comrades not only returned with the deep blue shadows and gentle moonlight, they were there in sunny afternoons. It seemed to Ian the echo of forgotten laughter, the music of better times, and voices forever silenced lingered in the still air.

One bright frosty afternoon shortly after his return, he drove to the Saxon colliery. As the Rolls proceeded through the coal-dusted streets of the village, he watched the ugly rows of terraced houses, grim as tombstones, flit by the car windows. He wondered, not for the first time, about the people who lived in those grotesque little dollhouses.

The women were worn and anxious, one ear constantly cocked for the dread sound of the mine whistle signaling some new catastrophe. The men peered through white-rimmed eyes and had coughs that rumbled up from blackened lungs, like the sound of the cage rising from the bowels of the earth, and to Ian it was the sound of tumbrels. Did they feel despair? Were they able to think original thoughts, enjoy music, books, in spite of their nightmarish toil? How could they bear to be sealed away from the sunlight each day?

As they reached the slag heaps adjacent to the pits, Ian felt his old claustrophobic horror of the mine return. The Saxons were gentlemen owners and it had not previously been their practice to go anywhere near the colliery. This fact was evident in the expression of the manager, who came hurrying from his pithead office as the Rolls drew to a stop.

"Good afternoon, Mr. McSuter," Ian said.

McSuter touched his cap. "Mr. Saxon, sir." He was as spare and craggy as the moors of his Scots homeland, but with an underlying hint of deceit in his eyes that Ian did not like. They went into the small cluttered office, and McSuter dusted off a chair.

Ian said, "I understand you've had some trouble with the men."

"They're agitating for nationalization again. I'll get rid of the troublemakers."

"There's going to be a Royal Commission. We shall have to sit down with the men and discuss grievances."

"There's been enough government interference all through the war. It's time you owners got control again."

"We can't go back to the old ways, McSuter. I'd like to know what their grievances are."

"Your father never butted in with the running of the colliery."

"My father is dead, Mr. McSuter, and so are the old ways and the old days."

McSuter gave him a resentful glare but answered the rest of Ian's questions with his animosity more carefully veiled.

In the ensuing days Ian found there was little time to keep as close an eye on the mine as he wished. The administration of tenant farms, the gravel quarry business, the maintenance of Saxon Hall, the welfare of family, servants, laborers, as well as various volunteer political posts the Saxons had traditionally held, all vied for his attention. But it was the colliery that weighed most heavily on his mind, and he had a recurring nightmare that he had been born down in the village in one of those miserable hovels and was doomed to choke to death in a hole in the earth.

During the five months that elapsed before the mother superior of the Convent of the Sisters of Mary sent word that the adoption formalities were complete, his mother gnawed constantly at his resolve, trying to dissuade him from bringing the child to England. When Ian found the slight stammer he had had as a child returned, he knew that if he weakened and gave in now, he would never be able to make a stand on any issue. That timid little boy had to be laid to rest. Ian reminded himself of this again when, on the day he was leaving for France, his mother said, "It still isn't too late to leave the child where she is."

"Good-bye, Mother. I shall be back in a few days." Ian gestured for his valet to take his bags down to the car.

"Ian, I have such a strong premonition that we're all going to regret this quixotic action of yours," Lady Saxon said. "Blood will always tell, in the end."

Spring had come to Saxon Hall when the Rolls bore Ian, a young nursemaid hired by Meredith, and the baby, Geneva, up the daffodil-lined drive. Over their heads the elms murmured a welcome. In the front seat of the car, next to the chauffeur, sat a ramrod-straight man in his fifties, with iron-gray hair, a somber and somewhat shabby suit, and facial muscles that twitched constantly.

There was an expectant hush as the Rolls came to a stop. The young nursemaid held up the baby, as though the infant would be impressed. The baby yawned, but the man in the front seat leaned forward, his eyes sweeping the house in the manner of one who has found what he has been seeking.

"Here we are, then," Ian said as the chauffeur came around to open his door. "Don't let my mother intimidate you, Rankin. She has a rather imperial manner, but I'm sure she'll be as pleased as I am that you've agreed to come to us."

Lady Saxon awaited them in the entrance hall. She nodded to her son, ignored the nursemaid, then gave a startled glance at the man standing respectfully behind Ian, hat in hand, facial muscles in an orgy of involuntary movement.

"Mother, this is Rankin," Ian said. "Our new butler. Ah—and here is Meredith. She'll introduce you to the staff, Rankin, and show you to your quarters."

Meredith bustled toward them, more intent on seeing the baby, but she paused to offer her hand to Rankin and murmur a welcome. She cooed over the baby. "Oh, Ian, I've never seen a prettier child—" she began.

"Perhaps you'll conduct Rankin belowstairs, Meredith," Lady Saxon said. "I'm sure he doesn't wish to spend another minute with a squalling baby."

Meredith's smile faded. She touched the cheek of the contentedly smiling baby and said to Rankin, "This way, Mr. Rankin."

Compressing her lips, Lady Saxon waited until they were gone, then said, "Ian, for heaven's sake. We can't possibly use him. That awful twitch—"

"Poison gas," Ian said. "He was gassed in the war. I found him in a military hospital. But he was in service before the war. Insisted on joining up when his employer did, despite his age. His employer is buried in Flanders. Mother, let me introduce you to your new granddaughter."

Confounded by Ian's authoritative tone, Lady Saxon moved closer to the nursemaid to peer at the bundle in her arms. Ian was drawing back the blanket from the baby's face, gazing at the child as though she were a fairy princess.

"Isn't she beautiful?" he whispered in profound awe.

"All babies are . . . appealing," his mother said stiffly. "Like kittens. Which unfortunately grow up to be cats. You'd better take her to the nursery." The last remark was addressed to the nursemaid, who bobbed a curtsy and made good her escape.

Ian said, "Excuse me, Mother, I must see Geneva has everything she needs."

Standing in the sunny nursery, looking at Geneva in her wicker cradle, the image of Celine giving birth amid the devastation of war came back to haunt him.

He had unknowingly killed Celine with his flu virus. Was it atonement that had engendered this fiercely protective feeling toward her child? No, there was more he had not yet grasped. He remembered how Celine's eyes seemed to implore him. Even clouded with pain, those eyes had tried to reach beyond the barrier of language to convey some urgent message. What had she wanted him to know?

Chiding himself for being a romantic, he wondered if he would ever know the answer to the enigma that took the young mother to the shelled cottage to give birth at that particular hour. He agonized over why she had not cried out to warn them when the wounded German outside sent the battalion into the ambush. But, of course, Celine probably spoke neither English nor German.

The doughboy, Ian thought, who had been mysteriously wounded far from his own lines—had the American been able to communicate with her? Their lives had all touched for a brief moment in time. Ian had obtained the address of the American hospital to which the wounded doughboy would be sent. But somehow the letter he had planned to write to John M. Lauren kept getting postponed.

Was it because of that faint suspicion that Celine and Lauren could have had a lovers' rendezvous at the cottage, and the baby was his? Was John Lauren at this moment wondering what had become of them as he lay in a hospital in New Orleans?

Chapter 3

New Orleans, Louisiana, 1919

The French Quarter of New Orleans, with its proud Spanish-design buildings, arches, courtyards, balconies, had been old when Andrew Jackson led his triumphant ragtag brigade beneath those same wrought-iron balconies a hundred years earlier.

Matthew John Lauren lived in a room on the second floor, above a restaurant on a narrow street, that was the closest thing to home he had known in his nine years of life. He was awakened by Specks' hand gently patting his cheek.

"Wake up, Matt. Your daddy come home from the war."

Specks fumbled with the blanket covering the window, and sunlight flooded the room. "We going to the hospital to see him."

"Hospital?" Matt struggled to come awake. Specks and the other Jazzmen worked every night until two, and Matt collected the nickels and dimes the people paid to crowd into the tiny hall and listen to their music. The two didn't usually arise so early.

"Your daddy got shot in the head. He's mighty poorly." Specks was feeling along the window ledge for the hairbrush he kept there, and Matt jumped out of bed and pushed it closer, saving Specks the embarrassment of asking for it. Matt knew with a wisdom beyond his years how difficult it was for Specks to accept his suddenly failed eyesight.

"Put on your Sunday shirt," Specks said. "And brush your hair."

He explored the wall above the stove, found an iron skillet, and reached into the adjacent icebox for eggs. "Looksee if they's enough grits left, Matt."

Specks was unusually silent during breakfast, but Matt put this down to the early hour.

Before the sun was hardly up over the slates, they were walking purposefully down Bourbon Street toward Dumaine. Already the streets hummed with activity as the cracked sidewalks in front of musty antique shops and novelty stalls were swept free of litter, and aromatic bake shops opened their doors to entice passersby while the praline lady hoisted her tray of golden treasures.

Street vendors attached to flocks of bright balloons, or pushing handcarts of ripe fruit, and grinning hawkers waving garish voodoo dolls parted to let them pass. Wending their way through the crowds, they were a striking pair. Specks, tall and sinewy, his skin the color of burnished ebony, tight curls on a well-shaped head, with a profile that could have graced an Egyptian tomb, carried himself like a prince, despite his eyes. At his side Matt imitated the proud gait, joined Specks in responding to the greetings of friends, and watched carefully to see that Specks did not stumble over an unexpected obstacle.

Matt had smooth dark hair, eyes almost as dark, and although his skin tanned easily, there was a chiseled leanness to his features that indicated Northern European origins, with enough of a hint of Cajun blood to make the boy's face interesting.

The black man and the white boy were well known to the street people and musicians and bedraggled artists in Jackson Square. One was rarely seen without the other.

Apart from the unexpected, in the form of a stumbling drunk or a wide-eyed newcomer, there was little need for Matt to guide Specks along these dearly familiar streets. Everyone knew that although Specks no longer wore the eyeglasses that had given him his nickname, he had only limited peripheral vision.

The doctor at the clinic had shone a tiny light into Specks' empty eyes and looked very grave. Matt had not understood a word the doctor said, but later Specks told Matt, "It's called . . . mac-u-lar de-gen-er-ation." He broke the words into bits that were no less baffling, then told Matt to hold his arms way out on either side of his body, wiggling his fingers.

"Don't move your head, Matt, look straight in front. Now, out of the corner of your eyes you can see your fingers moving. That's all Uncle Specks can see . . . just what's on the sides of his eyes. Everything in front of him is just a gray nothing. Now not to worry, Matt. I don't need my eyes to blow my horn. I could just walk like the crabs, sideways, only don't reckon I need to, so long as I've got you. You can be my eyes."

A friend who drove a delivery wagon gave them a ride part of the way to the hospital, then there was another long walk in a part of town unfamiliar to Matt, along streets that were still asleep.

The hospital proved to be a grim, barracks-like building. Matt was silent as they went down a long corridor reeking of disinfectant. They were intercepted by a white-coated orderly who took Matt's hand and directed Specks to a waiting room. Matt was ushered into a long ward with white walls and a dozen white-sheeted beds.

At the fourth bed the orderly stopped and pointed to the still figure beneath the sheets. Matt went to the chair beside the bed and sat down, looking at the ghost of his father. John Lauren's head was swathed in bandages. He turned slowly in Matt's direction, pain creasing his pinched features. Matt's heart lurched at the unfamiliar blankness of his father's expression. John Lauren blinked at his son without recognition.

A flickering image of his father, from long ago, flashed through Matt's mind. Big and strong, his expression animated, always laughing. "What the hell, Matt! What say you and me go fishing instead?" His handsome and happy-go-lucky father, always ready to forget work for play, always the shining light who brightened the world's dark corners; quick and volatile and sometimes too fond of brawling for his own good, but living life with a shout rather than a whisper, rushing at it full tilt—all that mercurial temperament was now lost in a vacuous shell.

Matt squirmed uncomfortably on the hard wooden chair. He cleared his throat. "Daddy? How are you feeling?" There was no response, just an unblinking, frightening stare. Matt waited, ill at ease.

When the orderly did not return for him after a few

minutes, Matt climbed down from the chair and went in search of Specks. Approaching a white-uniformed lady sitting at a counter in an adjacent waiting room, he coughed to attract her attention. Like the ward, the room was painted white. So much whiteness was beginning to make Matt feel as dizzy as his father looked.

"Where's my uncle Specks?" Matt demanded, his voice rising to a worried squeak. It was not like Specks to move far without Matt's guiding hand.

The nurse glared down at him from the height of the counter. "If you're referrin' to the Negra who brought you here, boy, he's been sent to the colored folks waiting room. This here waiting room is for white folks."

Matt was reunited with a strangely pensive Specks a few minutes later. Outside in the sticky heat of the afternoon Specks told him of the bewildering upheaval in their lives.

"You and your daddy is going to live in Natchez," Specks said, his voice tight.

"You too, Uncle Specks?"

"No. I'm staying here."

Matt looked up at his friend in panic. "No! No, I won't go without you."

"Tain't what I want neither," Specks said, his proud and handsome face set in tight lines of tension. "But your ma's folks is taking you and your daddy in. Your granddaddy Castleton got himself a fine house. He's a powerful rich and mighty fine gentleman. You'll be just fine, Matt. You'll like Natchez."

"I want you to come too," Matt protested. "Who's going to help you see? Ain't I your eyes? Didn't you say I was your eyes?"

Specks chewed on his lip, and his eyes slipped up under their lids in that way they had sometimes. "I can manage. Don't you fret none. And I'll come see y'all. First chance."

There was a note of finality in his voice that scared Matt. "What about my daddy? Why'd he look so funny and not talk?"

"The doctor say that wound done messed up your daddy's mind, Matt. He don't know who he is no more. Don't remember nothing."

There was a special poignancy to the performance given by the Jazzmen that night. Five rows of benches were filled with people, mostly white, crushed shoulder to shoulder. The

capacity crowd jammed the rear of the hall and spilled into
the dank courtyard. Stamping their feet and snapping their
fingers, their hearts pounded and their blood surged to the
sound of the music.

Behind the poster-covered orange crates that served as a
counter in the courtyard, Matt listened to the Dixieland jazz
filling the night air and tried not to think of his impending
journey.

Matt loved the music played in the hall, but he loved even
more the weddings and funerals, parades and marches,
through the narrow streets of the French Quarter. He would
prance along proudly at Specks' side as the soaring notes of
the trumpet dominated all the other instruments.

To both Specks and Matt, the trumpet was alive with its
own being. A voice that shouted pride at the coming of a new
life or wailed grief for the passing of a friend. It could tell of
the laughter and joy, as well as the sadness and strife, of a life
that was moving on to heaven. A heaven only the music could
describe.

When Specks raised his trumpet to his lips, threw back his
head, and filled the air with the clear true notes only he knew
how to find, his sculptured face acquired the peace of a dark
angel playing at the gates of paradise. His expression reflected
such inner tranquillity that those watching and listening felt
their own worries vanish on the strains of the melody.

Listening to "Honeysuckle Rose," Matt tried to sort out all
of the unexpected happenings of the day. He had never
known his mother or her family, and the man with the
bandaged head and shattered mind was equally a stranger to
him. Specks had been his family for so long that parting from
him was unthinkable. Having lived for three years with
coloreds and mulattoes and that special breed of prejudice-
free whites who shared the small area of the French Quarter
with them, Matt had no wish to leave his insulated world or
his best friend.

When the hall was filled to its utmost limits, Matt hid the
cash box under the tangle of vines climbing the brick walls of
the courtyard and went inside. He crawled through the forest
of legs to the stage, and the piano player eased his bulk to one
side so the boy could take his usual position by his knee,
under the keyboard. From there Matt could see Specks as he
stepped forward for his solo.

The melancholy cry of the blues, a new number that Matt
had not heard before, floated out over the hushed crowd,

growing in intensity and volume until it was a cry of loneliness and despair. The gaslight caught Specks' face, and Matt saw the tears streaming down his cheeks.

Matt and John Lauren traveled by riverboat to Natchez, high on the verdant bluffs above the Mississippi. Creole-style houses and mansions of Greek and Palladian influence, surrounded by formal gardens, lined the tree-shaded streets. The atmosphere of antebellum elegance was so well preserved that at first glance newcomers tended to forget both the city's industrial activity and the importance of Natchez as a trade and shipping center. It was a gracious queen of a city, slumbering in a hot Southern sun.

Most of its charm was lost on Matt, heavy-hearted since he had waved good-bye to Specks from the deck of the *Delta Queen* and watched the sad and solitary figure standing on the quay, unable to see him or hear his shouts over the blare of the boat's whistle, the jaunty rendition of *Dixie* coming from the steam calliope, and the churning of the paddlewheel.

A male nurse attended John Lauren, who sat in a wheelchair, remote and unapproachable, oblivious to his surroundings. Matt and his father were taken by limousine to a house so grand that Matt was sure he must be dreaming it. Two stories, an upper balcony and lower veranda, were outlined in fragile wrought iron, painted white and looking like lace on a wedding dress. Surrounding the house was a profusion of shade trees from which wisps of Spanish moss drifted languidly in the merest hint of a breeze from the river. Worked into a filigree arch above the wrought-iron gates was the name Greenboughs.

A black butler, resplendent in a starched shirt and black trousers with a knife-edged crease, directed the other servants to carry John Lauren to the room that had been prepared for him.

Slightly reassured by the familiar presence of a black man, Matt inquired as to the butler's name. His reply, stiff and formal, diminished any hopes of comradeship. "Nathan. This way, please, Master Matthew."

Matt followed to a drawing room that remained essentially as it had been during the War Between the States. The stern butler thrust Matt toward a massive desk, then departed.

Behind the desk sat a white-haired, white-whiskered old man with red cheeks and a pale fishy stare. He glowered at Matt for a few moments, examining him from head to toe. "I am your grandfather Castleton. Your poor departed mother was my errant daughter, God rest her soul. I cut her off as one cuts off a withered limb when she ran off with that Cajun." His voice had an edge like flint, scraping on Matt's ears and carving on his mind. Matt never, ever forgot anything his grandfather told him.

"I lost my only son in the war in Europe and, God help me, you are all that's left of my line. I'm going to turn you into a Castleton, boy. If you behave yourself and do as you're told, your father has a home here too. I believe his steamboating and gambling days are over for good. Not to mention his inglorious army career."

"Sir," Matt said, "my Uncle Specks don't see too good. I was fixin' to have him come live here too."

The old man's eyebrows came sliding down over his eyes in a frown that seemed to cover his face and slip down his neck. Blue veins appeared on the high-domed forehead. "Oh, you were, were you. Now I'm going to tell you this just once, boy, and I don't expect ever to repeat it. You will never tell anyone you've been living in shantytown with that Negra. You understand me? You lived with your daddy until I took you in. Is that clear?"

Matt clamped his mouth shut in the way Specks had instructed him. "If'n you feel yourself fixing to back-talk, make your mouth a fist. Don't say nothing until you've done a whole heap of pondering. Try to see if there ain't some better way than back-talking your granddaddy."

There was a better way all right, Matt decided silently. A riverboat brought him here; it could take him back.

Castleton rang a bell on his desk, and a woman in an apron bristling with starch came and conducted Matt to an indoor bathroom such as he had never imagined existed. To his utter mortification the woman stayed and insisted on scrubbing him from head to toe.

Dinner was a frightening ordeal of three kinds of meat and vegetables smothered in strange-tasting sauces, dispensed by silent servants. His grandfather advised him acidly as to which fork in the bewildering array flanking his plate he was to use. "Small fork for the shrimp. Not that one, that's for dessert. Work *outward,* boy. Place knife and fork together, center of the plate, to indicate you're finished." Apart from the instructions, the meal was eaten in total silence, with his grandfather at the head of the long dining table and Matt at the other end. As unlike the companionable meals Matt shared with Specks as the staid waltz his grandfather later played on the grand piano was from the exuberant jazz Specks played for his living.

It was a relief when his grandfather conducted him up the graceful spiral staircase to his room. "Some day you'll realize how fortunate you are, boy. Look around this room. That armoire stood there in 1840. Greenboughs was never occupied by Yankee troops like most of the rest of Natchez because my father was wily enough to convince them he was a British subject. This house and everything in it is the living testament that the Castletons were here—past and present and future. And that's why you're here. Don't ever forget it."

Matt blinked sleepily, his eyes fixed on the four-poster bed with its luxurious quilt of patchwork velvet, the main colors of which were reflected in the canopy. As though by magic, the woman servant appeared and began to fold back the quilt.

"Good night, Matthew," Castleton said gruffly. "I know it's all strange to you. It will be easier in time."

The next morning, before anyone was up, Matt slipped into the sickroom, patted his father's waxen hand, whispered, "I'll be back for you, Daddy. Specks'll know what to do," then went silently out of the house.

He followed the river until the house was out of sight, then waited on the levee, skimming rocks over the muddy surface of the water and watching the barges move their cargoes down to the sea. At noon a steamboat pulled in and he slipped aboard amid the confusion of disembarking passengers and boys carrying luggage.

Matt hid in a corner, deep in the endless cavern of the boiler room, where the air was so hot and wet it seemed to press him down like a great clammy hand. His mouth was parched and his face flushed. Cramps attacking his legs battled for supremacy with the hunger pains in his belly.

After a time he heard the engines start up, felt the vibration rattle his teeth. Then the paddlewheel churned the water, and from high above he heard the whistle blow and the calliope shriek its raucous tune as the steamboat pulled away from the levee.

The calliope's shrill wail reminded him, just a little, of the music his uncle Specks and the others made. Matt forgot his hunger and cramps, and even his thirst plagued him less when he told himself he would soon be home. Home . . . sleeping on the bed Specks made for him, eating the good grits and thick chicken gravy, black-eyed peas, fried okra, maybe even a juicy gumbo. His mouth watered in anticipation.

Two hours later thirst drove him from his hiding place. He crept through the semidarkness, wide-eyed, an uneasy prickling sensation plucking at his spine. All of the pipes and cylinders and pistons chugged and hissed, apparently of their own volition, metal monsters casting grotesque shadows and making unearthly sounds.

He could not remember the location of the ladder he had descended. Panic was upon him now. He felt like a mouse caught in a gigantic trap. His tongue seemed to fill his mouth.

There was a puddle of brackish water, trapped down between the ribs of the hull, and he bent to scoop it up with the palm of his hand. The oily water had scarcely reached his lips when a large knotted hand came out of nowhere and engulfed the back of his neck.

He let out a yelp of fright and cast a fearful glance over his shoulder. He looked up into an impassive black face atop an enormous body.

Chapter 4

The stoker passed him up to the engineer, who took him to the captain, in conversation with the pilot up in the pilot house. The captain scowled ferociously. "A stowaway, huh? You know what happens to stowaways, boy?" His eyes rolled alarmingly, conjuring up tortures beyond Matt's worst imaginings. He shook his head in dumb terror.

There was a long nerve-racking pause. The captain and pilot exchanged glances, then they both burst out laughing. "They get put ashore, the first time. Don't ever do this again, or I'll give you to that big stoker and he'll turn you into kindling for my engines."

The steamboat simply pulled over to the bank and put him ashore. He was told to wait on the levee until his grandfather came for him. Matt was too weak from dehydration to do anything but wait for retribution to descend. His punishment was administered by Nathan, the butler, while his grandfather stood by and explained that the small hexagonal brick structure beside the main house where the punishment was taking place was called a *garçonniere*.

"*Garçon* means 'boy' in French," Castleton said. *Whack* went Nathan's switch.

The bamboo cane had whistled through the air, and pain exploded in Matt's outstretched hand. It took all of his willpower to hold his tears in check and keep his hand from flying to the protection of his opposite armpit.

"In the old days visitors always stayed overnight, and if all the guest rooms were full, the sons of the family slept in the *garçonnieres*. There are two, one at each side of the house." *Whack, whack.*

When they were finished, Matt was taken to his room, where he remained locked in for a week. When he was released, it seemed there was always one of the servants hovering over his shoulder, except when he went into the sickroom to visit his father.

His father's condition did not improve. Once Matt crept to the door to listen to what the doctor was telling his grandfather.

". . . brain damage. He'll never be more than a vegetable. An institution would be a kindness. I could make arrangements with the National Home for Disabled Volunteer Soldiers."

Matt was at school when the ambulance took his father away. His grandfather was gone too and didn't return until late that night. Matt waited for him in the unlit study so that no one would know he was there. The moon sent ghostly fingers through the shutters, and on the mantelpiece over the dead fire the clock ticked away the minutes, growing steadily louder. When the door opened and his grandfather's silhouette moved into the room, Matt spoke before Castleton's hand found the light switch.

"What have you done with my daddy?"

"You mind your tone of voice. Your father is in a home where he belongs. Where are you hiding, Matthew?"

He could hear his grandfather's breath rasping in his throat and the beating of his own heart. The sounds pulsed through the room. The darkness surrounded them and separated them. Matt felt his own defiance and his grandfather's anger, like phantom warriors meeting somewhere in silent battle, in the hollow space between them.

The light snapped on. His grandfather was carrying a cardboard box. "These are his personal belongings— uniform, medals, papers. I'm going to put them away, and someday, when you're older, you can go through his papers. Then you'll understand why I don't feel bound by any family obligation to your father. You're too young to understand now. You are the son of my daughter's flesh and my only heir, so I'll not hold your father's bad blood against you, white trash though he is."

"Don't you call my father names! Why, I'll—I'll—"

"As for you, Matthew—" His grandfather's speech was unhurried, deliberate. He paused between syllables of longer words, emphasizing the first syllable and softening the last. "I'm putting you in military school. You'll go first thing tomorrow."

Matt was learning caution and cunning. He departed meekly enough the following day with Nathan, bound for the train station and then on to military school. Nathan had been lulled into a false sense of security by Matt's decorum by the time he said, "I need to go."

Nathan started toward the colored restroom, but Matt protested. "No! I'm too big to get took in there with you. I want to go to the white restroom. Chrissakes, Nathan, I'm nearly ten. I can take myself to pee."

"Yo' mind your language," Nathan said. "Go on then, but be right quick or we's going to miss the train."

Matt went in through the door, turned, and immediately followed a departing patron back outside. Nathan had his back turned, since only a split second had elapsed. Matt was quickly swallowed by the crowds.

Ten minutes later he reached the riverbend, where coal barges were negotiating a sharp turn, one pulling in close to the sandbank to allow barges coming upriver to pass.

Specks' trumpet wailed the plaintive strains of "Poor Butterfly," his hands caressing his instrument tenderly while his poor unseeing eyes rolled back into his creased brow. The former serenity of his face had been replaced by a lonely sadness that even his awesome mastery of impossible notes could not assuage.

Slipping through the crowd, Matt found a square foot of floor space near the stage at Specks' feet and sank down on the cold concrete. He was tired, hungry, and elated.

The moment the music ended and the crowd began to roar their appreciation, Matt flung himself at Specks' legs, hugging him so fiercely that the two of them almost toppled from the rickety platform on which the jazz players performed.

"Matt! Matthew John Lauren!" Specks laughed and cried and ran his callused fingertips over Matt's face. He pushed the boy to one side, trying to see him with limited peripheral vision.

Later, after Matt had led him back to their room and they heated leftover grits and side pork, Specks listened gravely while Matt related what his life at Greenboughs had been like. Specks drew in his breath sharply when he heard about the military academy.

"Matt, you can't never go there. Look what soldiering done to your poor daddy. Don't you never forget that the army is trained to do only one thing—kill. You don't never want no part of it." Specks pondered for a moment. "We can't stay here. This is the first place your granddaddy will look for you. Best we go now. Tonight."

For the next few weeks they kept moving. Specks would sometimes play his trumpet in a gambling house or private club. When there was nowhere else to play, he would play on a street corner and Matt would pass his cap for pennies.

Then one day, in a hot and humid little river town, Specks met a man named Zeke who played the piano at a place called Lottie's Lair. He told Specks maybe he could get him a job there, since Lottie had recently lost her banjo player. "She's always hollering at me to play louder," Zeke said with a sly grin. "Reckon that horn of your'n will be loud enough, Specks."

Lottie's Lair, despite its iniquitous name, proved to be a large but ordinary looking frame house on a rundown street that just missed being "downtown." Weed-covered empty lots on either side of the white-painted house showed evidence of neighboring houses having been torn down, with glimpses of broken foundations in the tall grass.

Matt sat on a satin-upholstered chair in a room with red and gold brocade wallpaper and gilt-framed mirrors while Lottie interviewed Specks.

Lottie was magnolia-skinned, red-haired, sumptuously dressed in floating purple trimmed with swishing feathers. Jewels flashed from a velvet headband, matching those that glittered around her throat and even on her ankles above the high-heeled satin slippers. Matt blinked as the lights from an enormous chandelier reflected on Lottie's jewels. She appeared to be surrounded by a radiant aura, dazzlingly befitting an angel of such breathtaking beauty.

She sat at a white desk that was suspended on delicate

curved legs. Her vermilion lips were pursed about a long black cigarette holder, and she blew heart-shaped puffs of smoke into the air as she listened to Specks' rendition of "Honeysuckle Rose." When the last note faded, Lottie said, "Zeke says you worked the houses of Storyville in the old days. Ain't that unusual for a trumpet player?" Her voice was a gravelly monotone, dispelling the illusion of an enchanted creature but making her more approachable and therefore more appealing.

Specks said, "I played cornet in them days, ma'am. When they closed down the district in '17, I joined up with three others and we found us a room to play in and the folks came and listened. We did weddings and funerals too. Called ourselves the Jazzmen."

Lottie grinned and cleared her throat suggestively. "Guess all them respectable folks don't know what it really means to 'jass' somebody, huh, Specks?"

"No, ma'am," Specks agreed politely.

Lottie turned her big blue eyes to meet Matt's wide-eyed stare, and her expression changed abruptly. "What about the kid? He's white, right?"

"An orphan, ma'am," Specks said quickly. "We's always been together."

"He can share your room then. Just keep him out of the way of the customers and the girls. And if the law comes around, he'd better vamoose. Mainly he'd better keep out of Mr. DeVore's way." She paused, and a cloud appeared on the horizons of her eyes, as though just the mention of DeVore's name brought with it uneasiness. Crushing out her cigarette, she added, "You can start tonight. I want that music loud enough to drown out the sounds coming from upstairs. 'Specially the toilet flushings. It spoils the mood of the clients, see."

Matt stared, fascinated, as she spoke. The movement of her full red lips was such a visual delight that her rough tones seemed less abrasive. Her words floated over Matt's head, undigested.

"We work six days," she said. "So long as we close up on Sundays, the town don't bother us none."

They were shown to a narrow room on the top floor. Zeke, it transpired, did not live on the premises but had a wife and family in a small house on the other side of town. The only other male was a doorman-bouncer, a monumentally proportioned ex-boxer who merely grunted when they were introduced. There was a gargantuan black woman who sang soulful hymns as she prepared food for Lottie and the girls. There appeared to be eight or nine other women, all pretty and young, though to Matt's eyes none in a class with Lottie. Despite the fact that it was late afternoon, they all seemed to be just getting up, and they came down the stairs to the dining room in varying stages of dress and undress. The bouncer hung around, exchanging intense glances with a rather shifty-eyed young woman.

Specks and Matt ate in the kitchen with the cook, then went up to their room, which was right under the roof, with a sloping ceiling and a tiny window overlooking the street. Specks put on his best shirt, then took his trumpet from its battered case. "You is going to school tomorrow," he said.

Matt grimaced. School was dull. He'd learned to read long ago, and anything he needed to know was in a book on the library shelves. Specks had taught him how to figure money, so he could count the dimes and quarters and share the proceeds equally between the four musicians. He knew that the big ocean liners sailed out of the lower Mississippi bound for places with exotic names, like Valparaiso and Sierra Leone. He'd talked to sailors who came to hear Specks' jazz, learned that the river was just the beginning of a vast water-borne network of commerce. Matt had learned from his grandfather that much of the Castleton wealth came from ownership of a fleet of big towboats that pushed acres of barges, transporting cargoes of wheat, corn, sunflower seeds, and soybeans to the grain companies for transfer to freighters bound for foreign ports.

"What kind of a place is this that Lottie has, Uncle Specks?" Matt asked, pushing aside the grim specter of school. "This a cafe?"

"This here is a sportin' house, Matt. They's some eatin' and drinkin' and card playin' goes on, but mostly the girls take the customers up to their rooms and do stuff with them."

"What stuff?" Matt asked, thinking all at once of the rosy mouth of the luscious Lottie.

"Just . . . stuff," Specks answered vaguely, making a great show of polishing his trumpet. "Now get to bed, 'cos I got to go to work."

Chapter 5

A Mississippi
River Town, 1920

"Come away from that window, Matt," Specks said sharply. "He'll see you."

Matt dragged his gaze reluctantly from the shiny black Chandler coupe parked in front of Lottie's Lair. He had caught a brief glimpse of a cadaverous-looking man with a thin straight mouth and hard unblinking eyes, dressed in black, with a slouch hat pulled low on one side of his head. There was a bulging valise in his hand and he held it as though it were all that kept him alive.

"Who is he?" Matt asked, letting the curtain fall over the window.

"DeVore. The boss man."

Matt shivered. "He went in Lottie's room. I saw him shove her real hard. I was on the landing, behind the statue. Why did he do that?"

Specks was polishing his trumpet with short angry strokes, and his jaw moved spasmodically with each wipe of the cloth. He ignored the question. "You just keep out of sight when DeVore's around."

Matt knew that Specks and Lottie liked each other. Matt often came home from school to find them in animated conversation, and sometimes Specks was summoned in the middle of the night to help unload the cases of booze that because of something called Prohibition had to be sneaked down to the basement.

The first time the truck arrived, Matt had followed, worried that Specks would not be able to see where he was going, but Specks had already memorized every inch of the house. Matt waited on the stairs behind the alabaster naked lady, poised forever in the moment before she stepped into a shell-shaped bathtub. He heard them come up from the basement, then Lottie whispered in her oddly appealing monotone voice, "Wait a minute, horn player. Listen, when you play the blues, it breaks my heart. I ain't never heard a man play the horn like you. How come you ain't making big money in some nice club or on a riverboat maybe?"

"I couldn't leave Matt."

"Yeah, I figured. You're a good-looking buck, you know that don't you? Half my girls say their knees turn to jelly when—"

"Ma'am, how'd a nice lady like you get into this business?"

Lottie laughed, a delicious tinkling sound, and said, "Guess I'd have been disappointed if you hadn't asked." Then her voice turned harsh and bitter and she added, "I ran away from home when I was sixteen 'cos my pa used to beat me. DeVore was just down here from Chicago on account he was getting too big for his shoes with the Mob. 'Course he's weaseling himself back in with them again now, and I guess thinks he don't need me no more. But he was good to me . . . at first. Now don't ask me about it again, not never." With bewildering abruptness, Lottie suddenly reached up with her pale hands and grabbed Specks' face, pulling him down to kiss his lips.

Matt's eyes widened as he saw Lottie, poised on one satin slipper, her other foot in the air behind her, press herself against Specks.

Specks' surprise was evident in the way his arms were stiff at his sides, making no move to touch Lottie. But she continued to explore his mouth and squirm against him until Specks' arms went around her, under her satin wrapper.

Matt ducked back behind the naked alabaster lady, his ears drumming and his knees weak, almost as if it were he who was being so thoroughly kissed. The stairs creaked and he realized they were coming toward him. He flattened himself behind the statue as they went by, arms entwined and oblivious of their surroundings. They went into Lottie's room.

He slept fitfully, awakening to find the dawn painting silver lines around the window shades and casting the room in lonely relief. Specks' bed had not been slept in. Alarmed, Matt crept down the landing and pushed open Lottie's door.

The first thing he saw was Specks' back, powerful muscles gleaming darkly in the half-light; then Lottie's arms and legs, all wrapped around Specks' body like climbing vines. They moved to an exciting rhythm, Specks thrusting forward and Lottie rising to meet him, clasping his buttocks in little white hands that clenched and unclenched. Her head was flung back, red curls bright against the pillow, eyes half closed, cupid's-bow mouth uttering soft little sounds each time Specks thrust himself into her. Matt watched, too fascinated to move, as Specks buried his face in Lottie's pink-tipped breasts and she moaned and spread her legs in the air, and their rhythm quickened to such a frenzied tempo that the bed squeaked and rocked on the floor and they panted and cried out. They did not hear Matt close their door.

After that it seemed there were many nights when Matt slept alone, and Specks had begun to smile and laugh and whistle under his breath all the time, while his music became an enchanted nocturne that told of something wonderful happening to him.

Lottie's girls mothered Matt, spoiled him, and unintentionally taught him more about their business than Specks wanted him to learn. They would casually walk about the house in varying degrees of nakedness and, when not on duty, would sit around gossiping about their clients' idiosyncrasies. Matt knew right away there was a difference in the way the clients treated the girls and the way Specks felt about Lottie.

The visit of the sinister Mr. DeVore that day had cast a pall of gloom over the entire house, but most of all over Specks. Matt had never seen him so downcast.

Specks had finished polishing his horn and replaced it in the velvet-lined case. "Listen, I found your daddy. But we got to be careful. Don't want no trouble 'bout a black man being in the white folks' hospital, so Lottie will take you. Tomorrow."

Lottie never left the house in the daytime, so Matt knew he was honored. He swaggered along beside her, enjoying the way the men all gawked at her as the women frowned and turned away. Lottie was resplendent in a brilliant green silk dress with matching cloche hat from which a rakish ostrich plume fluttered. A black eye-veil studded with glittering rhinestones added to the mystery of her eyes. Her shoes were alligator skin, high-heeled and pointy toed, and she carried a matching purse. Diamonds sparkled at her throat and wrists, and a little silver chain with a jingling bell adorned one slim ankle.

A hush fell over the waiting room when they entered. Then there was an audible gasp from one of the women. Ignoring the hostile stares, Lottie approached the reception counter and informed a wide-eyed nurse that they were there to see John Lauren. When the nurse replied that children were not allowed to visit, Lottie threw caution to the wind and announced, "This here is his kid."

"No one under sixteen is allowed in, not even family, in that ward," the nurse said with a self-satisfied smirk. "And if I might inquire about your relationship to Mr. Lauren . . . ?"

Lottie said, "I'm a friend of the family, honey."

"Only the immediate family may visit." The nurse's nostrils had closed up tightly, giving her face a funny pinched look, Matt noted, and making her eyes bulge out of their sockets.

Lottie tried to persuade the nurse to allow him just a peek at his father, but she was adamant. Then Lottie lost her temper and told the nurse what she thought of her, their hospital, and their stupid rules, punctuating her outburst with indignant cuss words. The nurse punched a bell on her desk and an orderly came running. Lottie and Matt quickly found themselves on the street.

"Maybe we could sneak in," Lottie said doubtfully.

Matt said quickly, "No. It's all right. I'll come back when I'm sixteen."

A cold rain began to fall, and thunderheads raced with night clouds across the sky when they went up the steps to the front door of Lottie's Lair. Later Matt thought that if it hadn't been raining so hard, they would have gone around to the back door and avoided at least part of what followed.

DeVore was pacing up and down the entry hall, a circular room furnished with couches and small glass tables. His lantern jaw and shadowed eye sockets were even more sinister in the dimly lit hall than they had been in the daylight of the street. His tall, angular frame was enveloped by a velvet-collared black overcoat, still damp from the rain. Matt remembered the moment they stepped into the house that Specks had gone across town to visit Zeke, who was sick. It was a Sunday, and the house wasn't open for business.

Lottie glanced nervously from the valise lying on the floor, open and obviously empty, to her office door, also open, although Matt remembered how carefully Lottie had locked it.

DeVore's deep-set eyes went slowly over Matt. "Who the hell is the kid?" His voice escaped from the corner of his mouth, lips barely moving.

Lottie licked her lower lip and her voice shook. "He's the horn player's kid. Honey, I just took him to see a sick relative."

"The kid's white. The trumpet player is black. Now you tell me who he is and where you went today, or I'll fix your face so your own mother won't know you."

"I took him to see his father—honest. See, his grandfather is a big man up at Natchez, name of Castleton, and the kid ran away—" Matt listened in horror as Lottie babbled on, giving DeVore the whole story.

"Castleton," DeVore repeated. "Barges, warehouses. He owns half the river. Reckon he'd pay good to get the kid back."

"Honey, please—" Lottie began.

"Or you got a better idea how you can make up your losses?" DeVore asked her in a voice that froze Matt's blood.

"Losses?" Lottie stammered, giving her gaping office door another frightened glance. "Oh no! That new girl—she didn't . . . honest, I locked the safe—"

"You stupid bitch. She took the safe too. And the bouncer's gone with her, so I guess we know who carried it for her. While you're out gallivanting." His arm shot out and he slapped her, knocking her backward so violently that she sprawled on the floor. Her eyes were wide and drowning. She cried out as DeVore's fist again smashed into her face.

Matt charged, fastening his arms tightly around DeVore's leg and hanging on tenaciously. DeVore was silently slapping Lottie and shaking his leg to dislodge Matt, who in desperation sank his teeth into a thigh as tough as old turkey flesh. DeVore did not make a sound. His body twitched slightly, as though troubled by a biting insect, then he stopped hitting Lottie and turned on Matt, grabbing him by the front of his coat and hoisting him into the air eye-level with the cadaverous face. DeVore shook him until his teeth rattled.

"Honey, please—don't!" Lottie shrieked. Her face seemed to have disintegrated. Dark green streaks ran from her eyes, which were swollen and smudged with black. Her pink cheeks

had white lines where her tears had washed away the rouge.
The jaunty feather on her hat was broken.

"Leave her alone! Don't touch her," Matt yelled, hoarse
with fear for her. He swung wildly and his fist connected with
DeVore's nose. Matt bellowed with both triumph and terror.

Something crashed into his jaw, sending him spinning
across the room. The pain sang in his ears and rushed around
his brain in a frenzied flood. He felt as though a giant hand
were squeezing his head, blacking the light from his eyes.
Then there was the dreamless darkness of unnatural sleep.

Someone was pressing an icepack to his jaw. Familiar
hands, strong and gentle, touched him. Specks' voice, urgent
and probing, broke through the smothering cocoon that
separated Matt from his senses.

"Matt, wake up. Come on now." The words were innocu-
ous, masking a hidden message.

"Lottie?" Matt asked, his voice cracking horribly.

"She's all right. Listen to me, we ain't got much time.
DeVore is getting a ransom—money for you from your
granddaddy. They'll take you someplace and dump you and
you jes' wait for him to come for you. Matt, you do what they
say, hear?"

Matt tried to sit up but could not move. His arms and legs
were tied. "Specks!" he cried in panic.

"I cain't untie you," Specks said gruffly. "We is locked in
here and one of DeVore's men is outside with a gun. They'll
be coming to get you soon. Now—just you don't worry."
There was something in Specks' voice pleading with him not
to ask questions now. Matt drew a deep breath, trusting
Specks to have a plan.

A moment later DeVore burst into the room and shoved
Specks roughly aside. He glowered down at Matt. "Now you
listen to me, kid, and you listen good. Your pal here can keep
his hide in one piece and his job, so long as you keep your
mouth shut, see? You tell your grandfather anything that
leads him back here and this darky is buzzard meat."

Still trussed like a chicken, Matt was tossed over DeVore's
shoulder. Viewing the room from a dizzy upside-down angle,
Matt's last glimpse of Specks was of a silhouetted windmill of
arms as he tried to find Matt in the fog that obscured his
vision.

During the long ride on the floor of the car, Matt was
convinced he would not live to see daylight again, unable to

imagine his grandfather actually paying money to get him back. One of DeVore's men amused himself by twisting Matt's ear every time he moved.

It was almost a relief when they dropped him out of the Chandler coupe on a dirt road that ended in a misty bayou. Nothing else the night offered could be worse than that ride. He was still bound, but they had not blindfolded or gagged him. There was no need since there was nothing to see and no one to call to. Just the splash of nocturnal animals in the water, the croaking of frogs, the shrill call of crickets, and the whine of mosquitoes.

Hopping to the nearest tree, he sank down on his haunches and leaned back against the rough bark to wait. His head and jaw ached and the rope bit into wrists and ankles, but he told himself thankfully that he was alive and Specks would surely come for him. Wearily he closed his eyes and slept.

The sound of a car engine, moving slowly along the dirt road, awakened him. He tensed, straining his eyes to see if his grandfather had arrived or if it was the Chandler returning. The car stopped and the doors swung open. A rough-edged female voice said, "He's over there by the tree. To your right." Lottie! Matt thought joyfully.

Specks' voice then, low, urgent. "You've got to come with us. You can't go back now."

Two shadows beside the car blended into one. There was a long pause, then a strangled sound. "He'd come after us."

"I'd take care of you, Lottie. I'd never let him hurt you again."

"Don't be a fool. It's too late. It was too late before we ever met." Despair and terror were in the words, and a terrible finality. The smaller shadow broke away, started to get back into the car.

Specks' shadow threshed the air, trying to find her to bring her back into his embrace. A metallic thud echoed through the stillness of the night as his groping hand smashed against the side of the car. "Lottie . . . Lottie, please—we can go someplace where he'll never find us—up north, maybe."

"And if he don't find us, some other black-hating white man will do his dirty work for him. For God's sake, there ain't no place on earth we'd be safe. They'd string you up to the nearest tree and you wouldn't even be able to see them doing it."

"You don't have to remind me I'm blind as well as black."

"Well, it's true, ain't it, for Christ's sake. Let go of the car.

I'm leaving and you can thank your stars I've enough gumption for both of us. It was nice knowin' you, Specks, but it's over."

"No, don't go . . . Lottie, I love you."

"Yeah? And will you still love me with my face cut up or burned with acid, like he promised me if I leave him? So long, Specks—" The rest of her words were lost in the roar of the engine, and the tires squealed against the dirt as the car was thrown into reverse.

Specks stood motionless for minutes after the sound of the car faded, then Matt hopped over to him and Specks dropped to his knees and began to fumble with the ropes. It seemed to Matt that something splashed gently down onto the back of his hand as Specks bent over him, and he wondered if it could be a tear.

Matt did not trust himself to speak about Lottie. Instead he asked, "Did my grandfather pay DeVore for me?"

"A whole heap of money," Specks confirmed in a strange tight voice. He was massaging Matt's wrists and ankles. "Can you walk?"

Matt stood up, flexing his shoulders. "Where we gonna go?"

"Find a trail along the bayou, like I showed you. Head south."

Matt took Specks' hand and they plunged into the dense growth of pine saplings, fought their way through tangled vines to the gravelly edge of the bayou, then followed the bank southward.

They froze at each unexpected sound that whispered across the water or rustled through the forest, fearfully expecting a shouted command to stop, or, worse, the baying of tracking hounds. But if grandfather Castleton was searching for them, he had not had the foresight to bring dogs or men with lights.

As a mist-swathed dawn crept up the river, they crawled wearily into a mossy clearing and fell into an exhausted slumber, Specks' arms protectively around the boy.

When they awakened, the sun was steaming the dripping leaves. Fading wisps of blue-green vapor danced dreamily on the placid surface of the bayou, like genies rising from submerged lamps.

Insects hummed and flitted, their ranks giving way occasionally to a brilliant flash of color as a dragonfly swept majestically by. The nocturnal animals were at rest, lulled by songbirds trilling in the interwoven branches overhead, so

dense the sunlight was merely a sprinkling of golden confetti
where they lay.

Matt said, "I'm hungry."

Specks fumbled in his pocket for the length of rope that had
been used to tie Matt. "Unravel it. Make us a line while I cut
a rod. Then we'll need a hook from your overalls and some
fresh-dug worms. We'll have fish for breakfast. Maybe a fat
catfish or a bluegill. Plenty of fish and game in bayou country,
Matt. Reckon it's time for you to learn some huntin' and
fishin' like them Cajun ancestors of your'n. They was the best
trappers ever lived, according to your daddy."

By sunset of that day the two were deep in the heart of the
eerily beautiful south Louisiana swampland. Shrimp boats
were moored at their owners' front porches, and skiffs darted
along the shallow passes that were the streets of the bayou
country. Castleton was not likely to follow them here, and
DeVore would be even more a fish out of water.

Just before they camped for the night, Matt said suddenly,
"I hate DeVore. Some day I'll go back and kill him."

Specks could not see the expression on the boy's face, but
there was a chillingly familiar ring to the iron-willed determination in his voice. "Now you listen up," Specks said, an old
fear stirring deep in his bones. "Revenge is the worst reason
for doing anything—especially for killing a man. Don't you
never forget that."

Matt was silent, thinking of the hated face of DeVore, with
its thin flat lips and merciless shark eyes.

Just before the stars faded into the dawn, they were
awakened by the baying of hounds. Specks sat bolt upright,
his body trembling. "God almighty!" he breathed. He listened for a moment, every muscle tense. There was no doubt.
A pack of dogs was approaching and their excited barking
meant only one thing. Pursuit.

"They coming after us?" Matt asked, jumping to his feet.

"Don't see how they'd know we was here. But reckon we'll
get across the first water we find, just in case. Don't leave no
sniffing trail in the water."

They stumbled through the trees, hearing the cry of the
dogs grow louder with each second that passed, until they
came to an island of cypress, separated from the bank by a
narrow stretch of water.

Specks broke off a sapling and probed the water. "See any
'gators, snakes?"

"No. Let's go. Quick," Matt said, hopping from one foot to the other as the shouts of men joined the full-throated cry of the hounds.

They splashed into the shallow water, scrambled through the cypress trees onto the tiny island, flinging themselves behind the trunk of an aged tree and into the gnarled roots just before the frantic yelping of the dogs announced that they were closing on their prey.

Panic clouded Matt's eyes, and his heart was thumping so hard that for a moment he did not realize that he and Specks were safely hidden from view and the hounds had their quarry cornered somewhere in the dense growth of trees on the other side of the protective strip of water.

Men's voices rose over the din of the dogs. "Hold them hounds. Let me through."

"You, boy—you move a muscle and them hounds is going to tear your black hide to ribbons."

There was a confused babble of voices, mixed with the crashing of boots and breaking of branches, that indicated a large group of men had now joined the yapping dogs. Although Matt and Specks could not see what was happening, the group was so close that Matt was sure if they quieted down for an instant they would hear him panting. Specks' arm was across Matt's back, and at that moment the only thought in Matt's mind was gratitude that some other unfortunate wretch had been caught by the hunters and their dogs, and he and Specks were safe.

Then one voice was raised above all the others. "Now, you filthy coon, we're going to show you what happens to niggers who gits a taste for white women."

Matt felt his heart thud against the damp ground. Next to him Specks' body tensed. The dogs were quiet now. A voice, pathetically young, unmistakably black, sobbed, "No, boss! Please, no, boss. Ah din' tech no white lady—"

There was a long drawn-out scream, heart-stopping, bone-numbing, turning veins to ice. Birds gave an echoing cry of fright as they fluttered aloft, leaving the branches whispering in their wake. Matt's head jerked up, but Specks slammed it down against the ground, keeping the boy prone in a viselike grip that drained all the blood from Matt's legs.

A second scream rent the air, more terrifying than the first; then there was a long interminable silence that was more nerve-racking than the screams. Matt struggled, but Specks would not let him move.

A voice, tense and uneasy, said, "Maybe we should finish him now? Where's the rope?" In the background a tortured sobbing played on the nerves like blood pumping from a wound.

Another voice, ugly with hate, shouted, "No! I'm not done with him yet. Strip the bastard. Gimme that knife."

Matt tried to burrow into the ferns and vine at the base of the tree, wanting to stop up his ears and shut out the screams.

At last there was no more sound. Eventually the birds sang again and the sun climbed high in the sky, but still they lay on the island, unmoving, as though turned to stone.

At some moment late in the afternoon, as though by prearrangement, they uncoiled stiff limbs and climbed unsteadily to their feet. Without a word they crossed the shallow water, now canopied with insects humming lazily in the hot still air. They pushed through the pine saplings to the trampled clearing surrounding a majestic oak.

From the lowest bough a figure dangled, moving almost imperceptibly in small circles. A black cloud of flies almost obscured the face, but not quite.

Matt felt the bile rise in his throat, gagged, and tugged at Specks' hand, trying to get him to move. But Specks was turning his head to try to see out of the corner of his eye what Matt wished he had never seen. Dragging his eyes from the mutilated body, Matt began to retch.

Chapter 6

Saxon Hall,
Lancashire, England

The hands of the grandfather clock moved inexorably toward the eleventh hour. Servants, from the stiffly erect Rankin, his facial twitch almost under control, to the lowliest scullery maid and stableboy, were lined up like troops at the ready, waiting expectantly.

At five minutes before the hour Lady Saxon and Ian descended the staircase. At the same moment Meredith ushered her charges into the hall. Heart thumping, palms clammy, Geneva followed her cousin, Terry.

A slender child, Geneva's large pearl-gray eyes and mass of shiny dark hair dominated her delicately lovely features. Her almost ethereal grace was often mistaken for vulnerability by those who did not recognize the thread of determination and steel core of stamina that occasionally showed in a flash of her eyes or a squaring of her diminutive shoulders. Nor was her courage the blind bravado of one who lacks the imagination to visualize danger. She simply refused to give in to fear in any form. Therefore, while her body trembled in anticipation of the eleventh hour and all the ghosts it harbored, her mind stood fast.

Ian caught her eye and smiled reassuringly. Thank you, Father, Geneva thought, wishing she could stand at his side and hold tightly to his hand. Earlier that morning he had

promised delicious things to come, presents and a huge
birthday cake, but Geneva would have gladly foregone even
the merest token of remembrance that it was her birthday if
she could have been spared the next few minutes of the day.
Why couldn't she have been born just a few days earlier, on
Guy Fawkes day; then her birthday would have been cele-
brated with bonfires and fireworks in honor of that old rascal
who tried to blow up the houses of Parliament.

Lady Saxon intercepted the glance she exchanged with Ian
and frowned. Geneva lowered her eyes, remembering the
terrible scene that had taken place on that other birthday,
when she had refused to leave her room for the eleventh-hour
ritual. Grandmarm had been furious. Geneva had questioned
her authority before, never cowering before her as everyone
else did, but this was the first time she had been openly
defiant.

When Geneva was not moved to obey her grandmother's
order to join the others in the hall immediately by threats of
withholding treats, suspending privileges, or even physical
punishment, she was driven to distraction. In one irrevocable
moment of lost control, nostrils quivering with revulsion at
the carnal indiscretion she believed had produced the child,
Lady Saxon thundered, "You are not one of us. You'll never
be one of us. Your mother was a French whore who convinced my gullible son he was the father of her bastard."

Geneva looked in the dictionary in Ian's study for the
words "whore" and "bastard." Then she asked Ian, "Why
didn't you marry my mother?"

He had wrinkled his eyes in pain, in that way he had
whenever Geneva was hurt or bewildered, and replied quietly, "I loved your mother . . . will you believe that? I would
gladly have married her, had there been time. Our love—hers
and mine for you—will surround you and protect you always.
Try to forgive your grandmother. There's been so much
tragedy in her life, her grief is like a festering wound. She
doesn't mean to hurt you."

Geneva tried to remember that, every time Grandmarm
made her life difficult, which was most of the time. Now on
this birthday morning the regal figure in black had reached
the foot of the stairs and was moving down the line of
servants.

In the distance, across the lovingly rolled lawns, beyond a
copse of trees, bare branches stark against the winter sky, the

bells of St. Agnes' Church tolled. Every year on Geneva's birthday the church bells rang.

She could perhaps have ignored the somber message of the bells. It was the shattering two-minute silence that made Geneva dread her birthday. The clock began to chime the hour. Nine, ten, eleven. . . . The church bells stopped pealing.

Geneva hated the silence that followed. It seemed as if every creature on earth had suddenly stopped living. After the interminable two minutes dragged by and the bowed heads of family and staff were again raised, she was convinced her heart had stopped beating and her lungs had collapsed for lack of air. She had never been able to tell anyone, not even her beloved Ian, how she felt. It was almost as if she had some prenatal knowledge of a tragedy so terrible that the effects of it had touched her in the womb.

No matter how many presents she received, or how delightful her birthday cake, nothing could dim the memory of that awesome, terrifying silence.

Even when she was old enough to understand that the silence was homage to a million dead English soldiers in a war that for some reason was called "great," she still could not in her heart celebrate the day of her birth, for if it had marked the end of the senseless killing, it had also marked the beginning of the death of her mother.

"Geneva!" Grandmarm's voice sliced into her thoughts.

Blinking, Geneva saw that the servants were returning to their duties, Meredith and Terry were already disappearing in the direction of the schoolroom, and Ian was in conversation with Rankin. Only Geneva stood, transfixed, still staring at the clock.

"You may go back to your studies, Geneva," Lady Saxon said. The air of brave martyrdom she wore for the two-minute silence still clung to her parchment-thin skin.

"Yes, Grandmarm," Geneva said automatically. She was about to follow Meredith and Terry into the schoolroom when there was a sudden commotion at the front door. Turning, she saw one of the footmen trying to prevent the entry of a ragged boy who obviously belonged at the tradesmen's entrance. Rankin moved to the footman's aid, but the boy was a strapping youth and more than a match for the two servants.

Twisting free of the footman's grasp, the boy sprang toward

Ian, yelling, "You'll see me, you bloody murdering bugger."
There was coal dust on his clothes and face, so that his eyes
stood out whitely and his fair hair appeared gray, giving his
features a wizened, aged appearance.

Ian stood perfectly still and his voice was calm. "I shall hear
what you have to say in my study. If you will calm down and
stop using foul language in the presence of ladies."

The boy spun around, red-rimmed eyes sweeping from
Lady Saxon to Geneva, who had flown to Ian's side as though
to protect him from attack.

"Ladies!" the boy said derisively. "An auld witch and a
little girl. Maybe it's time your women suffered like our
women, you flamin' parasite. Aye, that's what you are, living
off the blood and sweat of the likes of us. Well, I've come,
Mr. Bloody Saxon, for the price of a coffin."

There was a moment's silence as the echo of the words
hung in the air. The boy's voice broke slightly as he went on,
"You owe my mam that much. Your bloody pit took my
brothers and now my dad's gone too. Spitting up his life from
his black lungs."

"Ah, I see. You are Master Charlie Dutton," Ian said
quietly. "I was most distressed to hear of your father's
passing. Surely the colliery manager brought your mother my
condolences?"

"Stuff your bloody condolences." Charlie Dutton paced a
small angry circle around the hall, clenched fists flailing the
air. His eyes were polar blue, unnaturally bright. Watching,
Geneva thought he was going to cry.

"I instructed him also to see if we could offer financial
assistance—" Ian began.

"That bastard never came near us, nor will he. God strike
you, Mr. Ian Saxon, for sitting up here on your almighty
throne and never giving a damn what happens down the pit.
Why you—you—" Dutton's tears erupted in a great gust of
anguish. His fist went to his eyes, then to his mouth, in
frustration and humiliation. He coughed and gasped on the
salty flood.

Out of the corner of her eye Geneva saw the footman slip
outside. A moment later he reappeared with two of the
burliest stableboys.

"Won't you come into my study, Charlie?" Ian asked
gently. "We can talk it over privately. I had no idea—"

Charlie's wild sobs were choked back as he caught sight of

the approaching stableboys. Before Ian could prevent them, they had seized him from behind.

Ian was saying, "No, no—let him go," but his words were drowned by a bellow of rage from Charlie.

"Your turn will come, Ian Saxon. I swear to God." His eyes swept back to Geneva, lingering on her with a glittering malevolence that was a naked threat.

Geneva found herself suddenly enclosed by Rankin's bony arms and whisked away. When the schoolroom door closed behind them, Rankin, his facial muscles twitching violently, deposited her on her feet. Geneva tried to push past him to the door, but he blocked her way.

"Let me go—he's going to hurt Father," Geneva cried, her fear for Ian igniting every nerve in her body.

"What on earth is going on?" Meredith bustled over to them. Over Geneva's head Rankin said, "The Dutton boy from the village is here. He's distraught. Making wild threats. Keep Miss Geneva here."

Struggling in Meredith's stout embrace was useless. Gasping for breath against the lace jabot that adorned the governess' ample bosom, Geneva heard the door click shut.

That night, long after the rest of the household had retired, Ian sat in his study, the only room in the house that was truly his, from the Chippendale desk that was a gift from a favorite uncle while Ian was at Cambridge, to the rows of books Ian had collected and revered all his life. Everything else at Saxon Hall was held in trust for Terence Digby Saxon the third, firstborn son of a firstborn son, as tradition demanded.

Charlie Dutton had been mollified and accompanied back to his grieving mother by Rankin, bearing a gift of money to cover funeral expenses and tide the family over the crisis.

Geneva's birthday had proceeded under something of a strain, but then the child was always rather withdrawn on her birthday, Ian reflected. That damn two-minute silence, he thought.

Ian's numbing fear had been masked all day, but now it engulfed him. Surely Charlie Dutton's terrifying threat had been no more than a cry of pain? He couldn't intend to harm an innocent child? Ian paced his study in an agony of self-recrimination, cursing his part-time handling of the Saxon colliery. The manager must have pocketed all of those gifts of money he had sent to the families of sick or injured miners. McSuter would be sacked, of course, but what irreparable damage had already been done?

A discreet knock on the study door interrupted his thoughts. "Rankin? Come in. What happened with the Duttons?"

Rankin was still breathing heavily. "It was as you feared, sir. None of the money you sent to the families ever reached them. The Dutton family lost both of their elder sons in the explosion two years ago. The boy Charlie has been working down the pit for the past year. There are two sisters; one is mentally defective but kept at home."

Ian closed his eyes briefly. "We must get the boy out of the colliery. That poor woman has lost enough of her family. How old is he?"

"Fourteen, I believe, sir."

"A trade school, perhaps?"

"His mother will be relying on his wages now."

"Then we'll continue to pay his wages—but send the boy to school."

"I'll take care of it, sir."

The night before Charlie Dutton departed for a trade school in Liverpool, where lodgings nearby had also been found for him, Geneva awakened a little after midnight to see a red glow lighting up her window. The sound that had disturbed her sleep was an unearthly screaming. For an instant she covered her ears with her hands, wondering if she were caught in a nightmare, then she jumped out of bed and ran to lift the curtain from the window.

An orange pillar of flame, wrapped in black smoke, lit the sky, rising from the direction of the stables. That awful sound was the panic of trapped and terrified horses. She raced from her room, and by the time she was halfway down the stairs, the entire household was aroused.

Ian caught up with her as she was about to follow the army of servants rushing toward the blaze. He grabbed her arm, pulling her back. "No, Gennie. Go back to your room. You'll just be in the way."

"But the horses—my pony. I must save Patches."

"We'll get them out, don't worry."

Geneva went slowly back up the stairs. The house was unnaturally silent, even for the late hour, and she looked back over her shoulder as she reached the landing.

She sat on her bed, staring at the flickering light playing across the window, thinking of the bales of dried hay and aged wooden beams of the stables. A moment later, unable to bear the tension, she went back to the window. The flames had died, but smoke still rose against the moonlit sky. She strained to see across the tree-shadowed lawn where the stables were concealed behind a hawthorne hedge.

A figure moved across a pool of moonlight, leading a horse, then another and another. Geneva gave a deep sigh of relief. Then, inexplicably, a prickling sensation ran slowly down her spine. Her eyes dropped to the terrace beneath her window. Among the familiar shadows was one that leaped from the stone flags with the impact of a suddenly materialized spirit. The shadow was distorted by the moonlight and rough paving stones, but there was no doubt that a broad-shouldered figure was crouching behind the stone eagle. From the position of the silhouette, the figure was staring up at her room.

There was the sound of voices approaching the house. Geneva looked up to see someone running back toward the terrace. When she looked for the crouching shadow, it was gone.

A few minutes later Ian appeared at her bedroom door. His face was streaked with soot and his dressing gown was wet, but it was the desolation in his eyes that she saw first.

"Oh, Gennie, darling . . . I'm so sorry." He opened his arms and she ran into them, not wanting to hear what he was going to say. "The fire started in Patches' stall. It was too late by the time we got there. We saved the others. Oh, my dear—"

Chapter 7

Saxon Colliery, Lancashire, England

Ian was awakened by the shrill blast of the alarm whistle on a dismal December morning. By the time he reached the village, the narrow, rain-swept streets were filled with scurrying women and children. They gave way reluctantly to his vintage Rolls-Royce, casting reproachful eyes at the car from the depths of black shawls swathed about their faces.

From within the Rolls, Ian could hear the sound of their torment, like the low murmur of a fretful river struggling through a hostile land. A muted moan interspersed with the wail of younger children who did not understand what had happened but knew instinctively that this would be the worst day of their lives.

The column of women followed the men converging on the pithead; tired colliers only recently done with a long shift, answering the alarm blast and the code of honor of all miners that sends them back to help comrades in trouble.

At the pithead Ian's worst fears were confirmed by the foreman, his eyes white against his blackened skin and an ominous bloodstain soaking his shirt. Behind him the cage came rattling to the surface bearing a jammed cargo of men, some burned, others bleeding and dazed. All of them coughed in a rising cloud of smoke and dust.

"Explosion, sir," the foreman gasped. "Bad. Number four completely blocked and three and five on fire."

Ian's eyes swept the scene. A blanket of smoke laced

stanchions and girders, encircled the twin chimney towers, and hung heavily about the engine sheds and fitting shops. Only the top of the water-cooler pylon rose above the black cloud. A string of coal-laden tubs, like miniature railway gondolas, had halted their crawl into the gaping archway leading to the screening shed. The pulley wheels turned, and the steel rope slapped the block overhead as it lifted the cage. Even as he stared, there was another rumble from the depths of the earth and smoke shot up the main shaft. The men in the cage were tossed about like rag dolls.

The first of the women had reached the pithead and several screamed. Ian said, "Rope them off. Keep this area clear for ambulances. Have you sent for them? How many men below?"

"All the first shift—except for them." The foreman jerked his head in the direction of the men stumbling from the cage. "Ambulances are coming."

"At which level did the explosion occur?" Ian asked, desperately aware that he had not been near the colliery for months and all of his previous visits had been brief and above ground. That few owners went near their collieries did not occur to him.

"They're trapped a thousand feet down," the foreman said grimly, turning to help a collier with an injured comrade. "Them that's not already dead."

"I'm going down," Ian said.

The foreman's face was white eyes and white teeth, registering astonishment. Wordlessly he conducted Ian to the lamp cabin, handed him a safety lamp.

Clogs clattered onto the metal platform of the cage and the two wheels whined, lowering them on oily ropes. Surrounded by coal-grimed faces, Ian stared straight ahead as the cage dropped into the yawning mouth of the shaft.

Cimmerians, he thought as his stomach lurched; creatures of the darkest nightmare, dancing down to our tomb-world on the end of a thin steel rope; mindless marionettes. Jets of icy air plucked at trouser legs, whistled in frozen ears. Slimy walls shot upward. Down; falling endlessly.

His hands closed over the sturdy glass of his lamp, seeking its comfort, the last speck of light to remind him of the greater light. Once when he was a boy he had seen a blind pit pony, retired to wait for death, turning his nose upward toward a cool winter sun as though yearning for the light he could not see.

The pit bottom platform rushed up to meet them. The men in the cage surged out into the darkness, sweeping Ian with them. He fought the urge to retch as the foul air assaulted his lungs.

Overhead water dripped from the sweating roof, timbers reeked with mildew, feet dragged through a slaty quagmire. Grit had invaded every part of his body. Thoughts were cast in peculiar relief. *I didn't have time to kiss Geneva good-bye—to tell her all the truths she should know. Terry needs discipline, Mother spoils him. And why did I never write to John Lauren in America?*

The knot of rescuers came to a sudden halt. Stronger than the acrid fumes was the smell of blood; it came in cloying gusts. Lamps were held aloft, illuminating the two crushed men. Three hands, the tops of two heads—nothing else, except for the fall of stone that had mangled their bodies and spilled their blood.

"Where's the jack?" the foreman barked. "Come on—all together—heave!"

Ian put his hands on the giant boulder, feeling the cold rock lurch as they shoved, grumbling like some sacred idol about to be deprived of its human sacrifice.

"Shove the block in," someone hissed. "Now—quick, for Christ's sake—"

A pool of blood and dirt; that was all that was left of two men. One was face up, staring eyes reflecting the golden lamplight the way a cat's eyes shine in the dark.

A wave of panic passed through Ian. *Over my head is a hundred million tons of stone and clay and shale.* Perspiration lay in cold pools upon his body. Crouching, he followed the others through the narrow opening, wincing as the ragged roof tore the skin from the back of his hand as he lighted the way with his lamp. They inched past the buckled timbers and fallen shale, proceeded down a tunnel that ended abruptly.

"Here's the blockage," the foreman said. "Hear the tapping? Some of em's alive." The men in front were already hacking with their picks toward the sound.

"There's room for half a dozen to work. They'll do it in relays," the foreman said. "Begging your pardon, sir, but the men are a bit uneasy . . . with you being the owner and all."

Ian was thinking of his mother's chinchilla coat and men in

stiff white shirts drinking fifty-year-old wine and girls in bright dresses spilling onto ballroom floors and sunlight dappling playing fields. Did any of them care about what was happening here?

"Sir, there's nowt for you to do here, 'cept pray," the foreman prompted him again.

"Yes, of course. I'll try to get a doctor down here with morphine." He started back the way he had come, alone, feeling the darkness drive him in upon himself. *Guilt,* he thought, *is that the emotion that impels us? Is it the whip we use on each other? I should have included Nancy in my will.* Nancy was a village woman with grave brown eyes and soothing hands, who expected nothing of him but that he lie with her in softer darkness, sucking gently on dark nipples and probing milky thighs.

As he bent to crawl past the boulder and crushed bodies, he heard a low moan. Swinging his lamp in an arc, he watched in amazement as a heap of crumbled coal shifted and became the head and upper torso of a youthful collier. "Don't take the light away . . . please . . ." a voice, achingly young, whispered.

Placing his lamp nearby, Ian tore at the debris until his hands bled, succeeding in freeing all but the boy's lower legs, which lay beneath a fallen support pillar. "I can't move that alone—I shall have to go for help." He was panting with exertion.

A hand closed around his ankle. "Don't—let them—cut off my legs."

"Of course not." Ian hesitated, feeling the boy's panic. "What is your name?"

"Ted Corwin. Mister . . . you know, I had a presentiment. Last night—I went a-running on the hill and the air was sharp and clean and black clouds raced across the moon like all the colliers was running to the pit. I thought . . . it's all right— for a little bit I was here and saw the stars and the sun rolling over the hill like a great ball of polished steel—" he broke off, coughing.

Ian stared down at the boy, so acutely aware of his suffering that Ian's own legs began to buckle. "I won't be a minute, Ted."

He ran back, shouting, "Quickly—I need help." *Like a ball of polished steel,* he thought, and *I wondered about their thoughts, their sensitivities.*

The foreman and two men returned, and Ian dropped to his knees to cradle the boy's head. "We'll have you out soon, Ted."

A callused hand closed over Ian's arm and he looked up at the dust-blackened face. The foreman jerked his head upward, and following the glance, Ian saw that the support pillar was wedged against a large boulder. If the post was moved, the boulder would surely crash onto the boy's chest.

"Shore it up, and one of you go for a doctor." Ian tried to keep his voice steady, but he was finding it increasingly difficult to breathe, and the golden glow of the lamps had begun to turn an ominous purple. The three men were covering their mouths with their hands. Methane! Ian felt his heart stop. Gas . . . the deadly unseen enemy, creeping silently in to finish what fire and explosion and cave-in had not accomplished.

One of the men stumbled away, was swallowed by the darkness. The foreman said, "We move that boulder and the roof will come down. Mr. Saxon, sir, we've got to get some engineers down here and ventilate this tunnel—blow the gas away—before we can dig through." Behind him the other rescuers appeared, coughing and choking on the fumes. One of them carried a cage containing a canary, its yellow feathers lost in a coat of dust.

The buried boy said, "A hundred days I was here . . . in the mysterious shadows that I thought was hell itself . . . and the coal swooping down on me like a panther. And every time the timbers creaked I thought it was coming. But when it happened it was so sudden-like—I tho't a big blanket was dropped on me back, too heavy . . . oh, it was heavy."

The canary twittered in his lonely cage.

Ian could feel tears forming behind the film of dust that covered his eyes. "Get some of the other broken posts— quickly, man!" he snapped at the foreman, who leaped to obey.

They brought posts to shore up the sagging roof, working quickly, silently. Footsteps announced new arrivals and a calm voice announced, "Dr. Evans. Move aside and let me in."

A lever was pushed beneath the collapsed support pillar. Slowly, scarcely daring to breathe, the men inched it downward, raising the splintered wood and taking the weight of the boulder on their own backs. The doctor was administering morphine. When the pillar was clear, they looked down to see that they had freed one of the boy's legs, but the other lay beneath a solid trap of shale.

"Doctor," the foreman said suddenly, urgently, "we're running out of time."

Ian looked up to see that the canary had toppled from his perch. The dusty yellow feathers made a pathetically small corpse. The doctor was already rolling up his sleeves, reaching into his bag for a hacksaw and scalpels.

"No!" Ian shouted, feeling his stomach churn. "You can't."

The foreman grabbed him, pulling him back. "Gas is seeping in. He's got to. We can't get him out in time. It's his leg or his life."

Tears scalded his eyes. The sound of the hacksaw cutting through bone would haunt him for the rest of his life.

On the surface Ian raised his face to the rain-filled sky and listened silently to an appraisal of the situation. The fires had been smothered by closing off two shafts. The injured men who could be reached were being brought up; bodies would be left for later. At least a hundred men were entombed, and digging through to them would not resume until the deadly methane gas dissipated.

All Ian could think of was the boy, Ted Corwin, now on his way to hospital. That bright creative young mind, trapped, seeking the light just as surely as the boy's body yearned for the sun.

Ambulances clanged through the gloom of the morning. The women were silent now, an anguished, watchful circle behind the rope barricade keeping them at bay. When a husband or father or son emerged from that hell below ground, a woman would detach herself from the group, slip under the rope, and fall in step with the stretcher bearers.

As the hours dragged by, the anxious watchers grew in number. Ian felt their eyes, reproachful, antagonistic, begging for deliverance from the nightmare. He felt their pain more acutely than their blame.

Then sometime in the late afternoon he became aware of the magnetic pull of a stare so malevolent that as he turned to seek its source all of the hairs on the nape of his neck tingled. Pale eyes were watching him unblinkingly, expressing satisfaction as well as hatred. It was a moment before he recognized Charlie Dutton. Taller, older, with bulging shoulders and a boxer's biceps, but the look on his face the same as the day he forced his way into Saxon Hall . . . the day his father died.

Ian stood frozen, raindrops stinging his eyelids, thinking of the summer before Geneva went away to boarding school, and the reason he had agreed to his mother's suggestion. Under the onslaught of Dutton's fierce loathing, Ian remembered the dread that began that day.

Geneva had flung herself into his arms in customary greeting and, as always, Ian gave silent thanks to the benevolent fates that had brought them together. It gave him pleasure merely to look at the child, her lovely features, the perfection of her skin that was like a gossamer veil over exquisite bones.

Ian had said with studied lightness, "Meredith tells me one of the village boys stopped your horse when you were riding today."

Geneva looked up at him, watching for a sign that the incident concerned him unduly. "Yes, it was Charlie Dutton—the boy who burst in here on my birthday and cried because his father was dead." She shivered, knowing there could be no worse pain than to lose a beloved father. She had felt pity for Dutton, even when he lashed out at the Saxons as the cause of his grief.

Ian said, "Meredith wasn't sure what took place. Dutton didn't . . . threaten you?"

"He asked if I remembered that birthday—death day, he called it. There was the two-minute silence—"

"Yes. What else did he say?"

"He said he wanted you to feel as he did when they buried his father. He said he decided that day that the person you loved best would go into a hole in the ground too."

A pulse throbbed in Ian's temple and his mouth was dry. "Gennie, I want you to avoid Charlie Dutton like the plague. If he approaches you again, I want to know about it. Fortunately you'll be going away to boarding school in September."

"Did he mean he would try to push me down the pit?"

"I believe the hole he had in mind was a climate of fear. There is no worse pit a human being can fall into. I don't believe he will actually do anything, but he will try to frighten us. He is a rather disturbed young man, but also quite a remarkable one. He knows the persuasive quality of fear. We mustn't submit to it."

Geneva nodded gravely, not fully understanding, partly

because she was still a child, but also because fear had never been part of her makeup. She did not know either that Ian had long ago fought his lonely battle with the demon of cowardice, emerging with greater courage than men who had never fought the battle, but never fully realizing he had been the victor.

Later that day Rankin visited Charlie Dutton's mother, who informed him her son had had enough of school and was home for good. Rankin replied that in that event Mr. Saxon's support of the family would be withdrawn. Charlie had returned to Liverpool.

Ian gradually became aware of the rain driving against his face, the shape of the colliery chimneys and the elevated pulley wheels. He found moving toward the roped-off spectators. Other faces blurred, other sounds receded. For a few minutes even the drama being enacted around them was forgotten. Ian and Charlie Dutton might have been alone.

"I'm home for the Christmas holidays," Charlie said, curling his lip slightly in a way he had.

"While you're home," Ian said, "stay away from my daughter."

Charlie smiled a self-satisfied smile, then nodded his head in the direction of the pit. "Another lot of poor bastards choking to death for Saxon coal. I was surprised to see you down 'ere, Mr. Saxon, *sir*." His Lancashire accent had acquired a nasal intonation common to the Liverpool docks, Ian noted. There was also a veneer of big city toughness that hadn't been there before.

"Tell me, Charlie," Ian said, giving no indication he had heard a word the boy uttered, "what plans have you for when you leave school—next spring, isn't it?"

Charlie shrugged. "Been 'ard work, sloggin' away at school. Thought I'd rest up a bit."

"Take a month to find a job. I've a friend in Liverpool who may be able to help."

"Oh, I don't like Liverpool, I don't. I'll be coming home."

"A month, Charlie. After that my financial support ends," Ian said, and turned his back to return to the pithead.

The foreman was signaling that rescue operations could be resumed, and Ian realized with a stab of guilt he had forgotten the trapped miners.

Chapter 8

Liverpool, England

When the rescuers broke through to the trapped men on the third day of their entombment, Charlie Dutton's mother returned home from her vigil with the other women and caught Charlie red-handed. There was a row and Charlie stormed out of the house and took a train back to Liverpool.

He'd teach the auld witch a lesson. Stay away for Christmas. She wouldn't like that. Bloody hell, all he'd done was fondle Josie a bit. Josie was his younger sister and not quite all there, but she was soft and warm and had breasts like ripe fruit, and she loved to be touched.

When the pubs closed at ten o'clock, Charlie drifted in the direction of the Pier Head. He walked with hands thrust deeply into his coat pockets, woolen muffler pulled up over his chin against the chill of the night air. Vague shapes loomed in the misty shadows. A pair of stone lions, prone, ageless, guarding the wide steps ascending to St. George's Hall; but the building itself was obscured by mist so that the steps led nowhere. Like his life.

The stupid toffs up at Saxon Hall had never bothered to check on his progress at the trade school, so didn't know Charlie had stopped attending school the summer he accosted old Saxon's daughter while she was out riding. So long as he kept out of sight, his lodgings were paid for and his mam and sisters received his "wages." Blood money, he thought resentfully.

He hadn't inquired of his mam about relatives who might have been rescued from the pit. He'd seen that neighbor kid, Corwin, brought up. Someone said they'd cut off his leg. Didn't matter much, weird little bugger would rather read books than kick a ball about or chase girls.

Charlie chuckled to himself, thinking of the expression on Saxon's face at the pit. Probably credited Charlie with causing the explosion. Fair enough. By the time he was finished with Saxon, he'd have him believing Charlie Dutton could cause the Saxons misfortune simply by willing it. Maybe he could.

Someone had left an empty stout bottle on the curb. He kicked it into the street and heard it shatter. He hoped some toff ran over the broken glass and tore his tires to shreds. The fire in the Saxon stables now, that had been Charlie's doing. He'd have got into the house to the kid's room too, if they hadn't come back so soon.

At the Pier Head he sauntered down to the floating landing stage and boarded a ferry for Birkenhead. For a few coppers he could ride back and forth across the river all night so long as he stayed aboard. Charlie liked the river. It smelled of brine and fish and rust and rancid oil, but it was relentlessly going somewhere.

Charlie wanted desperately to be going somewhere too. But he couldn't do anything until the debt had been paid. He climbed up to the top deck of the ferry and watched the lights of the Cunard Building fade into the mist.

He had to even the score with Saxon, that was certain. His mam had told him that gossip had it that there was no love lost between Lady Saxon and her son. There was a rumor that he had a bit of stuff down in the village, but Charlie had never been able to find out who. There were several widows and old maids and one woman who took care of the colliers on Saturday nights. The little girl with the big gray eyes that looked like pearls—Geneva Saxon—she was all old man Saxon had. Everyone said he thought the sun rose and set on her. But one little girl wasn't enough to pay for a father and two brothers. Unless she suffered first, like Charlie's dad had suffered—sitting so still because each breath was torture— and Saxon would have to know she had suffered, have to live with it for the rest of his life, just like Charlie had to live with his memory of his father's filthy, miserable illness and death.

He walked briskly around the deck, inhaling the dank air. He worried constantly about his lungs, was given to frequently emptying his lungs of all air, to make a fresh start, then drawing in the air in slow, measured breaths.

Yes, Geneva Saxon would pay for the sins of her father. That was not only just, but it also gave Charlie a purpose in life, a direction. That she was only a child did not matter. In a way he and Geneva shared a special destiny. He was the avenger, she the victim. There was an almost unholy logic to it, something like a marriage.

He went down into the humid warmth of the saloon, blinking in the sudden light. Not many passengers this time of night. Over in a corner, face buried in a magazine, was a young girl wearing a secondary school uniform; black velour hat with her school colors on the band encircling it, school badge on the pocket of her coat, skinny legs encased in black wool stockings. She was about the same age as the Saxon girl. And alone.

He sat down opposite her, watching her covertly, thinking suddenly of his sister Josie and the bit of fun his mam had interrupted earlier that day. He wondered if the girl opposite him had the beginning of breasts, budding somewhere under her heavy coat.

Josie was well developed for her age, almost as if nature had compensated for not giving her any brains. The doctor at the clinic had told his mam that Josie had the mental age of a five-year-old and would never grow up. But the doctor was wrong, because Josie's body was already more womanly than his older sister, Millie, who was a shriveled old maid of thirty.

The girl in the school uniform gathered up her books and stood up as the ferry nudged the landing stage. They were back on the Liverpool side of the river, he realized, as he got up and followed her.

Their footsteps echoed behind them as they went up the tunnel to the street. The thin mist was now blossoming into a thick fog, and the schoolgirl stood uncertainly beside a tram stop, no doubt wondering if the trams would still be running. An old lady hobbled out of the shelter and approached her. "I've been waiting for ages for a number four," she said.

Charlie walked up behind them, forming a three-person queue.

"My mummy will be having fits," the girl confided to the old woman. "I stayed after school and missed the bus that takes me to the ferry. I was with a friend and didn't notice the time."

Charlie made a great show of pulling his father's pocket watch from inside his waistcoat and studying the time. The watch had not actually been working for years. "I'm in an awful hurry—would you ladies like to share a cab with me?" he asked. "Won't cost much, with the three of us."

They dropped the old lady off first, then Charlie directed the cab driver to take the girl home. The cab stopped in front of a block of flats near London Road. After the girl paid her share of the fare and stepped out into the fog, Charlie said to the driver, "Think I'll get out here too. I can walk from here." He flung a half crown at the man and leaped out of the cab.

She had just reached the front steps when Charlie's hand went over her mouth. Her books flew from her arms and fell with a soft flutter to the ground, hidden by the fog. Dragging her backward, he thought with some irritability how thin she was under her coat. Skinny as a little bird, and with about as much strength. She struggled weakly and made whimpering sounds in her throat as he pulled her across the street to the closed and shuttered shops.

In the nearest doorway he slammed her back against the glass of the shop window, still keeping his hand over her mouth, and tore open her coat. The serge of her gym slip resisted his tearing fingers, but the buttons on the shoulder broke. A school tie—good—something to choke her with to keep her quiet. He yanked on it until she was gasping for breath, then ripped open her cotton blouse.

At the touch of his hands on her flesh she struggled with renewed desperation. Out on the fog-shrouded street foot-steps and a burst of drunken laughter announced homeward-bound stragglers from the local pub. Charlie pulled the girl close and covered her mouth with his lips, turning his broad back to the street so that when the group of men stumbled past, they saw only the blurred outline of a couple kissing in the doorway.

When their bawdy comments faded into the night, Charlie flung the girl away from him in distaste. Her chest felt like that of a scrawny chicken, all delicate bones and childish flesh, and her mouth had tasted salty with tears. His hands went under her skirt, tearing at her cotton knickers.

She broke away, tried to run, but he caught her and pulled

her back, imprisoning her against the door with his body as he unbuttoned his trousers. Suddenly she raised her knee and caught him in the groin. He doubled over in pain, but not before one hand entangled her hair. Gasping and moaning his agony, he held on to her until the waves of pain subsided. Then he smashed his fist into her face, again and again.

When she slipped limply to the damp pavement, he flung himself on top of her, forcing her thighs apart with his knee and lying there, waiting for his erection to return.

The street was deserted now, silent except for the melancholy wail of the foghorns on the river. As his manhood again began to stir, the fog closed in around them like a blanket.

Chapter 9

Along the Mississippi

They had been vagabonds for a year. A tall sinewy black man with strange sad eyes and a boy with bold dark eyes, watching over each other with fierce protectiveness. They caught fish, trapped game, worked odd jobs. At night they slept under a woven canopy of cottonwoods and willows. The idyll came to an end at Mardi Gras.

A storm swept up the river, turning the sky to angry copper and tearing the moss loose to whirl over their heads. Finding shelter in an abandoned house, Matt had felt a strange surge of excitement as they huddled together in an upstairs room. Wind and rain were tearing the world asunder in an orchestrated orgy of violence that was somehow wildly beautiful.

Then suddenly, inexplicably, as though silenced by the descending fist of some mighty god, everything stopped. Where a moment before their shouted voices could not be heard, now the dripping of water from the eaves was loud and clear. "What happened?" Matt whispered, awed.

"We're in the eye. In a few minutes the other side of the storm will catch up with us." Despite the rising swamp waters and uprooted trees and even a pair of cottonmouths they saw swimming in the brackish water that now flooded the downstairs rooms, there was in Specks' voice the same euphoria Matt felt, as though he too had been charged with the electricity of the elements.

"You know what, Matt? If'n we live through this, we can live through anything. And if'n we do, I'm going back for Lottie. And I'm going to blow my horn in the big parade on Fat Tuesday. Lottie's going to be there and so are you. We's going home for Mardi Gras!"

They did live through the buffeting wind and rain; saw Spanish moss stand straight up on the cypresses like plumes of smoke. When it was all over, a bobcat, wet and stunned, sat in the crotch of a tree. Just below on a kneelike root was a large swamp rabbit. In the aftermath of the hurricane, predator and prey were oblivious to each other. And Specks and Matt went home to New Orleans.

Mardi Gras throbbed through the narrow streets of the French Quarter with music and laughter and the dancing feet of mummers. Matt stared at a carriage, bedecked with flowers and pulled by a high-stepping pair of matched bays. A huge red-feathered turkey bird strutted by, and then a tuxedo-clad tramp atop ten-foot stilts lurched playfully toward the crowd. Satin-draped horses pulled a dazzling float from whose fairy-land grotto leered ferociously masked devils.

"Throw me something, mister," the watching urchins yelled.

There was a mad scrambling as a handful of beads and doubloons was scattered on the street. Oh, it was a polished gem of a day. In the distance Matt could hear Dixieland, played as only Specks and the Jazzmen could play. They would be here soon.

Although the previous night Matt had tried to stay awake for Lottie's arrival, by midnight he was asleep from sheer exhaustion. He opened his eyes briefly when he heard the low murmur of voices. The room seemed to be filled with fresh flowers.

This morning there was a blanket hanging from a string across the room. Lifting a corner, Matt saw the sunlight gilding the brass posts of Specks' bed, painting the planes of Specks' bare chest so that it seemed he was a magnificent statue, cast in bronze. Nestled against the crook of his arm was the tumbled profusion of Lottie's red curls. One delicate white arm draped over Specks' chest like the neck of a swan against a dark lake. Her mouth was open, like a red heart.

Later, over breakfast, Matt learned that his grandfather had hounded Mr. DeVore right out of business. Matt was silent as the specter of both Grandfather Castleton and DeVore cast a shadow over the promise of the morning.

"We're going to leave New Orleans tonight, Matt," Specks said. "Soon as the parade is over. DeVore's going to come looking for Lottie, and your grandfather ain't never stopped searching for you."

Matt thought of that murdered boy, swinging from the tree, who still haunted his nightmares. Jumping to his feet, he said, "Let's go now."

Specks laughed and ruffled his hair. "No rush. Folks is packed into the Quarter like sardines. Nobody's going to find us till the crowd thins out some."

When night fell, it seemed the whole world was jammed into the narrow street, so that when Specks led the parade beneath the iron balcony where Lottie stood watching, and he stopped to play for her alone, the crowd swept forward, surrounding him, stomping their feet and yelling. The parade came to a laughing, jumbled halt. Smiling broadly, his unseeing eyes tranquil, Specks threw back his head and blew his horn until a great hush fell upon the other musicians and merrymakers alike.

He played "Muddy Water," "Coconut Dance," "Grizzly Bear," "Black Diamond," "Dill Pickles," and still they wouldn't let him go. It was a one-man concert. Then he filled the night air with "I'll Dance till the Sun Breaks Through." Finally he played "Dardanella" like it had never been played before, and the crowd was laughing and weeping for joy. Above Specks' head Lottie watched and listened, leaning forward on the delicate iron rail.

Matt felt a great surge of love sweep the street, rushing like a sparkling wave to spend all its electrifying energy on the horn player whose shining hour it was. More and more people jostled closer, and as adulation washed over Specks and his fellow musicians clustered about him in a tight knot, Matt felt himself shoved away, caught in an undertow that separated them. Lacking the advantage of adult height, Matt found himself drowning in a sea of legs and feet. Suddenly he lost his footing and went down amid boots and carriage wheels.

Someone stepped on his hand and he cried out in pain. Panic came, bubbling in his throat, pounding in his ears, squeezing the breath from his lungs. He yelled and tugged at his imprisoned hand. Another foot crashed perilously close to his head. He could see nothing but boots and legs, packed solidly around him.

The foot holding down his hand shifted slightly and he rolled toward it, jamming his shoulder into the man's calf. His hand came free and he dived under the nearest carriage. Clutching his swollen hand to his chest, he crawled to the back of the carriage and pulled himself cautiously to his feet. The crowd had swept by and he could almost breathe normally again.

Then he saw the gleaming black Chandler parked across the street and at the wheel a man in a black hat. DeVore! Matt ducked behind the carriage. Specks was surrounded by people. Lottie was up on the balcony. Matt glanced upward. She was gone.

Peering around the corner of the carriage, Matt saw DeVore lean over and open the passenger door. Then Matt saw the two men dragging Lottie toward the car. She was struggling, and one man had his hand over her mouth and the other had twisted her arms viciously behind her back. No one in the crowd was looking in their direction. Matt didn't hesitate. Bellowing at the top of his lungs for them to let go of Lottie, he charged across the street, head down, butting the nearest man in the stomach.

Surprised and winded, the man let go of Lottie and, swearing, reached for the boy. Lottie took advantage of the confusion to jab her high heel into the instep of the other man, and his hand fell from her mouth as he hopped in pain.

"Lottie! Quick—get Specks!" Matt yelled.

One of the men grabbed the flimsy material of her dress and it came away in his hand. Matt flung himself at the man's legs and hung on for dear life. He had a glimpse of Lottie's silk stockings as she pushed her way into the crowd. The second man started after her and Matt kicked out with both feet, tripping him.

They all fell heavily to the dusty pavement. Dazed, Matt felt iron fingers dig into his chest, lifting him by his shirt. Inches away were the shark eyes of DeVore. His thin flat lips barely moved, but Matt heard the words. "We'll get them later. Let's get the kid outa here. We finally got an ace in the hole to play against old man Castleton."

Matt never knew what happened during the rest of that night. He was never sure how long they had kept him tied and blindfolded. He knew only that after that Mardi Gras, he spent seven years in a succession of military academies. He was expelled from two of them for insubordination, ran away from two others. Once he returned to Lottie's Lair to question Zeke, but he was gone and the new madam slammed the door in Matt's face and called the police.

A trip to New Orleans to ask the Jazzmen for news of Specks was slightly more hopeful. "We ain't seen him since the night of the Rex Parade," they told him. "But there was a big important man from New York asking about him. Said he was producing a Broadway show and wanted to talk to Specks. Only Specks was gone someplace. Never did come back. We figured he'd met up with the man."

Matt rationalized that Specks had to get Lottie out of town and there was nothing he could do for Matt, so it made sense to go north to New York. But Matt was hurt that they hadn't sent him a note telling him they were safe. Lottie could have written, even if Specks couldn't see well enough to write. There was nothing to do but grow up, fast as he could, and go find them.

So he studied and drilled and spit-polished his shoes, and all would be well until someone gave a ridiculous order and Matt rebelled. At seventeen he was accepted by his grandfather's university and life improved considerably. Then, abruptly, everything changed.

October 1929. A week after news of the stock market crash, Matt was on a train in the company of one of his grandfather's clerks, a pale and wizened young man named Dooley who had appeared on campus and announced that Matt was to return to Greenboughs immediately. On the train to Natchez, Dooley said, "Your granddaddy lost most everything. You won't be going back to school." Dooley wheezed slightly as he spoke, giving all of his statements an unrelenting urgency.

At nineteen Matt was over six feet tall, with muscular shoulders and chest tapering to lithe hips and long legs that moved with the controlled precision of one accustomed to treading the uncertain and shifting swampland where he had spent his early childhood. He said slowly, "But his money wasn't all in stocks. What about the barges and tugs. Warehouses. All the properties he owned?"

"All owned by the various companies your grandfather controlled. There were loans, mortgages, some dubious investments. The only liquid assets were the stocks that just became worthless. By the time the creditors are finished with us, there'll be nothing left."

Matt thought of the iron-willed old man who had ruled his

life for the past seven years and, unaccountably, felt sorry for him. "The house too? Greenboughs?"

"Greenboughs is part of a trust he set up several years ago," Dooley said carefully. "Since the rest of the trust was made up of stocks in his companies, the house is the only tangible asset left. The trust was for you, Matt. I suppose you could say the house is now yours and your grandfather is living there on your charity."

Matt leaned back against the dusty upholstery of his seat, watching the countryside framed by the train window, not knowing how to react to this news. Unwillingly he seemed to have switched places with his grandfather. Whereas before Matt's only thought had been to escape from the old man's tyrannical rule, now it seemed that he was inexplicably responsible for the welfare of both of them.

If he expected to find a frail and broken old man waiting for him at Greenboughs, he was mistaken. Archer Castleton might have been down, but he was far from out. Feisty and cantankerous as ever, refusing to admit defeat, he was full of grandiose plans for the future.

Struggling through the early years of the Depression, Matt and his grandfather lived in faded splendor at Greenboughs, constantly at loggerheads. A battle of wills and wits raged that was secondary only to the fight for survival. Whereas Matt had no compunction about selling furniture and pictures and antiques to pay taxes, or even to put a meal on their table, Archer Castleton preferred to go hungry than to part with his possessions. Matt had to remind him that everything in the house now legally belonged to him and he wasn't going hungry; although the old man gave in, Matt felt no sense of victory.

Matt worked when he could find work, often on the river, while Castleton became involved with various enterprises—not all of them legitimate—that rarely made any money.

While they still actively hated one another, a certain grudging respect developed with the passing of time.

One evening, after a particularly grueling day rebuilding a washed-out levee, for which he had been paid twenty cents an hour, Matt returned to Greenboughs to find his grandfather in a strangely subdued mood. Nathan, the only servant still with them, who remained more because of age and infirmity than loyalty, was waiting for Matt in the hall and sent him into the study.

Castleton was sitting at his desk, staring at a battered cardboard carton. "You never asked me about your mother," he said. "What kind of son never asks about his mother? Did you know I found her in a gin mill—after that Cajun abandoned her? He even took her baby—you."

Matt could smell the whiskey on his grandfather's breath from across the desk. "Specks told me why my father left. My mother was an alcoholic. She would forget where she left me. They were both playing in a band aboard a paddlewheeler— Specks and my father. One night they came home and found her, drunk, with another man. I guess it was several hours before they found me."

Castleton came up out of his chair. "Shut your goddamn mouth. You speak of your mother with respect, you hear me?"

"Why don't we just change the subject?" Matt suggested.

The cardboard box was pushed across the table toward him. Inside the box Matt could see a bundle of letters, some other documents in tattered envelopes. He picked up a gold watch, a knife with a French name carved into the wooden handle. Medals . . . the Croix de Guerre and Distinguished Service Cross. At the bottom of the box was a khaki uniform.

"Your father is dead," Castleton said. "Last night. There's some insurance money. Those are his personal things—I told you about them, years ago."

Matt stood still, absorbing the fact that his father had at last escaped from his broken mind and body. Grief mingled with relief, gave way to regret, and nothing made any sense.

"Open that big envelope," his grandfather said. "Look inside."

Matt slowly withdrew a document issued in Paris in 1918, written in French, bearing a gold seal. A faded photograph fell from within the folds. The sepia tones showed a young girl, wearing a wide-brimmed hat over dark hair. Her gown was old-fashioned, with lace and a cameo brooch at the neck. Tapered fingers held long white gloves. Her features were breathtakingly, heartbreakingly lovely, but most compelling of all were her eyes. There was an eerily hypnotic quality about the eyes that, having captured his glance, refused to let go.

Reluctantly Matt turned to the official looking document, part of which was printed and part written in fading ink. His father's name was inscribed there, John M. Lauren. And on the other end of the same line, "Celine Thibault."

A marriage certificate. His father had married a French woman some time before the shell fragment wiped away his memory. There was a date, *28 Septembre, 1918.*

John Lauren had married Celine Thibault scant weeks before the war ended and he became a vegetable.

Chapter 10

Lancashire, England

Charlie Dutton crouched behind the privet hedge that bordered the most remote acreage of Saxon Hall, where the grounds met the cool dark woods. Through the polished leaves he could see an impromptu polo match taking place on the lawn.

Hooves thundered and turf flew to the accompaniment of snorting horses and the staccato crack of mallet against ball. Occasionally there was a burst of applause from the spectators sitting on deck chairs under the shade of oak trees that had been full-grown when a similar group of young men dropped their mallets to go off and fight the Great War. But Charlie was not watching the white-clad horsemen.

Geneva was home for the holidays. For once her father had not whisked her off to the south of France for most of the summer. Turning her into a proper little Frenchie, some said. Where the trees grew thickest, the grass gave way to beds of bluebells, nodding in thin beams of sunlight that penetrated the leafy roof of the copse. Seated upon a canvas deck chair amid the bluebells was Geneva. Charlie savored her beauty with his eyes, a trickle of saliva escaping from the corner of his mouth. She had been a pretty child, but now she was poised on the threshold of . . . not womanhood, but that mysterious time that precedes it, and there was a breathless, haunting, fragile quality about her that had surely belonged to the virgin sacrifices of countless pagan tribes. The aura of purity and goodness.

Charlie had not seen her for some time, due to a succession of misadventures, and he rejoiced that his revenge had been postponed until now. It was exactly the right time. The moment before the rosebud opens to full flower.

Shifting his bulk to a more comfortable position, Charlie shredded privet leaves impatiently. Where the hell was that blasted scullery maid? The longer he observed the scene on the lawn, the more difficult it was to restrain his impulse to run down there and grab Geneva Saxon. Already the swelling in his groin threatened to burst his trousers. His head ached as thoughts spun through his mind in bright kaleidoscopic shapes.

He was breathing slow deep breaths, filling his lungs and emptying them with rhythmic precision, aware of each separate breath. Sometimes he thought that all Charlie Dutton consisted of was a pair of delicate lungs, a great big sex organ, and that frightening cavern of his mind where ideas were born that never occurred to other men. Those parts of him dominated the rest and were, strangely, dependent on each other in a way he could not define.

"Charlie . . ." a voice whispered behind him.

He turned, crouched as though ready to spring. The scullery maid jumped backward in alarm.

Charlie grinned. He liked that frightened look that came to a girl's face. Frightened, but fascinated by him. Straightening up, he opened his arms and she came into them willingly.

"I'm sorry, I couldn't get away until now, Charlie. Old Rankin had me helping Cook with the refreshments. Refreshments—s'truth, you never saw so much food. Salmon in aspic and cracked lobster and the biggest bloody trifle, thought I'd never get enough cream whipped for it—"

"Shut up," Charlie said. He bent over her, his eyes so pale they reflected the shadows of the woods and her own face, like some haunted mirror warning the watcher to beware. She closed her eyes, shivering, and pursed her lips for his kiss.

His mouth devoured hers, tongue seeking the far recesses of her throat. She leaned against him, drained by his sheer masculine force. The other maids at Saxon Hall had been both envious and afraid for her when Charlie Dutton started to court her. She knew that he had just been released from reform school, that his sister was a mental case, and that it was rumored he'd got two girls in trouble in Liverpool. But crikey, he was so good looking, so big and strong. . . .

She was whimpering against his mouth when he slipped his hand under her knees and lifted her into his arms to carry her back to the seclusion of the woods. Placing her down on a drift of fallen leaves, brown and decaying yet pungently soft, he plucked at the buttons of her dress. Her eyes were glazed, staring up at him as she protested weakly, "Oh, Charlie, we mustn't. No, please . . ."

Her breasts were free, plump and yielding beneath his hands, and her skirts were already up around her thighs. She was pretending to push him away and he batted her hands away, thinking that all women should be like his sister Josie, who would let him do it to her any time of the day or night they were able to escape the watchful eyes of Mam and Millie. Josie needed no warming up. She was just a mindless female body.

Charlie took several deep breaths and played with the scullery maid, running his hands over her soft white body, exploring all of her silken hollows and dark moist places. She winced as he bit her nipple, his fingers pinching her vulva. "Charlie, you're hurting me." Tears swam to her eyes.

"When are you going to get me into your room?" he asked, relaxing his grip.

"I told you, I sleep with three other—ahh!" She gasped in pain as he bit her again, leaving the imprint of his teeth on her breast. Almost immediately he lay on top of her and kissed her mouth again, little fluttering kisses, his lips barely grazing hers, and his hands were gentle as he stroked her inner thighs.

"They all home for the summer now?" Charlie inclined his head in the direction of Saxon Hall. The girl in his arms nodded, still trembling with both fear and passion. He started to unbutton his trousers, rubbing her with the back of his hand as he did so.

Her eyes were half closed and she felt as though she were in a trance. "Master Terry's going to catch it if he's not careful. Stayed out all night, he did, and Mr. Ian tried to keep Milady from finding out." She drew a breath, squirming with pleasure as Charlie rewarded her with even more intimate caresses. Charlie liked to hear all the gossip from the hall. "They say Master Terry goes sneaking off to see some chorus girl in Liverpool."

"Never mind bloody Master Terry. What about Geneva—

what's she up to? Her dad not taking her to France this year then?"

"Charlie!" the girl said reproachfully. "You told me it weren't true what everybody said about you wanting to hurt Miss Geneva."

He smiled ingratiatingly and teased her, starting to penetrate, then pulling back, sliding against her until she raised her hips to try to bring him inside her. "I won't lay a hand on the kid. I just want old stiff-arse Saxon to think I'm going to. Come on, she must be alone sometimes, go somewhere by herself?"

She was moaning softly, twisting her head from side to side, her thighs damp against him. "Charlie, can you hurry up a bit? I've got to get back or Cook will kill me—they'll be serving lunch soon."

Both of his hands closed over her breasts, squeezing until sweat beaded on her forehead. Her cry of pain was cut off as his teeth tore savagely at her lips. When he released her bloodied mouth, she gasped out the words, "Sometimes . . . she walks . . . down by the river . . . early in the morning before anyone's up—"

Charlie filled his lungs with air and rammed into her so hard the dead leaves rose in a flurry around her hips.

Geneva shivered suddenly and glanced over her shoulder toward the woods. The bluebells still nodded at her feet, the sunshine was mellow, and Terry and his new friend were demolishing the other team, but a chill had wafted down from nowhere.

"Who is the rather Oriental-looking chap Terry brought home?" Ian asked. He was seated in a deck chair beside her. "Good thing they're on the same side or they'd be fierce rivals."

Geneva looked back at her cousin and his friend. Both were tall, with not a spare ounce of flesh on their long-legged bodies, but their physical resemblance ended there. Terry had an open-faced, cheeky grin and frank amber eyes that were incapable of deceit. His dark gold hair blew in untamed waves, but he was one of those carelessly elegant young men who never looked unkempt. His friend was black-haired, olive-skinned, with inscrutable dark eyes and flaring nostrils that gave him an intense and somewhat brooding look.

She said, "His name is Huw Wakefield. He and his

grandfather just returned from abroad—a retired colonel from the Royal Engineers. He bought the old abbey and is restoring it. Apparently Huw's parents were killed in India."

"Eurasian," Ian murmured. "Odd that a man back from the tropics would buy that drafty old abbey."

"He told Terry that his grandfather was an explosives expert, that he'd spent his life blowing things up, and restoring the abbey was his penance. I overheard Huw ask Terry, 'Don't you ever sweat? Isn't it done here?' and Terry said, 'You remain rather cool and collected yourself, but in your case I suspect it's from sheer arrogance,' and they both laughed and punched each other on the shoulder."

"From watching them play polo," Ian said thoughtfully, "I'd say there is a great deal of difference between them. Terry believes it doesn't matter who wins or loses, so long as the game is played fairly. Huw Wakefield seems obsessed with winning."

"You didn't tell me how Ted Corwin is. You went to see him this morning, didn't you?"

A worried frown knitted Ian's brows. "The doctors say he must have another operation on his leg. I hoped they would save the knee . . ."

"Oh, I am sorry. That letter that came from Germany, was that from the German surgeon you heard about?"

Ian nodded. "I think I'm going to send Ted to Germany. See if they can save the rest of his leg. They have new techniques—they want to try weaving the shattered bones together with silver wire."

"You should talk to Huw Wakefield then. He is leaving in the autumn for Heidelberg University. Perhaps he could travel with Ted?"

"Good idea. I will talk to him. Ted is a brilliant boy. I wish he were strong enough to go to university."

Geneva smiled. "Grandmarm would have a fit if you tried to educate him too." *Ian's strays,* Geneva thought, *that's what Grandmarm calls Charlie Dutton and Ted Corwin . . . and me.*

But she didn't really feel she was a part of that group, because she was her father's daughter and they were not his sons. Sometimes she wished her father had married, so that there could have been a brother or a sister in whom she could confide and who would be company when business took her father away from her, but then she wasn't sure she wanted another woman in her father's life; it seemed unfaithful to the memory of her mother. Terry wasn't really like a brother, Geneva felt; he was four years older and so different in coloring and looks and temperament that it was hard to believe he was even her cousin. She often mused about what it would have been like to have a real brother, perhaps a younger version of her father.

There was an exuberant shout from Terry as the game was won, and they came cantering over to where the footmen were serving cold lemonade to the spectators. Servants were now spreading white tablecloths over the trestle table and transporting from the house platters of cold meat and fish, trays of Cornish pasties and thick wedges of pork pie. Rankin himself carried out the crystal bowl containing the trifle, its whipped cream topping sprinkled with nuts and chopped angelica and cherries glistening like rubies and emeralds.

Lady Saxon walked with the aid of a cane, and as she approached, Terry swung down from his horse to offer his arm. Lady Saxon was pale and gaunt, each step costing her more effort than she ever would have admitted. A lace handkerchief was never far from her lips nowadays and she was often overcome by paroxysms of coughing, but she refused to see a doctor. She looked disdainfully at Terry's outstretched hand.

"Don't you dare touch me, young man, until you've washed away the smell of horse and perspiration."

Terry winked. "You mean the horse's sweat, of course. We Saxons never sweat, it's bad form."

"Don't be vulgar," Lady Saxon snapped, but her eyes watched him fondly as he ran back toward the house, calling for Huw and the other players to follow him. She allowed Rankin to assist her to a chair and bring her a plate of food, which she toyed with but did not eat.

Shortly after the trestle table was cleared and the guests drifted away, some to the tennis courts behind the sculpted privet hedge, others to walk in the rose garden, Terry found himself explaining his night-long absence to his uncle Ian.

"It was late when I decided to stay over, and I didn't want to wake anyone by phoning." Terry smiled engagingly.

Ian regarded him silently for a moment. "I take it there was a young lady involved?"

Terry winked and cleared his throat suggestively.

"I've lectured you often enough on the dangers inherent in

casual relationships with women, particularly women not of your class who seem to have an irresistible fascination for you. Therefore, I'll merely point out that it's inconsiderate to cause concern by being absent without explanation. Terry, you're almost an adult in the eyes of the law. I've been looking forward to placing the reins in your hands—the colliery, the farms. But this lack of responsibility on your part fills me with doubts."

"You know I don't give a damn about the Saxon holdings. Honestly, Ian, it's most unfair of Grandmother to do this to you. I mean, after all, dash it, you've been running things since Father and Grandfather were killed. Why should you turn everything over to me?"

"Because, my good chap, you are the firstborn son of a firstborn son, and that's the way the Saxons have always handled things. I believe it has something to do with a strain of ineffectual younger brothers in our line." Ian gave a tired smile. "Besides, I was thrust into the position of head of the household even more reluctantly than you."

Terry dropped to the nearest chair and surveyed his uncle gloomily. "I'll barely get my degree before my twenty-first. Not much time for sowing any wild oats."

Ian raised an eyebrow. "Terence, Terence. You've been sowing wild oats, to my knowledge, since you were fourteen years old. Now what about this chorus girl?"

"Dory? Oh, don't worry, she hasn't given me the time of day, so far."

Ian looked perplexed. "Then why did you stay in town all night?"

"Because, Uncle, old boy, although Miss Dory Gates finds me quite resistible, others in her troupe do not. And by the time I left Dory, believe me, I needed to find solace somewhere."

"Perhaps you should think about finding a wife to take care of such matters for you?"

Terry gave an exaggerated grimace of horror. "I say, come on!"

Ian paused and regarded Terry's expression with some amusement. "You'd better join your guests. But please be discreet with the chorus girl—what was her name? Dory Gates."

Terry made his way through the deserted corridors of Saxon Hall. The afternoon was hot, and a languid air of summer madness seemed to pervade the house. Everyone was outside, except for the distant clatter of dishes below-stairs that indicated the servants were hard at work.

Marriage, indeed! Although if the delectable Dory Gates had been a lady—but that subject was too serious for such a day. This was a day for carefree play, for stolen kisses and boyish pranks.

Whistling softly under his breath, Terry ran up the stairs to his room, anxious to change his clothes. He was aware of vague pangs of regret that could have been the result of Ian's grim reminder that youthful irresponsibility would soon be left behind. Perhaps that was why he remembered other prank-filled holidays and pink-cheeked scullery maids who giggled and protested while promising uninhibited delights with their eyes.

"Terry." Her voice was low, but he jumped, startled.

He had stripped down to his skin and quickly picked up his shirt to hold in front of him as he turned to face her.

Geneva stood in the doorway, her hand raised as though to knock on the door, which was ajar.

Terry said, "I was just changing," and immediately felt foolish for stating the obvious. The innocent trust in her eyes unnerved him. He felt a sudden urge to run, but stood still, his knees slowly turning to water as she came into the room. *She's going to be stunning when she grows up,* he thought. "You shouldn't be in here—while I'm undressed." His voice was hoarse. He cleared his throat.

"I had to talk to you for a minute. It's important. About Ian." Her gaze was deeply troubled, her lovely gray eyes more clouded than he had ever seen them. He wrenched his eyes from her and reached for his dressing gown, afraid she could see his most deeply buried thoughts. Longings he had never been truly consciously aware of rushed from some deep well inside him, touching nerve endings like liquid fire. He was appalled at his own carnal thoughts. Geneva was inno-cence personified, yet there was already a hint of that certain magnetic allure bestowed on only a few women.

"Father is in rather desperate financial straits," Geneva said. "Everyone—Grandmarm and you—just assumed he had been managing. But he hasn't. He borrowed money for new equipment for the colliery, didn't collect rents during that hoof-and-mouth disease period. But he never asked for any money from the trust funds. He used all of his own savings, and the pitiful amount he receives as an allowance barely covers his personal expenses, let alone payments on bank loans."

"But good lor' why the devil hasn't he said something?" Terry glanced nervously toward the door.

"He tried to tell Grandmarm. She said the Saxon holdings are self-supporting and he should learn to manage better. That all the money is in trust for you."

"I don't know what I can do."

"Talk to her. She'll listen to you."

"Well . . ." Terry said doubtfully.

Geneva gave a small cajoling smile. "Last night Father told everyone you phoned to say you were staying with a friend, and Grandmarm asked me point-blank if I knew which young lady was making you all moon-eyed. Terry, I didn't tell her the young lady in question is a chorus girl at the Liverpool Pavilion."

Terry regarded her with dawning comprehension. "I'm grateful. But why do I get the feeling I'm being blackmailed? It's not necessary, you know. I'll gladly speak with Grandmarm—I just don't believe I can influence her. You know, Gen, you're a proper little mother hen with Ian. You'd do anything for him, wouldn't you? I sometimes think you two would kill for each other. If you ever give that kind of loyalty to a husband, cousin dear, he's going to be a lucky man. Now you'd better leave before I get improper ideas about my lovely young relative. There's something about a fast polo match that brings out the beast in me."

Geneva was halfway down the staircase when she saw Rankin running across the hall toward the telephone. He was purple from exertion and his face twitched violently. The sound of raised voices outside followed him, and a moment later Huw Wakefield appeared, cradling in his arms the suddenly tiny and frail figure of Lady Sybil Saxon. Her waxen face hung limply over his arm.

"Send an ambulance," Rankin was saying into the telephone. "Lady Saxon has collapsed."

Geneva flung open the drawing room doors. "Bring her in here," she instructed Huw. The hall was rapidly filling with anxious guests and servants.

Huw placed Lady Saxon on a brocaded chaise and Geneva quickly rearranged her grandmother's gown to cover her knees, then wiped a smear of blood from the corner of her mouth. Geneva's eyes met Huw Wakefield's darkly inscrutable gaze. "Father has been trying to get her to see a doctor—her cough has been getting steadily worse. Where is Father, by the way? I didn't see him come in."

"Just before your grandmother collapsed, the gamekeeper came for him. They went off together toward the woods. One of the servants is searching for him now."

Lady Saxon moaned and stirred. Geneva dropped to her knees beside her. "It's all right, Grandmarm. You fainted. We'll take care of you."

"Ian? Where's Ian?" Lady Saxon murmured fretfully. "Bring him to me, Geneva."

Geneva beckoned one of the maids clustering about the door to enter the room. "Stay with her," she whispered. "I'll go and see what's keeping Father."

She was crossing the lawn when she saw Ian and the gamekeeper coming out of the woods. The gamekeeper was carrying a woman. Geneva blinked, feeling she was watching a reenactment of what had just taken place in the hall. First Grandmarm, now who else had been taken ill? But as they came closer, she saw that the girl in the gamekeeper's arms was not ill. She had been hurt. There was blood on her white apron and her face was swollen and almost unrecognizable, but the uniform proclaimed her to be one of Saxon Hall's scullery maids.

Ian called to her, "Gennie, run quickly to the house and call for an ambulance. Then call the police. This poor child has been assaulted."

Chapter 11

Natchez, Mississippi

Jobs were hard to find as the country writhed in the grip of the Great Depression. Occasionally there was work rebuilding the levees that were constantly eroded by the capricious changing of the course of the river. But some of the work bosses gave the jobs only to married men with children. Often Matt waited in line all night, only to be turned away.

When there was no work, he hunted and caught fish and worried about paying the taxes on Greenboughs. Much of the game and fish was sold to raise money and his grandfather and Nathan went hungry.

Quarrels flared frequently, especially on the subject of the marriage certificate Castleton had hidden away with his son-in-law's possessions. Matt stormed at his grandfather, "You knew. You had those things from the time he came back from France. There's a French woman somewhere who has no idea what happened to him. Didn't you even try to find her?"

"Soldiers in foreign countries often marry on the whim of the moment," Castleton said indifferently. "They suffer from a surfeit of sentimentality—especially if the girl tells them she's pregnant. The soldier thinks he might be killed, there'll be a son to carry on his name. Your father came back a hopeless invalid who didn't even know who he was. What good was he to a wife?"

"I'm going to try to find her. I'll write to the American embassy in Paris."

"And if you find her, what then? Are you going to bring her here to live with us—share our wealth?" Castleton gestured about the room. The best of the antique furniture had long ago been sold or pawned, the carpet was threadbare, and plaster showed through rotted wallpaper. "We're in the middle of a depression. Had you forgotten?"

"The army then—perhaps I could find out through the army where she is and how she's managing. If there was a child . . . I may have a brother or a sister." How many times he had wished for that. A sister, especially. He had never had a female relative and didn't remember his mother. Someone pretty and soft and gentle he could protect and watch over.

"No!" The word cracked with unexpected harshness. "Let sleeping dogs lie. Listen, boy, I never told you all the sordid details about your father. When he was hit by that shell fragment, he was absent without leave, far from his own company. If he'd not been so badly wounded he would have been court-martialed. He was lucky some British officer found him, or he would have died. And if he hadn't died, he would have been shot as a deserter. But he was taken to a British field hospital and the British contacted his outfit. The war was over by then, so they shipped him home."

"If he deserted, it was for a good reason," Matt said. He stared moodily in front of him for a moment. "That British officer—do you think my father told him anything?"

"When your father first arrived home, his army file was sent to the hospital. The name of the British outfit that found him was in it. But that file has probably been destroyed by now. Let it rest—and let him rest. What will you gain by stirring over old coals now?"

"Maybe a brother," Matt said to himself. "Or a sister."

"Your father probably sired as many bastards from here to the delta as any man alive. If it's brothers and sisters you want, I suggest you start off by searching every shanty-town—"

Matt was on his feet, eyes blazing. "Say one more word, old man, and by God I'll shut your filthy mouth."

Castleton's eyes were hard as flint. "I told you once I felt bound by no family ties to your father. You are the only reason I took him in when he came back from France. He took my only daughter and turned her into one of his whores.

She was pregnant with you before they ran off together—and dying in a waterfront dive before she was thirty."

They glowered at each other. The same territory had been covered before.

Castleton said, "What about the insurance money? It isn't doing us any good in the bank. Let me use it to buy a share in that ship I told you about. I can get a fifth share."

"I'll think about it," Matt said, not mentioning that he had already taken some of the insurance benefits to pay the Pinkerton Detective Agency in New York to find Specks.

Matt eventually gave in, and the remainder of the insurance benefits was invested in a decrepit merchant ship sailing between New Orleans and the other Gulf ports, ancient boilers wheezing, hull rusting, still bearing the name given her by her former Italian owners, *Bella Mia*.

His grandfather plunged back into the world of seagoing commerce with the enthusiasm of an old warhorse back in harness; rounding up crews, procuring cargoes, bulldozing port authorities, and bullying his partners until they let him run the vessel single-handedly.

Castleton, who had refused to sell the Greenboughs antiques to put food on their table, had no qualms about selling everything of value they had left to buy out his partners in the *Bella Mia*. He took her first real profits and bought one of the powerful tug boats used to push barges down the Mississippi, similar to the ones he had owned before the Crash. Matt was now forced to work with his grandfather since there was too much for the old man to handle alone. The years flew by, busy and productive, if still somewhat spartan.

The Pinkerton Detective Agency sent word that no one resembling Specks was playing the horn anywhere in New York or any major metropolitan center of the country. Matt replied that they were to keep looking.

In the winter of 1937 Nathan became ill with a deep wracking cough that lingered, a desperate wheezing in his chest, and became permanently bedridden. The year was also notable for a great flood in the Ohio River Valley, a bloody strike in Detroit, and the *Hindenburg* disaster. Amelia Earhart's plane had mysteriously vanished; a warlike prince became premier of Japan, while in Europe the English king had abdicated in order to marry an American commoner. Two dictators named Hitler and Mussolini were frequently in the news.

It was also the year Matt unearthed the old army records from the veterans' hospital and learned that Lieutenant Ian Saxon, of the Royal Lancashire Fusiliers, was the man who had found his wounded father. Matt sent a letter to the regimental headquarters and in due course was given Ian Saxon's civilian address. After a time, a response came to Matt's inquiry.

> Dear Mr. Lauren:
> I regret that I can add little to what you already know about your father being wounded in France. Your gratitude to me is quite without foundation. I merely summoned stretcher bearers to take your father to a field hospital. I was saddened to hear he suffered from amnesia for the remainder of his life and send you condolences on his passing.

The letter bothered Matt. He reread it but could not put his finger on what was wrong with it, yet he sensed something . . . evasion? He tossed the letter on the hall table and went to take breakfast up to Nathan's room. Castleton had already left for town, seeking a cargo for the *Bella Mia*.

Nathan's face was gray and convulsed with the effort to speak the moment Matt appeared at his bedside with a steaming bowl of grits. "Got to tell you, Matthew . . . cain't go to my Maker less'n I do—"

Matt said gently, "Take some food first. You'll feel better." Looking down at the wasted frame, Matt found it difficult to remember the times Nathan had hauled him out to the *garçonniere* for a session with the switch. Matt bore no grudge. The butler had been as much at the mercy of Archer Castleton as he was. Nathan shook his head weakly when Matt tried to press a spoonful of grits to his lips. "The horn player . . . got to tell you—"

"Specks?" Matt tensed, leaning forward.

"Letter came for you—horn player got somebody to write you. Didn't see what it said, your granddaddy burned it. Postmark—"

"You saw the postmark?" Matt held his breath.

"Town called Maple Ridge, Illinois."

Matt didn't wait to say good-bye to his grandfather. He called the woman who cleaned for them to come in and stay with Nathan, threw a change of clothes into a knapsack, and headed for the river. He made it as far as St. Louis by steamboat before his money ran out and he hopped a freight rolling through the endless snow-blanketed prairies toward the Great Lakes.

Small towns were strung along the railroad tracks, spaced by acres of farmland. The landscape was flat, unadorned, a sea of white snow and ice. Shivering in his threadbare coat, he tried to imagine what the same country looked like at harvest time when golden grain moved languidly in a hot sun.

Maple Ridge was on the Chicago, Burlington & Quincy line, southwest of Chicago. From the railroad depot Matt looked across the tracks and saw a cluster of red-brick stores. An ice cream parlor, paint store, dry goods. The rusted sign of a farm implement dealer marked the corner of the single street running through town; two rows of modest buildings, giving way to frame houses of appallingly similar and uninspired design. The awning of a movie theater jutted out at the end of the street. Walking toward it down the frozen and deserted street, Matt wondered with growing apprehension what Specks would do in such a place for a living. Everywhere was closed and shuttered. Bad timing to arrive on a Sunday. He blew on his deadened fingers.

Halfway down the block he passed a pharmacy and next to it a hole-in-the-wall shoe repair shop. In front of the latter was the inevitable shoeshine stand. He thought in passing that in a town this size, probably the only blacks in town would be Specks and the shoeshine boy.

The side door to the movie theater yielded to his shoulder. He slipped into the darkened auditorium to wait for the town's Monday morning awakening.

Breakfast was a handful of stale popcorn left in a carton under a seat. Outside a tentative sun gilded the frosty trees and sent rainbows dancing across melting ice. He walked warily, trying to keep from sliding on the disintegrating surface of the snow.

On Main Street store owners were busy clearing snow from the front of their premises. They nodded and offered greetings as he went by. In front of the shoeshine stand a boy was arranging his boxes of polish and rags. But he wasn't a boy. Despite the baggy overalls, the small figure moved with such grace that it could only be a girl.

Matt quickened his pace, sliding over slush and ice, oblivious to the stares of passersby. Reaching the shoeshine stand in a flurry of flying snow, he looked down at the little girl, his mind reeling. The child was a slender mulatto, with delicate features, gold-dusted complexion, and enormous brown velvet eyes. Now that he was close, he could see that the curls protruding from beneath a battered cap were tinged with red. She was eyeing his worn-out shoes scornfully.

"This your daddy's stand?" Matt asked. She shook her head.

"You know a man—a black man—who blows a horn? Name of Specks?"

Her eyes widened, then darted down the street as though considering flight.

"I'm a friend of his. My name is Matt Lauren."

The name obviously meant nothing to her. Matt was both disappointed and relieved. For a moment he had thought he was looking at Specks and Lottie's child. There was a hint of Specks' regal bearing, while Lottie's brash defiance seemed to be echoed in the little girl's arms-akimbo stance and reddish curls. She was looking up at him from beneath a curling fringe of eyelashes with that peculiarly beguiling glance of a child who is, unknowingly, a natural coquette.

"Mister, you want them ol' shoes shined or not?"

He heard it then. Lottie's gravelly monotone. Bending, he caught the child's hand. "Your momma's name is Lottie. Where is she?"

Her lip trembled. "No! Go away."

The shoe repair shop door behind her opened and a small swarthy man stuck out his head. "What's going on, Leah?"

Matt straightened up. "I'm a friend of Lottie—her mother. I was hoping she could help me find Specks Tobias, a horn player from New Orleans. I'm Matt Lauren, a friend of his."

The man bit his lip thoughtfully. "You'd best come inside. Leah, you run on home and bring your momma back here."

Matt followed the man into the stale smell of old leather and sweat and shoe polish. "My name's Tony," he said, avoiding Matt's gaze. "You're a bit late. Been years since Specks asked me to write to you. I want you to know, there wasn't a man in this town wouldn't have stopped it, if we could."

Matt caught his breath. Before he could speak, Tony went on, "Weren't no Negroes here before, see. When they first come there was some prejudice, you know, 'bout him being colored and her white. But they kept to themselves. Had a little place out of town and didn't come in together, so's not to get folks riled up. Fact, I never did see Lottie in town until—" He paused, his mouth a grim crescent. "See, Specks asked me if he could set up a shoeshine stand out front—"

"Specks? Shine shoes?" Matt repeated incredulously. "He was the finest horn player ever lived."

"Well, reckon if he could have resisted playing his horn—guess it was my fault, really. See, he never told nobody he was a horn player. Guess we realized why, when it was all over."

Tony searched his fly-specked ceiling, seeking words, while Matt thought of the letter from Maple Ridge that had been intercepted by his grandfather. "What happened, for Christ's sake?"

"We had this war hero, see. Won a Congressional Medal of Honor in the Great War. He was dying and he wanted to be buried here with his wife, but he wanted somebody to blow taps at his funeral. Kept fretting about it. I'll be honest with you, Matt, he was my brother. When I told Specks, he said he could blow taps. We went over to the hospital to show my brother that Specks could do it, so he'd die in peace, you know. And I don't know . . . Specks blew taps, then all at once he was blowing that horn like . . . like—"

"The angel Gabriel," Matt supplied for him, a tear glistening in the corner of his eye. "What did he play—'Muddy Water,' 'Dardanella'? Oh, God." His voice broke.

"It was a couple of weeks after my brother's funeral that the men came around. Oh, lord, if I'd only been here—but I was looking after my brother's house, settling things up. Gangsters, they were . . . hoods. Asking about a colored horn player they'd heard was here. Some drummer passing through had heard Specks play at the hospital and he'd told somebody else and they remembered somebody looking for him—"

"Never mind *how*. What happened to Specks?" Matt screamed the words.

Tony looked at his feet. "I told you, Specks and Lottie had a place out of town—just a shack, isolated. Next day she came walking up Main Street, in a daze, holding her hand up to one side of her face, blood coming out between her fingers—and she said—"

"Somebody help me. I got to bury my man and the ground is frozen hard," a rough female monotone said from the doorway.

Matt spun around. Lottie stood with her back to the

sunlight, the little girl named Leah holding on to her hand, and it was a moment before Matt saw the hideous scars that distorted Lottie's once lovely features.

"Funny thing, Matt," Lottie said with a sardonic little laugh. "I wouldn't write a letter to you. Maybe if I had, Specks wouldn't have asked Tony—and wouldn't have felt beholden to Tony. Matt, Specks tried to find you. He tore New Orleans apart that night, looking for you. He got me out of town and then went back. Next day he heard from Zeke that DeVore had taken you back to your grandfather. Specks worried about you, but I guess I kept him from coming back to see you. I was so afraid of DeVore."

"DeVore and his boys came to Maple Ridge?"

Lottie's scars pulled up one side of her mouth in a demented grin, adding to the horror of her flat statement. "They strung him up, Matt. Two weeks before Leah was born. Strung him up to a tree and made me watch."

Matt's strangled cry was trapped in his throat. Wordlessly he wrapped his arms around Lottie and held her, allowing waves of pain and grief to wash over both of them. After a moment Lottie jerked free. "Specks is lucky. He's dead. There's something worse than death. It's the state DeVore left me in."

Over her shoulder Matt looked into Leah's exquisite, too-old-for-her-years face. "You've got Leah."

"Yeah? And what's Leah got?"

Matt had not realized that he was gripping the back of a counterside chair so fiercely that two of the wooden posts snapped. He said, "Soon as I can, I'll have Specks' body taken back to New Orleans for a proper send-off, the kind he used to lead through the French Quarter. And you and Leah will come home with me. But first there's something I have to do. Where's DeVore?"

It was all so depressingly the same, Matt thought as he sat on a red velvet couch in the garish parlor of Darlene's Den, an aging mansion in a forlorn river town. The same erotic pictures and statues, the mirrors and carpets and all the tawdry trappings of the trade. The girls seemed younger, more beat-up looking than Lottie's girls had been.

Darlene undulated over to him. She wore a satin dress from the flapper era, years out of date. Her hair was frizzed about her soft-pudding face, and dark lipstick formed a cupid's-bow mouth where none had existed before. She leaned over him, exuding gin and pungent cologne and sex. "You back again, handsome? Reckon you must be some stud."

Matt grinned and winked at her.

Her eyes were hard as diamonds. "You been hanging around best part of three days. And I saw you this morning—across the street, watching the house. Now why don't you tell old Darlene what you're up to, kid?"

"Darlene, you seem like a nice understanding lady. I'm waiting for the boss-man to show up. He owes me ꞏome money for a job I did for him."

Her eyes narrowed. "What boss-man?"

"DeVore. He told me I could find him here, but I'm a bit late getting here."

"I'll say you are. DeVore ain't been around here for a couple of years. Where you been—inside?"

"Inside? Oh, yeah, I did some time. Darlene, I could sure use that money he owes me."

Darlene eyed him thoughtfully, thinking of her own son safely at school in the North. "Okay, kid. He's gone respectable, lives in a fancy house outa town. Now listen, I tell you where he is, you don't tell him I sent you, okay?"

DeVore lived in a carefully restored antebellum plantation house, and Matt stood beneath the Grecian pillars making comparisons with the dilapidated Greenboughs. The door was opened by a pugilist wearing a butler's suit.

"DeVore," Matt said.

"Get the hell outa here," the man responded just before Matt's left fist caught him under the ribs and his right arced in a clean uppercut to the jaw. A minute later he was striding across the entry hall.

The second door Matt opened revealed DeVore, seated at a desk. Shark eyes met his, thin flat lips barely moved. "How'd you get in here? Who the hell are you?" He was sliding open a drawer as Matt approached.

"Maple Ridge, Illinois. Remember the place? You'd have missed it if you'd blinked." Matt wheeled around the desk and slammed the drawer shut on DeVore's hand, holding it there.

DeVore did not flinch, nor did he glance in the direction of his trapped hand. "Castleton," he said.

"Lauren," Matt corrected. "Specks and Lottie—remember

them? You fixed them both up pretty good. How much of the job did you do yourself? You pull the rope? Slice Lottie's face?"

"Tough kid, huh? You got one minute to scram. After that you're dead."

Matt released the drawer and grabbed DeVore's shirt front, yanking him forward in his chair. A strong odor of garlic competed with the eye-smarting scent of the hair oil that plastered DeVore's thinning hair to his scalp. "We're going to the cops. You're going to confess to murdering Specks."

DeVore began to wheeze, his tiny deep-set eyes sinking into oblivion in their sockets. Several seconds passed before Matt realized DeVore was laughing. "You sure got a sense of humor, kid, 'specially for a Southerner. Christ, you rednecks *invented* lynching coons. Who the hell do you think is going to give a shit about some nigger getting his neck stretched—up north in some hick town—nine years ago? You think some Illinois lawman is coming down here to extradite me? How about the law down here? Hell, they'd slap me on the back."

Matt shoved him back in his chair, feeling helpless rage and a gut-churning need to get his hands on DeVore's throat and start choking him. If I touch him, I'll kill him, he thought, letting go of the shirt front and staring down at his hands.

The second's respite gave DeVore's foot time to find the button concealed in the carpet under his desk. The door burst open and a grizzly bear of a man shot into the room. There was a bone-wrenching impact, then no time to think; Matt could only react. As he struggled in a bear hug, DeVore whipped the gun out of his desk drawer.

Matt clasped his hands together and brought them up under the bear's chin, sending him sprawling backward onto the desk. Spinning around, Matt dived for the gun in DeVore's hand. For a split second they wrestled the gun back and forth, and into the red haze of Matt's mind flashed clear and distinct pictures. The lynched boy in the swamp—but now he was wearing the dearly beloved face of Specks with his blank unseeing eyes. Lottie's hideous, permanent grin. The pinched and undernourished features of the child, Leah.

Then the gun went off with a roar and there was a bloody mass where DeVore's face had been a moment before. The gun was in Matt's hand and he waved it at the man peeling himself from the top of the desk, who made no move toward

him as he raced for the open door. DeVore was crumpling, in
slow motion, to the floor.

Back in his room at Greenboughs, Matt rifled his drawers
for a clean shirt while he related the whole story. His
grandfather listened in grim silence. "I just wanted you to
hear it from me. I'm turning myself in, soon as I've cleaned
up. I don't know—maybe they'll let me plead self-defense,
though God knows I went after him with murder in my
heart."

Castleton looked suddenly much older. "I suppose you
blame me—for not giving you that letter that came for you?"

"What does it matter now? It's too late to change anything."

"Listen to me, boy. I've got too much of my immortality
invested in you for you to throw your life away over some
pimp who should have been exterminated years ago. I know
DeVore and his kind. If you get put away on a manslaughter
charge, you won't live to get out. The Mob will get you while
you're inside. No, you're not going to turn yourself in. But
you can't stay here, either, they'll come looking for you."
Castleton paced the room silently for a minute.

"The *Bella Mia,*" he said at last. "She sails from New
Orleans tomorrow. If you leave now you can just make it.
When she reaches Galveston, you can sign on any ship going
anywhere you choose. I'll fix up some seamen's papers for
you."

Matt considered. "Maybe you're right." He paused, his
hand on a leather writing case in his drawer, then with a
defiant look at his grandfather opened it and withdrew the
photograph of the French girl his father had married.

Castleton watched him slip the photograph between his
folded clothes in the open bag lying on the bed. "You taking
her with you?"

Matt felt himself flush and didn't know why it bothered him
that his grandfather had seen the value he placed on the
photograph. Defensively he said, "You got rid of all the
pictures of my mother. Maybe someday I'll go to France, find
Celine. She has a right to know what happened to her
husband."

His grandfather shrugged. "Just so you don't intend to
bring her back here—or return yourself until it's safe. Lay low
for a couple of years, until DeVore's forgotten. Travel; see

the world." Castleton was regarding him with an ironic expression of recognition. "That Negra ever tell you why your father suddenly up and hopped a freighter for Europe and joined up with the Allies to fight the Kaiser? We weren't even in their damn war at the time."

Matt shook his head.

"The Cajun got into a brawl—somebody insulted his darky pal and he killed a man. History sure repeats itself."

Chapter 12

Saxon Hall, England

The last lonely cry of the owl, deep in the woods, followed Geneva as she walked slowly along the riverbank, savoring the fragrance of the dawn. Ian had departed the previous day to take his mother to the warmer climate of Italy, since her sojourn in the sanitarium in the south of England had not helped in her long battle with tuberculosis. Already Geneva missed him desperately. At breakfast there would be no one to whom she could express indignation over the pages of coverage the newspapers would give to each lovelorn sigh of the American divorcée Mrs. Wallis Simpson, who wanted to be queen, while allotting two lines to the slaughter of a hundred children in the bloody war in Spain. But of more personal consequence was Geneva's need to talk to her father about the pressing matter of her education. Since her eighteenth birthday she had been experiencing a restless yearning to begin the quest she had set for herself, long ago, and she was unsure how her father would feel about her delaying going to university.

She wanted to go to northeastern France and trace her mother's origins. It was a longing that grew in intensity with each passing year. Her father had always been vague, evasive, about her mother. Celine had been young, beautiful, had told him nothing of her past, her family. They had known each other so briefly, he said, and looked so heartbroken that

Geneva couldn't bear it. Despite their almost annual holidays on the Riviera and visits to Paris, he adamantly refused to return to the old battlegrounds of the north. There was no point, he said, since Celine had no family. Such a trip would only open old wounds for him. He begged her to try to understand.

Then he had told her of her own birth, in a shelled cottage, where Celine had traveled to be with him when their daughter was born. Geneva had cried, for her mother, for him . . . for herself. But secretly she reasoned that although Celine had been an orphan, surely there was someone, somewhere, who had blood ties to her. If only she could find that someone, perhaps then she would understand why all of her life she had been haunted by a sense of someone lost to her.

Meredith had given her an embroidered motto on one of her birthdays, *Every day is a fresh beginning, every day is a world made new* . . . but at the gentle beginnings of each day on her solitary walks, Geneva felt acutely that her world was not complete.

She paused, waiting as a hare darted for cover. Beside her the river narrowed to little more than a brook as it passed Saxon Hall; shallow water singing over smooth pebbles. So accustomed was she to the sounds of the morning that when a twig snapped on the opposite bank, she was instantly alert.

Without looking around, she bent to pick a bright yellow buttercup and, admiring it, turned to retrace her footsteps. The brambles on the other bank rustled and she quickened her pace. Someone was following, closing the distance between them. Another few yards and she would reach the bridge leading to the Saxon Hall grounds. But her pursuer was on that side of the river. He would wait for her to cross the bridge. A poacher perhaps, after Saxon pheasant? But not at dawn, not close enough to the house that a gunshot would be heard.

The wooden bridge appeared ahead, shaded by willows that grew so profusely downstream that it became impossible to follow the river as it disappeared into the woods.

At the bridge she broke into a run, plunging instead into the trees. Branches tore her flesh and tugged at her hair as she scrambled through the tangle of foliage. She splashed into the stream, holding the slender willow trunks for support as her feet slid on the algae-coated stones in the shallow water. There was a flutter of wings as birds rose all around her.

The news item she had read the previous day kept hammering on her brain. She had been foolish to forget it this morning. Her ankle twisted over a slippery rock and she gave a low cry of pain, clutching at a willow branch to stop herself from sprawling in the water. *Just a little way ahead . . . keep going . . . the stepping-stones we used to play on when we were children—I can cross there and there's a way up the bank.*

Behind her she heard heavy footsteps thud across the boards of the bridge, then the crashing of a large body through the willows.

Her breath sobbed in her throat as she reached the stepping-stones. The water ran swiftly here, rushing toward a small waterfall. *Keep calm, slowly, don't slip . . . the water below the fall is more than waist deep; wet clothes will hamper your progress. One stone, two, three . . . careful. Will anyone hear if I call?*

Flinging herself on the opposite bank, she grabbed the nearest tree. A thick carpet of leafmold on the steep bank made climbing difficult and she had to pull herself from tree to tree. Few people followed the river into the woods, and even the animals chose a more accessible spot in order to drink.

Her fingers were reaching for tree roots at the top of the bank when she heard her pursuer splashing upstream. Turning, she saw Charlie Dutton leap from stone to stone. Despite his size, he moved with easy coordination, like a heavyweight boxer.

Grasping the roots, she tried to throw herself up to the safety of the meadow above, seeing a beckoning patch of sunlight. The roots came away in her hand and she tumbled backward, rolling through the dead leaves and landing at Dutton's feet.

He stopped in mid-stride, his face breaking into a grin that sent an icy ripple up her spine. He was breathing rapidly, somewhat in the manner of a diver about to spend some time under water, and he made no move toward her. She began to inch up the bank, in a sitting position, her eyes fixed on his face.

Apart from the manic grin and eyes that were so pale they appeared to be hollow, his features were even, almost handsome, if a trifle coarse. His light hair was untidy and in need of trimming. He was so close she could smell the odor of sweat and stale cooking on his clothes.

"Now then," he said, running his tongue over his upper lip,

"what 'ave we here? The posh Miss Saxon messing about in the dead leaves. Getting her nice clean frock all dirty." He clucked his tongue disapprovingly.

Meeting his stare unblinkingly, she said, "You are on Saxon property on this side of the river. I suggest you leave before the gamekeeper finds you here."

Charlie giggled. He had a high-pitched laugh that sounded almost girlish, but there was nothing feminine about his stance or the expression in his pale eyes as they went over her, lingering with insolent scrutiny. "Miss high-and-mighty. Been waiting a long time for this, I 'ave." His hand flew out suddenly and caught her ankle, pulling her back down the bank.

Geneva was trying to regain her breath. When she screamed for help, she wanted to be sure her lungs were operating at full capacity. She said, "I read in the paper that you'd been released from prison. I take it you enjoyed it so much you want to go back?"

"Oh, I'm not going back, love. They'll not catch me this time. Any stories you tell about me . . . well, it'll just be your word against mine. See, there's a girl in Liverpool who'll swear I'm with her today. And nobody's seen me in the village. Besides, love, what I'm going to do to you . . . well, you Saxons will make damn sure nobody hears about it. But you'll know—and old stiff-arse will know—and that's all that matters to me."

He dropped down beside her, pinning her to the bank with one arm and one leg flung across her body. His hand closed over her breast, and a trickle of saliva appeared at the corner of his mouth. "You know, years ago I thought when I got you I'd do it to you first, then kill you. Only I got caught a couple of times and I decided fuckin' you would be enough. See, they don't hang a man for fuckin' . . . and the thought of a rope cutting off my air was a bit hairy, see. Then I thought, wouldn't it be a lark if I got you pregnant. I've got three or four girls pregnant, you know, love. Three or four that I know of anyway."

Geneva opened her mouth and screamed, and almost instantly his mouth came down over hers, shutting off her scream as he forced his tongue deep into her throat. She fought the weight of his body as he rolled over on her, but was powerless to dislodge him. She clawed at the broad back, her fingernails catching on the rough threads of his jacket. A numbing realization of the disparity between a man's strength and a woman's caused her to stop struggling for a moment, and Charlie raised his head to look at her.

Looking up at him, her face livid with anger, she was a study in defiance, and Charlie frowned. They were supposed to cringe in terror, that was how he liked it. This bitch was looking at him like she'd kill him if she got a chance. He tore open the neck of her dress, ripped off the lacy wisp of brassiere, and, keeping one hand over her mouth to shut her up, sank his teeth into the delicate pink of her nipple. He felt the spasm of pain pass through her body. This was more like it; he took all of the areola into his mouth and sucked lustily, plucking at her skirts and pushing his hand between her thighs.

Now she fought him with all of her strength, and he was forced to remove his hand from her mouth to keep her pinned down. She yelled for help, but they were too far from the house for anyone to hear, and Charlie had seen the game-keeper heading in the opposite direction not half an hour earlier. Still, he slapped her mouth a couple of times to shut her up, then choked her until her eyes rolled and she started to go limp.

It would be a minute or two before she came to her senses, he knew from past experience, and he used the time to strip the remainder of her torn clothing from her body. Christ, he thought, but this one had a figure. Full breasts, tiny waist, hips that were feminine without being common-looking like the women down in the village; he hated the great globs of marble fat that undulated out of their underwear.

There were several bruises on her body and his teeth marks on her breast. She moaned and turned her head, and a shaft of sunlight caught the black swelling of her eye. Charlie went quickly to the task of unbuttoning his trousers before she came to and starting fighting him again.

For Geneva the world was spinning hazily into muted shapes and distant blurred sounds. A bird sang, water rushed over tiny pebbles, a bumblebee hummed nearby. She hurt all over. Throbbing eye, salt taste of blood on her mouth, a screaming ache in one breast, but all of it faded away in a single terrible tearing pain between her thighs that snapped her head up from its pillow of leafmold and brought a hoarse cry of agony to her lips.

Charlie Dutton held her wrists at her sides; trying to move her arms brought wrenching pain to elbows and shoulders. His knees separated her thighs and what felt like an iron rod was trying to work its way inside her. Dimly she heard him say, "Christ, love, your cherry's in there tighter than—"

Whatever simile he had been about to utter was lost as she brought her knee up to her chest and kicked him with all of her might. Something crashed into her face and she went plunging into darkness again. A long nightmare of darkness that she returned to in gratitude because when she struggled to the surface of consciousness, the reality was worse than the nightmare. *Alone . . . in our pain and terror we're truly alone.* The revelation was her last recognizable thought.

Dimly she heard Terry's voice. "Gen? Oh, Lord. Gen—oh, dear lord—"

She opened her eyes as far as throbbing lids would allow, peering at him through the slits. Terry was bending over her, and his own eyes registered a silent soliloquy that left no need to tell her what he was feeling. He had already wrapped the tattered remnants of her dress around her. "Gen, I'm going to carry you back to the hall. I'll try not to hurt you."

"No, Terry, wait. I—don't—want anyone to know."

"Was it Dutton?" he asked in a strangled whisper.

She nodded. Terry closed his eyes as though trying to make it all go away. "I'll get you to a hospital—send a wire to Italy to bring Ian home."

"No! Oh, God, Terry, no! Father is the last person on earth I want to know about this."

"But he'll find out—as soon as we go to the police."

"We're not going to the police. Terry, do you remember when Dutton was put on trial for assaulting that girl who worked at the hall? He was convicted—but that girl was just as much on trial as he was. The defense barrister paraded young men who said they'd been intimate with her too. Dutton's defense was that she'd encouraged him to beat her, that it was some sort of perverted sexual thrill she wanted—" Geneva broke off, breathing raggedly. Beads of perspiration oozed from her brow.

Terry looked away briefly, remembering only too clearly what the young girl in the case had suffered. And the way the Sunday tabloid press had reported the trial.

"Terry, help me get to my room without being seen . . . and swear you won't tell Father. I couldn't bear his suffering if he knew."

For a split second Terry battled conflicting emotions. Geneva was right: the price was too dear for letting anyone else know what had happened to her. *At the very least,* he thought grimly, *I can find Dutton and beat the swine within an inch of his life.*

"All right, Gen, don't worry. But we'll have to tell someone. You'll have to stay in your room until your face heals up. Meredith . . . we'll tell Meredith, she'll understand the need for secrecy." He hesitated for a moment, then added awkwardly, "Gen . . . you know, what Dutton did—it wasn't your fault—you shouldn't feel—" He foundered on the thought, flushing at his inability to express it.

Geneva stared at him with eyes that were suddenly too large for her fragile features, and too remote for him to bear. He could not know that, even then, some inner premonition was warning her that Charlie Dutton had left her with more than a battered body and a hellish memory.

Chapter 13

For several weeks Geneva's life seemed like an impressionistic painting—all broken brush strokes and muted colors, not quite in focus, yet not blurred enough to numb the ragged edges of her nerves. A metamorphosis was taking place, she knew, and the new self that emerged would have a more complex philosophy than that other Geneva. One brutal act had obliterated her inherent belief in the goodness of people. Early in her life she had learned that there were some who—through disappointments of their own—lashed out at innocent victims. Lady Saxon had been cold and unkind; a younger Dutton had blustered and threatened. But still Geneva had not learned the depth of human cruelty. Now she knew that the world outside herself was an adversary she must duel alone, and her only weapon would be her own inner strength.

When Ian returned from Italy, he was shocked by the change in her. She had lost weight, moved stiffly, and spoke in a wooden tone that was as unlike her former passionate concern for everything around her as the blank expression that now masked her once vitally alive features. She seemed to have erected an invisible wall between herself and the rest of the world. The dark shadows under her eyes were emphasized by her pallor, which she had apparently tried to hide with an unaccustomed layer of makeup. Closer examination revealed this was not all she was trying to hide. Ian placed his finger under her chin and raised her face.

"Gennie, darling, what on earth happened to your face? My dear, you have a black eye—and what's this?"

She winced as his exploring finger lightly touched a bruise along her jawline. "It's nothing, Father, really. I took a fall while I was riding. Clumsy of me."

"But you're so thin and pale. Have you been ill?"

"A little bilious, that's all. Must have eaten something that disagreed with me."

She hardly ate at all, Ian noted at dinner. Terry appeared ill at ease, covertly watching both Geneva and Ian. Later they sat around the drawing room fire while Ian told them about their grandmother's sanitarium in Italy.

"Did you see anything of old Mussolini and his Blackshirts—or is it Brownshirts?" Terry asked. "I haven't sorted out those fascist dictators yet—despite Huw's letters from Heidelberg. He seems to think Hitler is curing many of Germany's economic woes."

"I was only in Rome briefly, but I must say I didn't like what I saw. Frankly, it was worse in Germany, Huw's views notwithstanding. Hitler seems to have an open campaign of harassment aimed directly at the Jews. They wear armbands and their businesses are marked with a Star of David. There were those ghastly twisted crosses—swastikas—everywhere, and goose-stepping troops and secret police. Ted and I were glad to leave—I did tell you I brought him home? He's doing splendidly with the new prosthesis, barely limps when he walks. The doctor who saved his knee was Jewish incidentally —and he made the oddest remark, it's bothered me ever since . . . something to the effect that there had been few amputees to take advantage of his skills, and that in future there would be even less."

"What do you suppose he meant? Perhaps he was leaving the country?" Terry asked.

"I think it was a more sinister implication than that. There have been rumors that Hitler intends to 'purify' the race by eliminating all cripples and mental defectives."

"Good God," Terry exclaimed. "Huw never said anything about that."

Ian glanced at Geneva, who leaned back limply in her chair, watching him with haunted shadows in her eyes. "Gennie, I persuaded Ted to let me borrow one of his journals. You must read it. He's extraordinarily gifted when one considers he has only a rudimentary education. He went to work in the colliery when he was only twelve and apparently was immediately put to work as a cutter because they needed someone small to lie along a narrow ledge to cut the coal face above." He produced a battered notebook from his briefcase and flipped open a page. "Listen to this—written shortly after Ted started to work underground."

"'Last Sunday I went to town to hear a cabinet minister talk,'" Ian read. "'He had a deep, scratchy voice and bags under his eyes. I couldn't take my eyes off him, he was so impressive. I wondered if I could ever get such a voice, or bags under my eyes. I've never seen a collier with bags under his eyes. We get the scratchy voice sometimes, because we're always catching cold down the pit . . . but it isn't the same as his.'"

Terry looked puzzled. "Why on earth would he think bags under the eyes impressive?"

"Have you ever seen a fat collier?" Ian asked. "Or one with baggy eyes? Or any of the other marks of affluence or overindulgence or dissipation? They have pale taut faces and sinewy bodies—bent backs and bowed legs and black lungs."

Terry still looked perplexed. "I still don't understand."

Ian said, "Take, for example, Charlie Dutton. Had he continued to work in the pit, would he have attained his present physical stature?"

There was a sudden uncomfortable silence, broken when the grandfather clock in the hall chimed, reminding Ian of the two-minute silence they observed when Lady Saxon was in residence. Terry said hastily, "Gen, we've got some nice ripe pears, let me get you one. You hardly ate any dinner." He disappeared before Geneva could protest.

Ian watched him go with a thoughtful frown. Terry and Geneva had always been close, probably as close as many brothers and sisters, taking into consideration they spent the greater part of the year apart in different schools. But along with Geneva's mysterious malady, Terry seemed to have acquired a protectiveness toward her that was in sharp contrast to his former teasing banter. The month Ian had spent in Italy and Germany seemed to have wrought great changes in both of them. They're growing up, Ian thought with a pang of regret.

Because the silence was unbearable, Ian looked down at Ted Corwin's journal again and began to read.

"'Someone is walking down the dark passageways of my

mind. I hear him coming and I try to shake off the shackles of sleep to greet him. He's carrying a lamp. But the sound of his footsteps turns into the clatter of clogs on the road outside, and I must push away the blankets because it's five o'clock and the morning shift is walking to the pit. Someone is whistling softly, marking time with the beat of his clogs. *Whistling on the way to hell.'* "

A tear formed in the corner of Geneva's eye. "Oh, Father—" she said just as Terry returned with a bowl of fat yellow pears and an aura of false gaiety. Geneva asked to be excused because she was rather tired and yes, she would take one of the pears up to bed with her. After she kissed Ian's cheek and departed, Terry started to leave also but Ian said, "Wait a minute, Terry. Sit down and tell me what's been happening during my absence."

Terry avoided meeting his eye. "Nothing, Uncle—well, Gen took a fall and hasn't felt too well, but you know that."

"Was it a fall, really? Isn't Charlie Dutton due to be released from prison? Could he have been involved in any way? Terry, I insist that you tell me."

Terry's amber eyes flashed angrily, but all he said was, "Gen fell off her horse. We haven't seen Dutton. He's not in the village. I know, I looked for him."

"Oh? Why?"

"To be sure he didn't bother anyone at the Hall."

"Terry, my boy, don't imagine that a little boxing at university will do you any good in a bout with Dutton. He was prison heavyweight contender, I understand. I suggest you steer clear of him."

Dr. Evans' surgery hours were from ten to eleven in the morning and one to two in the afternoon, since he was semi-retired now. He saw patients in the sunny parlor of his home on the outskirts of the village, a detached house standing behind a low sandstone wall that barely contained a profusion of roses and lupins, already reluctantly yielding to autumn's chrysanthemums and Michaelmas daisies.

Geneva had waited in the parlor with several colliers. Two coughed into their blackened handkerchiefs. One boy had a bloodstained bandage around his hand; another had an injured eye. The doctor had taken Geneva ahead of all of them and now he faced her across his desk, his gaze accusing.

"Miss Saxon, I believe you know what ails you. Now before you say another word, let me explain to you that I realize why you came to me rather than going to your family doctor, but I'm sorry, I can't help you."

She had been holding her breath, and her shoulders slumped as she let it out. The doctor's hostility wafted over the polished surface of his desk in an almost palpable wave, and she shrank from the contempt in his voice. Staring at her hands, which pleated the folds of her skirt then tried to smooth them out, she felt even more acutely than his disgust her own embarrassment and shame. She drew a deep breath, trying to compose herself enough to speak without bursting into tears. "Dr. Evans . . . would you . . . change your mind, if I told you I had been . . . forced."

His lips compressed. "Apart from the fact that abortion is absolutely illegal and could put me in prison—to say nothing of ending my right to practice medicine—I'm personally opposed to murdering unborn children. No, Miss Saxon, you've had your bit of fun, now you'll have to pay the piper."

She stood up, holding the edge of his desk for support, wanting to sink to the floor and crawl away, wishing she were still a little girl who could run to her father's arms so that he could make everything right again. But Geneva the woman faced the doctor's outraged morality alone, and added another example of callousness to her knowledge of human nature. Her cheeks stung with rushing blood, and objects on the wall behind the doctor blurred and ran together; two framed diplomas, an oil painting of a madonna-like woman holding a cherubic infant, surrounded by an idyllic rose garden.

The bile rushing up from her stomach made it impossible to speak. What could she say that would lift that stonelike mask from the doctor's face? *It isn't supposed to happen like this—there should have been orange blossoms and champagne and two people wildly in love, so that their joining is a union of every part of their separate beings—and the child they create is eagerly wanted and loved, even before life begins. Oh, Doctor, for the love of God, have pity on me. I'm pregnant by the sperm of a great lumbering beast of a man who raped me and who may be criminally insane. . . .*

But the sanctimonious set of his mouth told her he had probably heard similar pleas and been unmoved by them. An inner voice warned her that the best she could salvage from the visit was a dignified withdrawal. "I'm sorry I bothered you. How much do I owe you?" She opened her purse, praying she could walk out of his office without losing the contents of her stomach.

The doctor's eyes flickered over her blue cashmere suit and fine quality leather handbag. "I've spent thirty years treating the men who cut Saxon coal," he said, flipping a chart across his desk toward her. "Look at that."

Geneva glanced down. There was a list of names, dates, then the nature of various accidents. Injured eye—flying piece of coal. Wrenched back—fall of coal. Internal injuries —caught between corf and prop. Crushed fingers—caught between tubs.

"Those are the minor accidents," he said. "I keep a separate chart of the amputations, and yet another for the men dying of black lung. Do you know what I've seen, as a doctor, for thirty years, Miss Saxon? I've seen men who aren't living—they're dying. They spend their lives dying. And you come and ask me to rid you of an unwanted fetus."

Geneva withdrew three pound notes from her purse, placed them on his desk, and walked silently from the room. In the parlor the boy with the crushed fingers gave her a shy smile.

The village street presented to the world sloping slate roofs, bristling with smoke-belching chimneys. Geneva knocked on the door of the next-to-last house on the row, acutely aware of lace curtains fluttering at every window and a curious knot of children who paused in their play to observe her. The brass doorknocker gleamed and the threshold of the house had been given a glowing coat of red-raddle. A moment later the door opened slightly and there was a startled intake of breath from the woman standing in the shadows beyond.

"Miss Nancy Whitaker?" Geneva asked. "Is this the right house? Please, I must talk to you."

The door opened wide and she stepped into a tiny room warmed by a coal fire, the flames illuminating a collection of horse brasses around the hearth, reflecting a Welsh sideboard on the opposite wall that housed blue willow china. In front of the fire a pair of well-worn easy chairs were draped with neatly embroidered antimacassars. A corner shelf held two faded photographs, a young man in army uniform, and an older man with the same gravely serious eyes of the woman who had admitted her to the house. Next to the pictures lay a well-used Bible and a carved music box. Geneva felt an inexplicable wave of sadness at the shrinelike quality of the corner shelf.

"Sit down, lass," Nancy Whitaker said. "You're looking a bit peeked."

Geneva sank gratefully into the nearest chair. Everything was an effort; just speaking seemed to take all of her strength. "I know I'm being presumptuous—I have no right to involve others in my . . . my shame. It's just that I didn't know where to turn, what to do. I haven't told a living soul, except Dr. Evans, but he won't help me. I'm so frightened. It's like a terrible nightmare that I can't wake up from—this feeling of dread and disgust and absolute revulsion that . . . that his seed is growing inside me—" She stopped, breathless, and ran her fingers through her hair, her eyes dull with despair.

Nancy waited silently for her to go on.

"I'm in trouble," Geneva said. "I must . . . get rid of the baby. They told me you might be able to help me. I have money—" The words were out in a rush and seemed to hang in the air.

Nancy Whitaker was not young, but she had fine bone structure and beautiful eyes. Her hair was a warm chestnut, coiled in a silky knot at the nape of her neck. She said, "Somebody's playing a very unkind joke. I think on the both of us. Who sent you to me?"

"One of the scullery maids at Saxon Hall," Geneva answered in a low monotone. "I pretended I was asking for someone else . . . but perhaps the girl guessed, I don't know. She said at first she didn't know anyone, but the following day she told me your daughter Lily had been to someone in Liverpool." She bit her lip. "I'm sorry—I gave the maid my best *broderie anglais* blouse . . . but all I really regret is that I've embarrassed you, Miss Whitaker. Please forgive me, I don't know what I was thinking about, coming here like this. I seem to be piling one mistake on another. Please forgive me."

Nancy patted the back of her hand gently. "It's all right. Let me make you a nice cup of tea and then we'll think what can be done. What about the boy—won't he marry you?"

"I wouldn't want to marry him."

As Nancy made the tea Geneva could not help noticing how graceful the woman was. She wore a simple skirt and blouse, and her only jewelry was a gold chain around her neck that disappeared into the collar of her blouse. "I live alone now," she said, pulling a tea cozy over the pot. "My daughter—Lily—went to work in a cotton mill and lives in Bolton."

She handed Geneva a cup and saucer, gazing at her with eyes that were filled with questions she did not ask. "My Lily knew a woman in Liverpool. I can give you her address. But lass, you must think of the dangers. Have you told your dad?"

Geneva shook her head. She took a sip of tea, put the cup down, and clapped a handkerchief to her mouth.

"The morning sickness?" Nancy asked sympathetically.

"All day long. I haven't been able to sleep either, yet I'm so tired."

"It will go away—at about four months. Try eating a bit of dry toast to settle your stomach."

Geneva nodded, grateful for the first advice she had received and feeling inexplicably drawn to this soft-spoken woman with the warm smile and loving eyes. It occurred to her that since "Miss" Whitaker was the mother of a daughter, Nancy was well aware of what she was going through. She wondered if the young man in uniform on the corner shelf was the father of Lily.

Following the direction of her glance, Nancy said, "He was killed in the Great War. It's hard having a baby all alone. I didn't know where to turn either." She paused, staring at the photograph of her lost love. "My mam always told me that bad girls didn't have babies—only good girls who make a mistake. But she was gone and so was my dad. When my young man was killed, I thought perhaps I should have his baby, so his life wouldn't be such a waste. But after I had my Lily . . . well, the other women treated me like dirt. And Lily grew up . . . resentful. Perhaps if I had it to do over again—" She gave Geneva an expressive shrug. "Bad enough for me, lass, but worse for you, I can see that."

"I can't tell you what a relief it is to talk to someone who understands," Geneva said, blinking so Nancy wouldn't see the tears. "You're very kind. I feel dreadful that I insulted you by believing . . . by listening to belowstairs gossip about your daughter."

"The gossip was true," Nancy said sadly. "But what Lily did, and what I did . . . well, there's other alternatives. But lass, I'm not the one who should be advising you. Your father is a wise and good man; you should tell him."

Nancy seemed suddenly ill at ease, her fingers tightened around her teacup and her color had deepened. Geneva wondered if she were merely generalizing about fathers, or if she could possibly have met Ian at some time.

The silence lengthened, and although Geneva was reluc-

tant to leave, she stood up and held out her hand to take
Nancy's in a warm grip. "I don't know how to thank you."

"I wish I could turn the clock back for you, so it wouldn't
have happened. But Gennie, before you do anything rash
. . . tell your father."

Geneva looked up, startled by the woman's use of the
diminutive of her name only ever used by her father.

She went directly to the address in Liverpool, paying off the
taxi driver outside a new tenement building that already had
the battered look of a fortress under siege. As she walked
across the interior courtyard, boys with the faces of hardened
felons dropped their football and surged around her, plucking
at her clothes and yelling obscenities. They stayed with her
until she knocked on a door and a woman with vivid hennaed
hair and a cigarette stuck to her upper lip came outside and
waved a mop at them. She gestured for Geneva to go inside.

"Bloody scum of the earth, them kids," she declared.
"Never should've been born, none of 'em. They're what
keeps the bloody oppressed workers in their places, see.
Struggling to feed an 'ouseful of kids, so they don't dare go on
strike. And us women is worst off of all. You should come to
our meetings, ducks."

The linoleum on the floor was cracked and filthy. Geneva
stepped over several dead cockroaches, her nostrils clenching
against a smell of onions and strong malt liquor. A man
wearing an undershirt and stained trousers was sprawled on a
settee, smoking a foul-odored pipe and listening to a variety
program on the wireless.

"Why, when we all stand up and sing 'The Red Flag' . . . it
don't matter if you're a man or a woman, see. You're equal,"
the woman was saying. "The Workers Party don't believe no
woman should 'ave kids if she don't want 'em."

For a moment the woman's sordid business seemed vindi-
cated. Geneva could accept a political movement that es-
poused a woman's right to control her own body. The man on
the settee roused himself and gave her a slow-motion wink.
"Got a bun in the oven, hey? Never mind, luv, the old
woman'll fix you up. Got the five quid, 'ave yer?"

The woman put a pudgy hand on Geneva's arm to turn her
around. Small glittering eyes went over Geneva's slim figure
with an unblinking snake's stare. "Youse not more than three
months gone, are yer? If yer are, I won't do it. And it's five
guineas, not five quid. Cash on the barrel. And yer can't stay

here after. You'll have to get yerself on home, soon as it's done. Did yer bring plenty of rags for the blood? I don't supply no rags."

The woman's teeth were tobacco-stained and her breath smelled of ale. Geneva looked down at the black crescents under the fingernails gripping her arm. Flowered wallpaper, covered with a yellow film of grease, swam dizzily. From the wireless came the disembodied shriek of Gracie Fields, singing, *"Oh, she fought like a tiger for 'er honor . . ."* The man was laughing and leering and scratching his scrotum. Geneva felt as though she had stepped into some mad sick stage comedy. Her sense of unreality was so overwhelming that she swayed on numb feet, blinking.

Then she was stumbling over the frayed doormat in her haste to leave. "I'm sorry," she said, "I've changed my mind."

Ian and Terry were waiting for her in the drawing room at Saxon Hall. They both jumped to their feet when Meredith brought her into the room. "Here she is, safe and sound. Come on, dear, sit down, you look exhausted."

"Gennie, we were worried to death," Ian said. "Rankin and the chauffeur are on their way to Liverpool to try to intercept you. Miss Whitaker regretted giving you that address the moment you left her. She came to see me."

Geneva looked at him with dazed and uncomprehending eyes as the horror of the day closed in on her. "I didn't—do it. I went to the woman, but couldn't stand the thought of . . ."

"Good lord," Terry said in a faint voice. "You mean . . . Gen? Oh, God, no!"

Meredith said, "Miss Geneva, you must tell your father."

Geneva looked from one to the other, fighting a blackness that threatened to pull her down into oblivion. She remembered she had not eaten anything all day.

"Gennie, are you going to have a baby?" Ian asked gently.

She was struggling to hold on to her senses, find the words to explain her shame, when Terry's voice came through the fog, announcing clearly, "Ian, the baby is mine. We want to get married, we were waiting for you to come home—because we didn't know if it was legal—you know, with us being first cousins."

Geneva couldn't speak; waves of nausea and weakness seemed to constrict her throat and the room rushed away, as though someone had turned a telescope the wrong way.

There was a long pause that seemed to fill the room with a pounding pulse beat. Ian's face was gray, stricken. At last a hoarse cry escaped from his lips and he sprang toward Terry and seized him by the throat. "You filthy young swine—I'll— I'll—" Ian shook him while Terry plucked at the choking hands.

Meredith was sobbing and Geneva rose unsteadily to her feet. "Father! No! Please, it wasn't Terry," she cried.

Ian's hands dropped to his sides and he stared wildly from Terry to Geneva. Terry recovered quickly. "She means we love each other and couldn't help ourselves. Ian, we would have got married first, only we're first cousins." He paused and gave Ian a questioning glance. "We are, aren't we? Despite what grandmother is always hinting about?"

Ian said, "Gennie—" broke off, shook his head. "I should have told you . . . years ago." He took a step toward her and his hands went to her shoulders to gently force her to sit down. He sat beside her on the sofa, his arm still around her shoulder, and looked up at Terry. "There's no impediment to marriage. You are not first cousins."

Geneva said, "But you and Terry's father were brothers—"

"Gennie, I'm not your father. I met your mother for the first time as she was about to give birth to you."

His stumbling explanation, interspersed with frequent self-recriminations, registered slowly on her mind. He told of the last hour of the war, of the German who sent his company into a bloody ambush, of his own illness and subsequent guilt over her mother's death and the losses needlessly sustained when the armistice was imminent. He tried to explain: the difficulties of adopting a foreign child, her grandmother's strong feelings about family ties, bloodlines, the rigid structure of their society. Geneva listened, disbelieving, not wanting to hear that the man she had loved more than life had lied to her all these years.

"I meant to tell you, Gennie, but somehow the years flew by and I came to believe you *were* my daughter, flesh of my flesh. You see, my dear, as my daughter you were protected from speculation, gossip—"

"About my real family, you mean," she said. "Why, I could have been the daughter of a monster—or perhaps my mother didn't go to the right schools. Yes, I can see it would have worried Grandmarm greatly."

"Please . . . don't judge us too harshly. In her own way Mother is very fond of you. And I . . . oh, Gennie, I love you so much, I couldn't love you more if there were blood ties between us."

"This is the reason we spent so many holidays in France, of course, and why you insisted I learn the language like a native. You wanted to fabricate a French heritage for me because you had no idea of my background. But why didn't you simply try to find my mother's family?"

"The nuns at the convent did try. But your mother had covered her tracks too well; they found nothing. Where she came from, what had happened to her before she reached the cottage near Valenciennes, I'm afraid will forever remain a mystery. Gennie, you must understand, the French authorities would never have let me bring you—a French citizen—to England if I hadn't told them I was your father."

There was pleading desperation written in his expression, his eyes; it conveyed itself in his touch, and she felt his abject misery that the revelation had to come now, under these circumstances, and in front of Terry. Meredith had discreetly withdrawn.

Geneva felt betrayed, angry, yet no less a daughter to this man who had so lovingly nurtured her than she had before. Nothing could change what he was, or what he had made her, but the shining image had lost some of its brilliance and for that she was not ready to forgive.

Terry said with a small embarrassed smile, "Well, there's one bright spot, Gen. There's nothing to stop us from getting married."

Geneva looked from her father to Terry, feeling a piercing shaft of pain so acute that she should have been aware of its source, but she was unable to define it. The revelation that she was an outsider? Her pregnancy? Dutton? It was as if her heart had shut down, cutting off the last strands of hope, so that even Terry's gallant gesture seemed suspect. Her soul wept for her mind's newfound bitterness.

Their faces blurred, and she slipped away to the misty nothingness that had been waiting for her all day.

Chapter 14

The delicate fragrance of wreaths and bouquets of flowers lingered in the air after the weeping servants carried the floral tributes to the black limousines lining the drive waiting to bear the mourners to church. Somber chamber music came softly from the gramophone in the drawing room, and everyone present wore unrelieved black, creating an atmosphere of sadness that hung in an invisible pall over the bright autumn day.

Word of Lady Sybil's death had reached the hall only days after wedding announcements had been dispatched and the first Sunday's banns called at St. Agnes' Church. The expected postponement of the wedding seemed to Geneva almost the hand of wise fates unwilling to allow the marriage to take place, but Ian quickly informed everyone that it had been his mother's last wish that Terry and Geneva marry as planned, a scant and, to the Saxon relatives, tasteless three weeks after the funeral of his mother.

At Ian's side Geneva offered her sympathy and support with every silent glance and gesture, while thinking of the stern and unyielding woman who had been the bane of her childhood. She sorrowed for what could have been between them, but never was, and for the impermanence of life, but most of all because Ian's mother was dead and he had loved her.

Sunlight blazed against the closed curtains at the windows, creating a soft golden light and casting the mourning clothes in even starker relief. Cook had predicted that on the day of the funeral the sun would scorch the heavens, never mind the lateness of the season. "Rain, now, that means they're happy to go. But sunshine . . . they weren't finished living."

Had Lady Saxon known her beloved Terry was marrying the French orphan, Geneva thought, the old lady probably would have found a way to go on living to prevent the match. And if she'd known about Charlie Dutton's child in her womb . . .

Terry was quiet, subdued. He stood on Ian's other flank, soberly shaking hands and occasionally glancing in Geneva's direction. She knew he grieved for his grandmother, perhaps more than Ian did. When news of her death reached them, Terry said only, "I feel as though someone just placed a large punctuation mark in the middle of my life."

Geneva had known what he meant. She was beginning to learn a great deal about Terry that she had not suspected. The depths of his emotions and his own personal code astonished her, in view of his facade of carefree youth. Uncovering the hidden side of him that spoke of integrity and honor had sharpened her sense of disappointment when she learned the real reason for his quixotic proposal of marriage. Yet hadn't she suspected an ulterior motive?

On the first opportunity they had to discuss the emotional scene with Ian, Geneva had stated flatly, "We can't go on with this charade, Terry. I simply won't let you sacrifice yourself because of what that animal did to me. It would just make it all worse."

Terry had studied her for a long minute, as though seeking something in her expression that he did not find. At length he shrugged with elaborate unconcern. "Look, Gen, it's like this. Ian, Grandmother, everyone would be shattered by the truth. We've always been fond of one another, you and me, haven't we? What would really change if we were to marry? We'd both go on living at Saxon Hall. You wouldn't even have to change your name."

"But, Terry, we're not in love. What if you wanted to marry someone else?"

"Gen, I *am* in love. Dory—the girl I go to see in Liverpool. But it's hopeless, she won't marry me."

"*She* won't marry *you!* But I thought she was a chorus girl—"

With a trace of bitterness in his voice, Terry replied, "Snobbery in reverse is the worst kind, Gen, believe me. But getting back to us—at least with a marriage of convenience I'd be free to go and see Dory without worrying about my conscience or your hurt feelings. Gen, I'm offering you legitimacy for your baby, and no one, including Ian, ever need know what Dutton did to you. Even Dutton himself— lord, can you imagine what it would be like if he knew? He'd be tied to the family forever."

Geneva had shuddered and seen the logic in the plan. A marriage of convenience: an understanding wife who closed her eyes to liaisons with chorus girls for Terry, and respecta- bility for herself. Another factor influenced her decision to accept Terry's terms—perhaps they were the world's terms, she thought—and that was her father's love of Saxon Hall. If she married Terry, Ian would never have to leave, or worry about money again.

The death of Lady Sybil seemed confirmation that she had been wise to consider Ian's place in the rapidly disintegrating pattern of things. Geneva steeled herself to accept what was and not lament what was forever lost.

As the line of mourners moved by, her hand unconsciously tightened on her father's arm. Near the front door Lady Sybil's brother, known affectionately as Uncle Dee Dee, was regaling long-unseen relatives with his views on the situation in Germany. The seventh earl of Steadwall, David Duncan Digby, was rather deaf and his voice shattered the muted murmur of conversation.

"Deuced Blackshirts have to be stopped, don't y'know. Herr Hitler will chip away bits of the continent until he has it all. I warned them back in '23, but they said Hitler had less than a thousand followers—boy scouts playing at being soldiers. Well, look at 'em now!"

Geneva moved quietly to Uncle Dee Dee's side and slipped her arm through his. "Come along, dear, I'll show you to your car," she whispered. Huw Wakefield was scowling at the old gentleman.

"Am I shouting again, m'dear? Sorry. Such a sad day. But a merciful release. Poor Sybil loathed being ill."

After she settled Uncle Dee Dee into his limousine, Geneva joined Terry and Ian to take her place in the car behind the flower-bedecked hearse. As the procession moved slowly forward, she saw the top of the letter that had arrived for Ian that morning protruding from his pocket. Another one with an American postmark. She had seen him remove it quickly from the silver tray in the hall. The same bold black script as on the other letters from America—and several foreign countries. She had wondered about those letters, but Ian had been vague in response to her questions, leaving her to believe they were business letters.

The sun was hot on the car windows; it was a relief to enter the cool gloom of St. Agnes' Church. The vicar spoke briefly of the dear departed, the organist played "Abide with Me," then, in accordance with Lady Sybil's instructions for her own funeral, the congregation sang her old school song. Uncle Dee Dee blew his nose loudly as their voices were raised in the sad but stirring melody:

> *"I vow to thee, my country, all earthly things above,*
> *Entire, and whole, and perfect, the service of my love,*
> *The love that asks no question, the love that stands the*
> *   test,*
> *That lays upon the altar, the dearest and the best."*

Lady Sybil must have expected to fall in battle, Geneva thought. The patriotic words rang about the granite walls of the church, and looking up at the stained glass windows, she thought that the church had stood here for two hundred years, was built to stand another two hundred years, and it was a comforting thought in view of the mortality of the humans who built it.

The refrain of Lady Sybil's school song lingered in her mind until they reached the cemetery, ending abruptly with the chillingly final rattle of earth falling on her coffin.

Late the following night, after everyone was in bed, Ian went to his study and collapsed into his leather armchair. The fire flickering in the grate sent changing patterns of light and shadow over the mantelpiece photograph of his father and brother, Terry, both in uniform, taken the last time they were together. They both gave him devil-may-care smiles.

"What am I going to do about your son, Terry?" Ian asked softly. "How can I in all conscience entrust Gennie to his care? Yet she carries his child."

His brother's unconcerned eyes regarded him blithely, and he blinked away an image of limp bodies, swagger sticks still clutched in lifeless hands, hanging over the front line wire. The ghastly song the soldiers used to sing in France called from the back of memory. *"Hanging on the front line wire . . ."*

Just before the Great War, Ian remembered, there had been a peculiar restlessness among the young men—brother Terry in particular. He saw it now in his nephew and his friends. *Am I rationalizing his behavior,* Ian wondered, *or am I unduly conservative in believing Terry should not go out so soon after his grandmother's funeral? Does his way of dealing with his grief make more sense than my lonely soliloquies?* Pouring himself a glass of brandy, he wondered if it was too late to visit Nancy. No, couldn't go tonight. Not with Terry gone too. Geneva might need something. But oh, how he needed Nancy's quiet guidance.

A discreet knock on the study door interrupted his reverie. "Excuse me, sir . . ." Rankin stood uncertainly on the threshold, peering through the darkness to see if Ian was asleep by the fire. "The telephone, sir. A young lady, sir." Rankin's face twitched furiously. "She says her name is Dory Gates and that you don't know her but she must speak with you on a matter of some urgency." Rankin sounded outraged and managed to convey his disdain for Dory Gates without uttering a derogatory word.

Dory had actually screamed at him in shrill Cockney rage that he'd better get Ian Saxon to the bleedin' phone right away for Christ's sake if he knew what was good for him snoopy old barstid 'cos there's a bloody crisis that's wot.

Ian went quickly to the telephone, knowing full well that Dory Gates was the chorus girl over whom Terry was making a fool of himself.

Chapter 15

Ian had forgotten about the letter from Matt Lauren until he was in the car speeding toward Liverpool and felt it in his jacket pocket. He switched on the light in the back of the Rolls and pulled the letter from its envelope, thinking perhaps it would distract him from worrying about Terry's condition. Dory Gates had told him merely that Terry had been in a fight and was in hospital.

Matt Lauren's bold handwriting leaped from the page.

I recently sailed to Cherbourg and managed to get to Paris. I checked on my father's marriage. I might as well get to the point. I know Celine Thibault Lauren gave birth to a baby girl at the Convent of the Sisters of Mary, on 11 November, 1918—the same day you found my father in the shelled cottage near Valenciennes. I'm convinced the imminent birth was the reason my father was far from his own company, absent without leave.

I also know you subsequently adopted that child.

This seems to be a dramatic gesture for a man who claims no prior knowledge of Celine or my father. I'm curious—and my curiosity is whetted still further by the fact that in all the time I've corresponded with you, you've never seen fit to tell me I have a sister. I'm anxious to meet her. One of these days I'll sign on a ship to England. If I can, I'll let you know when I'm coming. Meantime, please tell her of my existence.

Ian stuffed the letter back into his pocket. *Not yet, my friend,* he thought. *Not until I know what kind of a man you are and what you might possibly want from her.*

They were on the outskirts of Liverpool now, passing Picton Clock, and Ian peered at the rain spattering against the blackness of the car windows. They had turned onto Wellington Road and, almost before Ian realized they had reached the hospital, the chauffeur was unfurling an umbrella and opening the door, to the curious stares of night staff going on duty.

He had no trouble picking Dory Gates out of the crowd in the waiting room. She was a head and shoulders taller than any other woman present and her hair was bright as a beacon, commanding even more attention than her stage makeup and white-sequined evening dress. At her side was a dapper young man with a cheeky grin and a cleft in his chin, who looked vaguely familiar although Ian knew they had never met.

Dory pushed through the emergency room visitors to Ian. "I hope you didn't call the police, Mr. Saxon. Terry didn't want you to call the police." She had luminous eyes of a startling shade of blue that conveyed her emotions the way an open window emits light. Ian saw she was both afraid and angry.

"Where is my nephew?" he asked.

"He'll be fine—" Dory and her companion began to speak together. "Just an unlucky punch—but his nose's broken." They broke off and the young man gestured for Dory to continue. "He got Fred a good one too. Show him, Fred." Obligingly Fred turned his face to show the bruise on his jaw.

"I'll speak to you both after I've seen my nephew," Ian said.

Terry was in a private room, a nurse at his bedside and a thermometer stuck under his tongue. Above a swollen and discolored nose, his amber eyes still burned with fury.

Ian sat down to wait until the nurse was finished. After she made a notation on the chart at the foot of the bed, she said to Ian, "Five minutes, sir, all right? He should get some sleep. The doctor gave him something to calm him down."

Ian nodded. When the door closed behind her, Terry said, "This is utterly ridiculous. I don't know why the stupid doctor insisted on my staying overnight. It's just a broken nose, and the idiot can't do anything for it apparently—I mean one can't have a cast put on it like a broken arm."

Ian picked up the chart. "According to this, you were unconscious when your . . . friends . . . brought you in. You are under observation for possible concussion. No doubt you'll be discharged tomorrow. Now, before I exhaust all of the five minutes allotted, do you wish to bring charges against the young man who knocked you for six?"

"Good lord no!" Terry exclaimed. "I hit him first."

"Not too sporting of you, old chap. And strange behavior for a man who is shortly to be married. Not to mention being in mourning." Ian's feelings showed briefly in his eyes.

Terry bit his lip. "Does Gen know?"

"Fortunately she was asleep when I got the call. Well, you appear to be reasonably comfortable. I'll see you in the morning."

Terry watched him walk toward the door. "No questions? No lecture?"

Ian gave him a searching look. "Would there be any point? I can only leave you to your own conscience. I will, however, hope that you will tell Geneva yourself, *before* the wedding."

Ian half expected that Dory and her partner would be gone, but they had waited for him. *Cary Grant*, Ian thought. *The boy looks like the film star from Bristol.* "Perhaps we could go somewhere and talk?" he suggested.

They took him to a Chinese restaurant and were the only customers at the late hour. Dory ordered chow mein and Fred asked for bacon and eggs. Ian ordered coffee and sipped it as they demolished the food.

Dory was a surprise. It was easy to see why Terry had been bowled over by her. She was not beautiful in the classical sense, but there was an aura to her that dazzled, even as it disturbed him. Blatant sexuality? he asked himself, studying her. Every motion and glance seemed calculated to excite and entice. Her knee brushed his under the table, and her eyes sent an incendiary spark, mocking, daring him to recognize the invitation. She placed a small piece of chicken in her mouth and began to move her lips in erotic circles, her eyes never leaving his face. He noticed that she touched herself often, patting her hair, smoothing her gown, playing with the brooch pinned below the cleavage of her dress, drawing attention to various parts of her body with her long tapered fingers.

Embarrassed, he looked away, trying to shut out an image of what she did with Terry when they were alone. For one so young, Dory Gates exuded an air of sensual depravity it would have been difficult for any man to ignore. There was no doubt as to the nature of the hold she had on Terry.

Leaning forward so that her breasts pressed against the tight material of her dress, she said, "None of us wants the police in this, Mr. Saxon. I know Terry doesn't—even though he started the fight. Fred doesn't either."

"You've known my nephew for some time," Ian said. "What do you want from him?"

"Nothing!" she said, her mouth hardening. "He's been coming to see me dance. And hanging around the stage door. He took a couple of the other girls out."

Fred said, "A stage door Johnnie, your nephew. Made a right nuisance of himself, I can tell you."

"How did the fight begin?"

Fred swallowed the last of his eggs. "Your nephew made a scene when Dory told him she was busy. He wouldn't leave her dressing room—moaning something about needing to talk to her tonight. When I told him I was going to throw him out, he punched me."

"You won't go to the police, will you?" Dory said again. The fear flickered across her eyes again.

"There will be no police inquiry," Ian said. He paid the bill and walked out into the rain-washed street, now silvered with the cold touch of dawn.

Walking toward the Rolls, he passed a newsboy's placard that showed a picture of the German dictator addressing what looked like massed millions of Germans. Behind Hitler stood a tall row of ominous swastika flags.

Chapter 16

England, 1938

Matt went up on deck to watch the English coastline materialize out of the thin morning mists of the Irish Sea. At the bar a pilot would be taken aboard to guide them up the river, then, since Matt was first mate, he would supervise the docking and unloading of their cargo. He would probably be the last man ashore, he thought, a surge of impatience mingling with excitement that the conclusion of his quest was in sight.

To the starboard was a stretch of dun-colored beach at the mouth of the river, while to port, stretching endlessly, were miles of weatherbeaten docks. He shivered in the damp chill of the air, blood still tropic-thin after the voyage from West Africa; thinking that life had a habit of crowding events together, rather than spacing them at orderly intervals so they could be dealt with individually. At this moment he should in all conscience be sailing up the Mississippi, rather than the Mersey, because there had been a letter from his grandfather's doctor stating that Archer Castleton's health was failing and he was growing feeble with age. When the letter reached him, Matt had already signed on the vessel bound for Liverpool. He could, of course, sign on a ship bound for home the moment they reached port, but after waiting so long to meet Celine Thibault's daughter—his *sister;* it was a word he treasured—he was loath to miss this opportunity.

Ian Saxon had not replied to his last letter, or if he had the reply had not caught up with Matt. *I don't even know her name,* Matt thought. *She's my sister and I don't know her name.* Nor had he yet told his grandfather of his discovery. Although Matt had been in New York on several occasions, he had abided by Castleton's instructions to stay away from the South. DeVore's men had gone to Greenboughs looking for him, but that was two years ago.

A ferry boat churned by his ship and he looked down at the few hardy souls walking its upper deck. From their bowler hats, furled umbrellas, and business suits, he judged they were en route to jobs on the opposite bank of the river. The scene was a far cry from the dense and verdant foliage along the twisting lower Mississippi, but Matt felt strangely at home as they sailed up the Mersey. A kinship with riverbank dwellers, he decided.

The city of Liverpool loomed ahead; landing stages, large gray office buildings facing the river, the roof of one supporting a massive bird, wings outstretched, poised as though ready to haul the solid granite into the air. Other than the mythical liver bird, there was little to distinguish this from other seaports. After two years at sea, foreign ports no longer caused that quickening of the senses he had felt at first. A sailor's-eye view of the world, he soon learned, bore no resemblance to travel brochure tourist lures. Docks and waterfront bars began to look alike.

By the time he had discharged all of his duties, it was too late to visit the Saxons, so he spent his first evening in port in a pub near the Pier Head, drinking warm beer and trying to understand the nasal Liverpool accent. Finally he was able to obtain directions for his trip to Saxon Hall.

One old-timer, slower spoken than the rest, told him, "Take one of them buses marked 'Crosville' you'll see 'round the Pier Head. Look for a sign on front that says 'Wigan,' then tell the conductor where you're going. There's a village called Saxon Quarry—expect the Hall is nearby."

The double-decker bus did not stop anywhere near the village, so at the conductor's suggestion Matt rode on to Wigan then took a taxi back to Saxon Hall, bypassing a slate-gray village, a smoke-shrouded coal mine, and a gravel quarry.

When the taxi entered the ornamental gates of Saxon Hall, it was immediately evident that a party was in progress. Cars were parked on every available inch of space. A Rolls-Royce decorated with strings of tiny white flowers and red rosebuds was parked near the front doors. A wedding. Someone was getting married. His sister? He felt a stab of resentment that he had already missed so much of her life. Stately elms flew past the cab windows, gave way to a large country house of age-darkened brick and weathered wood, bathed in fault-forgiving sunlight. The Hall presented the same serene air of permanence that Matt had always associated with Green-boughs, but the impression was fleeting as he quickly paid off the cab driver and sprinted up the stone steps, his heartbeat noticeably louder.

Several minutes passed before there was a response to the doorbell. Matt waited impatiently, watched by a pair of stone eagles. At length the door was opened by a harassed-looking butler with a pronounced facial tic. Behind him the entry hall was crowded with well-dressed guests, spilling out from every available door. The butler's eyes flickered briefly over Matt's two-tone jacket and light tan trousers, which constituted the only "going ashore" part of his wardrobe of seaman's work clothes.

"Perhaps, sir," the butler suggested, "I could direct you to the tradesmen's entrance?"

"I'm Matt Lauren. Here to see Mr. Saxon. I can see my timing isn't exactly convenient, but perhaps if you explain I must return to America right away?"

"But Mr. Saxon is not expecting you?"

"Not exactly—at least, not today. I take it someone is getting married. Is it Miss Saxon?"

The butler's expression clearly indicated that he felt the question presumptuous, and Matt realized he must appear to be the worst kind of gate-crasher. "I'm sorry," he said quickly. "It's obvious my name means nothing to you. I'm Miss Saxon's brother."

While regretting the need for the blunt announcement, Matt admired the butler's poise in receiving this news with only a slight twitching of his eyes, but he was afraid the door might at any second be closed in his face.

"Would you wait here, sir, while I have a word with Mr. Saxon?"

He was gone for an endless few minutes, then the door reopened. "If you'll step inside, sir. The guests are waiting in the hall for Miss Geneva to observe the tradition of throwing her bridal bouquet to the bridesmaids."

Trying to ignore the curious glances cast in his direction,

Matt walked into the hall and stood as inconspicuously as he could in an alcove occupied only by a massive grandfather clock. A bevy of pastel-gowned girls giggled at the foot of the staircase and he studied his feet as they turned to examine him.

Faces stood out in the crowd. A distinguished-looking man who looked as though he should be running an embassy somewhere. He had silver hair and eyes that seemed to express resigned desperation, and he nodded to Matt, acknowledging his presence. *Ian Saxon*, Matt thought, *as I imagined him, surrounded by a crowd but not part of them. A man alone, with a secret.*

Nearby a querulous old gentleman was grumbling about their prime minister, Neville Chamberlain. Beside him stood a striking looking pair. A white-haired man with military bearing and that certain aplomb that belongs to those accustomed to command. At his side was a much younger man with olive skin and eyes and hair blacker than night. Eurasion; Matt's practiced eye noted the slightly Oriental features.

There was a murmuring among the guests, and Matt saw another young man run lightly down the stairs. Dark gold hair, amber eyes, a well-bred handsomeness that made Matt think of sleek racehorses. From the way the male guests slapped his shoulder as he reached the foot of the stairs, Matt assumed this was the groom.

All conversation suddenly stopped, and in the following breathless hush Matt looked up to see the bride at the top of the staircase. Was it, he wondered, her uncanny resemblance to the photograph of Celine that caused his breath to stop in his throat? Or was the impact of Geneva Saxon—whose name had not been changed by marriage—which caught him so completely unprepared and off guard, hers alone?

There was a split-second appraisal of flawless skin, pale as a white rose, delicately symmetrical bone structure, full lips that were both vulnerable and sensual, but most of all those enormous gray eyes, shining like pearls, their color lovelier than the light gray shantung suit she wore. Slender, above-average height, moving down the stairs with the grace of a ballerina. Matt felt a distant drum begin to sound, a pounding pulse beat that caused him to stare with an astonished thrill of recognition. In that instant he knew he had been waiting all of his life to meet her.

Her hair was dark, not as dark as his, but there was no other similarity between them. Her eyes swept the crowd, found the silver-haired man, and lighted up with a sweet, sad smile. Then she looked across the hall and saw Matt. A wave of electric tension passed between them, and he had time only to suppose it was the call of blood calling to blood before she wrenched her gaze away and tossed her bridal bouquet to the waiting bridesmaids.

In their scramble to catch it they all missed, and the bouquet fell forlornly to the floor. For a second it lay there, making a vivid impression on Matt's mind, one that came back later to haunt him. Then a laughing bridesmaid scooped it up, and the bride moved down the stairs to join her husband. The silver-haired man pushed through the crowd to them, whispered something first to the bride and then to the groom. Mounting several stairs, the older man held up his hand to still the excited babble of voices. "Please! Don't open your packets of confetti yet! Geneva and Terry are not leaving for a few minutes. Please, everyone, go back into the dining room and have some more champagne."

The surging crowd swallowed the three of them, and Matt strained over their heads for another glimpse of Geneva. The butler spoke at his elbow. "I'm to take you to the study, sir. This way."

Matt followed, feeling the eyes of the other guests, his nerves alive with anticipation, aware of the inappropriateness of his dress, of the patina of quality about the interior of Saxon Hall and its furnishings; intoxicated with both excitement and fear that his meeting with Geneva could not live up to his hopes; wanting to run but unsure in which direction.

Rankin pushed open the study door, and Matt stepped into a book-lined room and met the polite appraisal of three pairs of eyes. The silver-haired man stepped forward and offered his hand. "Mr. Lauren? I'm Ian Saxon. You've caught us completely off guard, I'm afraid. Myself in particular. You see, I haven't told my daughter about you." He was regarding Matt with a wary, questioning glance, but his handshake seemed cordial.

"Happy to meet you at last, sir," Matt murmured, his eyes on Geneva. "I know I should have written that I was coming, but it was a last-minute decision when the ship that brought me sailed." He was angry that Saxon hadn't told her but, oddly, understood why. *What were you expecting?* he wondered. *Some Neanderthal with whom you'd be ashamed to have blood ties?*

Saxon was introducing Terry, his nephew, who pumped his

hand enthusiastically while regarding him with baffled interest.

Finally Geneva was presented and, unlike American women, immediately offered her hand. The delicate fingers felt like orchid petals. "Mr. Lauren, we are intrigued by your sense of the dramatic in arriving at this particular moment," she said, her voice low and sweet, "and quite mystified. Father has told us only that we can't leave on our honeymoon because we have a very special guest and must meet him in private."

Matt felt as though he were sinking beneath the surface of her eyes. His throat was dry, and when he opened his mouth to speak he realized he was too overwhelmed to find words. Ian Saxon slipped his arm protectively around Geneva's shoulders.

"Forgive me, my dear, I should have told you . . . I had hoped to meet Mr. Lauren myself privately before presenting him to you. You see, dear, your mother was married to Mr. Lauren's father."

There were explanations, astonishment, shock, reassurance; but Matt was so intensely aware of Geneva that everything else rushed away in a vacuum. Then at last her voice broke through the babble of questions and answers. "Bur Mr. Lauren . . . this means . . . you're my *brother!*" She stood on tiptoe and shyly kissed his cheek, and he had to restrain himself from grasping her in his arms and holding her. Her husband was staring from one to the other in apparent shock.

Ian said, "Gennie, we can't be absolutely sure of that, but it does seem possible. You see, Mr. Lauren's father was with your mother when I found her. He was badly wounded and there were no Americans in that area. But there were many dead and wounded soldiers everywhere. There was not necessarily a connection between him and your mother. I suppose it's an old truism that we do indeed weave tangled webs when we practice to deceive. Forgive me, I had to add one lie to another once I pretended to be your father."

"Father, I know why you pretended, but let's not speak of that now. I'm stunned, but delighted, to find I have a brother. And that we've found each other at last. Although that's all your doing, Mr. Lauren . . . Matt—forgive me if I'm incoherent. I'm sure you must have felt as I do when you first learned of my existence."

Matt smiled. "In all the excitement I haven't offered my

congratulations to the groom and my good wishes on your marriage."

There was a split-second pause that was in sharp contrast to the earlier animated conversation. Terry and Geneva exchanged sidelong glances and a slight frown knitted Ian's brows, but he covered the tension by saying quickly, "I should have written you about the wedding. I do apologize, but we lost my mother . . . so much has happened recently, Mr. Lauren."

"Please, sir, call me Matt. I'd like to get on a less formal footing. I didn't intend to disrupt the occasion."

Terry said, "We do have a train to catch, Gen. If we aren't on the four o'clock we shan't get to Scotland tonight." He turned to Matt. "We'll be gone for two weeks on our honeymoon. But, of course, we'll look forward to seeing you when we return."

"I have to go back to America. I'll be sailing in a few days."

When Geneva started to protest, he added, "My grandfather is ill. But I promise I'll be back to see you as soon as I get things squared away at home. I'll be a little more considerate next time and let you know when."

"Terry . . ." Geneva began with a questioning glance.

His jaw moved slightly, but Terry's voice was light. "Come on now, Gen. A honeymoon isn't exactly something you can postpone."

Geneva flushed and Matt said, "Please, you mustn't miss your train because of me. I've caused you enough trouble; don't make me feel even more guilty."

There was an undercurrent between bride and groom he didn't understand, and although he'd pretended Geneva had been about to suggest taking a later train, he was sure from Terry's remark that she had been prepared to delay their honeymoon. He was disturbed and curious and, strangely, gladdened by this revelation. *The old male possessiveness,* he thought, *that resists sharing his women—be it wife, daughter, or sister. Perhaps I'm feeling it this strongly because this is the first time I ever had anyone to feel it about.*

The butler appeared with a tray containing glasses of champagne, and Ian Saxon said, "You must toast the bride and groom, Mr. Lauren—Matt—they have time for that."

"To your happiness," Matt said to Geneva. Regarding her across the shimmering surface of the champagne as he held the glass at eye level, it seemed to him she was surrounded by a delicate golden aura that was marred by a shadow that crossed her eyes—but, of course, it was a trick of the light playing on bubbling champagne and crystal glasses.

"Thank you," she said. "Today I'm doubly blessed. I gained a husband and a brother. I feel suddenly very safe."

Was it an odd remark, Matt wondered as they all said their good-byes, and had that been a hint of fear in those lovely eyes? Or was "feeling safe" the standard compliment a woman paid a man? There wasn't time to ponder. Ian had opened the doors, and bride and groom sped through a hail of confetti to the waiting Rolls. All of the guests followed, including Matt and Ian, and there was a confusion of good wishes and farewells.

Ian and Matt remained on the terrace steps after the flower-bedecked car had disappeared and all of the others had returned to the house. Matt felt a peculiar desolation he could not define. The elms rustled their leaves, and the stone eagles watched impassively while Matt stood frozen, staring down the driveway. At his feet, sprinkled about the stone flags, were multicolored confetti dots, the tiny bits of paper clinging to the rough surface.

"Terry is an extremely wealthy young man," Ian said. "He recently inherited all of the Saxon holdings—this house, the colliery, quarry, quite a bit of land. Geneva will be well provided for." The tone of voice seemed defensive, Matt thought.

"Are you explaining why you married my sister off to your nephew?" Matt asked.

"I have not, as you put it, married her off. As a matter of fact, she and Terry married against my wishes. Considering you've only had the briefest glimpse of them, I find your choice of words both curious and insulting."

"I'm sorry, but I saw her long enough to recognize that there was something missing. A sparkle, a hint that she loves him. That feeling was reinforced when you began to regale me with a list of his assets, as though trying to justify the marriage."

"You're a very perceptive fellow. Perhaps I was merely trying to determine if you were more interested in her fortune than in herself. In which case, you appear to have passed the test with flying colors."

Ian didn't sound particularly convinced of this, but Matt said, "Why didn't you test me long ago—when I first wrote to you? Why haven't Geneva and I met before today?"

"If there was time, I'd tell you about the last hour of the

Great War . . . about terror and confusion, and betrayal and guilt. Many men died or were maimed, needlessly, because I took the word of a German officer that a village was deserted. Celine—the girl your father married—was about to give birth, and I had influenza, though I didn't know it at the time. Two weeks later Celine was dead of the virus I'd given her, your father wasn't expected to survive his wound, and there was an orphan baby in a convent."

"Nineteen years ago. What about the last couple of years, since I've been writing you? You could have told her—invited me to come and meet her."

Ian's hand went to his brow as though to brush away the comment. "I don't find my doing so any more odd than the fact that your father's family made no attempt to learn what had become of Celine and her child after the war ended."

"We didn't know about them. They were married only two months before my father was wounded—"

Ian pounced on this information. "Two months! Then Celine was carrying Geneva at the time they were married. Can you even be sure he was the father? Please don't be angry. Let me explain. The casualties on both sides were ghastly. There were French women who were widowed several times over during the four years of war. I merely suggest that it was possible Celine had been married before. Sudden marriages were common. A soldier with a forty-eight-hour pass meets a girl and marries her . . . nine months was a long time in the trenches . . . I'm afraid it's difficult for you to understand what I'm driving at."

"I understand," Matt said, feeling a strange mixture of anger and hope. Anger that his father could have married a woman pregnant with someone else's child, and hope that if that were so . . . he backed away from the abyss over which his thoughts of Geneva wanted to take him. "You're hoping, for some reason that escapes me, that Geneva and I are *not* brother and sister."

"Perhaps I'm trying to justify why I've never told her about you," Ian responded with a sad smile. "Or again, perhaps I still feel you may be a fortune hunter with an eye on her wealth and, at best, a tenuous claim to blood ties."

That evening, after the wedding guests had departed and the American had been driven back to his ship in Liverpool, Ian drove the Morris he kept for his personal use to the village, parking it discreetly behind the pub before walking the rest of the short distance to Nancy Whitaker's house. She was not expecting him and, when his key turned in the lock, she appeared at the top of the stairs wearing a nightgown, her hair loose about her shoulders. "Ian? Is that you? Light the gas, I'll be down in a minute."

He struck a match, pulled the gas mantle down, and lit it. Waiting for her to don slippers and dressing gown, he prowled restlessly about the obstacle course of furniture, feeling a twinge of the claustrophobia that had almost ended his liaison with Nancy before it began, that first time he visited the tiny house and felt the walls close in.

Nancy had been engaged to marry a young lance-corporal who had died, wretchedly, of chlorine gas, shortly after Ian went to fight in France. Seeing the name and home village on the casualty list, Ian had gone to see the lance-corporal's mother on his first leave. She in turn sent him to Nancy, saying, "Will you go and see his young lady? I haven't seen her since the telegram came. I didn't want them to get engaged, what with the war and . . . we weren't close to her. But I heard she's in the family way. Tell her, if she is—" The woman had floundered, not knowing what to say.

Ian had no intention of asking Nancy if she was pregnant, but he did call on her because among the lance-corporal's personal possessions was a gold signet ring inscribed "For my love. Nancy."

Dry-eyed, Nancy had taken the ring and thanked him for his condolences. Ian had glanced about the small parlor and said, "Does your father work in the quarry—or down the pit?"

"He was a collier. We buried him last Whitsuntide—a year to the day after my mam passed away. It was right kind of you to bring me back the ring. Can I make you a cup of tea?"

"You're all alone in the world?" Ian tried to avoid looking at the bulge under her pinafore that said she was indeed in the family way. "Will you be able to manage?" He was thinking of Celine and women all over England, France, and Germany giving birth to fatherless babies, and he despaired anew at the mad waste of war.

"I do a bit of sewing. I'll be all right," Nancy had replied as he took the heavy iron kettle from her to lift it from hob to fire.

"Your young man's mother—" he began.

"No," Nancy said quickly, then smiled apologetically. "She didn't like me. I'm a fallen woman, you see, even though the baby's her son's. Mr. Saxon, if you'd like to help, you could keep me from being evicted from this house now Dad's gone. You're my landlord."

There had been Eccles cakes in one of the steel ovens flanking the coal fire, and he'd stayed for tea, inexplicably at ease with this quiet and composed young woman. Later he told her about Celine, and after he brought Geneva home and Nancy's own little girl, Lily, was born, he often slipped away to compare notes on child raising with Nancy. She was always there when he needed her, his refuge, his friend and confidant. Neither of them had, at first, tried to analyze their relationship.

Then one languid summer evening, after a particularly trying day at Saxon Hall, he had paced her tiny immaculate parlor and told her, "I'm appalled by the accidents at the colliery. We really need to spend more on timbering. I'm afraid my mother's health is failing, but she stubbornly refuses to see a doctor . . . and I'm at my wit's end worrying about that boy Charlie Dutton."

Nancy had let him talk about it all, then when he was finished, she took his hand and led him upstairs to her bedroom. Wordlessly she removed her clothes, unpinned her hair, and smiled at him with a shy gentle smile. Gratefully he went into her arms and made love to her, tentatively, awkwardly. But she had been sweetly responsive, patient and loving, and in the end it had been all right. He had never known such peace.

Afterward as they lay together he said, "Nancy . . . there's nothing to stop us from getting married," but she had quickly squashed that idea. "No, love, I'd be uncomfortable up at Saxon Hall. I'd not know how to talk proper, or how to act with all your posh relations and friends. Why, even the servants would frighten me to death. Let's just go on as we are."

She knew as much about Gennie, without ever meeting her face to face, as he did. Her own daughter, Lily, was a sensitive child who suffered the taunts regarding her illegitimacy from the village children until she was old enough to obtain a job in a cotton mill and live away from home.

Nancy was coming down the stairs on this, the day of Gennie's wedding, and Ian went to embrace her. "It's late, I shouldn't have come, but I had to see you for a little while. I brought you some wedding cake."

"I'll put it under my pillow—sleep on it and make a wish."

He smiled. "You'll make a pile of crumbs, superstitious old thing you. What will you wish?"

"Never you mind. Tell me about the wedding. I would have walked up to St. Agnes' Church, but I was afraid someone would see me and . . . you know. Was she a lovely bride?"

Ian sighed. "Heartbreakingly so. We had an unexpected guest. Matt Lauren—the American—arrived just as they were leaving. He said she lacked a certain sparkle and that was putting it mildly. Oh, lord, Nancy, is there anything worse than a forced marriage? I daren't think of their future."

Nancy drew him down onto the chair and sat on his lap, her arm around his shoulder. "You can't live her life for her. Perhaps they'll make something of their marriage. Tell me about the American. Do you think he's really her brother?"

"Frankly, no. There's absolutely nothing about Lauren that remotely hints he could be. Even beyond the differences of nationality, there is no physical resemblance. And he told me his father married Celine only two months before Gennie was born. I've been thinking, perhaps I should go to France, see if I can find any of Celine's relatives. There must be someone who can tell me for sure if Gennie and Lauren are brother and sister."

"Ian, dear, why is this so important now? Forgive me, love, but you've lost her anyway—to Terry. He's her husband. Why are you so afraid of the American? He can't take her away from you."

"Did you ever have a premonition, so strong that you believe it's actually happening in reality, rather than in your imagination? Lauren was standing in the hall—by that miserable grandfather clock that I really must get rid of—and Gennie came to the top of the staircase. She looked first at me, then straight at him—despite the crowd in the hall. He did rather stand out—he's a tall, striking looking fellow—and his clothes were very different from ours . . . but there was more that caught her attention. I can't explain it. One could almost feel the force of that look that passed between them. Then we went into the study so I could make the introductions in private, and he took her hand and they stood staring at each other, and the impact of their meeting seemed to fill the room. Oh, I know it must have been a moving moment for both of them—but there was so much more to it than that. I kept expecting cymbals to crash, or something. I've never seen two people so acutely aware of each other—the atmosphere was electric with it. I must sound like a fool; perhaps it's just the strain of the day."

"You're a wee bit emotional, it's only natural," Nancy said. "But you're a sensitive man and you've an intuition better than most women's. If you're worried about the American, then I'd do something about it. Find out all you can about him, and about Gennie's family in France, if you can still find them after all these years.

Ian stared at the corner shelf with its faded photographs and murmured, "Yes, you're right. My instincts tell me that a chain of events has just been set in motion that could bring tragedy to all of us."

Chapter 17

Geneva and Terry spent their wedding night playing draughts in a cozy bedroom in an old Scottish inn while a gale-force wind shrieked across the moors. Geneva was pale and exhausted, still reliving the day's events.

There had been a moment of desperate indecision just before she and her father left for the wedding ceremony at St. Agnes'. All of the guests and servants had preceded them to the church, and as they stood alone in the hall Ian said, "It isn't too late to change your mind, Gennie."

For a moment life beckoned her again, but then the weakness and nausea of early pregnancy and her emotional upheaval prevailed. She was no longer in control of her life. Its course was dictated by those who hated her and those who loved her—above all, by the child who needed her. She was too drained of feeling to speak and merely shook her head, avoiding her father's eyes.

During the long train journey north her thoughts were of Matt Lauren's surprise arrival, and she spoke of it to Terry until she sensed a slight resentment on his part and so had dropped the subject.

As the night closed in and she was obviously too tense to sleep, Terry gave her a conspiratorial grin and produced the draught board from his suitcase.

"I slipped it in when my valet wasn't looking. Can you

imagine what he would have thought? Cheer up, Gen, I'm not going to ravish you . . . oh, God, I didn't mean to say that!" He slapped his forehead with his hand in exasperation. "I'm a clumsy brute. I wanted to avoid reminding you of what Charlie Dutton did and—" He broke off, biting his lip.

She gave him a wan smile. "It's all right, Terry, I understand. You know, you don't have to stay here with me."

"Nonsense. Of course I want to stay with you. You always beat me at draughts when we were children. Perhaps tonight I'll win for a change. I've ordered dinner sent up here, just something light. You really must try to eat, you're thin as a stick."

To please him she picked at the boiled ham, then they spread the checkered board on the bed and set up the pieces. He was just her dearly beloved Terry, a brash, younger, more self-confident version of Ian, and she was not embarrassed to be sharing a room, or a bed, with him. Theirs was a marriage of convenience and she was sure they would never consummate it. The idea of willingly participating in what Charlie Dutton had done to her was unthinkable. She said, "Tell me about Dory. Have you heard from her since . . . since . . ."

"Since I had my nose bashed in by her dancing partner?" Terry finished for her ruefully. "No. Apparently they both got the sack and left the Liverpool Pavilion. I feel awful about it. I think perhaps Dory went back to London."

His amber eyes expressed such wistful longing that Geneva ached for him. She felt a wave of anger at the woman who could bring such abject misery to a man who could never hurt another creature. "Don't you have to go to London on colliery business soon? You should be able to find her easily by asking a few stage managers."

Terry regarded her quizzically for a moment. "I'd be better off trying to forget her. Just as you'd be better off trying to forget Dutton. You know . . . in time." He moved one of the black draughts on the board absently and Geneva immediately took two of his pieces. He did not appear to notice, adding, "After the baby is born and things get back to normal . . . oh, damn, what I'm trying to say is that even though we know each other too well for rockets to go soaring and waves crashing, you know—to fall madly in love—perhaps there could be a marriage for us? Lots of so-called marriages of convenience have ended up happy. The partners grow to care for one another."

Geneva felt a film slip over her eyes. She reached across the board and touched his hand. "Thank you, Terry . . . for I suppose just being yourself. Sweet and dear. I do care about you, I always have. But not in the way you're talking about. I'm afraid after Dutton . . ."

Terry studied the board intently and was silent for a while. "I suppose this . . . aversion to any physical contact with a man . . . explains your attitude toward the American this afternoon."

"What do you mean?" Geneva asked guardedly.

"Well, presumably he's your brother—half-brother, anyway. Therefore he isn't a threat—sexually. As Ian isn't and, I suppose, as I'm not."

"I still don't understand what you mean by my 'attitude' toward Matt."

The wind rattled the shutters on their windows and moaned in the chimney while Terry fingered one of the checkers. "Well, it was a bit much, wasn't it? Acting like Prince Charming just rode up on a horse—on your wedding day! I mean, dash it, he *is* a complete stranger. Even if it's true your mother married a man named Lauren, how do we know this is really his son? I should think you'd have been a little more restrained in your greeting. Didn't it occur to you that Ian kept us in the dark because he was worried about welcoming someone into the family whom we know nothing about? You heard him say they'd been corresponding with each other— yet Ian never said a word about it."

"Restrained? Can't you imagine how I felt? To be suddenly presented with a brother when I believed I had no blood relations." Her hand went to her brow in a gesture of tired incomprehension. "Could we stop playing? I'll concede the game. I'd like to lie down."

Terry was immediately contrite. "I'm sorry. I suppose I resented Lauren barging in and stealing my thunder—a chap doesn't get married every day, you know." There was a hint of his old banter, but his eyes remained troubled. He picked up her feet and swung them onto the bed so that she could lie down, then reached for her dressing case. "Where's your hairbrush? I'll brush your hair, perhaps it will help you relax."

She closed her eyes as the soft bristles of the brush smoothed back her hair. After a few minutes Terry began to speak of other things, recapturing the afternoon, the beautiful wedding ceremony in St. Agnes' Church, how the sunlight lit up the stained glass windows and sent bright spots of color dancing over her wedding gown. He didn't mention several raised eyebrows at the bride's choice of beige lace for the gown. Geneva had battled Meredith and Ian and adamantly refused to wear the traditional white.

"I was glad Huw arrived in time to be your best man," Geneva murmured. "You both looked so handsome, I was so proud of you. You're such a contrast—he so dark and you so fair. I've never felt completely at ease with Huw . . . I hope he doesn't feel you made a mistake marrying me."

"What nonsense! He thinks I'm a lucky blighter. He told me so. He had a crush on you himself once, though he never admitted it." The hairbrush paused, then resumed more slowly.

"Huw is finished with Heidelberg and taking a few months off before he decides what he wants to do. Lucky devil is taking flying lessons. He joined an aero club over at Speke."

Geneva knew that Huw Wakefield's mother had been a Hindu of high birth, daughter of a maharaja, and although there was no actual proof, Huw had confided to Terry that his parents died in a suicide pact, rather than in an accident as his grandfather had insisted. Huw's father had been ordered back to England and she had been afraid the prejudice she had encountered from British officers' wives in India would be even harder to bear far from her beloved country. "Are Huw and his grandfather getting along any better nowadays?" she asked, knowing how deep the friendship was between Terry and Huw.

"I'm afraid not. The colonel never forgave his son for marrying a Hindu—and I suspect he can't forgive Huw for being Eurasian. Damn shame, because Huw worships the old boy. Best part of it is, all the money he spends restoring the abbey is actually Huw's. Huw's Hindu grandfather settled a fortune on him. There's one room at the abbey that's a sort of shrine to Huw's father, set up by his grandfather, of course. Quite weird."

Geneva drifted off to sleep to dream about a dark horseman, silk turban on his head, riding toward a distant minaret-crowned palace, which was surely the result of Terry's conversation about Huw Wakefield.

The storms lashed the Scottish moors for a week, and when there was no sign of the weather improving by the eighth day, they took a train to London where there would be theaters and nightclubs and films with which to fill the time.

Geneva quickly became accustomed to sharing a room with

Terry and to sleeping beside him when only a double bed was
provided. She did notice that he became increasingly tense
and tight-lipped as the days passed, but assumed he was
somewhat bored by the inactivity and perhaps the knowledge
that Dora Gates could not be far away. She was not surprised
when Terry announced abruptly in the middle of the second
week, "Look, Gen, I've had enough of matinees and revues
to last me for a while. Do you mind if we go home this
weekend and declare our honeymoon officially at an end so I
can get back to work?"

She gave a sigh of relief. "I'll be glad to go home. I'm worn
out with all the false gaiety too . . . though in your case I
suspect there's more to it than that. You haven't run into
Dory, have you?"

"No and I haven't looked for her. I just want to go home,"
Terry replied with an unexpected testiness in his voice.

Puzzled, Geneva did not press the point, but something
was bothering the normally even-tempered Terry, of that she
was convinced. They took a train home to Saxon Hall that
afternoon.

Terry threw himself into the role of head of the Saxon
holdings with a vengeance during the early months of their
marriage, surprising Ian, Geneva, and everyone who had
known the previously fun-loving young man.

Letters came regularly from Matt in America, but due to
his grandfather's illness, he was unable to return to England.
Geneva eagerly awaited the letters and always replied the
same day. As she grew heavy with Charlie Dutton's child, she
was secretly glad Matt's return was delayed.

She never moved into that robust state of health most
pregnant women enjoy when the early months pass, and
when Ian called upon the family physician to express concern
about her, he was told curtly, "Some young women exhibit a
hysterical fear of delivery with their first baby. Offhand, old
man, I'd say your daughter isn't exactly thrilled to find herself
with child. State of mind, you know. Perhaps things will
improve when she gets closer to her time."

She was almost eight months pregnant when Charlie Dutton's mother died and he came home for her funeral. Charlie
had won several amateur boxing tournaments but had found
wrestling more to his liking since he took less punishment in
the choreographed bouts. He also enjoyed the flamboyant
role-playing of wrestling, the costumes, the posturing, and

the women who went bonkers over a certain wrestler. His ring name was the Turk and, at his manager's urging he shaved his head and grew a thin Oriental-style mustache and goatee, which were dyed black to add to the illusion. In the ring he wore a black satin robe and trunks, the former embroidered with a purple cobra, hooded and ready to strike. Charlie had chosen the design himself, although how it symbolized a Turk, no one dared ask. When he developed a boil over one eye that after lancing left an ugly scar, his manager suggested he wear a black satin mask and call himself the Masked Turk, adding menace to his presence as well as hiding the scar.

Charlie was pleased with the stir he created at his mother's funeral. Necks craned and eyes swiveled in his direction as he entered St. Agnes' Church for the services. His glance went immediately to the Saxon pew at the back of the church. The Saxons usually sent at least one representative to all of the village funerals. He saw the silver hair of Ian Saxon. Well, Charlie hadn't really expected Geneva to be there. She must be well along with the bun in her oven by now.

Taking his place in the front pew by his sisters, Charlie pondered again on the abrupt marriage of Geneva and Terry Saxon and allowed himself to count back to that day by the riverbank. Eight months ago. If she had the kid next month, he'd be almost certain it was his. Charlie chuckled and, catching Millie's frosty stare, hastily pulled his handkerchief from his pocket and smothered his amusement. At his side Josie grinned vacantly and rubbed her hand against his thigh.

The vicar was beside the coffin, speaking of the deceased in his droning voice. Charlie picked up Josie's hand and held it, afraid she would forget what he'd told her about not touching him in public. Christ, he'd have to get close to Geneva Saxon. He had to know if the kid was his. Hells bells, he was getting a hard-on just thinking about that day on the riverbank. The Saxon girl had a figure like one of those whores in a French postcard. 'Course it would have been better if she'd been petrified, perhaps fought more before she'd passed out. Charlie liked it when they fought and begged and cried. He didn't like it when they were eager. That spoiled it for him. Except for Josie, of course. But that was different.

Millie jabbed him sharply in the ribs with her pointy elbow and he jumped, realizing they were supposed to rise to sing the hymn. Auld witch was looking more like her mother every day. Thin, haggard, with a drooping, discontented mouth and streaks of iron gray in her hair. Nothing like the plump-breasted Josie with her little round buttocks that could work him up like no one could believe.

Across the aisle one of the village girls was watching him covertly while pretending to read the words in the hymnbook. Charlie stifled another grin. *Now Charlie,* he warned himself silently, *forget the village girls. Remember that blasted scullery maid at the hall. Don't want no more trouble like that.* The big cities were the place for fun and games. Besides, Josie would fix him up if they could get Millie out of the way for a bit.

Someone else was watching him. He turned to seek the eyes he could feel on the back of his neck. For a moment he didn't recognize the man looking at him. About his own age, with a frail body and delicate, almost girlish features. A high forehead and a contemplative look to the eyes that Charlie found unnerving, as though he were reading Charlie's thoughts. He frowned, trying to remember. He knew that face. Corwin. Ted Corwin. Of course, the weird little bugger who used to read books all the time. Lost half a leg in an explosion down the pit.

They were moving the coffin down the aisle now and Millie prodded him to follow. When they reached the cemetery he saw Corwin again, limping across the grass to the open grave. Curious, Charlie looked to see if there were two shoes under Corwin's trousers. There were. Must have a false leg.

When the earth rattled down on his mother's coffin, Charlie shuddered, not looking into the hole in the ground, impatient to be gone from this gloomy place. He'd already told his manager that when he died he didn't want to be put in no hole in the ground. He wanted to be cremated and put in a nice urn that would remain forever aboveground. He sighed with relief when the funeral was all over and they trooped back to the house.

Millie called him into the kitchen, cutting short his conversation with one of the daughters of a neighbor woman. "You look a fine sight," Millie said spitefully. "What did you go and shave your head for? Thought I'd die of shame, everybody staring at you. And what's that on your upper lip and chin? Bit of bootblack, is it?" She was slicing bread with short vicious strokes. "Here, give us a hand. Spread some marg on that and cut up the cucumber. And you listen to me, Charlie boy, 'cos things are going to be different 'round here from now on. No more of your tricks with Josie, or I'll call the coppers. Ought to be ashamed of yourself, you ought, taking advantage of your own daft sister."

"Shut up—don't call her that," Charlie said fiercely.

"I'll shut up when I'm finished. You're not staying here anymore. Get on back to your lodgings soon as everybody's gone home, see."

Charlie looked into Millie's malevolent eyes and decided not to argue. She meant it. "Christ, I don't need to come 'round here no more," he said with an offhand shrug. "Making more filthy lucre with my wrestling than I know what to do with."

"Mr. Saxon was at church," she said with a satisfied nod of her head. "Told me we could stay in the house as long as we liked, me and Josie. Said he'd have a word with Mr. Terry."

"Up theirs," Charlie said, whacking the cucumber in two.

"Watch your dirty mouth. And don't go near them Saxons making trouble for us. We've got to live here when you're gone."

"You seen Geneva lately? How far along is she?"

"What do you care?"

Charlie gave her a sly grin. "Maybe I've got a vested interest."

Millie put the bread knife down and looked at him, her features a study in crafty speculation. "Charlie . . . you didn't. No, you couldn't have . . ." She did some rapid mental calculations. "That day you came home—that's about eight months ago. You said the Saxon gamekeeper had chased you, swore Ma and me to secrecy if anybody came looking for you. Well, nobody did. We thought you'd just been poaching on their land again."

Charlie smirked. "I didn't expect them to come after me. Them Saxons wouldn't of wanted people to know."

"Shut up, they'll hear," Millie warned, with a jerk of her head in the direction of the mourners crowding the only other downstairs room. She piled sandwiches on a plate in nervous excitement, not knowing whether to be fearful or elated about the possibility of Charlie having fathered Geneva's child, unsure whether the Duttons had much to gain, or to lose. "What are you going to do?" she whispered.

"Find out for sure," Charlie answered.

Early the following morning Rankin approached Geneva as she stood on the terrace wishing she could walk along the riverbank but knowing that more than her lethargy held her back.

"There's a telephone call for you, madam." Rankin hesitated. "A woman's voice. She wouldn't give her name, but from her accent she sounds like one of the village women."

Nancy Whitaker, Geneva thought immediately. Nancy had called soon after they returned from their honeymoon to express her remorse about "tattletaling to Geneva's father," as she put it, and to inquire about her health. She had invited Geneva to tea, saying perhaps they could talk; she'd like to reassure her that "nothing is as bad as it looks."

Geneva had not taken her up on the invitation, not out of snobbishness, but simply because she barely had the strength to get through the day, let alone make any social calls. Nancy did not have a telephone in her house, and she had called from the post office, so later Geneva sent her a note thanking her for her solicitude and promising to call when she felt stronger.

"I'll take the call in the study, Rankin," Geneva said.

The voice on the phone was a hoarse whisper and was certainly not Nancy Whitaker. "Listen, you know what's good for you, you meet me—tonight, after dark. I know all about that baby and if you don't want the whole bloody village to know, to say nothing of your father—"

"Who are you?" Geneva asked, putting out her hand to steady herself against the desk. Her heart thudded painfully.

"Never mind. I'm just a woman what *knows*."

"Where . . . where shall I meet you?" Geneva's heart had skipped at the mention of Ian. No! She had endured too much to have him discover what had happened to her at this late date.

"The lane coming into the village from the hall—about halfway there's an old barn in the middle of a field. You know where I mean? You come by yourself and be there ten sharp."

The phone clicked in Geneva's ear. She stood still, trying to breathe normally. Terry was in London. Ian had grown accustomed to her retiring early, she was always so fatigued nowadays. Slipping out of the house would be relatively easy. Her child moved in her womb, kicking persistently against her side. She put her hand on her distended abdomen as though to quiet the restless baby. Blackmail? Had the woman on the phone somehow learned the truth? Was it possible? Charlie Dutton's mother had been buried yesterday, her father had attended the services. Had Charlie put two and two together and informed the woman? But why?

Geneva squared her shoulders. There would be no blackmail. If that were the plan, she'd have to tell her father the truth. But first she would confront the woman to find out for sure what she wanted.

The day passed slowly, measured by the ticking of the grandfather clock in the hall. Geneva glanced at her late grandmother's monstrosity of a clock every time she went through the hall. They no longer gathered around the clock for the two-minute silence on November 11, but Geneva still shivered each time she passed the clock, remembering. It had ticked away the minutes of her pregnancy; sometimes she felt it was ticking away the minutes of their lives, inexorably, irretrievably.

A few seconds before ten o'clock that night she was pushing through the hawthorne hedge bordering the field, feeling the sharp thorns tear at her clothes. The weight of the baby forced her to lean backward as she moved, and her progress over the stubble of the harvested field was slow. A light rain began to fall, plastering her hair to her brow.

In the dark barn gray shadows streaked for cover as she stood in the doorway and called, "Are you there? It's Geneva Saxon." Her only response was a scurrying amid the rancid straw. She stood still, straining to see through the misty gloom, suddenly fearful. Her hand went to her abdomen, where her child was strangely still.

She turned to leave and collided with a muscular chest. Large hands grabbed her shoulders, and she caught the odor of rum as a high-pitched laugh told her how foolish she had been to come expecting to meet the woman on the phone.

"Hello, love," Charlie Dutton said, giving her a squeeze that crushed the passenger in her womb.

"I should have guessed," Geneva said, trying to control the trembling of her voice. "That was your sister on the phone. What do you want?"

In the darkness she couldn't see his face, but the shape of his head was oddly globular, as though he didn't have any hair. He seemed ever bigger and heavier than she remembered. His hands slid from her shoulders, brushed her breasts, and rubbed insinuatingly on her stomach. He patted the swelling. "Not much longer now, hey, love? Till you and me's a mum and dad." He was convulsed with giggles now; she could feel him shaking and making little snorting noises.

"I don't know what you mean, but you'd better listen to me. I didn't tell anyone what happened before, but if you don't get out of my way and let me leave, I'll not only bring charges against you for tonight, I'll file a rape charge too. Do you want to go back to prison?"

He shoved her away from him viciously, and she slammed back against the wooden side of the barn. "Bitch. Bloody Saxon bitch. Shut your damn mouth. You think they'll do anything now—that was eight months ago."

She winced as pain shot upward from her lower back. "What is it you want of me? Haven't you done enough? You've ruined my life."

"Aha!" Charlie exclaimed triumphantly. "So the brat's mine! I knew it. You going to bring a paternity suit against me?" He guffawed at his wit.

"I'm not going to do anything if you'll just leave us alone. But if you make any more trouble for me, or my family, I'll . . . I'll kill you."

He moved in closer, pinning her between his bulk and the wall. "Come on now, be nice to me. I'm your brat's dad. Let's play house, shall we? Like we was married. I bet that posh husband of yours don't have a thing like mine."

She struggled, feeling the terrible fear return, trying desperately to think. The circulation in her legs had ceased and her body seemed frozen. "Wait—Charlie—just a minute," she gasped out as he tried to plant his lips on her mouth. "Please, just listen for a minute. I'm close to my time. You'll hurt the baby if you have intercourse with me now. You wouldn't want to hurt your own child, would you, Charlie? That's not like hurting the Saxons."

He stopped, considering. "All right—not a fuck then. But I'm all hard now, see, so you're going to have to do something else."

"I could . . . massage you . . ." she said, shuddering.

He laughed. "I know something better than that. Get down on your knees."

The fear was a snake, crawling up her body, strangling her. In her mind she raced in an endless maze, seeking deliverance. "First, could I go over there, in the bushes? I need to go to the bathroom. It's the pressure of the baby that causes it."

He found this even more hilarious and giggled as he took her arm and walked her over to the nearest bushes. "No funny stuff. I can see the top of your head in there. Though

Christ knows I've seen all of you, so I don't know what you
want to hide for."

"It's because I'm pregnant," she said, crouching in the
bushes and frantically exploring the ground around her.

"Hurry up. What's going on in there?" Charlie said
irritably.

Her fingers had found a fallen branch, solid, heavy, damp
from the rain. She drew a deep breath, straightened up, and
swung the branch with all of her strength. There was a
sickening thud as it connected with his head. She heard him
grunt, but he did not fall. Blindly she turned and ran, but a
glance over her shoulder showed that he was coming after
her. She turned as she heard his breathing behind her and
struck at him again, catching him under the jaw at the same
instant his fist smashed into her stomach.

She was still on her feet, waves of pain and dizziness
battling a blood lust of anger. The branch crashed down on
his head again and he went down on one knee, swinging at
her wildly. His fist caught her again, low in the stomach, and
she fell heavily, slipping away to merciful oblivion.

Rhythmic pains, radiating from her lower back, encircling
her stomach and squeezing painfully, then letting go, awakened her. Rain was falling on her face. She was alone in the
field.

She pushed herself up on her knees, the shadows spinning
about her head and the darkness closing in for a second until
she gritted her teeth and willed herself to stay conscious.
Trying to stand brought waves of pain. She began to crawl
toward the hawthorne hedge, her breath laboring in her
chest.

The Morris was parked on the lane; she could see the top of
the car. How much time had passed? Would anyone have
missed her? If Ian needed his car, he might have. Would he
come looking for her? No, better not to count on it. Keep
going—just put one knee in front of the other. *Oh, God, it
hurts. Please don't let the baby be born until I can get home.
Charlie Dutton must have thought he killed me. He certainly
didn't wait around. This pain . . . like no other I've known
. . . Please help me, please. Oh, God. Oh, Mother, Mother!*

Had she blacked out again? There was the hedge, not far
now. But the last few feet were an impossible chasm. She
couldn't move. Clawing at the mud and harvested stubble of

the field brought only a tightening band of pain and the feeling that she couldn't get enough air into her lungs. Panting, she lay on her side with the baby supported by the wet earth, her cheek cradled by her hand, hoping that a moment's rest would give her the strength to continue. She felt more alone than she had ever felt in her life, her terror as great as that day on the riverbank when the child was conceived, but now the fear was doubled because two lives were in jeopardy.

There was a pattern to the pain in her body, she realized as a new cramping began, low in her back, moving with increasing pressure around to her stomach, then surging in an agonizing wave until she wanted to scream. Despite the misting of cold rain, she could feel sweat beading on her forehead and her body felt hot, clammy.

She was in labor. The certainty of it crashed into her consciousness and, as the contraction eased, sent her up on her knees, desperate to reach the lane. The movement brought a rush of warm liquid from inside her. She rolled on her back, crying into her fist, knowing that the breaking of the waters was further proof that she was about to have her baby.

No, she thought—*no! Not here, in a muddy field, all alone. Please, not like this.* In the back of her mind she was groping back in time, seeking the moment of her own birth, knowing at last how her mother must have felt in that shell-ravaged cottage. A new pain began and she screamed. Her only answer was the mournful cry of an owl, somewhere in the woods surrounding Saxon Hall.

Lost in the grip of the contraction, she gasped for breath and felt her abdomen harden and strain downward. The pain began to recede, ebbing slowly like the tide that withdraws only to send even greater waves in an onslaught against the shore. She scrambled to her knees again to attempt to cross the last few feet to the hedge. Then she heard it—the soft purr of a car that could only be the Rolls, moving slowly along the lane.

"Father! I'm here!" she screamed, but the lights, muted by the hawthorne hedge, went slowly by. She put her face down in the mud and wept.

Now she dragged herself with her fingertips, squirming over the ground, oblivious to everything but the need to reach the lane. Thorns tore at her hair as she frantically sought a way through the densely grown hawthorne.

Then the glare of headlights blinded her. Thank God, they had seen the Morris parked a little farther down the lane and had turned back. Somewhere beyond the glare of lights were voices, muffled by her own sobbing breath and whimpers of pain. "Over there—by the hedge. Quickly, get out of my way, man."

Comforting arms went around her and she heard her father whisper her name and knew she was safe now. But then the worst pain of all began and went on without end. Dimly she heard Ian say, "Go directly to the hospital."

Chapter 18

1939

A year passed before Matt was able to return to England. Two weeks after Geneva's wedding he returned to Greenboughs to find his grandfather had suffered a heart attack. The old man was a brittle shell, hanging grimly on to life with sheer willpower. Nathan, so long an invalid himself, had rallied and was taking care of his employer with the help of a couple of new servants he bullied unmercifully.

There was no time to worry about DeVore's men coming around, or to long for a return visit to Geneva. Castleton now had four freighters and two barges, as well as several warehouses in New Orleans. He had begun to restore the house and hunt down his lost antiques. So much had been set in motion that Matt was swept along in a rush of work that sent him to bed exhausted after eighteen-hour days.

Several letters sent to Lottie in Maple Ridge had gone unanswered, so Matt telephoned Tony, in front of whose shoe repair shop Specks and later Leah had shined shoes. Tony told Matt that Lottie and Leah had left Maple Ridge shortly after he had found them there and no one knew where they had gone.

So Matt had Specks' body disinterred and brought home to New Orleans for burial in one of the city's aboveground cemeteries. Matt had always thought of them as small cities of the dead; the vaults had seemed taller when he was a boy, accompanying Specks on a funeral procession to listen to his horn bid farewell to a friend. Matt had been surprised to find there were cemeteries where the dead were buried underground, in the earth, until Specks explained that the ground in New Orleans was waterlogged and that underground graves were the usual kind. Still, Matt was sure Specks would rather rest above the ground.

The Jazzmen, older, grizzled, more frail than he remembered, gathered around the vault they had decorated with beads and brass wire twisted into the shape of a trumpet and played a last tribute, and Matt wept openly and unashamedly for the first time in his life. Then he went back to Greenboughs and threw himself into all of his grandfather's projects.

A year flew by before he was able to take the time to visit England. He sailed on a Castleton freighter, diverted to the New York-to-Liverpool run.

This time he telephoned Ian Saxon from the dock in Liverpool and was invited to spend the weekend at Saxon Hall. The chauffeur would be dispatched to pick him up at his ship.

Although Matt was ready to leave by early afternoon, the Rolls-Royce did not arrive until evening. Matt settled back against the smooth leather seat as the car passed, whisper-quiet, under the overhead railway running the length of the docks, then negotiated the traffic around the entrance to the Mersey tunnel and headed through busy downtown streets.

An hour later, the sun still high in the summer sky although it was almost eight in the evening, Matt was being greeted by Ian Saxon. "So glad to see you again. Geneva is looking forward to your visit so much, but our dinner guests were a little early and she's presently entertaining them in the drawing room. I thought perhaps you'd like to change before you meet the others. I took the liberty of having my valet lay out a dinner jacket for you, as I'm sure you have little need of one aboard ship."

Matt gave an easy smile. "Very kind of you, sir, but I did bring my own." He followed the butler, who carried his overnight bag, up the stairs, feeling considerably more in command of the situation than he had on his first visit. He was disappointed that he would again have to meet Geneva in the company of others, but the weekend stretched out, full of possibilities. In the pleasant room that had been prepared for him, overlooking the rear grounds where the soft green of the lawns met the darker green of the woods, Matt changed quickly and then went downstairs.

He was relieved to find the dinner party small. Some of the faces seemed familiar. A white-haired man was introduced as Colonel Wakefield, then his grandson Huw gave Matt an enigmatic stare as he shook hands. A fluttery young woman with a frizz of blonde hair clung to Huw's arm. She was presented as Binnie Barclay. Next came a young man with thoughtful eyes who limped across the room and was introduced as Ted Corwin.

Terry shook hands and smiled warmly. "Delighted to see you again. Gen has shared all of your letters, of course, and we were so sorry to hear of your grandfather's illness. How is he?"

"Determined to hang on, but fighting a losing battle, I'm sorry to say." Matt had been staring at Geneva even as he shook hands with everyone else. She had risen as he entered the room, fixing her lovely gray eyes on him with a look of wonderment he felt to his toes.

She placed her hand in his, hesitated, then kissed his cheek. He fought the impulse to wrap her in a tight embrace and hold her beyond the limits of propriety. She was saying, a trifle breathlessly, "I've been looking forward to this for a year. Now you're here I hardly know what to say."

They sat together on a satin-upholstered sofa, and the butler brought him a drink that he downed without tasting. Everyone asked questions and talked, and Matt replied but nothing was really said and none of it penetrated his mind and memory, because he had lived this moment so many times in his imagination that the reality, where it did not conform to his mind's picture, did not exist. Geneva was as he remembered her from her wedding day, but marriage had brought an added maturity that enhanced her beauty in a subtle way. She was intelligent and compassionate and warm, and he knew this from what she said and how her voice softened at times and became sorrowful at others, and from her eyes and the way they caressed him fondly—in the same way, he noted with an unexplainable pang, that she looked at her husband and her father.

When Rankin announced that dinner was served, she

slipped her arm through his as they rose to go to the dining room. "If we'd known you were coming today, we wouldn't have asked the others. But you said your ship would dock tomorrow."

"We made better time than I anticipated. But I do wish we could talk alone. I know they're all bursting with curiosity about me, but could we steer clear of personal matters?"

"Leave it to me," she said. "There's one sure way to change the subject nowadays—regrettably."

When café au lait and dessert were served, and Terry remarked on how chance encounters and apparent whims of fate sent people down unexpected paths, Geneva smoothly switched the line of conversation by asking Matt what his countrymen's feelings were on the current political situation in Europe.

"There's a strong feeling of isolationism," Matt replied. "Americans don't want to become involved in another European war."

Ian said, "I take it you don't believe Mr. Chamberlain's promise of 'peace in our time.' "

"No, sir. Do you?"

Before Ian could reply, Huw Wakefield leaned forward and said, "I lived in Germany. I watched the Nazi party rise to power. One has to realize what it was like there before Adolf Hitler swept the streets clean of debauchery. The German people will follow him through the gates of hell."

"And that's where he'll lead them," Ted Corwin said.

Matt noted there was a slightly rough edge to Ted's accented speech, which, although grammatically correct, lacked the polish of the others'.

"Debauchery, Huw?" Binnie exclaimed, raising painted-on eyebrows. "Sounds fascinating. Do tell. What was it like?"

"Decadent," Huw said. "Not for a young lady's ears."

Ted Corwin said, "It was nudity and cocaine and morphine—" He was looking at Huw as he spoke, rather than addressing a reply to Huw's vacant-eyed girl friend. "There were whores of both sexes. Cabaret and transvestite balls and thugs and gangsters. Private parties with waitresses in filmy panties who were paid to be fondled. Prostitutes strutting through the streets of Berlin wearing leather boots and wielding whips. Every kind of perversion known to man. And beneath it all the most appalling poverty because of currency fluctuations."

Into the awkward silence that followed, Binnie, apparently blithely unaware of the sudden atmosphere of tension, said, "And Hitler did away with the decadence?"

Ted said, "Hitler preached a twisted sort of puritanism. He shot homosexuals and put the prostitutes into state-operated brothels."

"Then he can't be all bad, can he?" Binnie said brightly, patting her dark red lips with a damask serviette.

Matt said quietly, "He also burned books, banned jazz, and is waging a reign of terror against Jews and other minorities. My father and my guardian were Dixieland jazz musicians, so I was naturally interested in that target of Hitler's . . . but I find everything he does sinister in the extreme."

"You had a father *and* a guardian?" Ted asked. He had an alert, concerned gaze that said he was genuinely interested.

"Consecutively. My father was wounded in 1918 and was an invalid until he died."

"And are you also a musician?"

"No. I spent a good part of my life on the Mississippi River and know good jazz when I hear it, but I haven't any musical talent."

Ian rose. "Shall we adjourn to the drawing room for liqueurs?"

Matt was glad the long English summer day was at last fading into twilight and the lamps had not yet been lit. He sat down to watch Geneva through the violet-tinted shadows, and to study and observe the people who had surrounded her and been a part of her life. It was clearly evident that the child born in a shelled cottage in war-torn France had enjoyed an insulated and luxurious family life, with an adoptive father who adored her, a cousin who became her husband and who treated her as though she were some remote goddess. Why, then, did that haunted shadow flit across her eyes occasionally, and why did he sense deep sorrow beneath the carefully tranquil manner? Replies to his letters during the past year had given no indication of anything of a tragic nature. Certainly the birth of her daughter must have been an occasion for joy, although Geneva had been quite ill following the birth and for a time Ian had responded to his letters. Matt was looking forward to meeting his niece.

Colonel Wakefield was the first guest to leave. He rose to make his apologies. "Forgive me, Ian old chap, but I've got the workmen coming at the crack of dawn to begin work on the last segment of the cloisters." He turned to Matt to explain, "I'm restoring an old abbey. You must come and see what we've done. Geneva will bring you over." He smiled at Geneva. "And bring that pretty little baby girl of yours."

Matt was watching Geneva and saw the shadow return to her eyes at the mention of her baby.

Although the colonel protested they should stay, Huw and his girl friend had driven him over to Saxon Hill and insisted they would take him home. The Wakefields dropped Binnie at her house and then drove the short distance to the abbey. Their butler immediately announced that a visitor had been waiting to see Mr. Huw. The butler had been Colonel Wakefield's batman in India, a wiry little Lancastrian named Higgins who was still more batman than butler. "A German bloke," he added. "Baron something or other."

The colonel said, "Thank you, Higgins." He raised a questioning eyebrow to Huw. "Willi? You were expecting him?"

Huw shrugged. "He's the only baron I know."

"Yes," his grandfather said thoughtfully. "I remember his hospitality that summer I visited you at Heidelberg."

Waiting for them in the drawing room was a spectacular figure: tall, Aryan blond, with vivid blue eyes, immaculately groomed. His heels clicked and he bowed as Huw reintroduced him to Higgins as Baron von Hegel. "Please, old friend," he protested, "my title is resurrected only when I must breach the bulwarks of protective old family retainers." He gave Higgins a dazzling smile that did not reach his eyes. "Let me now revert to plain Herr von Hegel." He laughed and pumped Huw's hand enthusiastically. "How good it is to see you again. Forgive the unannounced visit. I wasn't sure I would come this far north when I arranged to visit London, but I motored up today." He fingered a small scar on his cheek.

"I'm delighted to see you, Willi," Huw said. "I'll order supper for us. Higgins, would you mind seeing if Cook is still up?"

Higgins gave their visitor a baleful look and departed.

"If you two will excuse me, I'm very tired," the colonel said. "I'm sure you have a lot of talking to do. I'll see you in the morning."

When they were alone, Willi said reproachfully, "You promised to write. Why did I not hear from you?"

"I'm sorry. I've been busy." Huw went to the table, where decanters of wine and brandy had been placed.

Willi sat down, stretching his long legs out in front of him and regarding Huw with a faintly amused smile. "That isn't true. But we'll let it pass. Tell me, old friend, are you still at odds with the English half of your blood? Or are you settling down to be a country squire, shoring up two old ruins with the wealth of an Indian princess whose royal blood makes your English blood seem like water by comparison."

Huw handed him a glass of brandy. *"Two* old ruins?"

Willi gestured about the room. "This damp old monastery and . . . your grandfather." He laughed again. "Forgive me, I'm being my outrageous self. You have always appeared to me to be an exotic prince of the blood, rather than the offspring of some obscure army officer. Royal blood calling to royal blood, as it were."

"The question of blood seems to be obsessing you Germans at the moment. I doubt my particular mixture is acceptable, except to my more liberal fellow students at Heidelberg."

"And you do not number me among them?" Before Huw could reply, Willi added, "And I am a *Prussian,* my friend. Had you forgotten? There *is* a subtle difference."

"Why did you really come here, Willi?"

"To see an old friend, of course. Why else?"

"I feel bound to tell you that when we first met, I was in a somewhat disoriented period of my life. I'm no longer quite as confused, nor seeking an answer to my confusion by investigating every radical group—political and otherwise—as I was in those early days at the university."

Willi shrugged. "Of course not. But you cannot fail to realize that sooner or later you'll be forced to make a choice. India will eventually seek her independence from Britain. There will be more bloodshed in your lovely tormented land. You must choose your alliances with the long view in mind."

"If you came here to recruit me," Huw said, "I suggest you would probably be more successful looking up a certain Irish republican who was also a member of our group. In the event of war between Germany and England, there's no doubt as to which side he'd be on."

Willi laughed. "You do me an injustice. Ah, what have we here?" He turned his cool smile in the direction of one of the maids, who entered the room, blinking sleepily, carrying a tray of sandwiches.

Waiting for her to depart, Huw realized that Willi had made no mention of a military career, a tradition for the sons in his family. They ate some of the sandwiches, discussed mutual friends, diabolic former professors, unforgettable parties. Then Willi said, "You were always the best, the first in everything. Forever trying to impress your grandfather, win his affection. Did you know your grandfather feels guilty about the death of your parents? Do you remember that summer he visited you and we took him to my home for the weekend? I never told you of the long conversation he and I had after everyone was asleep one night."

Huw sat up straight in his chair. "What do you mean—guilty?"

Willi's vividly blue eyes gleamed, and Huw was reminded of sunlight catching the blade of a knife. "Your grandfather told me the two of them—he and your father—were working together, that he'd taken all the usual precautions. You had never told us that the explosion that killed your father was choreographed by your grandfather."

"Quaint choice of words, Willi. What are you getting at?"

"He told me your mother was the daughter of a maharaja. In the old days their women flung themselves on the funeral pyres of their husbands. In her depression and anguish over the death of your father, she committed suicide."

"So you know. Must we rake it over again?"

"Ah, but your grandfather told me he considered leaving you in India, but an Anglo-Indian faces great prejudice there, so he sent you to England, even while he remained in India to finish his army service. And you, Huw, must have felt he was shutting you out of his life. He told me you asked him once why he gave you the name of his Welsh grandfather rather than a Hindu name. I told him he should have talked to you—honestly—it would have closed the gulf between you. I told him you felt he resented your Hindu blood." His finger went again to the dueling scar on his cheek.

"You had no right—" Huw began angrily, half rising from his chair.

"The colonel said . . ." Willi's voice was as soft and deadly as a rapier slicing into vulnerable flesh. ". . . that he *did* resent your Hindu blood."

Huw slumped back in his chair, his lips drawn back as

though he were afraid if he parted them he would give a cry of pain. After a long pause he said, "Willi, as the saying goes, with a friend like you, I wonder if I need any enemies."

"It's better you know how the old man feels about you. Then you can be objective about your own loyalties."

Regarding him silently, Huw was unsure how he felt—admiring or appalled—at the cool logic that governed all of Willi's speech and action, which left no room for emotional reaction. Was that a preferred state—an evolution of mind over such trivialities as familial attachments? Willi had boasted in the past that he had long ago cast aside all outmoded traditions.

"I take it," Huw said, "that your family made good their threat to kick you out if you joined the Nazi party?"

Willi merely smiled.

"You did join—officially?"

Willi leaned forward. "You are in a unique position to be of service to us, Huw. The Führer will be most generous to those who serve the Third Reich. Do you not see yourself, one day, returning in glory to India to lead your people in revolution . . . with all the men and arms you need? Reclaiming your birthright?"

Huw reached for the brandy decanter again, thinking of his grandfather actually telling a stranger that he resented having a Eurasian grandson. Telling Willi von Hegel, of all people. Huw handed Willi a glass of brandy. They talked far into the night.

At Saxon Hall the following morning a hearty breakfast was served on the terrace to take advantage of the late-summer sunshine. Matt and Ian were alone and Ian had explained that Terry had business at the colliery, while Geneva had not yet returned from her morning ride. Matt asked about Geneva and Terry's daughter.

Ian said, "Dulcie is almost eight months old. An extraordinarily pretty child. Perhaps even more exquisite than Gennie herself was as a baby, if that's possible." He was rearranging the grilled ham and tomatoes on his plate, without eating.

"I'm looking forward to meeting my niece," Matt said.

"I'm sure Gennie will bring her down to the terrace shortly. On fine mornings she has the nursemaid put Dulcie's pram out here so she can be in the fresh air." He put down his knife and fork. "I've been thinking of going back to France

. . . the Valenciennes area. I would have gone months ago, but I felt Gennie needed me since Dulcie was born. Her strength returned so slowly and Terry is away on business frequently. Matt, I feel I should be frank and tell you I hope to trace Celine's family and learn if your father was indeed Gennie's father. I believe it would be better for all of us if we knew for certain."

Matt leaned back in his chair and studied his host. "I don't want anything from Geneva, other than to know her."

"But she lives in a different world from you; she has a husband, a daughter. I don't wish to seem unfeeling, but I don't see how you can fit into her life at this late date, nor she into yours."

"Yet you feel strongly enough to want to track down the truth about her parentage." Matt had a vague image in the back of his mind of Ian Saxon, dressed in a suit of armor, astride a horse, with lance at the ready to protect his castle, upon whose battlements stood his lovely adopted daughter.

Ian was staring at him. "You aren't anything like her, you know. Do you believe that our environment shapes us more than our genes?"

Before Matt could reply he heard Geneva's voice, inside the house, calling for someone to open the terrace doors. "Good morning, brother dear," she said as Matt opened the door. The baby was draped over her shoulder and she had a basket of berries in her other hand. She was still flushed from her ride, her hair tied back, wearing jodhpurs and a linen shirt. Matt felt his throat constrict at the sight of her.

"Say hello to Dulcie," she said. "Look, I picked some blackberries for breakfast. We'll all have stained teeth all morning. Cook is sending up some clotted cream."

A nursemaid in a navy blue uniform appeared, pushing a perambulator with a tasseled canopy. Geneva laid the baby down and Matt moved closer to look at the child.

Ian had been right about the porcelain prettiness of the child. Round violet-blue eyes studied the tassels of the canopy, fluttering in a slight breeze, with the remote air of a fairy-tale princess around whom every object has been placed to please, while perfect little hands lay like fallen stars on the satin coverlet. Dulcie lay still, in that perfectly relaxed state that precedes sleep, so Matt tiptoed away, afraid he would disturb her.

Geneva was concentrating on dividing the blackberries

when he rejoined her at the table. He said, "Dulcie is the most beautiful child I've ever seen. You and Terry must be very proud."

The dish of blackberries slid from Geneva's hand and crashed to the flagged terrace, shattering and sending a purple stain spattering over her leather boots. "How clumsy of me. Excuse me—" she stammered, then turned and ran back into the house.

Matt bent to pick up the broken pieces of glass, but Ian said abruptly, "One of the servants will attend to that."

The nursemaid stood beside the pram, but Matt realized that the baby had not been startled, nor cried out, at the sudden explosion of sound when the dish fell. He looked from the pram to Ian with dawning comprehension. "Is Dulcie deaf?" he asked quietly.

Ian said stiffly, "Gennie had a very difficult time with the birth. The doctors have various explanations for Dulcie's problems and apparent lack of progress. Deafness is only one of her afflictions. They think her oxygen was cut off for a time—during the delivery. Whatever happened . . . caused damage to her brain. Their prognosis for a normal life for Dulcie is not hopeful."

Chapter 19

The low murmur of conversation in the restaurant of the Adelphi Hotel in Liverpool was masked by the sad strains of "These Foolish Things," played with bored indifference by a substitute violinist to a small teatime crowd.

Geneva regarded Matt across their table, aware of the fragrance of the white rose in its silver vase, aware of his dark eyes probing her thoughts. Fleetingly, the question posed itself again: *How can I feel this bewildering sense of belonging when we grew up so far apart? And why does it bring both joy and despair?* The barren landscape of her life had been almost endurable until he came along. Now she yearned for all she could never be again, and for all that was forever denied her. A normal child, a marriage of love rather than convenience, above all to be whole, restored, a woman making her own destiny.

Aloud she said, "I haven't heard from Father since he left and I'm terribly worried. It's not like him not to send some word. Terry's in London on business and I spoke to him last night. He promised to wire the British Consulate in Paris."

Matt leaned forward, watching her intently. "What are your feelings on his trip to France? Are you hoping he'll bring back proof we are both John Lauren's children?"

"Of course. Why do you ask?" She twisted the stem of her

wineglass, disturbed more by the tensing of his jaw and the faraway flame in his eyes than by the question.

"You know why."

She closed her eyes briefly and swallowed. An elderly waiter materialized and removed their dishes. When he departed she said, "We're still a novelty to one another. It's that fascination we all feel toward a foreigner. I must seem quite as foreign and different to you as you do to me. There's a sort of glamour to it. This is only the fourth time we've met—we'll get used to it in time." She paused, waiting for him to comment, but he continued to watch her with that same raw question in his gaze. "Then, too, you are the sailor home from the sea. You drop in, then sail away with the tide. I wasn't sure I should come to Liverpool to meet you when you called today."

"If you hadn't, I wouldn't have got to see you this trip. I must sail tomorrow and I've that shipping agent to see tonight. Gennie, what if Ian learns that your father was *not* my father?"

She stared into the depths of her wine. "You will, of course, always be welcome to visit Saxon Hall. I feel we are . . . friends, no matter what. Perhaps friends are even more important than family. Besides, we'll always have that other mysterious bond—that your father loved my mother, and married her."

"We have an even more mysterious bond than that. You know it, you've felt it as strongly as I. Oh, we've been carefully proper, and God knows Terry is as decent a man as I've ever met and only a heel would—"

"Matt, stop it! We're brother and sister."

His mouth clamped shut. They stared at each other silently, neither daring to say any more, yet all the unspoken questions hung in the air. *What we feel for each other is wrong, hopeless. Even if by some random chance he's not my brother, there's Terry—and Dulcie. And always, forever,* Geneva thought despairingly, *Charlie Dutton, who stole a part of me.*

Matt motioned for the waiter and paid the bill. "Come on," he said. "I want to walk down to the river with you. We only have an hour. This is the first time I've been alone with you and I don't want to waste it in a stuffy cafe."

On Lime Street the homeward-bound workers had dwindled to an occasional clerk or shop assistant running to catch a tram. In the deepening dusk the peace that only a busy place can know crept over the streets in the lull between day and evening. Neon signs flickered on and buskers good-naturedly jostled each other for the best positions to entertain the expected queues of theatergoers. The cinema awnings shouted Hollywood's latest offerings with dazzling lights. English-made films were often relegated to second-feature status, a fact commented on by Matt as they passed the Odeon.

"I suppose the British studios haven't yet learned to make films with the . . . dash of Hollywood," she answered.

"Hollywood's depiction of life in America is hardly accurate," Matt said, taking her arm to steer her around a group of sailors converging on a pub. "I'd like to show you my country some time. Will you come?"

"Terry and Dulcie too, of course," she said, not looking at him.

They turned the corner and walked in the direction of the river. Matt said quietly, "Look, it wasn't hard to figure out that Dulcie was born barely six months after you and Terry were married. You're young . . . you were trapped. Let's talk about it."

"I'm not going to discuss my husband, my marriage . . . or my daughter with you, Matt," she answered in a tight voice.

The salt tang of the river grew stronger as they started down Water Street. A departing ship blew a lonely farewell, reminding her that he would sail on tomorrow's tide and enclosing her heart with an emotion she knew was more than regret.

"The saddest sound in the world," Matt said. "Sometimes I think I've been listening to ships' horns blowing good-bye to someone left behind all of my life. All right, Gennie, we won't talk about your family. You're right, it's none of my business."

She glanced sideways at him, surprised again that he had begun to use her father's diminutive of her name and that she had not forbidden it. Nancy called her that too. She had visited Nancy regularly since Dulcie was born, drawing on the older woman's strength and advice. That Matt also called her Gennie put him into that very small group of people she loved best.

They reached the Pier Head and stood looking at the ferries churning back and forth to Birkenhead, at gulls ushering a fishing boat shoreward, at the steamer inching in to Princes dock after crossing from Belfast; but seeing none of it, oblivious to the cold bite of the river air and the rumble of trams behind them, knowing only that when they were together something breathtaking and frightening and irrevocable took place.

Matt said, "Why do I have this feeling we're all players in some drama who somehow got handed the wrong parts?"

"I should go home—and you've an appointment to keep."

His hand slid along the iron railing and enclosed her wrist. His touch was warm and she didn't pull away. Nor did she really want to go home. She stood still, perplexed by feelings she didn't understand. This man was a stranger. Why did she look forward to his visits with an anticipation that did not precede any other event in her life? Why was he so important to her? And how had it happened so swiftly?

He said softly, "You emerged full grown . . . like a butterfly from a cocoon I never knew. Would you have been as dangerous if I'd known you as a child?"

Dangerous? she wanted to ask, but was afraid of what his answer would be, so she said nothing, afraid of where their conversation was leading, afraid of where everything about their relationship was leading. She looked down at the river as a gnarled branch of driftwood floated by, washed against the landing stage, now rising with the incoming tide. Caught in an undertow, the driftwood was sucked out of sight. The breeze blew a strand of hair across her eyes and Matt brushed it back with his warm, strong fingers.

"When a woman is told she's dangerous," he said, "and she doesn't deny it, I suppose she realizes it's true."

"I must go. When will you be back? Shall I write you in New York? I mean, to let you know what news Father brings back from France."

"Send me a wire," he said firmly. "I'll be back in a few weeks, but I want to know as soon as possible if he runs down Celine's family. I wish he'd told me he was going. I'd have found a way to go with him." He continued to hold her wrist, his thumb rubbing lightly against the slender band of her watch. "There's never enough time, is there?"

"No," she agreed. "We're still trying to catch up."

He bent and kissed her forehead lightly. "Don't be surprised if it takes the rest of our lives."

Geneva pushed open the bedroom door and was surprised to see that every lamp in the room was turned on. Her glance went from the suitcases standing in the middle of the floor to the figure of her husband, sprawled on the bed, fully dressed, a brandy glass in his hand. He looked up the moment the door opened. "Where the hell have you been?"

"Terry! I wasn't expecting you back tonight."

"That's obvious." He slammed the glass down on the bedside table, cracking the stem, and swung his feet over the side of the bed. "I asked where you'd been."

She stared, bewildered. His face was set in taut, angry lines. "Terry, what on earth is wrong? It isn't late, only a little after ten—"

He crossed the room in long strides, caught her arm, and pulled her close to him, staring at her face as though trying to see the answer to what plagued him. "Did you go to Liverpool to meet Matt Lauren?"

"Yes, but—"

"Why didn't he come here? Why did you go sneaking to his ship to see him?"

"I didn't go sneaking to his ship. We met at the Adelphi—"

"Good God, that's worse. A hotel."

"The Adelphi *cafe*," she corrected, her voice rising slightly. "We had tea, then walked down to the river. He had to meet a business acquaintance later and he's sailing back to New York tomorrow. Terry, I don't understand why you're so upset. This isn't like you."

His hand dropped from her arm. "No, it isn't, is it. Good old easygoing Terry doesn't fly into jealous rages, it's out of character."

"Jealous rages? Oh, you're joking."

"Am I? Gen, I don't know what's happened to us since Lauren came on the scene, but whatever it is, I don't like it."

She walked over to her dressing table, peeled off her gloves, and put them down with shaking fingers. "If you weren't acting somewhat irrationally, I'd be tempted to point out that even if Matt weren't my brother, you're hardly in a position to play the deceived husband. After all, we're married in name only, and I'm well aware you spend a considerable amount of time in London since you resumed your affair with Dory Gates. The jewelers' bills accidentally got in with my household accounts last month."

Even from across the room, Terry's discomfort was clearly evident. Geneva loathed herself for bringing up the subject, but felt so defensive about Matt that she couldn't stop. "I've known from the moment you started up with her again. Just after Dulcie was born. You had to go down to London. You've no aptitude for deceit, Terry. You left a theater program in the pocket of your dress suit . . . with her name and phone number scribbled on it. And tucked inside was a florists' card you evidently forgot to include with a bouquet, thanking her for . . . all the joys of the previous evening."

"Oh, God," Terry groaned. "Attack is still the best means of defense, isn't it, Gen?"

His reflection appeared beside hers in the dressing table mirror. "Perhaps I wouldn't go to London if I had a real wife at home," he said, a bitter smile twisting his mouth.

"That wasn't our arrangement," Geneva said, feeling a stirring of apprehension. She turned to look at him, to reassure herself that he couldn't have changed that much.

"For God's sake, don't look at me like that. Like I was going to force myself on you."

"Terry, what's happening to us? Why are we quarreling?"

"Oh, Gen . . . don't you know? Don't you know what's been taking place?"

He reached toward her tentatively, but she pulled open a drawer and began to rifle the contents. "If it's Dulcie . . . perhaps the new doctor can help. Perhaps—"

Terry looked at his outstretched hand, then stuffed it into his pocket. "It isn't Dulcie. Poor sweet little thing. Did you think I'd renounce all claim to her because she's retarded? No, Gen, don't look away from me—I know we all carefully avoid using the word, but the fact remains, Dulcie *is* mentally retarded, and I think we'd all be better off to consider what she is capable of accomplishing, rather than what we'd hoped she would be."

Geneva's eyes were wide and drowning. "It isn't hopeless! The new doctor—"

"Dulcie is a Saxon—my daughter, as far as the world is concerned, and I'm not ashamed of her. Don't you be, either, Gen. She's going to grow up surrounded by love, with the best care we can give her."

Blinking away a tear, Geneva thought of Terry's anger when she told him she was being blackmailed by Charlie Dutton's sister. Terry had gone to see Millie Dutton, alone, and that had been the end of the demands. Geneva had not told him what happened the night Dulcie was born, for fear he would also go after Charlie, now touring various cities in his role of wrestler. Everyone at the Hall believed she had foolishly gone for a drive in Ian's old Morris, the engine had stalled, and she had set off on foot, falling in the muddy ditch in the dark.

Terry was saying, "You know, I thought you'd shut yourself up in an ivory tower because of Dulcie . . . and what happened with Dutton. I believed that one day you'd break out of it and realize you're a warm, beautiful woman, with a husband who wants you so badly he works like a Trojan all day and drinks with his friends all night . . . so he doesn't have to come home and share a room with you, because he can't stand being near you and not touching you and why the hell am I speaking of myself in the third person?"

Geneva drew a deep breath, images hammering on her brain. Terry's expression when he looked at her sometimes, the way he allowed his hand to linger if he touched her in passing. She recalled the times she had looked up suddenly to find him watching her. "Terry, I had no idea. Why, you and I . . . we've always been like brother and sister. And what about Dory?"

His expression was bleak. "I see Dory maybe one night every couple of months, when I'm in London on business. I'm sure I'm only one in her stable. I see you, Gen, every night. I'm a normal male. I look at you, sleeping in my bed, your hair spread out on the pillow, your skin so soft-looking . . . knowing you're my *wife*. I'm sorry, I can't help my carnal thoughts." He turned away from her and walked into his dressing room.

Geneva raised her hand as though to call him back, but let it fall, knowing there was nothing she could say that would wipe that tormented longing from his face. She went quickly into her own bathroom and turned on the water in the tub.

Soaking in the warm comfort of the water, Geneva thought back over the times she had known Terry was in London with Dory Gates. Geneva's only reaction had been worry that he would be hurt—no, more than that, a curiosity about the woman who had refused to marry him. Wouldn't any woman on earth want to marry Terry? Dashing, wealthy, charming . . . Geneva's feelings had been those of an outraged sister whose brother has been rejected, not those of a jealous wife. Somehow this knowledge made her feel even worse about Terry's unexpected declaration tonight.

When she emerged from her dressing room, which lay between the bathroom and the bedroom, she was wearing her most substantial dressing gown. Terry was still fully dressed, seated in the chair by the window finishing his brandy.

"Terry . . ." He looked up questioningly, all at once very

young and vulnerable. She said, "I don't know what to say to you."

"You could say that you're ready to be my wife," he suggested with a sadly conciliatory smile.

"I'm sorry. Please try to understand. I love you dearly, but when I think of physical intimacy with a man I shrivel inside. I can only associate sex with pain and terror . . . not love."

His jaw moved slightly, but he didn't speak. He continued to stare at her with eyes that were all at once filled with accusation and hurt.

"Terry, do you want a divorce? I realize the withholding of conjugal rights is grounds—"

He stood up abruptly. "No, Gen. I don't want a divorce. God help me, I want you."

She shook her head in despair, not knowing what to say.

"How blithely we entered into this farce of a marriage," he said. "Idiot children, playing with the most dangerous fire of all . . . our own emotions. Oh, no, not yours, of course . . . you're the ice maiden who has no feelings. Except when it comes to your American half-brother, or whatever the hell relation he is to you."

"Terry, that isn't fair! It's only natural that Matt and I are curious about each other, want to learn all we can about our very different lives. To say nothing of wanting to know about the love affair of his father and my mother. I've been haunted all my life by my mother's death; since Matt came I've begun to wonder about her life. Somehow the yearning to have known her is less agonizing now."

"There's more to it than that between you and Lauren. I've seen the way he looks at you. There's nothing brotherly in that look. And there's that transformation in you when he's here. I think perhaps I could have stood it—the emptiness of our life together—believing you were incapable of ever feeling passion for a man, if it hadn't been for seeing you and Lauren together. And it wasn't just a jealous reaction to seeing desire for you in another man . . . because I've seen that look before, on Huw Wakefield's face, for one. No, Gen, it was knowing that Lauren brought you back to life just by walking into the room. Coming out of nowhere, when all the time, I was here . . . and it could have been me."

"I don't know what you're talking about." Geneva looked away from his accusing eyes. "Will you excuse me while I go and look in on Dulcie?"

"Ah, now we're on shifting ground so you'll retreat. Why

can't you acknowledge it—even to yourself? You're falling in love with him. It's written all over you."

She felt the blood drain from her face but remained composed as she looked back at him unflinchingly. "You know that's quite out of the question—even if it were true, which it isn't. I refuse to continue this ridiculous conversation. I'm going to the nursery."

Before she reached the bedroom door, there was a tentative knock and, opening it, she looked into the startled eyes of a young valet. "You rang, mum?"

Behind her, Terry said, "Yes. Come in. Take those suitcases to one of the guest rooms. Then come back and remove all of my clothes from the dressing room, wardrobe, chests— and my toilet articles from the bathroom."

The valet blinked uncomprehendingly as he looked from Geneva to Terry. "Sir?"

"You heard me correctly. I'm moving out of my wife's room."

Geneva went quickly past the valet and ran down the hall to the nursery. Standing in the room lit by a single nightlight, she looked down at the sleeping baby and felt utter desolation, knowing she had just lost something precious to her. She wished Matt were not sailing tomorrow, wished she had never met him, wished Dulcie were a normal baby. The child slept on her stomach, rose-petal cheek crushed against the linen sheet, small rump swanlike in the air. She was so beautiful that her nursemaid told stories of spellbound passersby who clustered around the pram when Dulcie left Saxon Hall. To see doctors, Geneva thought. So many doctors, in so many cities, all with the same dismal prognosis. She stood in the darkness, fighting the tears and terror again. After a few minutes she pulled a flannelette blanket up over her daughter, then went slowly back to the bedroom.

All traces of Terry had disappeared. Looking around the room they had shared, Geneva felt unutterably lonely. Downstairs in the hall the grandfather clock chimed midnight. She turned, unable to go into the empty room, and went down the stairs. In the kitchen she made herself a cup of cocoa and sat down at the scrubbed wood table to drink it.

If only her father were home. If only there were someone to talk to. Nancy? No, it was too late. Meredith was too old and forgetful nowadays to be burdened with any further Saxon problems. She kept confusing the generations, thinking Terry was his father, and Dulcie was Geneva.

A mental picture of Matt flitted across Geneva's mind, lying on his bunk aboard ship, his long legs stretched out, perhaps with his hands clasped under his head, those fierce dark eyes contemplative, searching . . . no, don't think about Matt now. At last her thoughts collided with exhaustion and she put her face down on her arm on the table and slept.

She was awakened by a gentle touch on her shoulder and looked up, wondering why her body felt as though it had been folded up in a drawer. Rankin was bending over her. "Madam? Are you all right?"

Struggling to clear her fogged senses, she nodded. "A little cold and stiff and feeling quite foolish. I suppose you know Mr. Terry moved into the guest quarters last night? I'll go upstairs, Rankin. Perhaps you could send up some tea?"

Rankin's face twitched furiously. "Madam, there is some rather grave news, I'm afraid. I heard it on the wireless in my room. The Germans have invaded Poland."

Chapter 20

Saxon Hall was in darkness when Ian let himself quietly in through the tradesmen's entrance. He had taken a taxi from the station without informing anyone at the Hall of his arrival, partly because of the lateness of the hour and partly because he was not yet ready to talk to Gennie.

The news of the declaration of war had reached him on his return crossing of the Channel, and he had then made an immediate decision not to tell Gennie what he had learned in France. But by the time he had journeyed to London, taken a taxi to Euston station, caught a train, and was rolling through the deepening shadows of the heartland of England, he was again filled with doubts. The countryside looked particularly lovely wearing the golden hues of autumn, softened by the twilight. Was there anywhere else on earth as tranquilly beautiful, he wondered, gazing from the train window as though seeing it all for the first—or last—time.

There was a delay at Crewe and he walked the busy platform, still undecided about how much he would tell Gennie, so wrapped up in his thoughts that he missed his train and had to wait for the one due at midnight.

Leaving his suitcase in the kitchen at Saxon Hall, he went to the entry hall just as the grandfather clock chimed two. Standing in the darkness, he looked at the towering ugliness of the clock, remembering his first sight of it on another homecoming . . . could it have been over twenty years ago? *Oh, God, it's all happening again,* he thought. Why? No country on earth is worth the blood of a single young man. How many will die this time? How many will be maimed, bereaved, homeless? How many babies will be born without fathers? *Gennie, oh, my dearest Gennie. I tried to shield you from all of life's abrasions, no matter how small. I told lies for you . . . to you . . . when I loathe the act of lying more than any other human weakness. And now? Shall I lie to you again? Would the truth be more damaging than a lie? How can I know, at this point in your life? How much suffering can you stand before you break? I know your torment about your baby. Do you blame yourself for going on an ill-advised drive the night she was born? I feel you do, yet you won't talk about it. And why did you go out that night? Was it because of Terry? I believe you two regret your marriage—must you persist with it, because of Dulcie? Because of convention? Because of sheer stubborn refusal to admit you were both wrong?*

The grandfather clock glowered silently down, its twin brass weights gleaming in the darkness and looking like shell casings. *When it's all over, there will be a two-minute silence for the victims, and then we'll all try to pick up the broken threads of our lives and go merrily forward until it's time for another war. Terry will join up, that's certain. Can their marriage stand a separation?*

There was a chair beside the hall table and he sat down, switching on a small lamp to see the letters on the tray. Several business letters, a note in the spidery scrawl of Uncle Dee Dee. The old boy would be in his element now that his dire predictions about the Huns had come to pass. A letter in Gennie's delicate copperplate handwriting was addressed to Matt Lauren in New York.

Ian thought about Matt. *If I don't tell Gennie the truth about her mother, then I cannot tell Matt either. And what if he decides to go to France to verify my story? France is at war; perhaps it's too late. I could pretend I didn't find Andre Thibault—wait until we're all so busy fighting the Germans. But Matt is American; they won't get into the war if they can help it. As a neutral, he'll be able to travel anywhere he pleases.*

It had been surprisingly easy to find Celine Thibault's surviving brother. Matt wouldn't have any trouble either. Twenty years ago France was reeling from the waning Great War and communications were not as efficient . . . *and no one made any real effort to find Celine's family then.* He leaned back, closed his eyes, and relived his visit to Andre Thibault.

At Valenciennes he had moved into a small pensione and, fanning out in a widening arc, had contacted every family named Thibault. He asked if they had heard of a relative named Celine who had left home during the Great War and never returned.

Two discouraging weeks went by before he found an elderly lady who was distantly related, by marriage, to the Thibaults he was seeking. A widow, she had not corresponded with her husband's family for years, but she remembered that his nephew's daughter was named Celine. Celine had left home in the spring of 1918 and no one in the family ever mentioned her name. The old lady was delighted to chat with the polite stranger with his charmingly accented French.

"You are perhaps Belgian, monsieur?" she asked with the disarming curiosity of the old. *"Anglais? Non!* I would not have guessed—you do not murder our language like the *Anglais."*

"I have spent a great deal of time in your country, madame," Ian replied, "and been the despair of several language teachers, but I try. Can you tell me where Celine's family lived before she left home?"

"Come and see me," she urged. "I seldom have visitors these days—they're all dead and gone now, my family and friends."

His visit lasted most of a day. He admired old family photographs and all of her relics of eighty years of living.

"My husband's nephew's family came from a tiny village between Calais and Lille. My husband was never close to them, you understand, but I remember him mentioning there was a daughter, Celine. Tell me, monsieur, will you go there, to the village, now? If you do, perhaps you would tell any surviving relatives about me? I get so lonely."

Ian insisted on taking her out to dinner and bought a bottle of cognac for her to take home. She gave him careful directions to the village, and it was a surprise to Ian that Celine had traveled only a relatively short distance to the shelled cottage where he had found her—so short that he wondered if she had been trying to get home in time for the birth of her baby.

The postmaster in the village informed him that the Thibaults had been prosperous farmers, but that their only surviving son, Andre, had sold the farm a few years after the war and moved to Paris. He had artistic inclinations and wanted to study art. However, he was not very talented and eventually married a girl whose father owned an art gallery. They had visited the village once or twice. She was a lovely slender woman of obvious breeding. Her name? No, he couldn't remember her name; to him she had been Madame Thibault. But he thought the art gallery was in Beauvais.

The ancient city of Beauvais stood in a verdant valley, enclosed by wooded hills, about forty miles northwest of Paris. Ian had once taken Geneva there briefly to visit the museum and cathedral of St. Pierre and to marvel at the antiquity of a town that had stood on that spot since the time of the Romans. Geneva had been fascinated by the tapestries and carpets for which Beauvais was famed. *And all the time we were here*, Ian thought, *Gennie's uncle was somewhere nearby.*

Of course, the art gallery would have been in the name of the wife's father. He would have to search the marriage records. The trouble was, he had no idea when the marriage took place, so he hired a young student to help him search the records for the marriage of Andre Thibault. Eventually they found it. He had married one Leontine Renet. There was also a Renet Art Gallery and Antique Shop listed in the telephone directory.

Andre Thibault was not at the gallery. A clerk told Ian that he might find Andre at his country residence, but that his employer traveled the country extensively, purchasing paintings. He was also called upon to appraise collections, catalog, and so on.

Ian was in luck. Andre Thibault was in residence at his country house in the tree-lined valley, a short drive from a tiny, picturesque village built around a lovely old square. The taxi took him to the Thibault house, set in formal gardens with beautifully sculpted topiary shrubs. The house itself was not large, a two-story modern disguised—no doubt to fit its setting—as a French Gothic.

A small plump woman answered the doorbell. Ian removed his hat. "Good afternoon. I am Ian Saxon. Is Monsieur Thibault at home? Or . . . are you perhaps Madame Thibault?" It didn't seem likely; the woman was considerably older than he expected Andre Thibault's wife to be.

She looked shocked. "Oh, no, monsieur! I am Marie Bouchard, the housekeeper. Madame passed away some years ago. Please come in. I will tell monsieur you are here. If you could tell me the nature of your business?"

"We have a mutual relative, I believe."

"Who is?"

"Geneva. She is the daughter of his sister, Celine."

The housekeeper stared, her mouth open, then retreated so hurriedly that Ian was left to show himself in. He stepped into an entry hall that on first glance resembled an antique clock shop. There were clocks everywhere. A row of wall clocks, pedestal clocks; a centrally placed table held a gilt clock under a glass dome whose pendulum was the delicate figure of a girl on a swing. At the foot of the stairs, one on either side of the staircase, stood a matching pair of grandfather and grandmother clocks. They all ticked independently, and when one began to chime it was several seconds before it was joined by another. By the time the housekeeper returned with Andre Thibault, the cacophony of chimes made speech impossible.

Andre Thibault was dark, leanly built, with an obvious flare for dress, from the silk cravat tucked into an impeccably fitted shirt, to the latest cut in trousers. But it was his eyes that Ian saw first. Despite the dimness of the clock-filled hall, he saw that Thibault had those same magnificent gray eyes that Celine, and now Gennie, had. Thibault was gesturing for Ian to follow him back through the door from which he had emerged.

The closed door muffled but did not shut out the chiming clocks. Mercifully it was only two in the afternoon; Ian wondered what it must sound like at midnight with all of the chiming clocks in full voice. Andre Thibault ignored Ian's outstretched hand. "My sister Celine? My housekeeper says you mentioned my sister. I had no sister. She was never born." His mouth twisted cruelly when he said her name, spoiling the handsome line of his features.

Silently Ian opened his attaché case and produced Geneva's birth certificate and adoption papers. He told of finding Celine in the cottage, about to give birth, on a battlefield east of Valenciennes. He told the story as fully as possible while Andre Thibault nervously wound a wall clock in what was apparently his study. Ian concluded, "But if I have the wrong Andre Thibault, I apologize. Perhaps you could tell me where I might find Celine's brother?"

Thibault slammed the clock key down on his desk and opened a cigar box. He brooded silently for a moment, then lit a slim black cigar. "You know that you have found the right Thibault." His tone was of grudging courtesy to a stranger. "Very well. Sit down. Since you adopted the child, I suppose you have a right to know."

Ian took the offered chair and waited while Thibault blew several clouds of blue smoke between them. "You were here, monsieur, you know how it was for a girl caught fraternizing with the Boches. We never learned how Celine met him. In the village they thought perhaps he had been spying behind the lines. Celine would say only that she met him while walking along the riverbank one day. She kept their meetings secret, of course, being well aware what happened to girls caught sneaking off to meet German soldiers. One other girl was found out. They dragged her to the village square, shaved her head. *Mon dieu!* The disgrace to the family. Already ten young men from the village had been killed in the fighting. For a girl to even smile at a Boche was the worst kind of betrayal."

"They were married?" Ian asked. "Celine and the German soldier?"

Andre regarded him pityingly. "Where would they find a priest to perform such sacrilege? No, monsieur, they were not married. But that did not stop them. When I came home on leave that spring, I found my family in turmoil."

Ian was horrified by the righteous indignation and lack of understanding in Thibault's story as he painted the grim picture. His sister in disgrace, their older brother killed at the front, nineteen-year-old Andre home on compassionate leave, their father broken-hearted, turning his back, vowing never to speak to his daughter again, their mother pleading, and Andre . . . the chilling tone of his voice as he described his sister's plight, twenty years later, rang with hollow finality.

"Celine confessed she was carrying the German's child. She told us he was the son of a Prussian nobleman, but since she also said he was only an *oberleutnant* in the infantry, this may not have been true. She did not know where he came from—we got from her only his name. A name forever burned into my brain. Wolfgang Rauch."

Ian felt the name slam into his consciousness. The last hour of the war came back, every detail still clear in his mind. The shelled cottage, the German lieutenant propped against the wall, bones protruding from his shattered thigh, ice-blue eyes scornful, derisive. . . . *The last of our rear guards left— perhaps two hours ago. The village is empty. Rauch, Wolf-*

gang, Oberleutnant, serial number. . . . Celine's lover, Gennie's father.

"I threw her out of the house. Her and her Boche bastard," Thibault stared defiantly, unrepentant at his act of righteous vengeance.

The picture clarified in Ian's mind: the frightened young girl, the wrathful family in the throes of bereavement. Distantly he heard himself tell Andre that her German lover had been with Celine as she went into labor, thinking perhaps this would somehow vindicate both of them. But then he remembered that John Lauren had also been present, and he had married Celine.

Andre's gaze remained bleak. "You did not let me finish my story. Shortly after I threw Celine out of the house, our village came under heavy artillery fire. The destruction and civilian panic were, I later learned, indescribable. My uncle, who survived, said the villagers ran in every direction as streets were reduced to rubble, blocking escape. Shells screamed into the streets, killing refugees in their flight— women, children, old men. My mother was buying stamps at the post office when the barrage began. My father rushed from our farm to the village to search for her. My uncle, who lived with us, had lost a leg early in the war and remained at the farm. As dusk fell and still the Boche guns pounded us, he stood at the door and watched the flashes light up the sky. The roar of the motorcycle was lost in the sound of gunfire and the Boche officer, Rauch, appeared out of nowhere. He had come for Celine."

"My uncle spat at him. Told him Celine had been sent away in disgrace. That she carried his Boche bastard. My uncle remembers no more. The Boche struck him, and when he came to his senses the farmhouse was in ruins, the village all but wiped off the map. My parents were dead."

Ian said, half to himself, "Rauch went in search of Celine . . . not knowing she had met and married the American." Remembering the lovely young woman in the cottage, he could understand how John Lauren must have felt about her. And she—driven from her home, ostracized for fraternizing with the enemy, pregnant with an illegitimate child . . . little wonder she had turned to Lauren. But then her German lover reappeared. There was a confrontation perhaps, between the three of them, in the cottage. Celine must have felt faint with her approaching labor, lay down. The two men went outside to settle things . . . her husband and her lover, enemy soldiers in love with the same woman. But then the shell exploded. Lauren crawled inside to Celine. The German, whose thigh was shattered, could not follow.

Ian said to Andre, "You didn't know your sister married an American? You never wondered what became of her and her child?"

"I told you, I have no sister. Her child is half German, therefore I have no wish to know more. Did you not hear what I said? My parents and my brother were killed in the war."

Ian tried to tell him about Gennie. About Lauren and his son. Andre listened in a curiously defiant way, eyes narrowed with suspicion, then asked, "What is it you want of me now, after all these years? You adopted Celine's bastard, that is your affair. All of the others—Celine, the Boche, and the American—are dead. Why do you come here now?"

Because, despite what I said to both of them, I really wanted Gennie and Matt to be brother and sister. Because if they know they aren't, he will take her away with him to America and I will seldom see her. Aloud, he said, "Are you not curious about your niece, Geneva?"

"Geneva," Andre repeated. "Celine named her, before she died."

"Yes. How did you know she chose the name?"

"She told me, before I threw her out of the house, that she hated war and killing and that, boy or girl, she would name her child Geneva—after the Geneva Convention—because the child was conceived by national enemies, and the Swiss convention was the only organization that seemed to want to end the suffering of war."

So that was how Gennie's name was chosen, Ian thought. The nuns had said the name seemed to have special significance to Celine.

"To answer your question, my niece—as you call her—is still half German. Are not the Boches again poised for attack? We shall be at war with them within the week."

At Saxon Hall the grandfather clock chimed the half hour. Ian stood up and was about to go up to his room when he heard someone fumbling with a key at the front door. He snapped on the overhead lights as the door opened, and Terry stood on the threshold, a white silk scarf about to slip from his neck, his hat askew. He blinked in the sudden light. "Oh . . . uh . . . Uncle, old boy, when did you get in?"

"A little while ago."

"How was France—" Terry tripped over his own feet, put out his hand to steady himself, and knocked the silver tray from the hall table. It crashed with a resounding echo on the marble floor. Looking about sheepishly, Terry said, "Shhh!"

"Give me your arm," Ian ordered. "I'll help you up to your room before you awaken the whole household."

Terry drew himself up with exaggerated dignity. "I've had a couple, but I'm not drunk," he protested, slurring the words. "I s'pose you know we declared war?" He hiccuped. "S'cuse me."

Ian pulled Terry's unresisting arm over his shoulder. "Keep your voice down, I don't want to awaken Gennie. I'll help you up to a guest room."

Terry made a sound that could have been a chuckle but was perhaps too bitter to express amusement. "Well now, Unk, it just so happens I'm already sleeping in a guest room on a . . . permanent basis s'marrafac'. My wife and I have separate rooms."

Ian digested this information silently as he steered Terry up the stairs, trying to keep him from crashing into the banisters. At the top of the stairs Terry indicated a guest room that was indeed filled with his things. Ian assisted him to the bed, then bent to remove his shoes. "I take it you and Gennie quarreled?"

"Oh, nothing as civilized as that, old boy."

"You're too drunk to make any sense. I'll talk to you in the morning." Ian unbuttoned Terry's dinner jacket, loosened his tie. Terry collapsed backward on the bed and closed his eyes.

Ian stood for a moment looking down at his nephew, putting pieces together. The strained relations between him and Gennie. The disturbing undercurrent between her and Matt. Before there had been that impenetrable barrier . . . the taboo of an incestuous relationship. If he were to tell them about Wolfgang Rauch, that barrier would fall. But then Gennie would be faced with other divided loyalties. What of her German heritage? Her father's country had again plunged Europe into war.

The tight band of tension returned to his brow. He made a quick decision as he slipped quietly out of Terry's room and back downstairs. Five minutes later he was backing the old Morris out of the garage.

He unlocked Nancy's front door, went up the stairs, undressed, and climbed into bed with her. She stirred and sleepily enclosed him in her warm embrace. "Ian? Did you find out anything?"

"Yes. They are not brother and sister. Go back to sleep."

"Have you told her?"

"No. And I'm not going to."

Eventually he fell into an exhausted sleep.

The sun had already begun its descent down the autumn sky when he awakened, still nestled in Nancy's arms. She smiled at him. "I didn't dare move for fear of waking you. I suppose they don't know at the Hall that you're back yet?"

Wordlessly he pulled her closer and kissed her warm sweet mouth, his hands traveling dearly remembered planes and hollows and soft swellings that were as familiar to him as his own body. Youthful passion had been wild and joyous, but maturity brought a savoring pleasure that was enhanced by shared memories, by the instant connection of touch and feeling and knowledge of every intimate secret of her entire being.

She sighed contentedly and pressed against him, her fingers making small circles on his back and bringing immediate arousal. "Oh, love, I've missed you so much," she whispered as he eased her nightgown down over her body, kissing each little piece of her as it was revealed. He marveled again at how beautiful her full breasts were. Naked, she could have reclined in a Renoir painting. They were so perfectly in tune that making love to Nancy was a ballet of the senses, intricately choreographed, so that each time, although the pattern was excitingly different, they were always in harmony. Ian never ceased to contemplate the magic; it was like the bright particles in a kaleidoscope that rearrange themselves into limitless designs, always fresh and new. The next time could never be as wonderful as this . . . but it was always better.

Downstairs the doorbell jangled, interrupting their kiss. Nancy sat up, looking at the clock. "Oh, love, it's past noon! That must be the insurance man, he's due today." She slipped out of bed while Ian protested in thwarted passion and reached for her to bring her back into his arms. She pulled a dress over her head and went downstairs. Ian stared resentfully at the closed door and recalled the previous evening. Terry would probably still be sleeping off his binge. No one would know Ian had returned from France.

He sat up abruptly. What had he done with his suitcase? Blast! He'd left it in the kitchen. A servant would have found it by now and Rankin would be frantically wondering what had happened to him. Swinging his feet to the floor, he reached for his clothes. Suit and shirt were wrinkled and travel-soiled. He opened Nancy's wardrobe door, looking for the change of clothing he always kept there. Only his dressing gown hung there.

Downstairs there was the sound of the front door closing. Good, Nancy had sent the insurance man on his way. Pulling on the dressing gown, Ian opened the door and went to the top of the stairs, looking down to the tiny entrance hall at the front door. "Nancy, where is my other suit—" he began in the same moment he remembered he'd asked her to take it to the cleaners.

At the foot of the stairs stood Nancy's visitor. It was, of course—he reflected with that split-second wisdom that comes after the event—inevitable that they would bump into each other. Reluctantly he met the startled eyes of Geneva.

Chapter 21

The wall clock dominating Nancy's tiny entrance hall ticked loudly. There was a crack in the plaster, creeping out from under the picture hung to cover it, on the blank wall to one side of the narrow staircase. They stood frozen, staring at each other, Geneva at the bottom of the stairs and her father at the top, tying the sash of an unfamiliar dressing gown. His silver hair was tousled, a faint shadow smudged his chin, and his bare legs and feet testified to a lack of pajamas.

An inner voice protested that this was not her father. Her father never emerged from his room this time of day unless perfectly dressed and immaculately groomed. This unshaven, half naked, untidy man who had obviously spent the night in Nancy's bed was some village lout with the morals of a tomcat.

"Gennie—" Ian said. "Gennie, I . . ." He gestured helplessly.

The voice was his, of course. There wasn't another as gentle and dear in all the world. She didn't answer; she could only stare, feeling betrayed by both of them, and worse, shut out.

Nancy touched her arm tentatively. "Gennie, come into the parlor. I'll make a cup of tea. This is a shock and you deserve an explanation."

Geneva shrugged away Nancy's hand. "An explanation? Please have the grace to spare me—and yourselves—any further embarrassment." She turned and stumbled to the door, hearing her father's choked cry as he repeated her name again and again as though it were a prayer.

The front doorknob turned in her hand as Nancy caught her arm, staying her progress. "Ee, lass, don't leave like this. Give us a minute to tell you it isn't as bad as it looks. We've loved each other for a long time, your dad and me . . . a very long time."

Geneva looked into Nancy's eyes and saw the deep anxiety there, but she was too stunned and hurt to feel anyone's pain but her own. "Really? Then why didn't you marry? Or at least acknowledge one another publicly? No, don't bother to answer. I really must go. I only called to tell you that I wouldn't be here for tea today because I'm driving Terry to the station. He informed me this morning that he has been accepted by his father's old regiment. And don't worry—I shan't be back to disturb your little love nest in future, either." She pulled the door open forcefully, not caring that it brushed Nancy's shoulder in passing. Geneva wanted to cry, to scream hurtful things. At the same time she knew she was judging them and she had no right to do so. She was acting like a child who cannot bear to share those she loved with anyone else, as though it would diminish her own share of love, when she knew this was not true.

The Vauxhall Terry had given her for her birthday was parked on the cobblestoned street, and she flung herself behind the wheel and turned the key in the ignition, not knowing whether she hated them for their deception, or herself for reacting in this way. She and her father had been so close; how could he have kept such a secret? Probably, she realized with a shock, in the same way she had been able to keep the secret of Charlie Dutton from him.

She barely remembered driving home. She was running up the staircase when Terry emerged from the guest wing, carrying a suitcase, and called to her. Not wanting to face him until she had composed herself, she pretended not to hear and went into her own room.

Seconds later there was a knock on her door and Terry pushed it open and entered. "Gen, do you know where I'll find the keys to the suitcases—" He broke off, seeing her face. "Good lor', are you crying? What happened?"

Geneva bit her lip and brushed the tears away. "I'm not. Honestly." Why is it, she wondered miserably, that on some days the sun never seems to rise? Terry was leaving. Rankin said virtually all of the young men on the staff were enlisting too. Meredith's doctor was recommending a nursing home for the old lady, and that morning Dulcie had a temperature. Nancy and her father's affair was just the last straw. "Oh, Terry," she said, needing to talk to someone, "I've been visiting Nancy Whitaker occasionally. Remember her? She was the village woman who told Father about me going to that abortionist . . . oh, God!" She paused, a sudden thought occurring to her. "Was that when it began? Was I the one who brought them together?"

She sat down weakly on the edge of the bed, thoughts and possibilities tumbling through her mind. She looked up at Terry, realizing he had no idea what she was talking about. "Father came home from France—apparently he spent last night at Nancy's house."

"Yes, I know. When I came to my senses this morning, I asked Rankin where Ian was, and he began to twitch and stammer and pretend he wasn't back yet. But when I insisted I'd seen him last night, Rankin gave up and admitted he'd found Ian's suitcase in the kitchen this morning and taken it upstairs. Then he told me Ian had a 'friend' in the village. I pried the whole thing out of him. I suppose it's foolish of any of us to imagine we keep anything from belowstairs. I expect the servants know more about our affairs than we ourselves do. But, Gen, don't worry, it wasn't you who brought Ian and Nancy together. According to Rankin, they've been 'friends' for donkeys' years—ever since Ian came home from the war."

Terry sat down beside her and tipped her chin with his finger so that he could look into her eyes. "Don't judge them too harshly. We don't know the whole story. Besides, surely the fact that their relationship has endured for so long takes it out of the class of a sordid affair? If you're thinking of it in the same light as my affair with Dory, for God's sake don't!"

"You're right, of course. But why did Father never bring her to the Hall? It all seems so . . . dishonest."

"Perhaps she wouldn't come? Gen, one day you'll realize that class snobbishness works both ways."

Geneva was remembering how many times she herself had invited Nancy up to the Hall, always to be refused. But, of course, that could have been because she was afraid of running unexpectedly into Ian. Geneva said, "You know, I was so shocked, I didn't even inquire what Father learned in France."

"You'll know soon enough, I'm sure. I believe I just heard a car pull into the driveway. I'd better go and finish packing; my valet is nowhere to be found and I haven't much time."

"Oh, Terry, forgive me! You're marching off to war and I'm acting like a sheltered schoolgirl. I didn't intend to be such a wet blanket during your last minutes at home."

He smiled and ruffled her hair. "You're never a wet blanket, Gen." He paused, his eyes searching her face as though committing every detail of it to memory. "God, you're beautiful."

There was an awkward silence that to Geneva seemed filled with memories, rushing past almost too swiftly to capture. A teasing little boy who pulled her hair and chased her, giggling, through the corridors of Saxon Hall, but who helped with her schoolwork and always ate her parsnips when Meredith left the room, though he hated them worse than she did. Terry, tall and debonair in his cricket whites, saluting her with his bat when he made a run; Terry on his polo pony; Terry bringing her a wilting bunch of violets, or seizing her hand to rush her outside to admire the first snowdrop pushing through the frozen earth. Terry in evening dress, leading her out onto the waxed floor for a fast foxtrot or a wicked tango. Terry winking at her across a room filled with the solemn upper-crust of society, reducing everyone and everything to perspective. He was leaving to join a wartime army, and she couldn't bear it.

Impulsively she flung her arms around him and hugged him, holding him tightly, wanting to keep him there, safe from guns and shells. For a second she felt his body tense, then his arms slipped around her and he pulled her closer, kissing her forehead, her eyelids, with quick little kisses, as though he had only moments to live.

She didn't pull away. She offered her lips in a lingering kiss that tried to express to him how much she had always loved him, how much she would miss him. But it was a passionless kiss and he knew it; she could see it in his eyes when he released her.

"Gen, it's all right, don't worry about me," he said quickly, sensing her feelings. "I'll be fine. Listen, who knows, perhaps when I come home in my dress uniform with my swagger stick

under my arm and my Sam Browne belt, you'll be so bowled
over by having a dashing young officer for a husband you'll
fall right into my arms. I can hope, anyway, can't I?"

She bit her lip, her hand straying to touch his cheek. "Oh,
Terry, you're so dear to me."

There was a knock at her door and when she called, "Come
in," Rankin appeared. His facial muscles immediately began
to jump when he saw Terry. "I'm sorry, madam, I thought
you were alone."

"What is it, Rankin? You needed me?" Geneva stood up.

Rankin twitched even harder as he examined the corners of
the room as though seeking escape. "A visitor, madam, in the
drawing room."

"Yes, Rankin. Who is it?"

He mumbled something unintelligible and turned to leave.
Geneva called after him, "I didn't hear—who did you say?"

Rankin turned slowly and looked at them with apologetic
eyes. "It's Mr. Lauren."

Something was wrong. Charlie Dutton's vision was filled
with flashing pinpricks of light, and the roar of the audience
seemed to have faded until it sounded like the fluttering of a
canary's wings against the bars of a cage. Christ, why was he
thinking about canaries? He hadn't thought about the pit for
years, or how he used to watch the little yellow caged birds so
carefully for signs that they were suffocating. He drew several
measured breaths.

Around the ring the packed stadium was filled with spirals
of blue smoke, rising toward the rafters and obscuring his
view of the excited faces and raised fists. Why the hell weren't
they yelling for his blood tonight? What was wrong with
them? The Masked Turk never played to silence. They
screamed for his blood.

Charlie tightened the armlock on his opponent's neck,
blinked to try to make the lights stop flickering, shook his
head to bring sounds through his plugged ears. Why weren't
they booing and hissing a sneak attack on his opponent?
Charlie loved to hear the women squeal. One night an old
lady actually jumped through the ropes and started hitting
him with her purse, yelling at him to "fight fair." S'truth, he
thought he'd wet himself laughing.

He idly placed a muscled leg over the rubbery back of
Handsome Harry, jerked his head until his neck made
popping sounds, then pushed the too-good-looking face flat

down. Had he kept him down longer than the required time for a fall? Funny how his mind kept wandering tonight. Being back in Liverpool probably had a lot to do with his state of mind. That and the row with his manager. He'd ordered the little twerp to find a way to keep him out of the army, and he'd had the gall to reply that maybe they should try for a disability exemption. "And me the picture of bloomin' health? Who could be in them adverts for body building? Are you daft?" Charlie had asked. "Oh, there's other kinds of disabilities—" his manager had begun, before Charlie slammed him across the room.

'Course there was no way the little bastard could know how Charlie felt about mental cases. His manager was new this year and hadn't met Josie yet. Charlie had brought Millie and Josie to live in Liverpool after that set-to with Terry Saxon. He'd been on the road since then. Stupid Millie had tried to blackmail Geneva Saxon and Geneva'd told her husband, and down to the village he'd gone and booted Millie out of the house and promised she'd go to jail for blackmail and Charlie for rape and assault if he ever laid eyes on any of them again.

Bloody Saxons always managed to have the last word. Christ, how he hated all the bloody Saxons. Still, one thing was certain, that kid of Geneva's wasn't her husband's, it was Charlie's. Otherwise why would Terry Saxon have threatened him with a rape charge? Geneva must have told Terry and the silly twerp had gone and married her to cover it up. Ian Saxon probably knew too, but they'd all stand together, that lot. That was the thing about them toffs, they closed their ranks and nothing budged them. Well, we'll bloody well see about that. That little girl was Charlie's own flesh and blood. Dulcie, they called her. Dulcie Dutton. The name brought a maudlin tear to his eye. Sounded nice, posh-like.

He supposed he'd better let old Handsome Harry up, he'd been down long enough. Charlie grabbed a handful of hair and shook him. Funny how quiet the crowd was tonight. Their sounds reached him then, as though a door had just been opened inside his head. Frightened exclamations, overlaid with a threatening muttering. A woman's voice pierced the fog of cigarette smoke: "Let him up, you filthy Turk. Get off him, you swine, you're breaking his neck."

Charlie grinned under his black satin mask. Silly buggers all thought the bouts were real, instead of the rough and tumble playacting they really were. The Masked Turk was always in demand because he played the sinister Oriental who resorted to forbidden holds and sly punches. They let him win sometimes, just to keep the outcome in doubt. Tonight he was supposed to lose to Handsome Harry, who was a favorite with the women, and pretty as a girl, despite his muscular build. But Harry lay face down on the canvas and didn't budge. His limp head rolled from Charlie's grasp.

Out of the corner of his eye Charlie caught the flutter of a towel being thrown into the ring, heard the referee hissing at him to get up so he could look at Harry. The seconds and the managers were ducking through the ropes now and everything was blurred and the lights kept flashing in his eyes.

Someone was tugging at his arm and he was standing up, feeling stupid because he didn't know what was happening. He could smell Harry's sweat and his own sweat and the faint but sickly odor of blood.

His manager's voice cracked in his ear like a whip. "What the Christ were you doing? It looked like you were trying to snap his neck. You shoulda stopped when his nose started pumping blood like that. Come on, get out of here before they come up and set about you. I don't like the look of the crowd."

The seconds were hauling Handsome Harry to his feet. They draped his arms about their necks. His head hung forward on his chest and his feet dragged as they pulled him from the ring. Over the loudspeakers the referee's voice boomed reassurances that it was all right, Harry had just fainted, he wasn't dead. But they were all on their feet, surging forward as Charlie dropped down from the ring. He saw their faces, felt the crush of them, heard their shouts and could almost feel their breath, sucking all the air from his lungs.

Panic came when one man pushed forward and spat in his face. Charlie bellowed at the top of his lungs and knocked the man aside with a single backhanded swipe of his hand. Then he was charging through the mobs of people, shoving them roughly out of his way, and they were falling back as he yelled and plowed into packed bodies.

He was still growling a warning when he was safely behind closed doors and his manager and seconds were restraining him while the doctor jabbed his arm with a needle. He felt them ease him down on his back on the massage table, and someone started to rub him down. Slowly everything came back into focus. He looked into his manager's anxious, lopsided grin. Coby was an ex-featherweight boxer and nothing about him matched. One eye remained permanently closed from a ring mishap; his upper teeth were large and uneven, the lowers missing and replaced by too small and perfect dentures. One ear dwarfed the other.

"Charlie? You all right now? Jesus, you gave us a scare. Listen, we got to get you out of here quietly. I've got a taxi at the back door. What come over you? You looked like you wanted to kill poor old Harry—proper spoiled his good looks you did. I mean, honest, Charlie, when you started bashing his head about, it looked real. Think you frightened the shit out of him. Passed out cold, he did. Now the doctor just give you something to quiet you down, see. You'll be all right. What you say, Doctor? Yeah. Charlie, the doctor says you pinched one of Harry's nerves and gave 'im a concussion and you've got to be more careful. Now, now, calm down, we'll talk about it tomorrow. I know you didn't mean it, you don't know your own strength, do you, Charlie boy? What? Okay, okay, I won't call you Charlie boy. Millie calls you that? Oh, yes, your sister. Hey, didn't you tell me she lives in Liverpool? Why don't I just take you over to her place? Better to lie low, the mood was a bit ugly tonight. Better than going to the Adelphi Hotel. Yeah, I know you wanted to stay there one night, but hell, that's a lot of lucre for one night just so's you can say you stayed at the poshest hotel in town. What, Charlie? Oh, all right. Yeah, righto."

Charlie's tension melted away beneath the soothing hands and rough towels, and by the time they slipped out of the back doors and into the waiting taxi, he was in control again and his breathing was normal. The cab sped up Church Street, turned the corner, and passed Central Station. Ahead rose the granite walls of the Adelphi Hotel.

The Adelphi wasn't just a hotel, it was the place whispered about in awe by anyone who knew Liverpool. The toffs stayed at the Ritz in Paris, the Savoy in London, and the Adelphi in Liverpool. Charlie used to walk up Lime Street as a boy, filling the hours he was supposed to be spending in trade school, watching the toffs going in and out of the Adelphi, promising himself he'd stay there one day, stepping out of a taxi, somebody carrying his bags while he just swept right in. God's truth, he'd earned at least one night there before he went to old Millie and poor daft Josie. He'd never had the cash until now.

"Hey! Stop the cab," Charlie ordered as he realized they were driving past the turn-in. "I told you I'm stopping 'ere."

"Now, Charlie, you don't want to go in there tonight," Coby said uneasily. "You're a bit upset tonight, not yourself."

"Stop the bloody cab," Charlie said. "I'm going in. Just to show 'em they're not too good for Charlie Dutton." He pounded on the glass separating them from the taxi driver.

"All right, all right. Don't get shirty. I suppose the crowd that goes to the Adelphi don't go to wrestling matches. Driver, drop us at the Adelphi. Yeah, you heard me."

Charlie leaned forward. "What's up with you? You think we're not good enough to go in a posh hotel?"

"Naw, Charlie, he don't think that. Come on now, here we are then."

The hotel foyer had a thick carpet and everything seemed muffled; footsteps were lost and voices reduced to whispers. Overhead chandeliers sparkled with hundreds of tiny prisms so that Charlie, blinking, was reminded of his feeling earlier, while wrestling: the flashing lights and distant sounds. He swallowed hard, feeling like he was suffocating, despite the high ceilings and faraway walls.

Not many people about. An old codger in a monkey suit and a woman in a long satin dress with a fur cape on her scrawny shoulders. Several frosty-faced old dowagers leaning on walking sticks waited for the lift. Four or five younger couples were disappearing through double doors. Uniformed kids carrying suitcases. The clerks at the reception desk were staring at him.

"How about it, Charlie?" Coby whispered at his side. "They want to know if we booked a room. You book one, Charlie?"

Charlie couldn't remember. He'd meant to tell Coby to do it. He shuffled his feet, intimidated by the way the clerks looked down their noses at him. What if he hadn't booked? He gave a sickly smile. "Got to use the lav," he said. "Back in a jiff."

He opened the door marked "Gentlemen" just as a man and woman crossed the foyer, not looking in his direction. He recognized the proud carriage and upswept dark hair of the woman immediately. Geneva Saxon still wore her hair long in a time when most women had theirs shingled or bobbed, but she put it up on top of her head and fastened it with little combs. Well now, that certainly wasn't Terry Saxon with her. The man at her side had coal-black hair and broader shoulders and his walk was different . . . so were his clothes.

Tingling with curiosity, Charlie waited until they had disappeared through the front doors, then hurried back to where Coby waited for him behind one of the fancy pillars. "See that couple what just left?" Charlie asked.

His manager nodded. "Nice bit of stuff."

"Get out there and follow them. There's a taxi rank outside if you need it. If they walk, don't get too close. And if they come back here, get the room number. Go on, don't argue. And Coby, I've changed me mind. We'd better get over to Millie's house tonight."

Chapter 22

Matt guided Geneva to the waiting line of cabs, helped her inside the first one, and slipped in beside her. "King Edward dock," he told the driver.

As the taxi pulled through the Adelphi gates Matt squeezed Geneva's elbow reassuringly. "Don't look so nervous. I promise I haven't any etchings aboard ship."

Geneva was silent, still wrapped in the sadness that had enveloped her all day. He had been unable to breach her air of reserve and was surprised when after a sedate dinner and a few liqueurs in the Adelphi she had agreed to go and see his ship.

"Gennie, hey, remember me? You still with me?"

"I'm sorry, Matt. I haven't been very good company, have I?"

"You have been a little preoccupied. I thought maybe it was because I came barging in unannounced yesterday—just in time to endear myself to Terry by timing my arrival to coincide with his departure. I guess if I weren't a brash Colonial, I'd have discreetly withdrawn. But I couldn't wait to hear what your father turned up in France . . . and, well, you know how much I wanted to see you."

"It was a disappointment that Father didn't find any of my mother's family."

There it was again, Matt thought. That hurt tone when she

mentioned her father that hinted they had quarreled recently. It confirmed his opinion of the somewhat strained atmosphere between them at dinner last night that appeared to have nothing to do with either Ian's trip to France or Terry's enlistment.

When after a few moments Geneva made no further comment, Matt said, "Do you believe your father couldn't find anyone who knew the Thibault family?"

"Of course. My father has never lied to me—" She broke off, as if remembering this statement was not entirely true.

"Gennie, it doesn't matter to me whether or not you're my half-sister. I can't get you off my mind. I've thought about you constantly. All the way across the Atlantic I wondered what I'd do if Ian came back with the news that we're blood-related—and all the time I knew I didn't really give a damn."

Geneva glanced at the back of the taxi driver's head. "Matt, please. Not now. We'll talk later."

His hand found hers in the darkness and held it. "It's sad to see all the lights turned off," he said. "I suppose Liverpool will be a prime target for the Luftwaffe. I noticed when I traveled up to the Hall yesterday there weren't as many children about. Are the schools closed?"

"Many of them were evacuated before war was actually declared. The others are leaving every day. It's up to the parents whether they go to the country or not. I heard some of the evacuees are being sent to America. I can't help but wonder what will happen to young children who may spend years away from home, forming new associations."

"There are going to be plenty of partings and absences. You and Terry, for instance. Many lives are never going to be the same."

The taxi pulled into the dock area and dropped them. They walked toward the gangplank of the battered and rusty hulk of a merchant ship. "The old girl herself," Matt said with a smile. "The *Bella Mia*. She isn't much to look at, but she's my favorite. She was the first freighter my grandfather bought. She was due to go into dry dock—she must have more barnacles on her hull than ballast in her holds—but I picked up a cargo and here we are." He placed his hand under Geneva's elbow to guide her up the gangplank.

Like the seaport, the ships were subject to blackout regulations, and they stood in shadowy silence as though the almost total darkness had also muffled all sound except for the

gentle lapping of the river. Matt and Geneva stood on deck,
curiously moved by a world lit only by moonlight, seeing the
stars again and remembering how small and insignificant a
planet they inhabited, despite the enormity of the problems
of their world. Geneva's eyes were luminous in the soft light
and Matt felt himself grip the smooth wood of the ship's rail
to keep from grabbing her. He wanted to hold her so badly he
looked away, scanning the black water touched by moon-
silvered waves.

"I guess I could give you the grand tour, but I'm afraid
you'd twist your ankle in the darkness in those heels. Besides,
there's not much to see. The engine room, galley—I wouldn't
inflict the crew's quarters on you. We could go down to my
cabin if you like."

He turned back to her and groaned. "Oh, God, Gennie."
Then his arms went around her and he was kissing her, feeling
her body melt into his, her arms cling to him, loving the feel
of her and the taste of her and the way she responded to him
and yielded and returned his kiss and they were out there
somewhere, two comets fusing in the cosmos, and how could
it be like this if it weren't right and good and inevitable.

"Gennie, I love you. I've loved you from the instant I saw
you. Not as a sister—passionately, overwhelmingly. Right or
wrong, I can't help it. I want you so much. I need you with me
every minute. I started to live when we met and I can't go
back to the emptiness of being without you."

A shiver passed through her body. She placed her hands on
his chest and gently pushed him away. "We must talk. There
are things you must know. Could we go down to your cabin?"

They went silently down the companionway, and he pushed
open a cabin door, flipped on a light, and hastily kicked his
used work clothes under the bunk as he cleared the only chair
of a pile of books so she could sit down. Opening a cabinet
fastened to the bulkhead, he produced a bottle of wine and
two glasses. She smiled as he displayed the cobweb threads on
the dusty bottle. She took the wineglass from him but placed
it on his desk untouched.

"I have to tell you about Terry and me. And about Dulcie.
And about a man named Charlie Dutton."

The house was on a street in the Old Swan district, a row
house with bay windows and a small walled area in front just
large enough for a neatly clipped privet hedge. Millie Dutton
came to the door with a coat over her nightgown and her hair

tied up in little rags to make curls. She opened the door only a crack. "Oh, it's you, is it," she said to Charlie. "Well, don't just stand there, come in quick before the bloody air raid warden gets after me for showing a bit of light."

Charlie had to turn sideways to pass through the grudgingly offered space. There was a long hall leading to the kitchen; parlor and dining room doors on the right, a blank wall shared with the house next door on the left. She'd used the money he'd sent her well, old Millie. Place wasn't half bad. Nice Indian carpet runner down the hall and matching stair carpet. An aspidistra plant on top of the gas meter cupboard.

Millie closed the front door and shuffled down to the kitchen in slippers too battered to lift from the floor. "Couldn't you come at a decent hour? I was in bed. You might of dropped us a card. Didn't know if you was bloody dead or alive. You want something to eat? Who's got your ration book? If you're going to eat here, you'd better hand it over."

When he could get a word in, Charlie said, "You go on back to bed, Mil. I told my manager to come here. I'll wait up for him."

She switched on the kitchen light and peered at him as he dropped into a chair. "Still shave your flamin' head, I see. And that stupid muzzy and stringy little beard make you look a proper clot, I must say. I don't know about no managers coming here. Josie gets upset with strangers."

"She in bed, is she?" Charlie asked, squirming under Millie's scrutiny.

"Yes. And you stay away from her, 'ear? I catch you laying a hand on Josie and I'll cut it off for you."

Charlie shivered, a boyhood memory stirring. He'd been about five or six years old and Millie had seemed big and powerful. She's caught him playing with himself and told Ma and they'd held him down on his bed while Ma brandished a knife, threatening to cut off his thing if they ever caught him at it again, and Millie had looked disappointed when Ma didn't cut it off.

"Now, now, Mil," he said ingratiatingly. "How about putting the kettle on if you're staying up? I could do with a cup of char."

She dropped the aluminum kettle on the gas stove with a clatter and struck a match to light the burner. "If you'd been in touch, you'd have heard some news I had for you."

"Oh? What news was that, Mil?"

"Nothing much. A bit of something I heard when I ran into one of the maids from Saxon Hall. Got the sack, she did, and come to work in Liverpool. I met her in the ladies' lingerie at Blacklers' stores." She pronounced "lingerie" the way it was spelled, scorning the French vowels.

"Something about the Saxons?" Charlie prompted.

Millie looked at him, her deep-set eyes gleaming with anticipation, tiny jet beads in a face like a frying pan. "About your brat, Charlie. The baby, Dulcie."

"Go on! What about 'er?"

Millie hesitated, her thin lips going up at the corners but not forming a smile, her eyes darting about. He recognized that look; he'd seen it before on her dried-up old cow's face when misfortune befell someone, particularly if it befell some woman younger and better looking than herself, which was every woman on earth; or some man who'd looked at her with indifference, which was all of them too. She licked her lips and said, "The baby's daft, Charlie. Just like Josie."

Charlie was on his feet, hearing strange noises coming from his own throat, advancing on Millie with his fists jammed up against his ears, shaking his head back and forth and that pounding in his brain he couldn't stand frightening him as much as the lack of air to his starving lungs.

Millie grabbed the carving knife from the breadboard and waved it under his nose. "Sit down, you big lump. Don't you dare come near me, I'll cut off your balls."

Charlie's hands dropped limply to his sides. "You're just making it up, aren't you, Mil? She's not—the kid's not—" He backed away from the knife.

"Yes, she is. They've taken her to all sorts of Harley Street specialists and everything, but she's retarded and there's nowt they can do." She smirked, enjoying his reaction. "What do you think of that, Charlie boy? The toffs can have idiot brats just like anybody else."

"But I saw pictures of the baby, at her christening at St. Agnes'. She was a pretty little thing. Didn't look like no Mongoloid," Charlie protested.

Millie gave him a scathing glance. "They can be not all there without being a Mongoloid."

The doorbell rang and Charlie said, "That'll be my manager. I'll let him in. Listen, don't say nothing about Dulcie."

Coby slithered around the doorjamb and informed him in a stage whisper, "They went to a Yank ship in the dock, the bloke was the skipper. Name's Matthew Lauren, according to the dock watchman."

Matt paced back and forth in the small space of the cabin of the *Bella Mia,* his jaw set in angry lines, fists clenched. Stopping, he slammed his fist into the bulkhead, rattling the lamp and a set of framed photographs that were behind Geneva's head and out of her range of vision.

"Matt, please calm down," Geneva begged. Her eyes glistened with tears, silently telling how much it had cost her to tell him the painful story of Dulcie's conception and birth.

He went to her, pulled her to her feet, and held her tightly. "I want to kill him. God help me, I've already killed one man and I'm filled with that same red fog of hate that tells me if I ever cross paths with Dutton, I'll kill him for sure."

"No, Matt, you mustn't let yourself hate like that, it will destroy you. You can't know what you're saying."

He released her and drew several deep breaths. "I hadn't intended to tell you about DeVore yet. I wasn't expecting to bring you here—or to show you your mother's photograph, not yet. It's on the wall behind you, Gennie. I planned to try to find someone to restore it for you."

Geneva stared wordlessly at the sepia tones of the beautiful sad-eyed woman, hardly more than a girl really. She felt her heart contract.

"It belonged to my father," Matt said. "The picture was what got me started on the quest to find Celine. But in view of what you just told me about Dutton, I think perhaps I'd better tell you about that other picture hanging beside your mother's. It's the only one I have of Specks. One of the Jazzmen took it the day Specks led the Mardi Gras parade in New Orleans."

Not really wanting to take her eyes off her mother's portrait, Geneva glanced at the second picture. A handsome black man, trumpet to his lips, striding out at the head of a parade. She looked from one photograph to the other as Matt told her of his own encounter with evil, and the awful consequences. Then Geneva turned to him and he enfolded her in his arms, holding her close, stroking her hair and knowing she was reliving his pain, just as hers was a searing spark that traveled his veins, igniting passions he'd sworn never to give in to again.

"Specks was a tremendous influence on my life," he said.

"He taught me that violence only begets violence. That killing is wrong, whether in war or in personal vendettas. No exceptions. There was the example of my father to back up everything Specks said. My father killed a man in a brawl, ran away to hide in the army, and had his mind blown away with a shell fragment. The vicious unbreakable cycle. Yet when I faced DeVore I forgot everything but a primitive driving need to obliterate him from the earth, like a piece of diseased vermin. I wasn't a rational thinking being, Gennie, I was all blind hate."

She looked up at him with smoky gray eyes, reached up to stroke his cheek. "You're so gentle—with me—that I can't imagine such rage. And yet, perhaps only a man capable of caring so much would be capable of acting as you did. But Matt, that's the past, and DeVore was a man you'd known a long time, who had harmed you before. You've never met Charlie Dutton. I hope you never will."

"I've never met Hitler either," Matt said grimly, "but I don't think that would stop my blind fury from erupting if I came face to face with the little bastard. My rational thinking tells me war is evil and the military is a mindless killing machine—but my blood boils when I see the newsreels of the strutting Nazis."

"You're torn between intellectual morality and an emotion as basic to our kind as the need to breathe or sleep. Women can feel it too, Matt. Don't you think the desire to kill Dutton crossed my mind? Of course it did! But an act of violence can't be isolated from the sum of our lives and loves. Too many other people are involved . . . and would be hurt."

Matt let his lips drift across her hair, held her closer, wanting to protect her, wanting to wipe out what could never be removed from her life.

"Father doesn't know about Dutton," she whispered against his chest. "I don't want him ever to know. Oh, Matt, what are we going to do? I'm afraid I'm falling in love with you and I don't know how to stop it from happening. Tell me you're going away and we'll never see each other again. Tell me you can't accept what Dutton did to me—tell me anything —but make this terrible longing go away."

He pressed his lips to her forehead. "There isn't any way to make it go away, Gennie. We have to be together, no matter what. As for what Dutton did—that's his shame, not yours. I think you should have told your father and I think Dutton should be behind bars, but I understand why you, and Terry, kept it secret." He broke off and his jaw moved in a sardonic grimace. "With everything else Terry had going for him, he had to turn out to be a noble gentleman too, didn't he? When I pick a rival, I sure pick 'em. But Gennie, you have to get your marriage annulled—you can, it hasn't been consummated, that's grounds. Then marry me, come home with me."

"Please let me go. I can't think clearly when you're this close."

"No, I don't ever want to let you go again," he said, but he reluctantly released her. She sat down, her hand shaking as she pushed back a long strand of dark hair that had come unfastened. Framed by the background of his small cabin, with its spartan furnishings and rust marks around the porthole, she seemed to him like a beautiful portrait painted in oils that had somehow become superimposed over the wrong picture. Her life should have been carefree, fulfilling. He wanted to make her future so perfect it would compensate, a little, for the past. "Gennie . . ." he began.

She interrupted breathlessly. "It would be so easy to forget everything but what I want—which is you, Matt. I'll never love anyone else as I love you. I want with all my heart to go with you, be with you, forever. But I can't be that selfish. Terry just left for the army. I can't write and ask for an annulment, it would be too cruel. And my country is at war. I'd feel like a traitor, leaving now."

"Then we'll wait."

"No. Matt, more than anything else, we haven't resolved the question of whether or not we're brother and sister. If we are, we could never have children together. I couldn't make that kind of demand of you, nor you of me. Besides, it would be illegal for us to marry; there would be all sorts of terrible complications. And as for getting an annulment from Terry —to plead nonconsummation would mean exposing the fact that Dulcie is not Terry's child . . . to my father, to the world . . . to Charlie Dutton."

"A divorce then," Matt said hoarsely, knowing he was losing.

"The only legal grounds in this country are desertion, seven years' absence, or adultery. Matt, accept it, it's hopeless. Darling, I'm sorry, I'll love you until I die, but we can't see each other again. I came to your ship tonight knowing I must tell you this. I'll be honest and admit I thought perhaps we would spend the night together . . . but I know now we can't, because afterward I wouldn't be able to leave you. Oh, Matt, I've been terrified of having a sexual relationship with a man, yet when you take me in your arms and kiss me, I can imagine it happening—want it to happen."

"Then stay with me, sail with me tomorrow. We'll pick up Dulcie and—"

"No! I can't. Will you please get a cab for me? I must go. If I stay another minute, I'll weaken, I know I will—and then I'll hate myself."

"Gennie, why did we come together if not to be lovers? Do you feel like my sister? You know you don't—and brotherly thoughts are the last thing on my mind. There's got to be some grand design for us somewhere, or why did we meet? We could have lived all of our lives apart and never known the existence of the other, but we didn't. We're here, together. Stay with me, be with me."

She brushed past him, her eyes filled with tears. "Write to me, Matt. I couldn't bear to lose touch completely . . . but for God's sake, don't come back."

Chapter 23

Matt took the *Bella Mia* back to New York and from there sailed to New Orleans with her, partly because of the illness of the skipper he'd hoped to put aboard her, and partly to give himself time to think.

Geneva was right, they shouldn't see each other. Their chemistry was altogether too volatile. There would be no half measures in any relationship between them.

The war at sea had begun immediately and devastatingly for the Allies. The *Athenia,* a passenger liner, was sunk on the first day with a hundred lives lost, including twenty-eight Americans. The British battleship *Royal Oak* was destroyed at anchor by German torpedoes. During September of 1939, 137,000 tons of Allied shipping went down, as well as 42,000 tons of neutral shipping, and Matt considered himself lucky to have completed the return journey across the Atlantic without sighting a German sub. Poland had been quickly overrun by the Germans and their Russian allies, and now Russia was giving valuable assistance to the Third Reich in the war at sea.

Upon arrival in New Orleans, Matt received a wire asking him to come to Greenboughs immediately; his grandfather's condition had worsened.

Sailing up the Mississippi brought back memories. The riverbanks were lushly green and there were new sandbars where the untamed torrent of water chose fresh paths to conquer. The lower Mississippi had changed its course but not its nature's feast of beauty along the banks. No hint of the presence of people or towns was visible beyond the dense growth of trees, except for an occasional boy with a fishing pole. Matt thought of Specks and the hours they had spent fishing and talking.

"The good lord don't count the hours a man spends fishing," Specks used to tell him. "They all get added on to our spell on His good earth." And the little boy at his side had replied, "Reckon he won't count the hours you play your horn neither, 'cause you make everybody feel good."

But men of integrity didn't always prevail and the meek rarely inherited the earth, Matt thought bitterly. He had a permonition that gloomy news awaited him at Greenboughs. His grandfather had watched over the ships from his sickbed, freeing Matt for an occasional voyage when the call to adventure—or, lately, the need to see Geneva—became irresistible. But if his grandfather was no longer capable, then Matt would have to settle down ashore and run the business. It may be he'd have to honor Geneva's wish not to return, whether he wanted to or not.

Nathan was waiting on the levee when the boat pulled in to Natchez, sitting erectly at the wheel of a well-shined Ford that Castleton had insisted they buy, although the old man never rode in it. Nathan eased his lanky frame stiffly from the car as he saw Matt approach, duffel bag over his shoulder. Nathan seemed to have taken a new lease on life following the recovery from his long illness, and although he moved with the cautious deliberation of age and his hair was battleship gray, he ran Greenboughs with a firm hand and Matt did not interfere.

Matt saw from the expression on Nathan's face that the news was worse than he expected. "I'm sorry, Mr. Matthew," he said with a catch in his voice. "We done lost him, last night. He tried to hold on till you came, but . . ." He smeared a drop of moisture from the corner of his eye with a gnarled finger.

There was no immediate sense of loss, rather of confirmation of the expected and the question of how it would affect his life. He tried to conjure an image of his grandfather in his prime, to make his death seem more real, but the only memories that came were of military academies and his mother's photograph face down, and his father hauled away to the Veteran's Home.

But then Matt thought of the frail old man propped on pillows in the massive four-poster bed, dispensing sage business advice and wry observations. Matt had resented the years spent in military schools, which had left in him a horror of regimentation and a fear of the type of personality able to give blind obedience to orders, but he knew Castleton had believed he needed the discipline. Perhaps he had. He wondered now if the relationship they had shared as adults compensated for those early years. He was probably, in part, the man his grandfather had made him. Matt was unsure if he would miss the old tyrant or not.

He briefly considered sending for the surviving Jazzmen to play at his grandfather's funeral. Somehow a funeral didn't seem complete without the melancholy wail of a clarinet or the stirring dirge of a trumpet; but he knew his grandfather would have been appalled, so did not. The old man was laid to rest in the family crypt and the will was read. It left everything to Matt, and all that was asked of him was that he take care of Nathan and endeavor to hunt down the rest of the furniture and antiques sold during the Depression, to restore Greenboughs to her former glory.

A note scrawled in Castleton's own hand was attached to the will, urging Matt to have a son with all speed and adding, with poignant simplicity, "and Matthew . . . I'm sorry I couldn't find it in my heart to forgive your mother or accept your father. Life is too short for rifts with those we love." The note was dated one month before he died.

Matt threw himself into the running of the Castleton freighters, and the final quarter of the year slipped away despite the hollow space in his life that was, he knew, reserved forever for Geneva. A long letter arrived from her, with no mention of their last meeting or its revelations.

. . . the newspapers are calling it "the phony war" because virtually nothing has happened—on land, at least. The air raid sirens sounded in Liverpool, but it was a false alarm. Ian is running the colliery and he joined the Home Guard—a volunteer force with little in the way of weapons to defend us from the expected German invasion. All of the young men are gone except Huw Wakefield, who was turned down because of a bad heart. We were all shocked—he seemed so healthy—especially his grandfather, who seems to be taking it personally.

Matt, please stay away from the North Atlantic—
don't risk the U-boat packs. Shipping losses are fright-
ful.

No mention of her husband, Matt noticed, wondering if
Terry had been home on leave, and where he was stationed.
He agonized for several days, then wrote back to her that he
couldn't stand not seeing her. Then he searched for someone
to replace him so that he could return to England.

He found the man he was seeking working for another
company. An old acquaintance, Alvin Dooley, who had been
his grandfather's most trusted clerk years ago, and who had
brought Matt home from school after the Crash of '29. Alvin
still wheezed as though coming to the end of a strenuous run,
but he knew shipping inside out, river and deepwater. He
promptly dashed Matt's hopes of taking a cargo to England.
"The Neutrality Act, Matt. Forbids credits to belligerents.
Means shipments have to be paid for in cash, and also states
transportation has to be provided by non–U.S. nationals.
Cash and carry, in other words. Then there's the National
Munitions Control Board—"

"Passengers . . ." Matt began.

Alvin shook his head. "The Neutrality Act states we're
forbidden to carry passengers, articles, or material to belligerents."

"Damn. I'll have to sail on an English ship then. Soon as
you're able to take over here."

Geneva was sitting on the terrace with Dulcie on her lap,
the child cooing contentedly, when Huw Wakefield came
cantering up the driveway on a sweat-streaked horse. Morning sunlight dodged scudding rainclouds on the horizon, and
the grounds smelled fragrantly of early summer flowers.
Huw's black eyes were hard and his mouth seemed to have
taken on a permanent cynical twist these days, Geneva
thought, watching him toss his reins to an elderly groom.

Striding toward the terrace, Huw looked strong and vital. It
was difficult to imagine a faulty heart beneath those hard
pectoral muscles. He had refused to join any of the volunteer
organizations and seemed to do little these days but drink and
frequent lower-class clubs. "Good morning, Huw. I don't see
a gas mask over your shoulder. Don't you know you're not
supposed to leave home without it?" she asked in mock
horror.

"I'd rather get gassed than wear that foul mask. Rubbery tasting abomination."

"Rankin was gassed in the Great War—that's what caused his twitch."

"I'd rather twitch than wear that mask. Besides, Rankin's twitching was caused by mustard gas and our masks are no protection against that. I doubt they protect against anything. We were issued the stupid things to keep us calm. You notice the police and firemen have real oxygen masks, not little rubber things with filters taped on."

"Oh, dear, we are in a bad mood this morning, aren't we?" Geneva murmured. "There's a letter from Terry."

"I got one too. He's in France. We worked out a code before he left." Huw paused, scowling. "I'm sick of the abbey and everything around here. I'm going into Liverpool for dinner. Will you come with me?"

Geneva carefully smoothed Dulcie's bright curls back from the baby's lovely but vacant eyes. "Had a spat with Binnie, Huw? I can't imagine you being reduced to taking an old married woman out to dinner."

"She joined the WAAF," Huw said with studied careless-ness. "She's a trainee plotter in the Operations Room that controls four fighter squadrons. They use long-handled plot-ting rods and trace suspected German raiders on a big glass screen. Only there haven't been any raiders to plot. I understand some of the RAF pilots are getting pretty bored with the whole thing. They've been dropping leaflets on the enemy. Binnie says some of the pilots are forgetting to untie the bundles before they drop them, hoping to hit some German on the head."

Geneva was uncomfortable, knowing how desperately Huw wanted to join the RAF. He had taken flying lessons and been on the verge of getting a pilot's license before the war started. "I'm sorry, Huw, I can't leave tonight. But why don't you join us for dinner instead? Matt should arrive today. Of course, I can't be sure with all the secrecy about ships' movements, but I think he'll be here." Actually she knew he would come, it was one of those intangible bonds they had. She could sense Matt was not far away in the same manner some people foretold a change in the weather.

Huw was on his feet. "No thanks. I don't think your American friend cares for me. He's from the South, isn't he? Shades of *Uncle Tom's Cabin*. Probably sees me as some sort of untouchable."

Indignation flared in Geneva's eyes. "Huw, that's unfair and completely untrue and you know it. Matt is not in the least bit like that. If you're feeling sorry for yourself, I suggest you blame the person responsible for your state of mind. Yourself. Can't you find something useful to do instead of moping about?"

"I'm sorry I'm such a nuisance. I'll be off," he said stiffly. On the second terrace step he paused and looked back. "Have you noticed all the activity in the fields on the other side of the woods? Army engineers are swarming all over the place and they're throwing up prefabricated buildings. Sentries are posted in an almost solid ring around the place. Whatever they're doing is very hush-hush."

"Yes, I know. I tried to ride along the lane and they sent me back the other morning."

"Geneva, have you considered taking the baby and going somewhere really safe? Scotland or Wales, into the countryside?"

"Whatever for? We live in the country here."

"But we're only fifteen miles from the outskirts of Liverpool, and with that new army installation just across the woods, we may not be as safe from air raids here as we imagine. It will happen, Geneva—England will be bombed."

Geneva could not help feeling he spoke with an insider's knowledge. She thought of his years at Heidelberg, his friendship with Germans who were at this moment planning the attack on England.

After he left, she hoisted Dulcie to her shoulder and went into the house. Rankin had just answered the telephone and offered her the receiver. "It's for you, madam. Mr. Ian." He took the baby from her arms.

"Hello, Father, where are you?"

"In a phone booth in a village that is now nameless. We've removed all the street signs for miles around too, to confuse any invaders. Gennie, I'm going on maneuvers for a day or two, drilling a few old codgers like myself with broom handles in lieu of guns. Darling, did you try to reach Uncle Dee Dee again? I'm really worried about the old boy. He shouldn't stay down there on the south coast."

"I tried an hour ago. Still no answer. I called the gamekeeper's house and he said Uncle Dee Dee is so deaf nowadays he simply refuses to talk on the phone and won't let his butler act as go-between either, so has instructed him to ignore it."

There was a long pause, then Ian's voice, low and urgent, came over the wire. "Gennie, could you travel down there and get him? There's a train at eight in the morning. I just learned how bad things really are in France. They're keeping the news from the civilian population, but the Expeditionary Forces are in full retreat. There are rumors we may have to try to evacuate them from French beaches."

"Oh, my God," Geneva breathed. "Terry—"

"Try not to worry, dear. But if the Germans reach the French coast and there is an invasion . . ."

"I'll go for Uncle Dee Dee tomorrow," Geneva promised.

She moved through the rest of the day in bursts of nervous activity, trying not to worry about Terry nor be resentful of dear old Uncle Dee Dee, who would take her away from Matt the moment he arrived. Unless, she thought late in the afternoon, Matt were to go with her?

As the day wore on, his imminent arrival drove away all other thoughts. That evening she took particular care with her appearance, choosing a shot-silk dress that cast mysterious lavender shadows in her eyes and set off her shining dark hair. She touched perfume to pulse spots and felt that certain weakness that Matt's presence caused begin to creep luxuriously along her veins. It was a magical feeling that brought a soft glow to her eyes and communicated itself to everyone around her, especially the baby, who was always contented and lovable but blossomed even more when her mother played with her so happily. Not even Dulcie's lost little mind could mar Geneva's wonderful mood of anticipation. Even though it was she who had insisted he stay away, she had missed Matt desperately these past months.

When his taxi arrived, she opened the front doors before Rankin appeared and ran down the steps to meet Matt. They stopped seconds before they were in each other's arms. She felt Matt's dark eyes penetrate her thoughts, sending a silent message of adoration and receiving one in return. He took her hand and squeezed it and although they ached to hold one another, propriety was observed and that one glance conveyed all they needed to know.

"You get lovelier each time I see you," he whispered as they went into the house.

"And you more handsome." She smiled mischievously. "Are you the tall dark stranger the gypsy is always warning me about? If so, I'm afraid the spell is already cast. Come on, we're going to have dinner for two tonight and I don't care if

Rankin twitches furiously all night!" *How easy it is to forget everything else when he's at my side,* she thought. *The hopelessness of loving him, the fear of losing him that drives me to retell our story in my mind and make it all come out right. Only it never will.* A stab of conscience reminded her of their last conversation aboard his ship. Why hadn't she been completely honest with him then? Because, she realized as she watched him hand his coat to Rankin, she couldn't bear any more pity. Nor could she have diminished herself any further in Matt's eyes than had already been accomplished by telling the bald facts of Dutton's monstrous act.

Rankin stood like a sentry beside the table throughout the meal, directing the one remaining footman with silent gestures, never taking his eyes from Matt. Geneva ordered coffee and liqueurs to be served in the drawing room, and as soon as the butler reluctantly left, she gave Matt a conspiratorial smile, took his hand, and led him outside.

They walked down the path through the rose garden, intoxicated with the scent of the flowers, the sheltering canopy of the night sky, and the nearness of each other.

"Two weeks, Gennie," Matt said, slipping his arm around her waist as soon as they were out of sight of the house. "I can stay two weeks. You've got to come away with me."

"The south coast . . . there's a train tomorrow morning," Geneva answered unexpectedly. From her tone it was obvious they were not speaking of the same kind of journey. She told him briefly that she must go and bring Uncle Dee Dee up north in case there was a German invasion, which seemed more than likely.

"Okay, we'll go get him. Shouldn't take more than a day or two. Then we'll take off by ourselves. Say yes, Gennie, please."

She turned and placed her arms about his neck. "Yes, Matt. As soon as Uncle Dee Dee is safely at Saxon Hall, I'll go away with you. I can't go on living unless you're completely mine."

Chapter 24

Geneva and Matt took an interminably slow train south, coming at last to a seaside resort that was as deserted as a ghost town: shops boarded up, streets empty except for primitive roadblocks manned by unarmed police constables and air raid wardens.

"Invasion preparations," Geneva remarked. "The church bells will be the signal that invaders have landed. The bells haven't been rung since war was declared." She was thinking that she for one would not miss the church bells on November 11—nor the two-minute silence that followed, presuming that custom would be discontinued until there was another batch of war dead to mourn.

They found a taxi still running, and as they went through a roadblock consisting of a concrete pyramid and a pile of scrap lumber, Matt glanced at the lone policeman on duty. "What's he going to do if the Germans invade? Hit them on the head with his truncheon?"

"At least we won't go under begging for mercy like our French allies," Geneva replied, remembering the plea that Paris be declared an open city, to escape the German blitzkrieg.

"I didn't mean to poke fun, but it's obvious you haven't anything to fight with. And yet everyone is so calm you'd think this was a Sunday afternoon cricket match. The phony war can't last, you know. All hell will break loose soon. I wish you'd bring Dulcie and come back to America with me."

"You sound like Huw Wakefield with his dire prophecies. We shan't be beaten. England has never lost a war."

"Well, there was the small matter of the American colonies," Matt said, grinning.

"English settlers fighting German mercenaries—one of our greatest victories." She laughed softly.

They both knew that the banter helped mask a feeling of impending disaster that seemed to hang in the air.

"Uncle Dee Dee lives within shouting distance of the French coast. He served in the Royal Navy for about a hundred years and loves to sail his boat, even today," Geneva said. "We're nearly there."

The deserted town gave way to a narrow lane, bordered on either side by hawthorne hedgerows, beyond which a patchwork of meadows from deepest green to light gold stretched toward a summer horizon of palest blue. The pastoral scene was so tranquil that it seemed quite likely at any moment they would realize they had awakened from what was only a dream of war.

Uncle Dee Dee, the seventh earl of Steadwall, was as deaf and crotchety as ever, but obviously delighted to see them. He bullied a small group of elderly servants into preparing a gala dinner, ration books be damned, and spent the meal bemoaning the fact that the Admiralty had declined his offer of reenlistment in the navy. His grandsons and granddaughters and even a couple of great-grandsons had duly responded to the call, while his son, who, he added darkly, "Is in actual fact older than I am," was serving aboard the aircraft carrier *Illustrious*.

His lament was interrupted, halfway through dinner, by an ancient butler. As he handed his lordship a note, Matt was thinking that there had to be a special reserve of retired old butlers somewhere in England for service in time of war. This one was even older than his master.

Holding the note at arm's length in order to read it, Lord Steadwall rose abruptly. "I'm sorry Geneva, but I must leave right away." Glancing at the impassive butler, he barked, "Be off, man. You know what I need. Oilskins and flasks of rum."

"What is it, Uncle? A boat in trouble?" Geneva asked.

"The fishing fleet is putting out into the Channel. There's been a call for sailing boats, pleasure yachts . . ." He blinked in Matt's direction, new purpose in his faded eyes. "I've a small sloop. Auxiliary engine is a bit temperamental, but I should think it will do."

"Do for what? You're not going sailing at this time of night?" Geneva said, her heart beginning to flutter as she remembered Ian's telephone call.

"Everything that floats will be out in the Channel soon, my dear." The old man's voice was suddenly firmer, his posture more erect, as the years seemed to slip away from him. "Our expeditionary force is stranded on the beach at Dunkirk. Small boats are needed to ferry them to transport vessels. There's a gentle slope of sand into tidal waters—I know that beach—we can pull in and ground in knee-deep water."

"Uncle—no, please, you can't go—" Geneva began.

"Stop acting like a woman," her uncle snapped testily. "We're not leaving our men to the mercy of the Hun. We're going to rescue them."

Matt was on his feet. "I'll go with you, sir, if I may. I can handle a boat."

Geneva turned to him with gratitude on her face. "Thank you, Matt. I wish I could sail, I'd go too. Terry is probably one of those poor souls waiting at Dunkirk."

The mention of her husband's name sliced into Matt's senses like a knife-thrust.

The mist was dissipating, drifting off over a flat sea, leaving the beach bleakly gray and vulnerable in the early dawn light. Under Terry's cramped body the sand was cold, hard. He crawled wearily toward his fallen sergeant.

The sergeant was dead. His last words had ordered what was left of their company to move forward to the sailing boats that bobbed invitingly offshore. Incredibly, the men maintained orderly lines, as though they were waiting in bus queues; the lines snaked out from the beach until soldiers stood waist-deep in water. They could hear artillery fire pounding the shrinking perimeter of the British and French lines.

Easing himself over onto his back, Terry loosened the tourniquet on his leg for a moment and watched his blood pump out and be swallowed by the sand. Tightening the sodden bandage again, he pulled his steel helmet over his face as the drone of approaching aircraft drowned the other sounds.

A Stuka dived for the beach, bomb ports open, and the

lines of men went down like collapsing dominoes, scrabbling in the sand for cover. Where the hell was the RAF? There'd been some air cover but nowhere near enough. The engines of the German planes throbbed with a peculiar pulsating sound. Even with his face under his helmet, Terry knew the Luftwaffe was alone up there.

The German planes moved off, scattering death in their wake, to hit another section of the beach. Terry sat up and looked at the astonishing profusion of vessels in the channel. Navy ships and merchant ships, trawlers, yachts, sailing boats, anything that would float. There were even Thames barges.

Into this flotilla scrambled dead-tired troops, hungry, thirsty, unaware of how much time had passed since they arrived. The small boats ferried the troops to the larger craft. Organized chaos, Terry thought, watching as one boat's keel dug into the sand when the sodden men climbed into it. They slid back into the water to push it free. Further offshore another group were frantically bailing water from a rapidly sinking pleasure yacht, using their steel helmets.

Water. Oh, God, why didn't they think to bring water? He rolled his dry tongue around the inside of his mouth and watched in despair as men continued to die.

A week had gone by and Dunkirk must fall soon. *How many of us will see England again,* he wondered. They had come through a nightmare of roads crammed with fleeing humanity, retreating soldiers, frantic civilian refugees; past demolished houses lying under a pall of smoke, dead animals, scarred trees. An inferno filled with rumbling gunfire and the whine of falling bombs. Great columns of black smoke probed the sky from blazing oil storage tanks, testifying to the destruction already wrought by the Luftwaffe.

At first weak cheers had greeted the arrival of English Spitfires and Hurricanes and the sight of the approaching ships—until it dawned on them that the evacuation of all the English and French troops crowding the beach would take days, and there were far too few RAF planes to keep the bombers at bay.

Boulogne and Calais were in German hands. While Allied troops still held a weakening perimeter around Dunkirk, the armada of little ships braved unpredictable weather and the treacherous currents of the English Channel. Sleek yachts jostled rusty tugs to creep closer to the lines of soldiers waist deep in the choppy water. There were groans and curses as a string of the rescue boats were ripped apart by strafing German planes.

What day is it? Terry wondered, trying to bring everything into focus. *The Channel appears reasonably calm now although the skies are cloudy. Smoke is helping to camouflage the beach. The men seem more confident of rescue this morning, hunger and thirst and untreated wounds apparently forgotten as they patiently inch forward in their orderly lines.*

"Walking wounded only," was the order. Terry's leg would no longer bear his weight, and he had been unable to hobble even with a makeshift crutch. He lay in the hollow of a sand dune, a badly wounded senior officer beside him. Their blood had mingled as it seeped into the sand.

"Panzers are closing in. The evacuation must end soon," the officer said, his words slow, measured, requiring considerable effort. "I'd like to order boats to take only English troops. Saw bloody French pilots sipping wine . . . brand-new Curtis planes parked outside . . . refusing to fly with a sky full of Germans." He coughed and a trickle of blood oozed from his nose.

Terry was experiencing a strange calmness. His leg no longer hurt; it was numb. Except for his raging thirst, he felt quite removed from the miseries of his body. His mind was suddenly remarkably clear. He was aware of the passage of time, but in some mystical way he was glad of the opportunity to simply relax after the frantic fighting of the last weeks. To his wounded companion he said, "I don't think the boats are picking up too many French pilots, sir. The French troops who are going to England fought well. Besides, those boats ferrying the men to the transports are manned by civilians for the most part."

"You wouldn't have any water left, would you, old boy?" the senior officer inquired apologetically.

"Sorry, sir."

"Quite all right. Still say we should leave the French behind. Better off to take some of the equipment going up in smoke."

Terry rolled over, pulling his helmet down over his eyes again, as the Stuka wheeled back, whining earthward in its fearful dive. Bullets sprayed all around him. He felt the flying sand sting the mangled flesh of his leg where his trousers were torn.

The German plane droned away, circling in a leisurely fashion to choose another target. Like a sharpshooter in a fairground arcade, Terry thought, shaking the sand from his helmet. He turned to speak to the senior officer and saw that several new holes had appeared in the body that now lay inert, eyes staring, fists slowly unclenching.

Rolling away from the corpse, Terry shaded his eyes to watch a sailboat tack unerringly through the clutter of small boats to the shallows. A sloop, like Uncle Dee Dee's. A black-haired man in the stern was helping water-logged soldiers to clamber aboard, while a white-haired old chap stood ready at the helm. *Must be going bonkers*, Terry thought, blinking. *That old codger looks a bit like Uncle Dee Dee. But, of course, it isn't. Delirious, old bean, that's what you are.*

Whirling smoke obscured his view of the boat. *Funny how the old man resembles Uncle Dee Dee. Good lord, he's about eighty. Disgraced himself by falling asleep during our wedding. Sitting at the end of a pew, on the aisle, inches from where Huw and I stood waiting for Ian to bring Gennie to us. Snored like an old hound.* Terry grinned, remembering, until his wife's face blotted out the other memories and an old pain made itself felt. There hadn't been any letters since the retreat began.

Her early letters had been full of encouragement and reassurance that everything was going well on the home front. She chose carefully the incidents to relate and the people to mention. Nothing about Matt Lauren—and that was more of a worry than if her letters had been full of him.

The stretch of sand between where he lay with a group of men too badly wounded to be moved and the troops moving slowly toward the sea had broadened. There now seemed to be a vast plane of gray sand separating the two groups. *Must move forward somehow*, he thought wearily, *get into one of those lines, or I'll be left behind*. He forced himself up on one knee, collapsed as he tried to crawl forward.

"Damn," he said aloud. He looked down at his blood-soaked leg curiously, as though it belonged to someone else. Ted Corwin had managed without a leg for a long time now. Hardly even limped. Geneva had written that Ted was a reporter for a small southern newspaper. *The loss of a leg isn't the end of everything. The end of cricket and rugby, of course. Perhaps not polo. Besides, got to keep cheerful; perhaps medical aid will arrive before the damn thing rots on my torso.*

He tried to move again and fell on his face. Spitting the sand from his mouth, he was aware that the shriek of Stukas and the distant rumble of artillery had stopped. A new sound intruded. A slow grinding noise that was coming from the ground beneath him. *Tanks,* he thought. *They've broken through. Got to get moving.*

Pulling himself forward with one arm, dragging his leg, he found he made progress, agonizingly slow. He wanted to curse in frustration when he came to an unconscious corporal with a head wound lying directly in his path. A detour around the man meant going up the side of a sand dune. He considered crawling right over the inert form.

The corporal groaned and stirred, but before he could speak there was a burst of conversation nearby.

"Come on, sir," a voice overhead said. "Let's be 'aving you. We've got a stretcher here. We're going to try to set up an aid station. We'll rig up a red cross if we can." Two silhouettes loomed over him, carrying something.

"Take the corporal," Terry said. "I'll be able to get out to the boats. I'm just resting." When they hesitated, Terry said, "That *is* an order, private."

The corporal opened his eyes and grinned at him from the stretcher and gave a thumbs-up sign.

Terry didn't reply. Resuming his slither toward the sea, he realized he could no longer see ahead for the thick pall of smoke hanging over the water. He crawled blindly, losing his sense of direction. After a few minutes he was forced to rest. He lay on his back, a faint drizzle of rain drifting across his face, and succumbed to that peculiar sense of drifting away. Try as he might, he could not bring the beach back into focus. As consciousness faded, Terry thought about Geneva. The way her dark hair shone in the moonlight, how he felt when he looked into her eyes.

Lying on the cold wet sands of Dunkirk, he was dreaming about her after the last rescue boat had gone and the rumble of German tanks blotted out all other sounds.

Chapter 25

The black headlines on the newsstands screamed of the miracle of Dunkirk: OPERATION DYNAMO PLUCKS 338,000 ENGLISH AND FRENCH SOLDIERS FROM SMOKING BEACHES. Many of the rescued soldiers acquired flashes for their sleeves that read DUNKIRK while others simply chalked BEF on their steel helmets. Civilians patted them on the back as they strolled by and, down in the village near Steadwall Manor, Geneva saw one middle-aged woman impulsively hug a red-faced sergeant.

Lord Steadwall had been outraged by the first news reports of the evacuation when he and Matt returned, scruffy and unshaven. Geneva had turned on the BBC news as she supervised breakfast. The old man exploded, "They think they're heroes! And what's worse, the civilian population does too. Don't they realize Dunkirk was a *defeat?*"

"Perhaps they see it more as a deliverance?" Matt suggested.

"It certainly isn't a German victory," Geneva put in. "And perhaps we need a sense of something accomplished at this point." She was anxious to get them both to bed, as they were trembling with fatigue but still wound up and exhibiting that brittle hyperactivity that comes in the last stages of exhaustion. She added, "Tomorrow, after you've slept, Uncle Dee Dee, I'm taking you back to Saxon Hall."

She didn't add that he couldn't stay on the south coast now because the Germans were sure to invade, but she wondered how much time they really had left.

"Oh, no you're not," the old man snapped. "I know I can't stay here; I'll move up to my London club. But I won't go and live in Lancashire. God forbid!"

He meant it, she knew. He had often chided his sister Sybil for marrying into a family of northern merchants, as he called them in his more charitable moments. He viewed the industrial north as some sort of outback, culturally deprived, its denizens speaking a foreign tongue.

Matt said tactfully, "Perhaps we could make plans after we've slept, sir?"

After they had gone to their rooms, Geneva and the butler set about packing and putting dust covers on the furniture. The morning slipped away and it was late afternoon before she had a moment to sit down and rest. Her uncle and Matt were still sound asleep.

The telephone rang almost immediately and she grabbed it, afraid an extension might ring upstairs and wake Matt. Her father's voice said, "Gennie? Is that you?"

"Hello, Father, yes. I'm sorry, I should have called you, but we've been so busy. Uncle Dee Dee is all right. You won't believe what he's been doing all night. He won't come to the Hall with us, but—"

"Gennie." The interruption was sharp, unexpected. "I'm afraid I have some very bad news."

A pulse started to throb in her throat. "No, no, please, not Terry!"

"He didn't come back from Dunkirk. He's probably been captured. Officially he's listed as missing in action. We may know more when all the reports are in. Gennie, are you all right? Darling, you mustn't give up hope."

"I'm coming home, Father," she said in a small flat voice. "I'll be on the next train. Uncle Dee Dee is going to his club. His butler will take care of him."

She replaced the receiver and pressed her fingers to her temples. The room seemed suddenly to be filled with Terry's presence, shutting out other images. *He's alive,* she thought, *he has to be.* A newly defined anger at the Germans surfaced. Now they were no longer a vague and faceless enemy. They were a people who had hurled another generation of young men into battle, twice in twenty years, who had killed Terry's father and his grandfather.

Horrified by the fury of her resentment of an entire race, she told herself that this was how wars and blood feuds were perpetuated. *If I could go and fight Germans myself, now, I'd do it. To wipe out my fear for Terry. Then, having killed another woman's husband, or son, would I learn that Terry is safe? And is my fear for him rooted in guilt? Don't die yet, Terry, because I still owe you too much. Some gesture of gratitude—a small portion of loyalty perhaps?*

After a while her resolutions crystalized. She couldn't rescue Terry, but she could at least keep her marriage vows until he returned.

She went into her uncle's study and sat down at his desk. Her note to Matt was brief.

> Forgive me for leaving while you're still asleep, but it will be easier for both of us not to have to say good-bye. Terry is missing. I'm going home and you mustn't follow because I won't see you again—I can't. You'll understand why.

She closed her eyes, squeezing back the tears.

The cinemas were showing newsreels of Hitler triumphantly riding through the streets of Paris over a carpet of flowers, proclaimed Field Lord and Leader of Battles. A man with a sneering voice and a British accent was broadcasting propaganda messages from Germany to England. He was dubbed Lord Haw Haw and became the butt of comedians' jokes. His actual identity was soon discovered: William Joyce, born in New York City of a naturalized father, he had spent most of his life in Ireland and England. More items of food were rationed. Despite world opinion that the conquest of Britain was merely a mopping-up operation after the fall of France, the RAF raided German transportation centers and ports. Pilots brought back news of massed invasion craft.

Ian observed and listened and was saddened, remembering France not only during the first war, but on peacetime holidays. How swiftly the years had flown, from one war to the next. He had tried to show Geneva part of her heritage without giving in to her wish to see the part of the country her mother had come from—allowing Geneva to think his reluctance was due to his not wishing to revisit the battlegrounds and the place where Celine had died. He had seen to it that she learned to speak fluent French; he'd even learned the language himself, wishing a thousand times he had been able to speak with Celine. If he had known her story would anything have been different? He would not have gone to meet Andre Thibault. Andre . . . how would he feel, now that his beloved country was flying the hated *croix gammée*—the twisted cross. He could not imagine Andre Thibault collaborating with the Boches.

Ian managed to keep any of the news from affecting him deeply until Geneva announced she was moving to Liverpool to take a flat and join the St. John's Ambulance Brigade. They were in desperate need of drivers. Dulcie would remain at Saxon Hall in the care of her nursemaid. The child responded lovingly, but without recognition, to anyone who cared for her. Ian said good-bye to Geneva with a feeling of something forever lost. He knew she worried about Terry and felt compelled to do something for the war effort, but he worried that what drove her was more complex than that.

But there was the Home Guard, and the colliery, and the endless problem of maintaining the house and the tenant farms with the drastic shortages of materials and labor, and Ian had little time to spend wishing for happier times to return.

One evening after a particularly grueling day he returned to Saxon Hall to find Huw Wakefield climbing the terrace steps leading to the front door.

"Hello, Huw. Make yourself comfortable, I'll be with you in a moment, soon as I've looked in on Dulcie," Ian said, gesturing for Huw to go into the drawing room.

When Ian joined him a short time later, Huw had poured himself a brandy, obviously not his first, and was staring moodily at a sturdy aspidistra plant whose glossy leaves filled a corner of the room. He glanced up as Ian entered the room. "I was just contemplating the ubiquitous aspidistra. Look at the strength of those leaves, the sheen of health. What an incredibly ugly creation is the aspidistra." He raised his glass in a mock toast to the plant.

Ian stifled a sigh, wishing he had chosen some other time to return to the Hall. He sat down and said, "I have some idea of what you're feeling, Huw. But you won't find your answers in a brandy glass."

Huw turned and regarded him with eyes like black mirrors. "You know what I'm feeling, do you? You know what it's like to be the only man in England not in uniform?"

"An exaggeration, but yes, I do know. I didn't join up in the Great War until 1917. For nearly three years I was a conscientious objector, much to the horror of my family. Far more of a pariah than you could ever be, with medical grounds for deferment. I was berated by old ladies, called 'slacker' and 'coward' to my face by complete strangers. I lost count of the number of white feathers I received."

"But you eventually gave in to the pressures and enlisted," Huw said. "Despite your convictions. Unfortunately I can't follow suit."

"That was my true act of cowardice," Ian said quietly. "War is evil and has never solved anything. This one won't either. Wars just beget more wars, they don't end them. But this really isn't what I started to say to you. I wanted you to know that no one will send white feathers to you. Frankly I think you'd do well to go to work—perhaps in a munitions factory, if you feel some overwhelming urge to participate in killing Germans." Ian paused, studying the young man who was Terry's best friend. "Or . . ."

"Yes?" Huw asked. His eyes were without hope but his nostrils flared in anger, as they always did when someone chided him for his idleness. His handsomely hewn face was somehow symbolic of his sadly beautiful homeland.

"You know about the army installation across the woods? I'm sure you must have seen the practice parachute jumps there? An old friend of mine is running a highly secret show. I can't tell you much about it, except that he was an Intelligence officer in the first war. If you're interested, I could speak to him. I happen to know he's in desperate need of people who speak German fluently."

Huw put the brandy glass down slowly. He drew a breath. "Why . . . yes. Thank you, I'd appreciate it."

"His name is Captain Phillip Jefferson. Career man, bit of an odd sort, but that's probably due to his job. I'll invite him over soon and you and your grandfather can come and meet him. By the way, Jeff—as we used to call him when we were boys—is in need of a local billet for some of his officers. He approached me about using the Hall, but of course it was out of the question, with Dulcie and all. I don't suppose your grandfather would consider allowing them to use part of the abbey?"

"I'll ask him," Huw said. "He's fiercely patriotic, as you know. But the abbey is an inviolate shrine to the memory of my father—I don't know about army boots stamping on the sacred ground."

"Now if you'll excuse me, I'm frightfully tired, Huw."

Chapter 26

Charlie Dutton, still incongruously masked and wearing his black satin robe over his wrestling trunks, stared down at the white mound of the sheet covering the body on the bed.

"No. No-no-no!" He turned to Millie at the foot of the bed. "I come right away. Honest, Mil. I dropped everything. I was up for the next bout, but I swear to Christ—"

"Shut up." Millie hissed the words from lips that looked like rubber bands. "She's gone. The doctor signed the death certificate more than two hours ago—before I sent for you. I didn't want you here, making a scene, till they was all gone."

"Josie, oh, Josie, don't leave me!" Charlie screamed, flinging himself down on top of her, pulling the sheet from her face.

"Jesus Christ!" Millie exclaimed. "Pull yourself together."

He stared down at Josie's immobile features, which looked more intelligent now than they had in life, and felt the same sense of abandonment and fear he had felt when their father died. It frightened Charlie to think of his own death and angered him that they had reminded him of it by dying themselves. He felt a tearing fury swell and grow inside him. Josie had no right to die. She wasn't old, she wasn't ill. She was plump and affectionate and she worshiped him and never laughed at him or looked down her nose at him. He didn't want her to be gone forever. He grasped her rigid shoulders and began to shake her. Vaguely he felt Millie plucking at his back.

"Stop it! Charlie! Do you hear me? Stop it."

Josie's body felt different, smelled different. He began to gasp for breath, choke on the smell of death. He released her, jumped to his feet, and reeled about the room trying to catch his breath.

Millie followed, thumping him between the shoulder blades and berating him in a high, shrill voice that might have been speaking a foreign language for all Charlie understood. He staggered to the bedroom door and went down the stairs two at a time.

In the hall he leaned against the gas meter cupboard, chest rising and falling. He heard the bedroom door close and Millie's slippers dragging down the stairs. "Come on, I've a drop of brandy in the kitchen."

The fiery brandy caused another choking fit and brought tears to his eyes. Millie was telling him what had happened. He didn't want to hear, but she went on anyway. "Just sitting there, she was, having her dinner. I was always after her to cut up her meat—you know that, Charlie. We only get one joint of beef a week, with the rationing, and the butcher let me save the rations for two weeks, on account of we was expecting you. But of course his lordship didn't come. Better things to do than visit his poor sisters, he has. And we waited and waited—she was hungry. I was getting the Yorkshire pudding out of the oven—I'd have cut up her meat for her in a minute. But no, she couldn't wait."

A low moan escaped from Charlie's lips. "Oh, sweet Jesus. She didn't choke to death? Not fighting for 'er breath—like Dad? Oh, my God, Millie . . . not like that!"

"A damn big piece of meat went down the wrong way. She was blue in the face and couldn't speak. I didn't know what was up with her. By the time I'd got the doctor, she was gone. It's all your fault. If you'd come 'ome for Sunday dinner like you promised—"

Charlie blinked, shook his head. "But it's Monday today, Mil—"

"When you didn't come yesterday, I didn't cook the meat. But I had to cook it today; it would've spoiled. I thought you'd come today."

She went on and on. Charlie shut out her voice. He'd been touring the country. They hadn't wanted him back at the Liverpool Stadium again for a while after that bout with

Handsome Harry. He'd given exhibition bouts at private clubs mostly. There was also the tricky situation about him not being in the army. Coby had taken care of it, and Charlie had the uneasy feeling his deferment was a result of the time he'd served for assaulting those girls. But he didn't press for details; he was too relieved he didn't have to go. He hadn't wanted to leave Liverpool right away after the Handsome Harry incident, because he wanted to find out more about Geneva Saxon and that Yank sailor.

Thinking about Geneva Saxon brought her baby to mind. Dulcie. He wondered if she was sweet and loving as Josie had been. Bound to be a family resemblance. He'd seen that photo in the Sunday paper of the baby at her christening. Prettier than Josie. But just as affectionate, he was sure. Another tear slipped down his cheek. It wasn't fair that he couldn't see his own flesh and blood, hold her like he used to hold Josie. How she used to snuggle closer, stroke him so gently. . . .

"Charlie, are you listening to me? I said the undertaker will be here shortly."

"No! You're not going to bury her in the ground." Charlie was on his feet.

"What do you suggest we do with her? Send her to the taxidermist?"

Charlie's hand caught Millie full in the mouth. She went down heavily, screaming with pain and rage. He stood over her, feeling suddenly free of her. She was just as frail as the rest of them. One blow and she was down. He hadn't even hit her hard. Well, he'd needed her to take care of Josie, but he sure as hell didn't need her no more. "Don't you make fun of Josie, you auld witch. She's going to be cremated. She's not going in any flaming hole in the ground with a concrete slab on top of her."

Millie watched him warily, her deep-set eyes sending him lightning bolts of hatred, but she didn't answer him back. What would she do without him, anyway? Who paid the flaming rent on the house, put the grub in her mouth?

She wiped a streak of blood from her lip. "I'm just as upset about Josie as you are. But you talk so daft sometimes. Besides, I'll miss her more than you. You know they're going to start calling up women? I'll have to go into a munitions factory or some essential job. I could have got an exemption while I was looking after our Josie."

Charlie considered this. "If you had a little baby to look after, you wouldn't have to go then, Mil, would you?"

The skin between her eyes puckered. "What you driving at?"

"I've got a kid, Mil. Me very own daughter. I've as much right to her as the bloody Saxons."

Millie snorted. "And what judge do you think will give her to you?"

"I was just thinking about it. We could go down south, take the baby with us. I know a bloke what makes identification cards and ration books. We could just change our names. They'd never find us in wartime."

"And what about the Masked Turk? You think nobody would notice him?"

"I could grow me hair out again—shave off the muzzy and goatee. Nobody's seen my face in the ring for years anyway."

"All that trouble for a kid?" Millie's frown deepened.

"*My* kid. And paying back the bleeding Saxon family for all they done to us."

"And if you're not wrestling, what do we live on?"

"I've a tidy penny put away. And I know a few people what can get things that are very scarce now, with the rationing."

"Black market? You got black market connections and didn't bring nothing home?"

"Are you game, Mil?"

"Maybe. I'll have to see. How you going to get your hands on the baby?"

"I couldn't do anything for a while. There's arrangements to be made. And I need time to grow me hair."

He went into the parlor and switched on the wireless. The BBC announcer said German Heinkels, Junkers, Dorniers, and Messerschmitts were bombing the southern coast from Portsmouth to the Thames estuary. Shipping in the Channel was hard hit. The Luftwaffe, he continued, was meeting spirited resistance from the RAF Spitfires and Hurricanes. There had been civilian casualties.

Charlie sat down beside the wireless. They were in for it now, all right. The long-threatened blitzkrieg of Britain had begun.

Rankin complained to Ian that dinner parties would have to be forgotten for the duration. There simply wasn't a way to stretch rations to accommodate guests. A couple of ounces of meat a week per person constituted *one meat dinner a week,* did the master understand that? Rankin was growing frail and crotchety with age, but Ian hadn't the heart to suggest he retire.

"Oh, perhaps some vegetables from the garden, and fish for the main course?" Ian suggested. "And no dessert, of course."

Muttering and grumbling and twitching furiously, the butler had withdrawn to arrange a small dinner party for the Wakefields and Captain "Jeff" Jefferson.

Jefferson was the first to arrive: a tall, stoop-shouldered man with a long jaw and hooded eyes that gave him an excessively gloomy countenance. He had actually been more a friend to Ian's brother, with whom he had joined the army at the same time. Jefferson had decided to stay in at war's end. As Rankin took his coat and gloves, he glanced about the hall appreciatively. "Pleasure to come here again, Ian. You wouldn't believe what my digs look like. I don't suppose . . ."

"No. We have a baby and nursemaid and my daughter comes home when she can. No, Saxon Hall is quite unsuitable for your purpose," Ian said firmly, gesturing toward the drawing room. "But perhaps the colonel will let you use the abbey. There's just he and Huw and their butler there now; they use only a couple of rooms." He crossed the room to the decanter and glasses waiting on the sideboard while Jefferson closed the door behind them with what seemed unnecessary stealth.

"Before the Wakefields arrive, Ian—and incidentally your recommendation is all I need to give young Huw a job as civilian interpreter, so that's a foregone conclusion. His father and grandfather had distinguished army records; I looked them up myself—but I'd like to talk to you privately about another matter entirely."

Ian handed him a glass and took his own over to the fireplace.

"The last time I saw you, you mentioned being in France, just before the war started . . . in some of the places you'd seen action in during the first war," Jefferson went on. "You said you'd a sickening sense of history repeating itself, seeing the countryside again. And later you mentioned the Renet-Thibault art gallery in Beauvais. I gathered you knew Andre Thibault. Forgive me, old chap, but I put two and two together—an occupational hazard, I shouldn't wonder, along with my impeccable memory. Do you remember the dinner party your mother gave when you first returned from France? When we were all astounded by the announcement that you had married a French girl and she had died giving birth to your daughter? You see, I wondered if Andre Thibault was related to her mother's side of the family."

Ian looked at him with astonishment. "I must have had a little more brandy than usual, to have told you so much. Please, I'd prefer you not mention Andre Thibault to anyone else. He is Geneva's uncle, her mother's brother. But Geneva doesn't know of his existence. Her mother was estranged from her family before Geneva was born."

"But you sought him out after an estrangement of twenty years," Jefferson mused. "You've had your finger in several pies since young Terry went away, haven't you? The colliery and so on. Of course, since coal is an essential industry, you can get all the help you need. Then there's the Home Guard—and you're far too old to be conscripted."

"Not that old," Ian demurred. "What are you driving at, Jeff? I feel I'm being interrogated. You've acquired that policeman's way of ruminating that we ordinary souls find most disconcerting. I feel as though I've been dissected and sewn up again, and I'm not sure what the result was."

Jefferson laughed. "I was just thinking that it would be relatively simple to have the Home Guard release you on loan to us. You speak French, know a part of the countryside we're interested in."

"How do you know I speak French?"

"Don't you?"

"If it's another interpreter you need, Huw Wakefield speaks French as well as German."

"Ah, yes, well . . . as a matter of fact it's Andre Thibault we're really interested in. Look, Ian, I've been a bit evasive. I didn't learn of your relationship from your chance remarks. You see, Thibault was something of a hero in the last days before Dunkirk fell. A group of our chaps were cut off from their company and found themselves surrounded by Germans. Andre guided them back to their own lines. When they tried to thank him and suggest he might want to come home with them to fight again, he said he had an art gallery he had to get to before the Boches looted it. He also told them that if they wanted to do something for him, they should take a message to one Ian Saxon, of Saxon Hall, Lancs. The cryptic message was that he had later realized—after you left him—that he had been both ungracious and ungrateful. He wanted you to know he really did appreciate what you did for his sister and her child."

"I see," Ian said. "Now why don't you tell me what it is you want of me?"

"Last summer Churchill founded a group called Special Operations Executive. SOE. Winnie realized that it might be years before we could invade the occupied countries, and in the meantime he wants clandestine warfare. It's a subject that's fascinated the PM for some time. He sent a memo to the chiefs of staff to the effect that it would be wonderful if the Germans could be made to fear where and when they would be struck against, instead of England just trying to wall in our island and roof it over."

"Attack being the best means of defense," Ian said. "But we're hardly in a position—"

"He's conceived of commando parties that would harass the coasts with hit-and-run raids, and of secret agents parachuted into occupied countries to gather intelligence, plan sabotage, and train underground armies to revolt against the occupying forces. He's given his brainchild an inspiring mandate. 'Set Europe Ablaze.'"

"Very interesting, but—"

"Our organization is having some birth pains, Ian. There was the inevitable power struggle between the War Office, the Foreign Office, and the secret services. And, of course, our haughty friend de Gaulle is the biggest headache of all. As Churchill says, the heaviest cross he has to bear is the cross of Lorraine. So . . . the SOE came into being with, incidentally, a separate French section reporting to de Gaulle. They're particularly vexed at us for poaching on their preserves, and everyone is at cross purposes, working against each other. We need reliable people in France to coordinate all of the activities. At the moment our worst problem is our lack of contacts in the occupied countries. We need to know who will help—get radio transmission started, send people to train saboteurs, arrange for weapons to be flown in. Our first agents have been dropped into France with nothing more than a name—someone who might or might not help them, or knows someone who will. The prospects are usually gleaned from a fellow countryman who has made his way here when his country was overrun. The contacts are dicey, to say the least. If an agent is lucky, he'll find an embryonic resistance movement already in existence, but mostly we're finding we have to start one."

"And you think Andre Thibault might be a possibility? You're probably right. He appeared to be extremely patriotic, and I know he hates the Germans. He's also a prosperous businessman. I don't know if that makes a difference. I suppose it depends on whether the Germans allow him to continue running his art gallery. But in general I'd say Andre Thibault is as good a prospect for your purpose as anyone."

Jefferson cleared his throat. He placed his forefinger on his upper lip and tapped it in a way Ian thought indicated the desire to keep a comment in—or perhaps force a statement out. Which possibility was correct Ian did not have time to learn, since at that moment Rankin knocked on the door and announced the arrival of Colonel Wakefield and Huw.

A battered convoy had limped into the river Mersey and Geneva was picking up wounded men and transporting them to hospital. One group were survivors from a torpedoed tanker, plucked from the flames of an oil-covered sea. The worst of the burned sailors had not lived to be hauled aboard other ships in the convoy. The survivors had minor burns; their faces were oil-blackened, dazed. Was there such a thing as a minor burn?

Geneva drove the ambulance and tried not to imagine Matt in a ship being set afire or sunk by German U-boats. She had regretted a hundred times sending him that impulsive letter, written in a moment of desperate loneliness, asking him to come back. She had a two-day weekend this week, so would be going home to Saxon Hall. She had missed Dulcie and Ian desperately and was looking forward to seeing them.

Ian had come to Liverpool and they'd had a hurried lunch together one day. She had been glad to hear Huw was working as a civilian interpreter at the nearby army installation and surprised to learn that Colonel Wakefield had also turned over part of the abbey to be used as a billet for some of the officers. He'd spent so much time and money restoring the abbey, she couldn't imagine him allowing army officers all over it.

Her shoulders ached and her feet seemed permanently attached to accelerator and brakes. Driving her car on short trips had not prepared her for handling the much heavier ambulance for hours at a time. She drove down Water Street toward the docks for what she hoped would be her last trip of the day.

All of the injured had been taken to hospital, and she was asked instead to take some of the sailors who had been picked up after being in the water to a naval outfitter on Church Street so they could be given clothing. Most were nearly naked, covered by blankets. They crowded into the ambulance, and two of them jammed themselves in front with the driver. Their tired eyes brightened as they received the full force of Geneva's sympathetic smile.

"Reckon it was worth it, getting my ship shot out from under me," one man drawled in an accent that caused Geneva to tighten her grip on the wheel. "I think I jes' fell in love."

"You're an American?" she asked.

"A Texan," he corrected with a grin. "How'd you guess?"

She smiled. "I have an American half-brother. I don't suppose there were any other Americans on your ship?"

"No, ma'am. I figured I was the only crazy man aboard. Back home the folks worry about England being all alone against Hitler, but nobody seems to be doing anything about it. Figured maybe I'd lend a hand."

"We're grateful," Geneva murmured, braking to avoid two small children crossing the road. In the long months of the phony war many evacuees had returned from their banishment to the country. "But you're certainly not the only American helping out. I'm expecting my brother's ship any day . . . of course, I don't know when."

"Hope he makes it okay, ma'am," the Texan said as he alighted.

Geneva thanked him and settled back to wait while the group went into the naval outfitters'. She was worried that she had not heard from Matt but reasoned that he must be on his way to England. Her nerves were taut and she counted the hours until she reached the peace and tranquility of Saxon Hall.

Early the following Saturday morning she took a bus from Liverpool. There was no ration of petrol for civilian use. Rankin had found an ancient cart in the stables and harnessed one of the horses to pull it to come and meet her and take her the last couple of miles from the bus stop to Saxon Hall. His face twitched alarmingly the moment he saw her, but Geneva knew from the twinkling eyes that the involuntary movements were because of excitement, not stress. He burst forth with the news the moment he saw her. "Oh, Miss Geneva, a telegram came from the Red Cross just before I left. It's Mr. Terry. He's all right. He's a prisoner of war."

Chapter 27

The sky was yellow, the air hot and still. Nothing stirred in the uneasy silence beyond the ramparts of cypress knees marking the boundary of Matt's campsite beside the Mississippi. He could almost hear Specks' voice. "Big storm coming, Matt. Time to get going."

An alligator floated to the surface of the bayou, its snout nudging a delicate blue water hyacinth, and an egret winged overhead, seeking shelter from the open sky. But Matt still sat, fishing rod across his knees, staring moodily across the dusty water. The real storm was half a world away, in Europe, and nothing he did erased it from his mind.

Long ago he and Specks had been caught along the river in a near-hurricane. Surviving it, a false sense of bravado had sent them back to New Orleans, into the glory of Specks' last Mardi Gras parade—and the waiting jaws of DeVore. Matt thought about it as the sound began. At first it seemed to come from the branches of the trees far down the river, as though the swamp itself wailed. Matt recognized it a moment later. The cry of birds—herons, warblers, blackbirds—all of the swamp birds shrieking in unison.

"I heard tell the birds cried out before a big storm. Never heard it though." *Go away, Specks, I don't believe in ghosts.* Matt reached into his backpack and fished out a bottle of whiskey. He'd never been much of a drinker, but the summer of 1940 was surely driving him to the bottle.

The sky was now an angry copper color and the leaves fluttered as the first rain slanted through the trees. The wind roared toward him. He stood up, bottle to his lips, and made his way through a tangle of vines, skirting a great pyramid of resurrection fern, brushed aside ghostly gray tendrils of Spanish moss festooning a lordly cypress. Seconds later he was in a dense growth of sycamore, ash, and cottonwood that formed a vaulted green cathedral over his head, mysterious and sepulchral. He had been here before, but memory refused to recall when.

By the time he reached the skiff he had borrowed, it was too late to escape the fury of the storm and he was forced to backtrack to an abandoned house he had seen a short distance down the river. It had appeared sturdy enough to withstand the wind. The air was now so hot and clammy that it squeezed every last drop of vitality from him. *Hey, Geneva . . . what are you doing now? What would you think of this humid heat—would you be afraid of the swamp? The gators and snakes and bobcats and bears? Hell, got to get a hold of myself. Should have invited Alvin to come with me. Been too long on my own.*

Listen to me, old John Lauren, wherever the hell you are . . . you shouldn't have killed that guy—not even for Specks. 'Cause then you wouldn't have gone to France and met Celine and your only son and heir wouldn't be roaring drunk in a derelict house in the middle of a storm wishing he was dead . . .

What was it all for, anyway? What in hell was it *for?* Back during the Depression when he was a boy and had to go to bed hungry, he had had a recurring nightmare that he was drifting endlessly down a dark river. In the dream he never reached the shore, nor did he sink beneath the black surface of the water. Feeling nothing in the limbo of sleep, he was neither alive nor dead, oblivious to everything but the current, taking him where it would, mindless as a floating log. Waking in a cold sweat, he would prowl the house, searching for something to gnaw on to quiet his growling belly.

He awoke suddenly to find himself in the empty house.

The wind was a continuous shriek, rising and falling. Every few seconds something thudded against the walls or roof of the house, and the windows of the upper story where he sat were already covered with debris. Christ, he hadn't had that dream since he was a kid. It unnerved him more than the storm.

Specks would have said it was a sign he should take note of—that the body and the mind gave us plenty of warning of forthcoming disaster, if we were sufficiently in tune with ourselves to pay heed. Well, it wasn't difficult to recognize what he should *not* do with his life, Matt thought, crossing the empty room to the window. He should not give in to the urge to go back to England and Geneva. She was his sister and she was married, and it didn't take a psychic to see the double madness of that situation.

A chink in the debris over the window afforded a view of a flow of water, tossing uprooted trees and dead animals, a shapeless mass that approached the house and made him glad for the insulating lower floor. Trees surrounding him were now half submerged.

He was beginning to feel that euphoria a violent storm causes, and fought against it. The walls shook under the impact of a tremendous gust of rain-filled air. An explosion and roar from the other side of the house announced that one of the windows had blown in. On the roof a bird screamed and died in the wind.

"Goddamn everything to hell," Matt roared at the top of his lungs. "I live through this I can live through anything."

In the eerie silence that came as the eye of the hurricane settled about him, the echo of his words rang in his head. Specks had said that very same thing, just before he went back for Mardi Gras.

The storm abated the following morning, and by nightfall Matt was driving through the wrought-iron gates of Greenboughs.

Nathan was already in bed, and a sleepy-eyed maid told Matt the storm had kept them awake all the previous night.

"Me too," Matt said. "Where's the mail?"

The pale blue envelope bearing Geneva's copperplate handwriting leaped from the stack of typed business letters and handful of social invitations. Matt tore it open

Dear Matt,

I'm all alone at Saxon Hall tonight . . . exploring, in my mind, the mysterious bonds that unite human beings . . . the forces that divide them. My thoughts are too complex to explain. I'm in the drawing room and the door is open so I can see the grandfather clock . . . it just chimed eleven. I've always hated that clock and especially the eleventh hour—though the one of childhood nightmare was eleven in the morning, November 11.

All at once I realized that Lady Sybil's old monstrosity of a clock is only a symbol for another clock . . . the invisible one that is ticking away our lives . . . that won't stop for anything, doesn't care about whys and wherefores, or meanings and resolutions—it just keeps measuring the time left to us. And when it's gone, what else matters?

Come to me, Matt. Please.

Gennie

Matt sailed aboard an English ship, in convoy, the following week. The ship carried American rifles, machine guns and cannon, World War I equipment purchased and paid for under the "cash and carry" provisions of the Neutrality Act. Matt had argued unsuccessfully with Alvin that they should transport a cargo of guns to England on one of their own ships, telling him of the unarmed constables and Home Guard who stood ready to face highly mechanized German invaders. But Alvin pointed out that a lone ship in mid-Atlantic, even flying an American flag, was a certain target for U-boats.

Unwilling to waste the voyage in idleness, Matt worked as a deckhand. Time would pass more quickly with physical activity to occupy him, and perhaps he'd be too tired to lie awake worrying about all the moral implications of his relationship with Geneva.

They sailed full-steam despite rough seas and gale warnings, constantly checking the deck cargo and keeping an anxious eye on the other ships in the convoy to be sure they were not left behind. The crew were a mixed bag of Englishmen, Norwegians, and a fair number of Hindus. Matt was accepted without question, in the manner of merchant mariners, and he was careful not to mention the Castleton freighters. Somewhere down below, he thought, his grandfather was probably smiling up at him as he toiled as a common seaman.

Two days after joining the Royal Navy escort vessels in

mid-Atlantic, they ran into the expected storm. Heavy seas snapped cables and sent dishes skittering from tables. Every man aboard worked four-on and four-off watches, staggering with one foot on the deck and one on the bulkhead to and from the forecastle to snatch a few hours of uneasy sleep. Matt awoke from his dream of floating down a dark river to an unnerving silence. There was the sound of the wind, and rain pelting portholes, and swells slapping the hull—but there was no reassuring grinding of engines or thudding of screws leaving the water as the ship pitched forward on the heaving seas. The engines had stopped.

The engineers worked all night while the ship rolled helplessly, but the malfunction had not been repaired when a sullen dawn broke over an empty sea. The convoy stopped for nothing, every skipper knew the consequences of dropping out; he would be left behind.

Just before noon the engines throbbed to life and the ship headed after the convoy as fast as the ailing engines would permit.

Night came and they were still alone. Matt went down to the galley before turning in for his four hours' sleep. The cook was a grizzled Hindu named Arshad and he was seated before a formidable plate of beef and rice, a large shaker of curry powder in hand.

"Guess I'm not the only one with a nighttime appetite," Matt said.

Arshad motioned for him to help himself. "Better to have full stomach tonight, just in case," the cook said in his soothing singsong accent. Matt wondered if it was a tone cultivated to placate the tempers of irate sahibs.

"Just in case of what?" Matt asked, picking up a crusty roll and layering beef on it.

"Probably nothing. Tomorrow we catch up with convoy. Anything going to happen, it be tonight. Whatever comes—is our kismet."

"I guess we are sitting ducks tonight. I heard you'd been torpedoed before. That right?"

Arshad chewed a mouthful of food carefully. "You just remember, always go over *opposite* side of ship from torpedo hole. I see men sucked into the hole in the hull. Then, swim away from oil or flame on sea's surface. Stay in the largest group you can—more bodies in water, easier for ships to spot. If there's time, fill your canteen before you go over side.

Thirst will plague you more than hunger. And don't drink
seawater, or urine . . . or blood. It will drive you mad."

"I'll try to remember," Matt promised. "Now how about a
more cheerful topic?"

Matt finished eating and went to his bunk. The trouble with
these short stretches of sleep was that they were filled with
dreams, he thought just before he closed his eyes and
immediately began a confused dream in which Arshad the
cook suddenly became Geneva's neighbor, the aristocratic
Huw, and their skiff was being chased up the Mississippi by a
German U-boat with Terry Saxon riding the deck, sword in
hand, hunting him down.

The roar of the explosion awoke him. He was flung from his
bunk amid unseen flying debris. Somewhere above were
muffled shouts of pain, indistinguishable orders. Great con-
vulsive sighs seemed to come from the ship herself, followed
by wrenching noises and collapsing decks. A portion of the
bulkhead blew in, bringing squirting water.

In the darkness Matt fumbled under his bunk for a life
jacket, but his hand found instead an icy jet of seawater. He
lurched across the sloping deck through a foot of water.
Groping blindly, his hands closed around a steel rail and he
thrust himself upward toward a night sky that met a dizzily
angled top deck.

The ship was going down rapidly, bow first. The deck cargo
had torn loose and was careening about. Some of the pieces
had smashed into men trying to lower boats and they lay
bleeding and moaning. Matt picked up the nearest wounded
man and dragged him to the side just as a second explosion
ripped through the hull, pitching him over the rail.

Cold water, breath-stopping, mind-blocking, closed over
his head. Pinpricks of light exploded in the turbulence-caused
phosphorescence. Something caught his ankle, gripped it,
and pulled him down. He tried to jerk his leg free, but it was
like being held in the coils of a snake. Down, down, endlessly,
his lungs screaming for air.

His foot suddenly connected with a large piece of debris,
and the pressure around his ankle eased. He kicked free and
felt himself rise to the surface. There were sharp pains in his
chest as he gasped for air, then a rush of seawater from his
mouth.

The sea around him was filled with bodies, some dead,
others flailing wildly with arms and legs to escape the pull of

the sinking ship. Flotsam whirled by on a rushing wave. He clutched a sodden floating board and began to swim. The cold was a fire that seared his bones.

He swam until his legs were numb, then floated. The ship was a barely discernible outline, half submerged, with several fires flickering in the stern, which appeared to be almost at a ninety-degree angle. He could taste oil in the water and that sense seemed to be the last one functioning. He forced himself to tread water, keep moving.

Oddly, he was aware of the blood still moving in his veins. As though flesh and muscle and bone were gone, leaving only the veins hung like jellyfish tentacles in the cold sea. He found that if he concentrated hard enough, he could actually feel his blood pump faster, whereas if he let the heaviness of sleep begin to overtake him, the sensation of movement would cease.

The first probing fingers of a steel gray dawn were reaching for the sea when he bumped into a boat and felt hands drag him over the side. He looked up into the unperturbed face of Arshad. "Kismet," the cook said.

Shivering violently, Matt looked at the other occupants of the lifeboat. Three of the Hindus, a young blond Norwegian with blood in his hair, and an Englishman who lay on the bottom of the boat moaning softly. There was space for more and Matt looked at Arshad questioningly.

"Hawser snapped as boat was being lowered," the cook explained. "Dumped all into sea. We swim to boat, like you. Except for two wounded men. They had on life jackets and we saved them—for now."

Matt scanned the gunmetal surface of the sea. There was no sign of other lifeboats, of their ship, or of the submarine that had sunk them. His body ached with cold and fatigue. He put his head down on his arm and slept.

The sun came up, its brilliance against his eyelids awakening him. The man on the bottom of the boat was still moaning. Arshad offered him a flask of water and he took a sip.

There was a ghastly choking sound from the Englishman and the moaning stopped. Matt bent over him, then looked up at Arshad. "Dead. Help me get him over the side. Any of the others speak English?"

Arshad shook his head, taking the dead man's feet as Matt picked up his shoulders. "Tell them to start bailing. We won't stay afloat long if we don't get rid of the water that's seeped in all night long."

There was a sickening thud as the dead man's head struck the side of the boat because of an unexpected swell. He disappeared beneath the surface as the others began to bail water that was red with blood.

"What about fresh water? Food?" Matt asked.

Arshad held his hands palms upward in a gesture of resignation. "Most fell into sea when the cables broke; boat hung sideways for a time. There is enough for this small group for a week if we're careful."

"A week! Smile, you old sinner—we'll be picked up by then."

Arshad's expression remained solemn. "Last trip I torpedoed also. In boat three weeks. Atlantic big ocean—boat small."

Chapter 28

Geneva sat bolt upright in bed, still caught in the grip of a nightmare that faded from memory before she could recapture it. She was in her bed at Saxon Hall. The room looked vast and palatial after so many nights of sleeping in her small Liverpool flat or sitting behind the wheel of the ambulance. Her heart was still thumping madly. She got up and went into the bathroom to splash cold water on her face and thoroughly awaken.

She wondered if her father had returned home yet. She had been disappointed when he went out immediately after dinner on her first night home. They had rejoiced together that Terry was safe, drunk a toast to his speedy return, then Ian had departed without explanation.

When Geneva questioned Rankin, he replied, "The master has been going out at odd times on mysterious little journeys, madame. He works far too hard, in my opinion. There's an army officer, a Captain Jefferson, he sees frequently—the one billeted at the abbey. Mr. Huw works for him too. I thought the master was going off on Home Guard duties, but apparently I was mistaken." Rankin conveyed with a twitch of his nostrils and upraised eyebrow that he disapproved of secrecy, intentional or unintentional deception, and employers who managed to outwit their butlers and keep the nature of certain of their activities to themselves.

Geneva glanced at the clock. Nearly seven, later than she imagined. The days were growing shorter; dark winter mornings and days that ended in midafternoon would soon be here. She dressed and went downstairs, hoping her father had returned from whatever rendezvous he'd had, convinced, despite Rankin's speculation, that it was probably nothing more than a tête-à-tête with Nancy. Perhaps, after all, they knew what they were doing, those two. No prosaic marriage for them. Life was a series of romantic interludes.

Dulcie and her nursemaid were in the morning room playing with wooden blocks. Geneva swept her daughter into her arms, and Dulcie gurgled happily but looked at her mother without recognition. Geneva held the child close and fought the urge to cry. Sometimes, when Geneva was away from her, she thought of Dulcie as a normal baby. It was easier to think that she was just a little slow in learning to walk and talk than to face the truth. But the denial made the reality harder to bear. When Dulcie was in her arms and she was overwhelmed with a fiercely protective love, she wanted to give her child everything, make her a part of the world, and Geneva became angry that no one, not even her mother who loved her so, could make Dulcie whole.

After a few minutes she handed the baby back to her nursemaid and went to the breakfast room, relieved to find her father sitting at the table reading the morning papers. Pale sunlight painted a trellis of light over the room as it moved across the diamond-paned windows. Her father looked up and smiled, held his cheek for a kiss.

He looks tired, she thought, *and preoccupied. He's shut me out of his life in some way. But, of course, he had to—I went away. Absences do that.*

Ian returned her kiss and said, "I've just been reading Ted's account of the air raids down south. He feels Hitler has just lost the war by switching the Luftwaffe to civilian targets—that there'll be no invasion now and that although we English are a bit slow to arouse, the civilian casualties have at last got our dander up to the point we'll really begin to fight. It's a real blood, sweat, toil and tears, à la Churchill type article. Unlike Ted's previous writing. I suspect he's been recruited to write propaganda—but he may be right."

Geneva helped herself to toast and marmalade and sat down opposite her father. The sunlight filling the room had that fragile quality of autumn impermanence and she felt chilly in her linen dress. She had not bought any clothes for herself since rationing began, partly because the standardized "utility" clothing was so depressingly ugly, but mostly because Dulcie was growing so rapidly she needed both of their coupon allowances. Her father had folded up the newspaper and put it down.

"What are you up to, Father?" Geneva asked. "What's all this about some mysterious Captain Jefferson who is billeted at the abbey and whom you see without explaining where or when to Rankin?"

Ian smiled but his eyes were evasive. "Oh, Jeff is just an old friend. I'd run into him occasionally at the club. I put him in touch with the Wakefields, that's all. Now, tell me all you've been doing in the sooty seaport?"

They talked while Geneva ate breakfast, lingered over a pot of tea. Their conversation was warm but not intimate. They both had secrets and each was aware of it. Geneva wanted to confide in him but knew he would be hurt and ashamed for her if she were to tell him that her need for Matt was an endless aching yearning that never lessened, no matter how much she tried to fill her days with work. It was important to her that her father be proud of her. Especially so since she had found out about Nancy. Geneva wasn't sure why.

There had been no reply from Matt, and she was unsure if this was due to the uncertain nature of wartime mail, or to Matt exhibiting better judgment than her own.

"Gennie, have you seen your doctor recently?" her father asked unexpectedly. "Are you taking care of your health?"

"Funny, I was just thinking *you* looked a little tired," she replied. "I suppose we're all feeling the strain—and showing it."

"I'm particularly concerned about meat rationing. You know you're a little anemic. Are you taking the iron tablets the doctor prescribed?"

"I'm healthy as a horse. Don't worry about me."

Her father frowned slightly. "Darling, you know that isn't quite true. I know you hate the thought of your body failing you in any way, but don't rationalize away what needs to be dealt with."

"Are you suggesting I ignore what I don't want to acknowledge? Perhaps I do, sometimes. On the surface at least. I know we have to accept what we can't change. But do we have to dwell on it constantly?"

"Of course not. I suppose I worry about you wearing yourself out driving that ambulance. And I'll admit there are times when it crosses my mind that you and Terry have no son to whom you can leave the estate."

"I thought perhaps that was what was at the back of your mind. Father, when the war's over and Terry is home, we'll worry about heirs."

His eyes searched her face, his expression troubled. "But—"

"Please, Father! I just don't want to talk about it now."

After breakfast Ian retired to his study with the promise that he would rejoin her as soon as he'd gone over some reports from the colliery. Geneva went upstairs to unpack winter clothes and was shaking out a woolen cardigan riddled with moth holes when the telephone rang downstairs. Minutes later she heard her father's step on the stairs. As he knocked and entered the room, she saw the deep sadness in his eyes even before he spoke.

"Oh, dear God, Gennie. The air raids, the casualty lists—"

"Father, sit down. You're white as a sheet. Someone we know has been hurt? Killed?"

"Uncle Dee Dee. A direct hit on his club. Some of the members were trapped in the basement for several hours and eventually were dug out, but he was dead when they reached him. Oh, lord, he should have died in his own bed . . . didn't he deserve that at his age?"

Geneva grasped her father's hands and held them tightly, thinking of the old gentleman swathed in oilskins dragging himself wearily home from Dunkirk, and her insistence that he leave Steadwall Manor on the coast for a safer place.

Her father said, "I shall have to go to the funeral. I must have Rankin see about trains."

"I'll go with you," Geneva said. "I'll call St. John's and tell them I need an extra day or two. They'll understand."

They set about the ritual of calling relatives and friends, unpacking black suits and stockings and coats, and all of the other somber tasks attendant upon death. But there was another name on the previous night's casualty list that was not reported to them until late that afternoon. A German bomber had apparently strayed out of formation, possibly due to engine failure. It had jettisoned its load of bombs over the quiet countryside before crashing. The nursing home had been completely destroyed. Meredith was killed instantly.

Geneva and Ian were numb with shock. They embraced each other wordlessly, trying to keep from giving in to grief and anger in front of the baby and the servants.

London was scarred by bombed buildings and great piles of rubble. Many streets were impassable. Geneva and Ian were appalled by the swollen obituary columns of the newspapers. They did not mention that the dead had been killed in air raids, stating only, ". . . died very suddenly."

The day after Uncle Dee Dee was laid to rest, they attended Meredith's funeral. Before the first handful of earth was dropped onto the casket, the air raid warning sounded. It was ignored as the minister continued with the graveside service.

Bombers droned overhead, bound for the city. Geneva raised tear-filled eyes to see two squadrons of Spitfires take off from a nearby RAF field. They were ludicrously outnumbered by the Luftwaffe, but she said a blasphemous prayer that they would shoot down great numbers of bombers, surprised at the blood lust she felt.

Before the mourners left the churchyard, columns of smoke were visible and the distant din of exploding bombs could be heard. One of Meredith's elderly friends clutched Geneva's arm and nodded toward the sky over London. A German bomber spiraled toward earth, smoke pouring from its tail. "That's one for Miss Meredith," the old man muttered with a grim nod.

Geneva felt a surge of grim satisfaction that the RAF were winning the dogfights despite the odds and thought how much easier it might be to go and fight Germans rather than stay home and worry about those who did. Or to bury their victims. Yesterday Uncle Dee Dee's funeral, today Meredith's. Geneva's grief and depression deepened.

Then something Meredith used to tell her when she was a child came back to her: often when life seemed to have reached its lowest ebb, that was when good fortune was on the way. "There's always something worthwhile on the way to us, if we've the courage to endure and wait for it. Geneva, I sometimes think the most wonderful surprises of all come after a period of the worst despair. Almost as though we're being rewarded for bearing it."

The thought was one to cling to at this moment in her life, Geneva decided as she placed a bouquet of roses and lilies of the valley on Meredith's grave.

Chapter 29

Matt's face was blistered by sun and wind, his body caked with oil. He'd wiped most of the oil from his eyes and so was not half blind with infection as some of the others in the lifeboat were. They'd been drifting for eight days, their water finished two days earlier. His tongue was swelling behind cracked and puffy lips; his throat burned.

The first day they'd sighted several other boats on the horizon and paddled frantically, but a sudden squall blew up, and when the seas subsided they were alone in the vastness of the Atlantic. Arshad and a Hindu named Scrini began an almost trancelike session of meditation and prayer while Matt and a Norwegian, Peder, dangled fishing lines and tried to learn each other's language. Both endeavors were abandoned when the seas began to roil again.

When the meager rations of food were gone, they lay still and silent, conserving strength. Matt's mind felt as numb as his body. All the threads tying him to the past were slowly unraveling. Nothing mattered. Not the past certainly. And the future lay behind a closed curtain. Thoughts occasionally penetrated the continual craving for water. He thought of Specks, then tried not to think of Specks. Arshad said he spoke Gennie's name in troubled sleep and asked if she was his wife. Matt shook his head.

On the ninth day the swells increased and the boat pitched,

standing almost vertically with each wave. Matt took down the blanket-sail they'd rigged and shook Arshad out of his trance. "We've got to find containers to catch rainwater . . . lash ourselves to the boat."

The old cook's head rolled up from his chest and he squinted through oil-ringed eyes at the scudding clouds. "Go to hell, Yank." Matt forced lifeless muscles to obey his brain's command, and eventually Arshad and the others helped. By the time everyone was secure, waves were breaking over them, but there was no rain. Saltwater stung Matt's face and splashed into his mouth. He wanted to swallow but heeded the warning that it would drive him insane.

All night long the storm battered them. Their arms ached from bailing water that came back with each wave. When the rain at last began to fall, mouths were turned skyward. Nothing ever tasted sweeter. But by morning the boat had been tossed so violently that their precious containers were fouled with saltwater. What little rainwater they'd caught was gone the following day.

Time was meaningless. Matt gave up counting days. Some of the others hallucinated. One man pointed to the empty horizon and babbled. Arshad translated, "Jamini thinks he sees a bus coming for us." They restrained him from jumping overboard.

Several nights later Jamini, whom they suspected of drinking seawater, suddenly went berserk, struck everyone who tried to hold him, and leaped over the side. Matt began to tie a line around his waist, but Arshad grabbed his arm. "No. You haven't the strength. He would pull you down. Let him go."

Straining to see through the darkness, Matt couldn't tell which direction Jamini had taken. Slumping back, he was more discouraged than ever, knowing he had just witnessed the ultimate despair. The blackness of the night was like that other darkness that awaited, where thirst ceased to plague and muscles no longer ached nor skin tormented as salt sores formed. He could understand a man's longing for the nothingness of death.

Arshad shook him awake just before dawn. The sea was calm, mirror-still. "Tell me, Yank, do I see something not there? Look to starboard."

Matt raised leaden eyelids. A large shadow on the horizon hovered, unmoving. A faint creaking sound that was not coming from the lifeboat penetrated hearing dulled by oil and sores. Sitting up slowly, Matt stared at the dark shape. "It's a ship. But she's dead in the water."

Arshad aroused the others, prodded them to paddle. The sky lightened and they saw the ship clearly, listing heavily to port. Her decks were deserted. The surrounding water was coated with a film of oil in which life jackets and debris floated. Several life jackets held bloated bodies, probably killed by falling debris or panicked shipmates jumping on their heads. Matt half expected to find it was their own ship, that they'd drifted in a circle and she hadn't sunk. But it was another freighter from their convoy, a torpedo hole in her bow.

"Tie up alongside," Matt said. "Maybe there's water, food aboard."

Arshad looking at the listing vessel doubtfully. "She's sinking slowly, but she's going down."

"Then we haven't much time," Matt muttered irritably. No point in trying to persuade the other Hindus; the pidgin English he'd heard them use aboard ship appeared to be forgotten. He swung stiffly to the ship's rope ladder, wincing as it bit into flesh softened by water.

Peder followed, then Arshad. The ship hissed faintly, shuddered as it swayed slowly back and forth. The eerie sounds sent Arshad back to the side.

"It's certain death back in the boat," Matt said. "There's a chance if we find water." The words were a painful croak. He stumbled across the sloping deck, Peder at his side.

Belowdecks it was almost completely dark and awash with water. They found the galley and the storeroom, water almost shoulder-deep with all sorts of things floating in it. Including two dead bodies that sent Arshad topside again.

They found a water cask and several canteens. A couple of sacks of flour and sugar were of no value, but there was a bag of rice, soaked and swollen. Matt called for Arshad and passed water and rice up to him. Peder wrenched open a jammed door and a large tin floated out. He passed it up to Arshad.

The ship lurched suddenly with another almost human moan. They were flung across the galley. They could hear a fresh stream of water pouring in, somewhere close. Matt fumbled in the darkness, found Peder's shoulder, and shook him, pointing to the small circle of light to indicate they should get out.

Back on deck they heard the men in the lifeboat calling to them. Arshad had already lowered the water cask and bag of rice. He had also found a flask of rum and a tin of biscuits on deck. "We go now. She's going under." He pointed to the side of the ship. "The rope ladder fell into the sea when she settled. They could not catch it in time."

The ship was making more noise than before, and swells were again rising on the surface of the sea. Matt looked around, found a hawser, and tossed it over the side. He nodded for Arshad to go first. The Hindu grasped the steel cable, started to slide, then let go and dropped to the sea. He was not far from the lifeboat and they threw him a line.

Peder was next, sliding the length of the hawser although his features contorted with pain. When Matt began his descent, he understood why as pain ripped through his hands. Their palms bled as they paddled away from the ship. The bow was now awash, the ship wallowing in deepening troughs of water. The hissing sound of escaping air was stronger, as ghostly as a dying breath.

They were less than a hundred yards away when she went down. Matt felt a lump in his throat. Was there any sadder sight than the end of a ship? he wondered as she slid under the gray surface.

Surveying their haul, he saw enough water for several days. The bag of rice. Peder's tin contained flaked fish. Biscuits and rum. They were hard put not to gorge themselves. *Another reprieve,* Matt thought. *Got to get them fishing while they've got the strength.*

With careful rationing the water lasted a week. Strengthened by the rice and canned fish, they diligently dropped lines baited with some of their precious food over the side. The raw fish at first made Matt and Peder vomit, until Arshad said sharply, "Is in your minds. Cut into small pieces. No! Do not throw away the heads. There is water in the eyes."

By the following week Matt and Peder had learned to swallow the eyes too.

Matt thought they must have been in the boat a month when mountainous seas bore down and the boat began to ship dangerous levels of water. Shrieking winds plucked at their lifelines, and they came so near to capsizing that they were washed into the sea and then slammed against the side of the boat. When Scrini failed to clamber back, they grabbed his shoulders to haul him aboard only to find that his skull had been smashed in. They cut his body free and it disappeared.

When darkness fell, Matt realized they were sinking. "She's breaking up," he yelled over the wind's howl. "Hang on to line—planks." *Maybe we can make a raft,* he thought. A huge wave broke over him, exploding into phosphorescent flashes of light. His feet went out from under him and he found himself struggling in the water. He was clutching a coil of rope that snaked away in the rushing sea. Treading water, he hung on to the line, gulping air between breaking waves.

The fury of the storm swept on, leaving rolling seas and inky darkness. He shouted, hoping to hear an answering cry, but the only sound was the fading roar of wind and wave.

"Good-bye Gennie." He wasn't sure if he said the words aloud or if they were inside his head.

Saltwater splashed into his mouth and he held it there a long time before spitting it out. Thirst maddened as the long night wore on, and at last he succumbed to the temptation and swallowed several times. The seawater only increased his thirst and he gulped more. Legs and arms ached and he turned onto his back to rest.

Storm clouds raced across the sky, leaving in their wake a blackness so dense it seemed to press against his face. Eyes stinging from the salt spray, he blinked, thinking he could see a neon light winking at him. No, a star . . . it was a star. A not unpleasant lethargy was stealing over him, crawling over his body, relaxing his limbs. It suddenly seemed very quiet. The star had disappeared. He jerked his head up, realizing his face had been underwater; choked and gasped for breath. A second later he vomited seawater.

All the miseries of his body assaulted him at once. How peaceful it had been, just under the surface. How easy to just slip away. He wasn't going to be picked up; why prolong it? If they couldn't get picked up in a lifeboat, what chance for one man alone?

He floated on his back again, wanting a moment first to collect his thoughts, one last second to think of a love affair that would never be; to wonder why human beings insisted on being the instruments of their own unhappiness. *We deny ourselves . . . find a hundred reasons why we can't have what we want . . . throw up obstacles and barriers and taboos. And in the end . . . for what? For this . . . for release to emptiness, where we'll feel nothing. Gennie, you were right . . . there's*

*only so many minutes on that clock, and when they're
gone . . .*

*Am I delirious? I must be. I could swear I see a steamboat,
paddlewheel churning, colored steam rising from the calliope.
Oh, sure, a Mississippi steamboat in the middle of the Atlantic.
Hallucination. I'm about at the end . . . might as well give up.
How long can I keep swimming before I die of exhaustion
anyway? Better to go now, before the pain gets any worse.*

"*Hang in, Matt. Ah never raised a quitter.*"

Matt's eyes flew open. He had heard Specks' voice so
clearly that he thrashed about in the water, trying to find him.
The rope he held seemed all at once taut, as though there was
something on the other end. He strained to see in the
darkness. Was he still attached to the wreckage of the
lifeboat? He pulled gently on the line, allowed his body to
relax and hang in the water. He didn't sink.

When the dawn peeled the night sky from the horizon, his
hands were gripping the rope so tightly they seemed bonded
to it, skin white, bones standing up sharply. His body felt
buoyant, yet when he scanned the sea around him he saw no
evidence of the lifeboat or any wreckage from it. Just the
length of rope trailing along behind him in the water.

He began to swim, to revive his circulation, not thinking
about the previous night. Some time later he bumped into
something and looked up to see Arshad, bobbing beside him
in a life jacket, several loose planks floating about him. The
old Hindu attempted a smile but his lips were too swollen.
"Still here, Yank? Not your time to die yet."

Matt grabbed a plank, hung over it to rest. "The others?"

Arshad shook his head. Matt thought of the brave and
uncomplaining young Norwegian.

"But we make it, Yank. Look . . . ships coming."

Matt didn't bother to turn his head. It would have required
too much effort and he remembered the steamboat he had
been convinced he saw. Poor old Arshad was probably
hallucinating too.

Arshad began waving his arms and shouting with all of his
remaining strength. Matt heard the throb of the engines and
felt the turbulence in the water before he turned to look at the
approaching convoy.

Chapter 30

October was almost over and November loomed ahead, bleak and ghost-ridden. The days grew shorter. In London and the south the Luftwaffe continued to pound the cities, but the north had so far been spared. Home for a weekend at Saxon Hall, Geneva approached her father with the suggestion that they donate the grandfather clock to some servicemen's club.

"If it's still here on my birthday, I shall go mad thinking of all those two minutes of silence we used to suffer every November eleventh, and this year will be worse than ever, because . . ."

"Because you'll be mourning Meredith and Uncle Dee Dee," her father finished for her. "By all means, give it away. I don't know why we didn't heave it out after Mother died."

They walked across the marble floor to survey the clock, glowering at them from its alcove.

"It's eerie how it just keeps going," Geneva said. "I know Rankin pulls up the weights each day and has it cleaned regularly, but—" She broke off, wanting to broach another subject that had been on her mind. "Father, would you like to go out for lunch today? Remember that old inn where we used to go when I was a little girl and I'd done something to make Grandmother angry and you'd spirit me away from her wrath?"

"The Boar's Head." Ian smiled, remembering.

"You could invite Nancy to join us," she said carefully, not looking at him.

"Yes," Ian said. "That would be nice. I'll slip down to the village and tell her to put her bonnet on. Never could get her to let me install a telephone. She said her neighbors don't have phones, none of the villagers do except for the postmistress. Nancy was afraid of what people would think."

Geneva walked with him down the driveway. All of the wrought iron had been torn down and donated for the war effort, so the gatekeeper's lodge now stood beside two stone columns that no longer held the gates that had shut out the world.

There was no need for her to tell her father that the three of them having lunch together was both an apology and a gesture of acknowledgment that Geneva understood and approved of Nancy.

"Huw came over last night after you left." She had come to expect her father to be gone much of the time she was home. "He was full of himself. Hinting about all sorts of hush-hush stuff he's working on. Even suggesting he might be instrumental in helping Terry in some way."

"Several shot-down RAF pilots were recently returned from France," her father said. "But don't let him get your hopes up about Terry. It's one thing helping a shot-down flyer who hasn't yet been picked up by the Germans, and quite another getting a POW out of a camp. And Huw's part in the intelligence operation is peripheral in the extreme. He was trying to impress you."

"Yes, of course," Geneva murmured, wondering not so much about her father's apparent knowledge of the secret operations across the woods and in the abbey, but at that veiled hint that he knew more than he was saying. She had met Captain Jefferson briefly one evening and had been oddly disturbed by him. "Will you and Nancy come back for me, or shall I meet you somewhere?"

"Well, we'll have to ride over on our bikes. Perhaps you could borrow one from one of the servants and meet us at the Boar's Head. It would save a double trip for me."

And preclude Nancy having to come to Saxon Hall, Geneva thought. But it made sense, since the cars were laid up for the duration because there was no civilian ration of petrol.

Geneva walked back toward the house after her father disappeared down the lane in the direction of the village. It was a fine morning, but the sun was low in the sky and the air brisk. She was envious of her father and Nancy. No matter what lay before them, they shared precious moments together. Months had gone by since she had last seen Matt, yet the longing for him had not diminished.

She had sent letters and parcels to Terry, care of the Red Cross, but she had no idea how he was faring either. She felt very lonely.

The staff of Saxon Hall was now reduced to Rankin, Cook, Dulcie's nursemaid, a young scullery maid, and an elderly gardener and his grandson. They had closed most of the rooms, and the house was taking on a forlorn and shabby appearance. She walked under the trees lining the drive, some still clinging to their leaves, red and gold and saffron in the sunlight. A pair of Land Army girls strolled by with hoes over their shoulders. They smiled shyly.

Very little of the rolling lawns were left; most of the carefully nurtured soil had been given up to vegetable gardens that were tended by Land Army girls who were billeted in the servants' quarters. Some of them had formerly been shorthand-typists and salesgirls wanting to escape the city, and there were comical stories about their misconceptions of country life. Others were fresh-cheeked farm girls, cheerful and willing to work in all weather, not averse to mucking the pigs that now inhabited much of the stable area.

A shaft of sunlight broke through the trees and blinded Geneva for an instant. She paused, her spirits suddenly rising. A sense of expectation, of something about to happen, came out of nowhere. Where moments earlier she had been filled with sadness, she now found herself quickening her pace toward the house.

Dulcie's nursemaid was feeding the child in the breakfast room. "Oh, Miss Geneva, St. John's Ambulance people have been trying to get you on the phone. They say will you please call them back right away?"

Geneva felt let down. She flipped through the letters on the tray, but there was nothing from Matt or from the Red Cross about Terry. She picked up the telephone receiver and asked the operator to connect her with Liverpool.

The harried St. John's clerk who answered the call had to track down the person who placed it. Geneva waited so long for someone to come back on the line that she missed the first words of his message.

". . . the convoy had survivors they'd picked up from a

couple of their own ships. Usual—fractures and burns and oil all over them. Some of them blind from infections in their eyes. But most remarkable was that they picked up two men who had been torpedoed five or six weeks earlier. Geneva, are you sitting down? One of the two refuses to let anyone touch him until we contact you. He says his name is Matthew Lauren."

Everything rushed away, came slowly back. His voice was low, husky. "Gennie? Gennie, it's Matt."

She was laughing and crying. "I'll be there in an hour. Oh, Matt. Matt!"

It took longer than an hour to reach Liverpool because of disrupted train and bus schedules. Geneva waited all afternoon for a train that arrived jammed with servicemen, and she was among those turned away by the conductor. The buses were running once an hour and she had just missed one. She stood in a long queue in an agony of dread that it too would be full when it reached the village. When it arrived, fifteen minutes late, a pert young female conductor, newly recruited to fill a job formerly done by a man, declared, "One only, please. I've already got too many standing inside."

Geneva was second in the queue, but a young soldier ahead of her stood aside. "I'm just going back to camp, love. You can go," he offered with a grin. She was ridiculously grateful, almost sobbing her thanks.

By the time she reached the hospital, it was dark. The ward sister at the desk in the dimly lit corridor looked over her list of patients in response to Geneva's query. A comfortable, caring hush hung in the air as nurses went silently about their duties, settling down wards full of patients, speaking quietly to visitors and doctors and each other.

"D Ward, down to the left," the ward sister said. "He put up a bit of a struggle, but we managed to clean most of the oil off him and treat his sores. He's had some gruel and he's fighting to stay awake until you get here. You can go right in."

Matt was in the first bed, a curtained screen around him proclaiming him to be the last admitted to that ward. Geneva tiptoed to the side of the bed, unsure if he was asleep. His blistered eyelids flickered and he struggled to try to sit up. "Gennie . . ."

She enfolded him in her arms, just holding him, too overcome to speak. His body trembled and she released him, pushed him down gently on the pillow. Tears streamed down her cheeks as she saw his burned face, the cruel sores on arms and hands.

"No, don't cry, Gennie," he whispered. "I'm okay, honest. I'll just rest tonight, then tomorrow we'll go away, just the two of us."

She sat beside his bed, holding his hands, speaking softly, trying to ease his passage to exhausted sleep. When at last his eyes closed, she gently unwound his fingers from hers and sat watching him. He lay still for a short time, apparently sleeping deeply, but then his legs began to move, doggedly pushing his feet up and down. His fingers curled with determination around some unseen object.

Oh, God, Geneva thought, *he thinks he's still in the sea. He's treading water, trying to stay afloat. Oh, my poor darling, what hell have you been through?* She bent over him, whispering in his ear. "You're safe, Matt. You're on dry land, here with me. Matt, my darling, I love you. You're safe."

Matt slept for forty-eight hours and awakened demanding to be released from hospital immediately. He was told he would have to remain for several more days of observation. Yes, he would be fed shortly. A bland diet to start. Mrs. Saxon would be allowed back during the normal visiting hours, as he was not on the critical list.

That evening when Geneva arrived she was wearing a uniform as unfamiliar to him as the tiny purple daisies of the bouquet she brought for him. His strength was returning and he was full of questions that she laughingly tried to answer simultaneously. "It's the uniform of the St. John's Ambulance Brigade. Would you believe we had our origins in the eleventh century? When military hospitals came into being along traveled routes, pestilence and disease felling more Crusaders than the Saracens. In those days St. John's was called the Knights Hospitallers of the Order of St. John, surviving through the centuries as the St. John's Ambulance Brigade. I'm an ambulance driver. The flowers are Michaelmas daisies. I picked them at the Hall this morning in the one bit of land not producing vegetables. And yes, I do have the weekend off." Her smile faded. "But no, Father doesn't know you're here. I haven't told him. He thinks I had an urgent call to return to my duties."

Matt nodded, understanding why. "I must let them know

I'm okay. Nathan at Greenboughs, and Alvin Dooley—" he began.

Her hand closed over his on the white sheet. "I took care of it." Her eyes were so luminous with love that he wanted to take her into his arms, despite the nurse at the next bed adjusting a bottle of glucose over an inert arm. He swallowed, eyes fixed on Geneva, willing the minutes to fly until they were alone.

She was waiting for him when he was discharged from the hospital. Grinning, he held up his arms to display the mismatched, ill-fitting, donated clothing he wore. British army trousers, a civilian shirt, and a navy jacket. She smiled and said, "You're the most handsome man in the world, no matter what you wear. Come on, I've a taxi waiting."

The taxi took them to the Pier Head, and Matt expressed mock alarm when she steered him toward the gangway leading to the floating quay where river-crossing passengers awaited the busy ferryboats crossing back and forth between Liverpool and the Wirral peninsula. "I'm not sure I'm ready for another shipwreck," he said as the New Brighton ferry nudged the quay. "What if we're torpedoed?"

Geneva placed her hand solemnly over her heart. "I absolutely guarantee safe passage. Come on, let's go up on the top deck. I managed to get two days off and we aren't going to waste a second of it."

"You have a destination in mind, I take it?" he inquired as they emerged into a chill wind and cold salt spray on the top deck. "I mean, I'd hate to think I'd turned into some latter-day Flying Dutchman, doomed to sail endlessly . . ."

She slipped her arm through his and snuggled closer, her cheeks pink from the bite of the wind. "A small hotel in New Brighton, practically deserted at this time of year; that's why I chose it. Let's walk around the deck before we freeze."

New Brighton proved to be a small Coney Island type resort, with a stretch of deserted beach and a cluster of cafes, gift shops, arcades, and carnival rides, all retired for either the duration of the winter or the war, or both. The hotel was a Georgian mansion with a small paved courtyard in front on a street of similar structures. Some of the rooms would have a view of the mouth of the river and the Irish Sea. They crossed an empty foyer to the reception desk, where a gray-haired old lady blinked at them nearsightedly and greeted them with the stern reminder that everyone was to observe the five-inches-of-water-in-the-bathtub rule. It certainly did help the war effort.

Geneva took the pen from her outstretched hand before Matt could accept it. "I'll register for us, darling," she said. She looked into the proprietress' horn-rimmed glasses, trying to find her eyes beneath the thick lens. "My husband is still weak from his ordeal. He was torpedoed."

The old lady's expression relaxed and she murmured sympathetically. Geneva boldly signed the register "Mr. and Mrs. M. Lauren." She had brought an overnight bag, and Matt's few personal belongings were in a paper bag.

"The lift isn't working," the proprietress said. "But it's only three flights up. Nothing for a young couple like you."

The room was cozily old-fashioned, with a knitted patchwork quilt on a high double bed, a cushioned windowseat in the bay window, and a marble-topped washstand complete with porcelain bowl and pitcher. A rather odd-looking chair with a tapestry seat stood beside the bed. Matt peered at it, head on one side, trying to decide what was strange about it.

Geneva blushed, reached out, and lifted the tapestry seat. It concealed a chamber pot. "The bathroom is down the hall," she said, not meeting his eye. "But don't you dare . . ."

They laughed and Matt caught her about the waist and pulled her to him. "I can't believe you're here," he said huskily. "I'm going to wake up and find myself back in that boat."

"I'm starving," Geneva said. "Let's have lunch and then go for a walk along the beach."

Sensing her nervousness, Matt nodded and released her.

They found a cafe open and had fish-paste sandwiches, which Matt valiantly ate without comment. The hotel dining room opened only for breakfast and dinner, they were informed, somewhat reproachfully. Then they walked down the steps to the beach and kicked off their shoes. The sand was icy cold. The tide had gone out, exposing algae-covered rocks and pools teeming with marine life. Picking their way carefully over the slippery rocks, they examined several tide pools, moved on to the hard ridges of sand left by the retreating tide.

Geneva said, "It must seem like a busman's holiday, Matt, I know—bringing you here. But it's close to Liverpool, yet remote somehow, in that way a summer resort is in winter. I wanted to be away from everything and everyone."

He took her hand, warming it in his. "It's perfect. Well . . . except could you maybe arrange for it to be thirty degrees warmer?"

They dined by candlelight. There were a few elderly guests and one other young couple, an airman and a girl who was close to tears. Matt had no idea what he ate. He stood up and took Geneva's hand, holding her fingers tightly all the way up the three flights of stairs.

In their room Geneva said, "The maid hasn't been in to turn the bed down, and the blackout curtains aren't closed." Her voice shook slightly. She paced about, not looking at him.

Matt turned the key in the lock. With the solemn dedication of a gladiator he saluted the window, pulled the cord to close the heavy black drapes, then flipped the patchwork quilt back from the bed with a single sweeping gesture. He gave a ceremonial bow, then sat down majestically on the commode-chair.

Geneva collapsed, laughing, at the edge of the bed. "Oh, Matt, is it you, or are all Americans so wonderfully droll? When I'm with you I feel so lighthearted. You have a marvelous knack for finding the funny side of the most serious situation."

His dark eyes held hers for a long moment before he replied. "I know just how serious this is for you, Gennie. Perhaps I'm clowning around because . . . I don't want you to be afraid of me. We don't have to do anything, but just lie in each other's arms, be together. I don't know how to tell you how I feel, the love I have for you . . . the desire that has nothing to do with lust—it's a part of all the ways I want to express to you that you are my whole and entire reason for living. But Gennie, I don't want to do anything to cause you pain or embarrassment or—"

"Matt, I love you," she said softly. "I want you to make love to me."

He got up slowly and went to her, drew her up into his arms, and kissed her lips, allowed his hands to drift over her back. "Oh, God, Gennie, I love you so much . . . stop me before I say something crazy, something that's been said so many times it's got to be a cliche, yet it's never been said before, because there was never you and I . . . until this moment. No one ever loved like this, not since time began. I've waited for you for so long." He reached up and pulled the combs from her hair so that it flowed about her shoulders in a shimmering curtain that reminded him of a moonlit field moving in a soft summer breeze. Fragments of half-forgotten poems hovered in the back of his mind and he wasn't sure if he murmured them against her hair. When he breathed he drew in her scent, and when she sighed he felt her heart beat.

His fingers slipped around to the front of her blouse and he unbuttoned it slowly, then unhooked her skirt, not hurrying, because this night was destined for a special place in memory. When she was naked, he picked her up and laid her on the bed, and she watched shyly as he removed his own clothes. He knew instinctively that she had never looked at a man before. She had married one man and borne a child by another, but she was as virginal as a temple sacrifice. He was her first and only lover. It was all there, in her eyes, as he went to her and lay beside her.

"Matt . . . the light," she whispered.

He reached over and switched off the bedside lamp. The room was plunged into deepest darkness. His hand traveled the wall until he found the blackout curtain cord. The curtain fell back to allow a rising crescent moon to dust the bed with silver light and find the creamy perfection of her body. Bending to kiss her lips, he sighed like a man who comes to sweet clear water after crossing the desert.

Stroking her hair, tracing the slender column of her throat with a fingertip, he said, "Gennie, I'm so afraid of hurting you. Stop me . . . if—"

For answer her arms went around his neck and her mouth searched for his. Her kiss was innocent, yet promised sensuality. It told him she loved and wanted him, that she was without fear.

He made love to her slowly, his touch gentle, his kisses tentative, until he was sure of her response, holding back his own blinding need, controlling his desire until she could catch up with him.

For Geneva it was as though she had just been born. She was running down a long tunnel and it was filled with lovely warm winds and floating petals and drifting music and the sweet musky scent of the earth itself. She was borne along on a current of caresses that inflamed her senses, and her mouth tasted fiery wine and she was lost in a spinning universe of exploding stars that was exciting and abandoned and filled with the promise of some heady peak not yet reached.

She could hear herself murmuring his name, moaning

softly as he kissed her breasts and inner thighs; could hear him tell her that her skin was like silk and whisper his love and his need, but she no longer knew or cared where she was or who she was, because she was part of him and they were earth's last living things. When he began to enter her, so gently and carefully, there was no pain or embarrassment or shame, no sense that this could be anything but beautiful and right. And at the end of the journey was fulfillment so heart-stopping that she felt its aftershocks long after passion had ebbed and he held her in a tender embrace.

The evening was still just beginning, and they talked, then made love again and slept briefly and awakened to pour out their hearts to each other again. Eventually, because she sensed his unspoken questions, she told him what he wanted to hear.

"Matt, I didn't know how it would be. I *was* afraid, but you were so patient and loving. I want you to know—that other time—when I conceived Dulcie . . . I didn't really know what was happening. He hit me—I was half unconscious—and afterward I had only fragments of memories. It was so different that I can't even imagine the two experiences being even remotely similar. I'm not saying this very well. I no longer remember him clearly, and what he did seems as though it happened to someone else. But more than that— tonight you gave me back something I didn't know I'd lost. Oh, darling, am I making any sense at all?"

"Yes, Gennie, oh, yes," Matt breathed.

Chapter 31

Reality returned shortly after midnight. Geneva awoke to the sound of the air raid siren. Matt was lying propped on one elbow, looking down at her. She sat up, hearing the distant throb of aircraft engines. "I must go. I'll be needed," she said.

"Gennie, no. You have the weekend off." He tried to catch her wrist as she slipped out of bed, missed her, and stumbled after her. The room was fiercely cold.

She closed the blackout curtains before turning on the bedside lamp. "Matt, we haven't had any air raids yet, not in the north, but those planes are German. I was in London recently when the bombers flew overhead." She began to dress rapidly. "Their engines pulsate—sound quite different from ours."

"One night, Gennie? Is that all we get?"

"I volunteered to be an ambulance driver and I must go. Why don't you stay here? I'll call you as soon as I can get away."

"How will you get back to Liverpool? Assuming that's where the Luftwaffe is heading?"

"The ferries run all night from Birkenhead. I'll have to get there somehow—walk if I have to."

He reached for his clothes. "I'll go with you."

"Matt, I wish you wouldn't. You've been through a terrible ordeal and I want you to rest. Besides, what will you do? They won't let you ride in the ambulance with me."

"All right, I can at least see you safely on the ferry. I'll go with you as far as Birkenhead. Then we'll play it by ear."

The hotel proprietress solved the problem of getting to Birkenhead by loaning them a pair of rusting bicycles. They rode along the waterfront until the bombers reached the river and the docks on the opposite bank exploded into fire and billowing smoke. An air raid warden stopped them then, ordering them to the nearest public shelter, a solid-brick structure with a foot of concrete for a roof.

Matt paused before entering, looked across the river. The skyline over Liverpool was brilliant with sweeping searchlights, hanging flares dropped by the bombers to illuminate their target, and the flashes of exploding bombs. Ghostly silver barrage balloons drifted upward, and antiaircraft batteries came to life in staccato accompaniment to the whine of planes and bombs. The flashing lights and glow of fires were reflected on the dark surface of the water so that the scene seemed like a surrealistic depiction of the end of the world.

There were few people in the air raid shelter. A pair of foreign seamen, not quite drunk; an old man with bicycle clips on his trouser ankles who looked as though he were returning from an evening job; and two middle-aged nurses no doubt on their way to a hospital. They all smiled sheepishly at one another.

"Most people have their own shelters," Geneva explained. "Steel Anderson shelters if they have a garden to bury them in, or the indoor Morrison shelter if they haven't. I suppose we were getting too complacent up north—thought we'd never have to use them."

"It looked like all the action was on the other side of the river," Matt said. "Maybe we should just go back to the hotel? Better than standing up in here for the rest of the night."

Geneva nodded. "I probably won't get a ferry—even if we can run the gauntlet of air raid wardens between here and Birkenhead. As soon as this warden turns his back, we'll slip out and find our bikes."

Returning to the hotel, they were intercepted by the proprietress and sent to join the other guests in the basement. The next morning they returned to a scarred and still smoking Liverpool.

* * *

Now the Luftwaffe returned nightly as soon as it was dark. The short English winter days meant that the air raids began as early as four in the afternoon. Geneva was put on twelve-hour shifts that frequently lasted even longer. In between she returned to her flat where Matt waited for her. They made love, but the rapture had been muted by a hungry need that had to be satisfied too swiftly, a snack instead of a banquet, because Geneva had to go back on duty or was so tired Matt would find her asleep before she had undressed for bed. He would quietly remove her clothes and lie beside her, silently cursing the war and every other intrusion that came between them. She was his, but she was not his.

He felt guilty too that he lived off her, including sharing her rationed food. That he would have to return home was inevitable. He needed clothes, money. Besides, in a land where it seemed everyone was employed in the war effort, he felt like a parasite. The idea of another Atlantic crossing through the U-boat wolf packs brought a cold knot to the pit of his stomach, but there was nothing else for it.

Then one late afternoon, when he was prowling the shops for unrationed food, he was caught in an air raid and had to spend the night in a public shelter. Geneva was working. The next morning when he returned to her flat the building was a pile of rubble.

When Geneva came off duty, she was beyond caring. Exhaustion was written in the dark smudges under her eyes and the tired lines of her brow. "I've got the weekend off, fortunately," she said wearily. "I really should go to Saxon Hall, see how Father and Dulcie are."

"I must go home too, Gennie. There are things I must do. But I'll be back as soon as I can."

They wrapped their arms around each other and stood beside the bomb debris in a long, wordless embrace. They had always known another parting was inevitable.

Geneva held on to him as though she were drowning. There was no need for him to know she had been given time off because Dulcie wasn't well. She couldn't let herself think about U-boats and torpedoes, of Matt crossing those deadly waters again. Sometimes there was nothing to do but endure.

She went with him to the docks, and he signed on a freighter. Few ships had full crews these days. She didn't wait until he sailed, but took the bus directly from the Pier Head to Saxon Quarry.

Entering the Hall, Geneva was confronted by Dr. Evans descending the staircase. He stopped, one hand on the carved balustrade, and regarded her silently. Geneva recalled that the younger doctors who had formerly treated the family had both gone into the army. She had not been face to face with Dr. Evans since he had refused to abort Dulcie. She searched his expression to try to fathom what he was thinking. An atmosphere of diffused embarrassment seemed to hang between them. Did he wish now that he had not allowed Dulcie to be born? Did he even remember how she had begged him to end the pregnancy?

He said, "Your daughter has a bad cold, some fever, and congestion in her chest. There's a slight inflammation of the ears that will require watching. There's no cause for alarm. Rankin, however, really should be in hospital."

"Rankin? I wasn't informed he was ill."

"He fell down the stairs last night. Broke his leg. I've put on a cast, but he's an old man and sometimes the shock of a fall and a fracture can cause complications. Especially if he catches the cold Dulcie and Cook and the nursemaid have. However, he's refused to leave Saxon Hall."

"Thank you. I'll go to him as soon as I've looked in on my daughter." *Poor old Rankin, he probably feels we'll sink without him,* Geneva thought, *and intends to run the Hall from his bed.*

The doctor had reached her side. She noticed that he avoided meeting her eyes. She was tempted to say, "It's all right, Doctor, I'm glad I have Dulcie. She's brought so much love into my life." But she merely asked for instructions on the care of the two patients, listening to his advice, then held the door as he departed.

Dulcie was deep in a fevered sleep, but Rankin flushed with embarrassment that Geneva was seeing him in bed in his nightshirt. He assured her he was quite all right, her father had left the Hall only minutes before her arrival and had gone to the village to try to enlist the aid of a woman to help with nursing chores.

Her father returned briefly to check on the invalids and tell her he'd persuaded a woman to come in. He squeezed Geneva's arm. "Glad you're home, Gennie. Sorry, I've got to leave again." He gave her a tired smile. "Ships that pass in the night."

"Yes, we are, aren't we? I'll take care of everything. See you at dinner?"

"I'm not sure—I'll try."

But he didn't return all evening, and at length Geneva went to bed, feeling depressed. It wasn't fair; she was in love for the first time in her life and she wanted to relive in her mind every minute she had spent with Matt, recalling the way he smiled, the tenderness of his touch, every word he had uttered—but there was no time. She had not even had time to miss him. It was as if part of her basked in warm sunlight while another part was buffeted by icy winds. There was the magic world of being in love, and there was the reality of a world torn apart by bombs and death. There had been times when she thought she could not bear the suffering of the maimed and burned air raid victims she took to hospital. The children were the worst . . . oh, God, the children . . . why had their parents brought them back from the safety of the country? But, of course, many of the young evacuees had simply been too miserably homesick. Some had run away, and there were harrowing stories of youngsters trying to make their way back to their parents.

The previous night an air raid warden and two police constables had turned her away from a church in the Edge Hill neighborhood that had received a direct hit. There were fifty people in the cellar, many of them children, and there was no way to reach them before they suffocated. Their haven would become their tomb.

Every time she saw a mangled child, she thought of Dulcie, of the anguish of the parents. She turned restlessly in bed, trying to drive away images too cruel to allow sleep; clinging desperately to her last memory of Matt, looking down at her from high on the deck of the ship, his black hair blowing in the wind, his broad shoulders straining the borrowed jacket. The day had been filled with gray drizzle, and they had detoured around so many debris-filled streets. She fell at last into uneasy sleep.

She awoke thinking she was back in her Liverpool flat, but the wail of the air raid sirens that had broken her sleep was a distant one, miles away. The eerie shriek echoed across the surrounding fields and woods and she sat up in bed, thinking the winds must be just right, or the night particularly still, to hear the warning here, so far into the country.

A quick check of the nursery disclosed that neither Dulcie nor her nursemaid had awakened. Back in her own bed, Geneva was just drifting off to sleep again when she heard the drone of a plane, coming in low over the woods.

Chapter 32

Dr. Evans had been making a late call on one of his patients who lived on a farm several miles from Saxon Quarry and had just reached the woods bordering Saxon Hall when the lone plane came out of the dark horizon.

At the same instant he saw the flash of light from the ground. It came from the direction of the army installation. The doctor thought at first it was another of their planes making a practice run to drop parachutists to the field, since this activity was no longer a secret in the village. But they didn't usually light the landing area, since there would be no lights for agents dropped behind enemy lines.

Bewildered, and suddenly apprehensive, the doctor slowed down. A moment later the first bombs fell, some exploding in the woods and others on the landing field. Two fires started immediately. The plane circled and came back. This was no lost bomber jettisoning his load. He was after the army installation, and by God, someone had shown him where it was.

He braked to a complete stop as a dark figure emerged from the woods and hesitated for an instant before plunging through the hedge on the other side of the lane. In the pinpricks of light allowed to show through blacked-out headlights, it was difficult to be sure, but the man who darted across the lane was tall, lean, black-haired. Huw Wakefield was the only man the doctor knew who wore his hair that long. In the village it was whispered that if Huw had remained in India, he would never have cut his hair but worn a turban at all times.

The side road leading to the abbey was only a little farther down the lane. Dr. Evans jammed the accelerator to the floor and roared away. A man on foot could cut through the fields and be there before a car, but if he hurried . . .

Oblivious to the bumps in the rutted lane, the doctor took the corner with reckless speed. The German bomber was diving again, directly overhead. It swept over the car and went in low over the abbey. The sound of bombs whining to earth brought the car to an abrupt stop. The doctor slid from the driver's seat, rolled into the ditch, and buried his face in dried leaves as the ground shook with the roar of the explosions.

For a man his age, stiff with arthritis, he told himself he had reacted with astonishing agility. Incredible what a surge of adrenaline will do for the human body. Now it was imperative that he be sure who that man on foot racing toward the abbey was.

He threw himself behind the wheel and went hurtling toward the smoke-shrouded abbey. Within the smoke were flickering tongues of flame. As he approached he could just make out one end of the cloisters. Several of the arches were still standing; the rest had collapsed and lay beneath a pall of dust and smoke, crumbled almost to powder. The abbey had received two, perhaps three direct hits. The incendiaries would finish the job.

Dr. Evans was so appalled at the total destruction that he did not at first see Huw Wakefield. Huw stood with his back to the approaching car, and the sound of the engine was lost in the roar of flames and the fading sound of the plane's engines. Huw watched as another wall fell, sending up dust and mortar flakes to join the smoke. His hands were hanging at his sides, each holding an electric torch.

The doctor stopped the car and flung open the door. "Where is your grandfather? Is anybody in there?" he shouted.

Huw's head jerked around as he shoved the two torches into his pockets. "No. There's no one here. My grandfather and Higgins are away, visiting friends."

"What about the army officers you had billeted here?"

"They went down south for the weekend. There's no one here but me."

"And me . . . you bloody flamin' traitor." They both turned to see an old man wearing an overcoat over a nightshirt hobbling toward them.

"What are you doing here?" Huw demanded coldly. "I specifically told you there would be no need for you to work this weekend since everyone would be away." He turned to Dr. Evans. "He's a handyman who works for us occasionally. I don't know what he's doing here."

"Sleeping in the lodge, that's what. And at the window when you flashed those lights at the Jerry plane. You was over there in the field, flashing lights at the abbey. May God forgive you, Master Huw, for what you've done this night."

Huw said, "The man's a halfwit."

"You did have torches in your hands just now."

"To light my way across those blasted fields—" Huw began, but his words were lost in another series of explosions a mile or two away in the direction of the village.

The three dropped instinctively to the ground. As Dr. Evans lay there he thought of two things. One was that if Huw was indeed a German agent, then he and the handyman had better tread warily. It would be prudent not to accuse Huw now, but to inform the army at the first opportunity of what they had seen. Lying on the cold earth, listening to the plane's engine fade away, the doctor also thought of almost two decades of painstaking reconstruction that had gone into restoring the abbey. If, as they said in the village, it had been a shrine to the memory of Huw's father and an atonement for all of the buildings the old colonel had blown up during his army career, then there was a certain irony in tonight's events.

The plane was turning, coming back this way. No doubt now that this was a planned target. At the doctor's side, Huw lay propped on his elbows, searching the sky with eyes that mirrored the flames of his grandfather's endeavors. *You hated him that much,* the doctor thought, amazed as always at the depths of human passions. *You blamed him for your mother's suicide—for your own alienation from the world? Or did you strive for acceptance for your mixed blood only to have your grandfather withdraw even further from you?* Whatever the motives, there was little doubt that Huw Wakefield had chosen the ultimate revenge on the fiercely patriotic old warrior. How would the old man live with the knowledge that his grandson was a traitor to his country?

The first stick of bombs had jolted Geneva out of bed, and the floor still shook from the blast as she clutched the bedpost for support until the shock wave passed. Plaster fell from the ceiling and there was the sound of glass shattering behind the blackout screens.

Then she ran for the nursery, meeting her father halfway along the landing.

"I'm going to turn off the gas at the main," he said. "You take Dulcie down to the cellar. I'll bring blankets and the fire extinguisher down to you, then I'll go to Rankin. I don't like the idea of moving him."

Geneva nodded, intent on reaching the nursery. Within five minutes the small group of servants were settled in the wine cellar, and Dulcie, wrapped in several blankets, was sleeping in her nursemaid's arms. "I'm going upstairs to Father. All of you, stay here until we come for you."

She found her father seated just inside the door to Rankin's room, which was on the ground floor. The room was in darkness. Looking up as she approached, her father said, "Gennie, you should have stayed in the cellar. Would you believe Rankin is sound asleep? I don't think he heard anything."

Geneva found a chair and pulled it close to her father's. "I only heard one plane, didn't you? Perhaps it's just a straggler jettisoning his load."

"Yes, I'm sure of it. I hope none of them fell in the village."

"You're worried about Nancy, aren't you?"

He was silent for a moment. "She was disappointed, you know, when you rushed to Liverpool that day we planned to have lunch together at the Boar's Head."

"Yes. I'm sorry. We'll do it some other time."

"You never told me what the emergency was—I'm sorry, I don't mean to pry. Gennie, in wartime everything is accelerated—the pace of living . . . and dying. Everyone catches that let's-live-for-today mood. I'm trying to tell you . . . don't get hurt."

"You suspect me of having an illicit relationship? Father, that really is priceless, coming from you."

"I wanted to marry Nancy. From the very beginning. You'll never know how many times I asked her. She felt she would be a burden because of her class, her lack of education.

I couldn't seem to convey to her how meaningless my life would have been without her."

But you had me, Geneva thought, *how can you say that?* A faraway voice answered that the love of father for child, child for parent, was beautiful and pure and selfless . . . but incomplete. The mystical union of man and woman fulfilled all human needs, expressed all that was noble and fine in human relationships, carrying us beyond the limits of earthly experience to a realm of spiritual and sexual blending that fused souls. Such loves were rare, and fortunate were they who found them. *Father and Nancy,* Geneva thought. *Matt and I denied ourselves for so long. Is it too late now? Have we missed that time when we should have come together?*

Another series of explosions shattered the night. Ian flung himself across the room to shelter Rankin's body with his own as a Grecian urn in the window bay cracked and fell in pieces. Ceiling plaster showered them with a choking cloud.

"Dear God, that was close," Geneva said. "It sounded as though they fell just across the woods." The plane droned away, the sound of its engine fading in the distance. "Is Rankin all right?"

A faint voice, filled with astonishment, asked, "Is something wrong, sir?"

Ian was trying to wave the cloud of dust and plaster flakes away from the butler's face. "Sorry about the rude awakening, old chap. I'm afraid we've had a bit of an air raid. But it's all over now, go back to sleep."

Geneva went to the window, tipped the slats of the shutter to look out through the cracked glass. The night horizon in the direction of Liverpool glowed red, but there was a column of fire even closer. One of the jettisoned bombs had hit a target not far away.

"He's asleep again," her father said. "I believe the doctor gave him sedation. Let's go and get a drink, shall we? We'd better leave the others where they are for the time being until we're sure it's over."

They went through the silent house. Pictures had fallen from walls, and in the dining room both chandeliers had shattered. When they came to the entry hall they both stopped, staring. Lady Sybil's grandfather clock had crashed forward on its face and lay like a broken coffin on the marble floor.

I was going to see about giving it away, Geneva thought, *just before Matt arrived.* She said, as lightly as she could,

"Well, Jerry seems to have solved one problem for us. We shan't have to gather around the clock mourning the dead when it's all over."

Ian did not appear to have heard her. "It's all quite mad. Why do we put up with it? Aren't there enough rational men in the world to prevent it? It doesn't solve anything. The seeds of the next war are being planted in this one, just as this one was born in a railway carriage in France twenty years ago when the Germans signed the armistice. Old men beat the drums and young men spill their blood. But this time the horror is even greater—women, children . . ."

She placed her hand on his arm. "Father, don't . . . please." She hesitated. "I think I should go and see how Dulcie is. I'm worried about her being in that damp cellar."

"Gennie, wait a minute. You don't blame yourself because of Dulcie, do you? It's an odd thing to ask at this particular moment, but I'm tormented by so many unanswered questions tonight. I don't mean about her catching cold. I mean about her being retarded."

"I used to blame myself for going out the night she was born. But she might have been born retarded even if the birth had not been so . . . difficult. I'm not a terribly religious person, Father, not as much as my upbringing should have made me. It just seemed that your God was too vengeful, if he existed. Why did he punish us in such cruel ways? But I always felt there was something in life we haven't quite grasped. The answers are there, elusive but tangible. In Dulcie's case, we all love her as we would love an exquisite flower, or a perfect piece of music, or an unforgettable book—and even more than that, as a little human being who is without flaws, who loves us in return so completely that it doesn't matter that she isn't like the rest of us. I've accepted the fact that her body will grow and mature but her mind won't. It grieves me, but I have accepted it."

She heard his long sigh in the dusty dimness of the hall. "Yes, you're right. We have to love her for what she is. I was so afraid you thought perhaps there was some genetic defect."

Geneva thought of Charlie Dutton's sister, Josie, and she froze. Surely her father didn't know? But he went on, "I know there must always be unanswered questions for an adopted child."

Adopted. He's thinking of my *family*, Geneva thought, relieved.

"The doctors didn't think it was hereditary, Father," she reminded him gently. "Lack of oxygen during the birth, or perhaps some virus that attacked the baby in the womb in the early stages of development. It never occurred to me to wonder—"

"Of course, quite right. You know, Gennie, when the war is over you must think about more children. Saxon Hall cries out for heirs. Perhaps you and Terry could adopt a son."

No, Geneva thought, *not now. I can't think about that now.* "Father, I'd better go and see to Dulcie."

"Yes, and I must go out. You'll be all right?"

"You're going to the village, to see Nancy?"

It seemed he paused, considering, before he answered, "Yes, I'm going to see Nancy."

Chapter 33

Rankin developed pneumonia and died suddenly only days after the lone German plane bombed the area. Ted Corwin had returned to Saxon Quarry the day before the funeral. Now he limped through the churchyard behind the small group of mourners to see the Saxon butler buried in the family plot beside the ruined remains of St. Agnes' Church. The steeple still stood, but it would have to be pulled down in the interests of safety. A bomb had exploded directly over the altar.

Bombs had all but destroyed the abbey too. Ted pondered on this as Colonel Wakefield and Huw walked stiffly ahead of him, side by side, as though to dispel the rumors Ted heard the moment he returned home: that Huw Wakefield had "spotted" the lone plane that had caused all the destruction in this quiet part of Lancashire. Wasn't he involved with that hush-hush operation across the woods, working there as a civilian? Weren't army officers from a wide conglomeration of different regiments billeted at the abbey? Hadn't Huw gone to school in Germany? Had German friends? One of whom actually visited him just before the war started? Hadn't there always been that conflict between Huw and his grandfather? He was more Hindu than English, wasn't he? And that story about him not being in the army because he had a bad heart!

Why, he looked fit as a fiddle. No, there was something fishy about that German bomber picking those remote targets, camouflaged as they were.

"You're a newspaper reporter, Ted," they'd said in the local pub the previous night. "You ought to look into it."

Rankin's casket was being lowered into the ground. Ted glanced at the mourners, his eyes coming to rest on the bowed head of Ian Saxon. Ian Saxon had saved him from entombment in the pit, given him a life he never would have had. It had cost him his leg and he would gladly have given it again to have escaped to the life he'd had instead. Oh, there'd been times when he felt the lure of a socialist Utopia that had no place for landed gentry; when he'd resented the opulence of Saxon Hall, the Rolls-Royce, the teams of servants and sleek horses and the power. But when he looked at Ian Saxon, all he saw was a man whose only real concern was for those he loved and those fortunate enough to be his friends. It was clear from the presence of the Wakefields at Rankin's funeral that Ian didn't believe the rumors, and Ted wasn't interested in a story about Huw. The army would no doubt hear the rumors and investigate. Ted felt that perhaps Huw's main crime was in being such an arrogant bastard.

Ted caught a glimpse of another face. It startled him by appearing suddenly in the shadow of the ruined church just as the minister sprinkled the earth into the grave. What kind of mourner lurked in the background, hiding himself? Ted blinked, sure at first that he imagined the large, pale face that dodged back behind the crumbled wall like a moon retreating behind a cloud. No, there it was again. A big, coarse-featured face, vaguely familiar, gone again before he recognized it. Had anyone else seen it? He looked around the circle, but all heads were bowed in prayer. Was the watcher in the shadows perhaps more interested in the mourners than in the deceased? Why? *My own instincts for drama,* Ted thought, *want to weave something sinister into a barely glimpsed face.*

He looked back at the bombed church. It had stood for two hundred years on that spot. It was symbolic of the end of an age, he decided, just as Rankin's passing was.

When the service ended, Ian Saxon approached him, shook his hand, and invited him back to the Hall. Ted declined but promised to call before he returned to London. He watched Ian hurry to catch the others as they went to the waiting cars. Ian's silver hair—they said he went prematurely gray shortly after returning from France in the first war—tended to add years to his age, unjustifiably, since he was still in his prime. He moved with a strong, sure step and spoke with quiet authority, but tended to separate himself from the crowd in some mysterious way Ted could not pinpoint. Perhaps it was that which made him appear a patriarchal figure of venerable years, no mean feat for a man who was only in his early forties.

Ted made a pretense of studying the inscriptions on some of the age-blackened tombstones, waiting for everyone to leave. He was careful to stay between the ruins of the church and the lane, so that the figure he had seen lurking in the shadows could not leave without him knowing. There was a tall monument over one grave, a trio of angels atop a column that had escaped the bombs. He drew close, hiding behind it.

Minutes later a large man dressed in a tan mackintosh emerged from the church. He had a sprouting of blond hair on his massive skull, as though it was growing after being shaved. Charlie Dutton. He'd shaved off the Masked Turk's mustache and goatee too. What the devil was he up to, spying on a funeral?

Ted stepped out from behind the tombstone as Charlie approached.

"Christ!" Charlie exclaimed. "You frightened the shit out of me. Thought you was a bloody ghost. What you hiding behind there for?"

"I was reading the inscription. Two hundred years ago a man buried his young wife and stillborn son here. How about yourself, Charlie? What were you hiding in the church for? I didn't know you were a friend of the Saxons' butler."

Charlie's pale eyes squinted down at him; his lips moved soundlessly, as though he were rehearsing what he was about to say. Then he blinked and gave an ingratiating grin. "Come over to see the bomb damage, you know. Didn't know they was having a funeral today. Ducked out of sight when I seen 'em coming."

Ted waited. As a journalist he'd learned that people grew uncomfortable with any long pause in the conversation and tended to give more information.

"Come on, Corwin, you know as well as anybody that the Saxons threw us out of our house after my dad and my brothers died cutting coal for the bastards."

"You lived there for a couple of years after your father died, Charlie. You were asked to leave quite some time later. Ian Saxon even let your sisters stay on when you were put away for assaulting that scullery maid. Seems to me there were rumors that you were hanging around the Hall, making a nuisance of yourself. You wouldn't be back with more mischief in mind, would you?"

Charlie's eyes went contemptuously down the length of Ted's slight frame and came to rest on his artificial leg. Charlie gave a snort and spat on the gravestone. "Can't a bloke come back home where he was born? You don't live here no more neither, but you come back. Why can't I?"

"Leave the Saxons alone, Charlie, if you want to stay out of jail." Ted turned to walk away but found himself sprawling on the ground as Charlie's foot went in front of his prosthesis and tripped him.

"You little twerp. Nobody threatens Charlie Dutton. Not you nor the bloody Saxons."

He swaggered away, leaving Ted to adjust the prosthesis against his stump. *The pen,* Ted told himself ruefully, *is not always mightier than the sword.*

Still, he didn't see Charlie again in the village for the remainder of his visit.

Geneva returned to Liverpool shortly after the funeral, glad to be busy again and secretly relieved to leave Saxon Hall. Apart from the sadness of Rankin's passing, her father had closed down all but the essential rooms in the interest of wartime economy and fuel conservation, and the house had a lonely and deserted atmosphere, especially when he was gone—which was much of the time.

November slipped away and December crept in on frostbitten feet that sank ever deeper into the mire of war. Air raids, streets blocked with rubble, shortages, rationing, long queues for food. Merchants vied with each other to create jaunty signs that scoffed at their blasted-out shop windows and Hitler's bombs. Over the radio Churchill hurled growling defiance at the Nazis.

Geneva worked long hours, growing a protective facade that enabled her to pick up a mangled child and place her in the ambulance when the need arose—without thinking of Dulcie, safe at Saxon Hall.

Days went by in a jumbled blur. Nights meant falling bombs and mad dashes about the city, fast U-turns on blocked streets, jamming on the brakes as a building collapsed dead ahead. Smoke and fire and the rattle of shrapnel hitting the roof of the ambulance as ack-ack batteries pounded the sky. The antiaircraft guns were now manned by women of the "auxiliary" army, as were the barrage balloons. Neither defense was particularly effective at bringing down German planes, but the rapid fire and ghostly floating balloons trailing their nets were morale boosters to the weary citizens. And when the nights ended, Geneva and the other ambulance drivers stood by in the cold dawn as victims were dug out of the smoking rubble of their houses.

She was sound asleep at her newfound flat early one afternoon when her doorbell rang. Struggling into a dressing gown, trying to make heavy eyelids stay open, she opened the door to find her father standing outside. He wore his Home Guard uniform, a greatcoat, and gauntlets, and carried a satchel.

He kissed her cheek. "Forgive me for waking you, Gennie. But I'm going away for a while."

She wasn't completely awake. "On colliery business? Come in, I'll make a cup of tea."

"No tea, thank you. I haven't time." He followed her into the small room. "Not on colliery business actually. We get a lot of help from the Ministry nowadays, coal being so essential to the war effort. I can safely leave everything in the hands of the new manager. No, I'm going on Home Guard duties down south. It's a special training course. I'll be gone several months—probably won't be here for Christmas. I may not be able to call or write for a while, and I didn't want you to worry."

She tried to read in his expression what it was he was not telling her. Their bonds were close enough for her to know it was something essential. "But I thought the danger of invasion was over."

"Well, actually I'm on loan to the army. You know how they are. Always have to do things by the most inconvenient method they can devise. Gennie, there's a favor I'd like to ask of you. Would you . . . would you mind looking in on Nancy for me when you're home? See if she needs anything, keep her company when you can."

Geneva sighed. "Of course. But wouldn't it be simpler all 'round if you just married her?"

His eyes clouded and he gave a deprecating shrug. "I'm afraid the lady still refuses me. I know you understand the army's methods, but Nancy might not realize I'm incommunicado."

Geneva pushed several angry thoughts down into her

subconscious as her father prepared to leave. She insisted on accompanying him to the station, and there wasn't time to talk as she hurriedly dressed.

As they emerged into the street her father said, "I don't think I'd better chance trying to get a taxi. The trams are still running and this is all the luggage I have."

A double-decker tram rattled toward them minutes later, and since it was crowded on the lower deck, they went up the narrow stairway to join the cigarette smokers on top. Geneva had a fleeting vision of her father in a chauffeur-driven Rolls as he stood aside to allow a rough-clad docker to pass along the tram's narrow aisle, and a small smile curved her lips. They were forced to take single seats on opposite sides of the aisle. A young female conductor came around selling tickets, and two older women remarked that it didn't seem right, these bits of girls doing men's jobs.

Alighting at the corner of Lime Street, they hurried past the Adelphi Hotel. Geneva glanced up at the gray walls but resolutely pushed aside thoughts of Matt. Minutes later the railway station greeted them with the shriek of a departing train, an ear-splitting burst of steam, and the cold damp smell peculiar to trains and travel.

Ian looked at the corrected time chalked in beside the next London train on the board. "Don't come down the platform. I'll probably sit on the train half an hour before it leaves, and we'll just stare at each other through the window and run out of small talk. Did it ever occur to you that train travelers never come to Liverpool en route to somewhere else—unless they're catching a ship. All the train lines end here, so people are coming home or leaving. What nonsense I'm talking!"

They had reached the ticket collector's barrier. As Geneva stopped, glancing toward the window where she could buy a platform ticket, her father added, "Please, Gennie, I feel guilty enough for having deprived you of your sleep. Go home now."

She gave him a quick hug, pulled away because they were surrounded by people, mostly in uniform, and was surprised when he held on to her. He whispered, "Gennie, I love you very much. Take care of yourself, my dear."

Then he was gone, and she watched him walk down the platform, swept along by the crowd, yet not part of it. Her heart ached with love for him, and she wished there had been a moment when she could have expressed her feelings.

Wartime partings had such a poignant air of finality, and everyone was aware they must not let an opportunity pass for reaching out to one another. Geneva blinked back a tear, unable to dispel the memory of Terry boarding a train, leaving her for an unknown hell she could not even imagine.

There was a brief telephone call from her father the following day, assuring her of his safe arrival. A week later there was a letter giving no indication of where he was or what he was doing.

She was given a week's leave at Christmas and went home to spend the holiday with Dulcie, saddened to realize this would be the first Christmas she had ever spent away from her father. Then, on the twenty-third, there was a call from Matt. His voice came crackling over the telephone wires and suddenly everything was wonderfully, gloriously, all right.

"Gennie? I made it with my clothes on this time. It's great to hear your voice. I've missed you like crazy."

"Matt! Oh, how marvelous you're here for Christmas. Can you come to Saxon Hall immediately—this minute?"

There was a slight pause. "Are you sure? I mean, about me coming there. I don't want to cause any trouble."

"Father's away. But even if he were here, I'd want you to spend the holiday with us. After New Year's Day we'll go back to Liverpool. I found another flat."

"I'm on my way."

He came bearing a large box of incredible treasures.

The elderly gardener had hauled a log to the drawing room fireplace and cut a small fir tree from the woods, which was awaiting decoration in a corner of the room. Red-berried holly swathed the mantelpiece and stood in bright copper pots, and a large bunch of mistletoe hung from the chandelier. All the greenery vied with the aromatic smoke rising in the fireplace for a fresh, clean winter smell. Dulcie sat on the rug and watched wide-eyed as Matt produced a floppy rag doll, gaily attired in red and white gingham, followed by a fluffy pink teddy bear.

"Matt, they're beautiful!" Geneva exclaimed, putting the doll into her daughter's arms. Dulcie gurgled ecstatically.

"There's some stuff for the kitchen too, I'll leave it in the box," Matt said. "Except for this." He pulled out one brightly wrapped package and slid it under the tree. "That one isn't to be opened until Christmas Eve."

Geneva was peering into the box. "Tinned fruit and chicken and—Matt! Oranges! Real ones. I don't remember when I last saw one. And what's this?"

"Canned pumpkin. Don't you make pumpkin pie this time of year?"

She looked blank. "You mean they still exist? I thought they were semi-mythical things in fairy stories, or extinct at least. You know, Cinderella's coach was made from a pumpkin. I don't think Cook will know how to make it into a pie."

Matt laughed. "I guess I'll have to bake it myself."

"Oooh . . . I see a bottle of cherry brandy and dried fruit and nuts. We can have a Christmas pudding!"

"Now I thought *that* was something that only happened in Dickens," Matt said, slipping his arm about her shoulder. "I just had the cook at Greenboughs fill up the box with whatever struck her fancy. The fresh fruit is from my ship."

"Your ship? You mean the ship you came on? American ships are still barred from the war zones, aren't they?" A small frown knitted her brows. It was well known that British funds in the United States were rapidly running out, and Germany was counting on American supplies being cut off. English factories were constantly hammered by the Luftwaffe, while Germany now exploited all of the industry of the occupied countries, most of which were beyond the range of retaliatory raids; but the American position on cash-and-carry commerce remained firm.

"I came on a Castleton freighter. My own ship," Matt replied. "I figured if I have to worry about wolf packs, I want to be the one in command. I did a little probing into the situation. My ship is registered in Liberia—though there's little chance she'll ever see Monrovia, which is that country's only deep-water port. I retain ownership, but I'm now free to sail where I please, carrying whatever cargo I choose."

"I see." Geneva smiled. "The *Bella Mia?*"

"No. She's newer, faster. I called her the *Geneva.*"

Geneva gave him an impulsive hug. He looked down at her fondly. "And as far as other American ships bringing supplies are concerned, Roosevelt is trying to work out a lend-lease bill. People are beginning to realize that if Britain collapses, we're probably next on Hitler's list."

"We won't collapse." She looked into the flames dancing along the top of the log in the fireplace. "My father feels wars aren't the antidote, they're the cause. He's officially in the army, by the way. I had a letter confirming what I'd suspected. He was given a commission as a captain. Someone must have been very persuasive."

"People change their views," Matt said. "Perhaps he thought even war is preferable to living as a slave. I can't see any other reason every generation fights a war to end all wars. But let's forget about it—for a little while—and enjoy Christmas and being together, shall we?"

They looked at each other over the top of Dulcie's head. The firelight shimmered in Dulcie's soft golden curls and gave her face an angelic glow, and they both admired her silently for a moment, enjoying the pleasure of her guileless beauty; thinking she should be perched on top of the Christmas tree. Then they looked up simultaneously, and in the look they exchanged was a yearning they both felt but could not express. A moment later a young maid came into the room precariously balancing a tray of hot toddies, and Matt leaped to help her. Geneva almost expected Rankin to appear, twitching disapprovingly. How empty the Hall seemed without her father and his butler. It was difficult for Geneva to realize Rankin was gone forever, and her father's absence caused a continual nagging worry she had to fight to suppress.

The following day was Christmas Eve. It dawned bright with frost under clear skies. After breakfast they wrapped themselves in their warmest clothes and went for a stroll. The bleak furrows that had housed the last crop of potatoes ran down what had formerly been the lawns, and where Terry and his friends had once played polo, beanpoles protruded from the frozen earth.

They picked their way along a trampled dirt path to the edge of the woods. The bare trees were painted on the sky like charcoal line drawings. A redbreasted robin observed them from a drooping branch as they went by.

Matt took Geneva's hand and slipped it inside his pocket, enclosed by his warm fingers. "I want to take you in my arms, make love to you," he said. "I want to carry you off astride my horse, float you down the river on a barge, lock you in my castle. Gennie, I want you . . . I love you so much I can't think straight."

She looked at him and smiled, her eyes expressing her feelings. "Now that you're with me, I can stand anything. Oh, Matt, now I know this is how it's meant to be. Each little pleasure is enhanced when it's shared with one we love. Disappointments are easier to bear, danger is less frightening."

"Gennie, we haven't talked about something that needs to be talked about. Your husband. Has there been any word from him?" He had been both relieved and apprehensive at the news that Terry was a prisoner of war.

A cloud shadowed her eyes, hovered in their depths. "No. The Red Cross has been forwarding some letters from POW's, but I haven't heard from Terry. Matt, you know we can't do anything until he's home. And even then . . ."

Matt stopped, grabbed her shoulders, and spun her around to face him. "And even then . . . what, Gennie? I'm not the kind of man content to see you when you can sneak away from your husband. I want all of you, all the time. I want to take you home with me. No offense, but I can't see myself settling in England. I want, in other words, an old-fashioned, all-inclusive commitment—marriage and all that it entails."

"There's something I haven't told you." She hesitated, her face torn with more despair than her next words warranted. "Terry loves me. He may not agree to a legal separation."

Had she been about to say something else, changed her mind? "But you don't love him. God, Gennie, you wouldn't sacrifice yourself—"

She closed her eyes, trying to shut out the memory of Terry's face, naked with emotion. "Please try to understand how I feel about him. It doesn't diminish the way I feel about you. Terry was my childhood companion, always the gallant knight who protected me, and I suppose there was always that certain resemblance to my father. And Matt, Terry sacrificed himself in marriage to me, to save me from disgrace when he found out I was pregnant. I can't just cast him aside like an old shoe. I want to be with you all the time too. I'd gladly go anywhere with you. But don't ask me to destroy Terry."

Matt's hands fell from her shoulders. He glanced across the furrowed ground to Saxon Hall, mellow in the winter sunlight. "Perhaps I'm afraid of the competition. I knew he loved you. I saw it in his eyes."

"Perhaps . . . there's a girl in London, he loved her once. Perhaps she's the answer, I don't know. All I'm asking, Matt, is that when Terry comes home, you give me time to try to undo the wrong I did him. I must be sure his life isn't scarred. Do you understand?"

"Too well. I guess part of what I love about you is that caring. But Gennie, I feel there's more to your reluctance than not wanting to hurt Terry. More than all of the other excuses—your baby, your father—Dutton. I don't know what

it is you're not telling me; perhaps you're not even sure of it
yourself. But there's something and it's tearing my heart out
that you won't confide in me, whatever it is. Nothing could
change the way I feel about you."

Her eyes darted about as though seeking escape. "There
isn't anything else. I've told you everything."

"No, Gennie. Not everything. Because it doesn't add up."

"I told you that the only grounds for divorce in England are
desertion—seven years' absence—or adultery. I can't do that
to the Saxon family. And an annullment means telling the
world about Dulcie. And how can we ever be sure, really,
that we aren't half-brother and sister? That would make
marriage between us illegal."

"We've been over all this," Matt sighed in exasperation.
"You're holding something back. Is it Dutton? Are you afraid
he might come after me, or I'd go after him? I swear I won't,
if that's what's worrying you. And he's not likely to find you
in America."

"No, no! There's nothing else!" Geneva almost screamed
the words. *There is something else,* a distant voice whispered
in her mind, but she ignored it because it didn't really matter,
did it, not if Matt were her brother. Didn't one thing cancel
out the other?

"We'd better start back. I forgot to mention, we'll have a
couple of guests for dinner. I felt I should ask the colonel and
Huw at least once over Christmas. They've been ostracized
by everyone since that night the abbey was bombed, as
though they haven't suffered enough in losing their home.
They're living in a cramped little bungalow on the outskirts of
the village. There were rumors that Huw signaled the
German plane that wiped out the installation across the
woods, as well as destroying the church and the abbey. I felt
we had to show everyone we didn't believe the rumors. Huw
was Terry's best friend. Oh, yes, Ted Corwin is coming too.
His mother died and he's all alone for Christmas."

Matt thrust his hands into his pockets as they turned to
retrace their steps. "Sure. I understand." He looked straight
ahead, his mouth set in tight lines, and Geneva felt that some
of the sparkle had just left the day. She wished with all her
heart she could have told him what he wanted to hear.

Dinner that evening was something less than festive despite
Matt's contribution of scarce items of food. A pair of scrawny
chickens were augmented by the canned chicken he brought

and plenty of sage-and-onion stuffing. Geneva sat at the head
of the table, looking lovely but tired in a dark red dress that
was two years out of style.

The colonel and Huw sat side by side, not looking at each
other, while opposite them Ted Corwin tried to keep the
conversation going almost singlehandedly. Attempting to
lighten the mood, he told of some of the more amusing
aspects of the war he had observed while living in London
and freelancing for the news services.

"I was fire-watching on the roof of one of the office
buildings one night, and it occurred to me I should try to find
something different to say about the blitz. It seemed like
everything that could be said about the stoic acceptance of
almost continual bombing had already been said. Then one
night I saw an aerial torpedo drop. It came down on a
parachute big enough to cover a house. Somehow it missed
hitting any buildings, but went through the street-level window of a basement. The chute was draped all over the street.
Well, I flung myself down waiting for the explosion, but
nothing happened."

He paused to take a sip of wine, and Geneva said, "An
unexploded one? Set to go off later?"

Ted nodded. "Next morning the area was cordoned off and
everyone evacuated, and the bomb disposal crew arrived to
defuse it. I managed to get close enough to talk to the
sergeant who was first down into the basement. Big, tough-
looking bloke with a ruddy face and handlebar mustache. His
officer told me the sergeant had dug up eighteen bombs.
Well, down he goes into the cellar and next minute up pops
his head again and he's white as a ghost. He says, "I'm not
bloody well going down there—there's a dirty great rat in that
basement!""

Matt laughed and everyone else smiled politely. Geneva
went to bring in the Christmas pudding, resplendent with a
sprig of holly on top and afire with brandy burning with a cool
blue flame. There was a rum sauce to pour over it, and then
Geneva announced that it was time to pull the crackers. Matt
had been wondering what the brightly colored crepe paper
tubes at each place setting were. Ted picked his up, holding it
by one end and offering the other end to Matt.

"You grasp it firmly and pull," Ted instructed, seeing
Matt's blank expression. The paper tube was divided into
three segments, so that when they pulled the end segments,
there was a loud pop of an exploding cap and Matt was left

holding the middle part as well as the end. "There you are—you win. Open it, and you must read your motto aloud."

The cardboard reinforcing the center of the tube peeled open to disgorge its contents; the spent strip of explosive cap, a gaudy paper hat, a tiny toy whistle, and a curled slip of paper that Matt unwound and read, " 'Tis impossible to love and be wise.' " He looked around the table and added, " 'Attributed to Francis Bacon.' "

Ted grinned. "You're supposed to take the advice of the mottoes in the cracker."

The rest of the Christmas crackers exploded as they were pulled, and paper hats were donned. Ted insisted on hearing everyone's motto. Geneva read, " 'Tell me who you live with and I'll tell you who you are.' Fascinating. They say it's from a Spanish proverb, quoted in a letter from the Earl of Chesterfield to his son." She held up her prize, a tiny silver bell.

Ted's proclaimed, "Seldom any splendid story is wholly true." Everyone laughed, and the colonel turned to Geneva and said, "Did you insert that particular motto into his cracker after he told the rat and bomb story?"

Geneva shook her head, still smiling. "You know I could never put one together so that the cap would explode. That's your department, isn't it? Didn't you blow up things in the army?"

"Touché, m'dear. Here's mine. 'There's nothing permanent except change.' Hmmm . . . Heraclitus was not my favorite philosopher."

"Come on, Huw, what's yours say?" Ted asked.

Huw's dark eyes turned slowly to regard him. "Probably some similar nonsense—or perhaps in my case there will be something about treason and disgrace." He crumpled the motto and tossed it on the table.

There was an awkward pause. Then Ted picked up the slip of paper and read, " 'For all sad words of tongue or pen, the saddest are these. It might have been!' "

Geneva stood up. "We seem to have picked a box of crackers with depressing mottoes. What happened to all the amusing ones we used to get? Or at least those that promised tall dark handsome strangers entering our lives, or sudden wealth? Come on, let's go into the drawing room for liqueurs."

She lingered until everyone but Huw was out of the room, then went to him and slipped her arm through his. "Huw, I've never mentioned those vicious lies being spread about you, because I didn't want to dignify them with a comment. But I want you to know that I don't believe a word of those awful rumors. I know you are fine and decent and honorable. Furthermore, I believe you are as patriotic as anyone else. Now let's not have any more gloom—it's Christmas Eve, after all. Will you join the others now while I slip upstairs to say good night to Dulcie?"

The baby was already asleep, and Geneva came from the nursery and stood on the dimly lit landing for a moment, trying to recapture the mood of the previous evening. Matt had seemed so distant all day. She knew, of course, what he was suffering. She felt it even more acutely. But there was honor, as well as love and need, to be considered. To say nothing of continuing bloodlines.

"Geneva."

She jumped, startled, as Huw's voice spoke from the top stair. "Please, may I have a word with you in private?"

"Well . . . yes, all right. Let's go into the gallery. It's rather cold, I'm afraid. We're only heating the rooms we use."

He followed her along the line of portraits, not looking at them. Stopping at the end of the row, under the portrait of Ian's father and brother, Huw said, "Did you know your father was going on a rather risky mission?"

Geneva felt the walls pulse inward for a second. "He told me he was going for some special training. What . . . what is he really doing?"

"Look, Geneva, I'm not supposed to talk about this. But damnit, you and your family are the only ones who don't believe I spotted that German plane. I feel obligated to you. Besides, Terry is my best friend. You know I've been working for the army. I'm attached to a new group that's called Special Operations Executive—SOE. They're using a motley group of people . . . civilians from all walks of life, some servicemen loaned from other regiments—and a certain Home Guard volunteer, your father."

"What is it he's doing?"

"Well, I'm sure he *is* being trained at the moment, as he told you. You see, the SOE's objective is to recruit resistance fighters in German-occupied countries. The fields across the woods were used for night parachute jumps, to prepare men for dropping behind enemy lines, but the main training centers are in the south."

Geneva felt a flutter of apprehension. "Surely not my father?"

"I don't know. I do know Captain Jefferson approached your father because the SOE is most anxious to have a Frenchman in the occupied zone do a job for them. There have been isolated outbreaks of resistance in France; some guerrilla activity, but nothing on an organized basis. Still, our intelligence turned up that one man is a definite possibility for leadership. And your father is acquainted with that man."

"Who? Do you know who he is? I can't think of anyone in France my father knows who might be a possible saboteur. Besides, we spent our holidays in the south of France. He hasn't spent much time in the north since he was in the first war. Except for . . ." her voice trailed off as she remembered her father's visit to try to find her mother's family. "Occasional visits to Paris," she finished.

"Geneva, listen. Go to Captain Jefferson and give him some pressing reason to send your father home before it's too late. A compassionate leave, perhaps. Say you're ill— anything to prevent him from going to France."

"Huw, I can't do that. It isn't true. Besides, if my father volunteered for such a mission, I can't prevent him from doing what he wants to do. No matter how afraid for him I am."

"Does the name Andre Thibault mean anything to you?"

Geneva swayed slightly on her feet. "Thibault was my mother's maiden name," she whispered. "But I don't know who Andre is."

Matt's voice, calling to her from the bottom of the staircase, interrupted. Later, when the guests had left, Geneva presented him with a handsome antique leather dressing case and then opened his present and sighed over the white angora sweater and gold locket he had brought for her. But she knew he was watching her with a puzzled hurt in his eyes that said he was aware of the wall of reserve that had suddenly sprung between them. She decided not to add to the tension by telling him about her father.

"I was going to stay home for a day or two longer," she said, to break one of the silences that fell between them, "but I think I'll go back to Liverpool tomorrow. Will you come with me?"

"Of course." He watched her for a moment. "Why don't you go to bed now, Gennie? You look beat."

"I am rather tired. We can talk more privately at my flat."

"Sure. Good night."

He senses my change of mood, she thought as she went up to her room. *I should have told him what Huw said about Father.* Despite her brave words to Huw and the very large question in her mind about Huw's motives and loyalty, she was worried about what her father was really training for in the south. At the same time she felt a surge of pride in him that was almost envy. Did she, she wondered suddenly, secretly wish she could go to her beloved France herself and strike a blow, no matter how small, at the jackbooted invaders?

Chapter 34

The day after Christmas, which Geneva called Boxing Day, Matt accompanied her back to her Liverpool flat, an austere two rooms near the university. She gave no reason for cutting short her holiday at Saxon Hall, but Matt hoped that like himself, she wanted them to be alone to straighten out all of the knots in their relationship. He was dismayed when instead she abruptly left him, again without explanation, and did not return for several hours.

She seemed withdrawn, introspective to the point of being mysterious. He put it down to grief over the death of so many people near to her—her uncle, Meredith, Rankin—but Matt was beginning to wonder if her feelings toward him were changing.

Had she really been ready for a sexual relationship? he wondered. Was it ever possible to recover from rape, to dissociate sexual assault from the lovemaking of a man who truly cared for her? He'd clung to the thought that the past didn't matter. But it did matter. It was there, reaching out to taint the future, interlocking events and people, weaving together and then unraveling lives, so that dreams and nightmares became part of the same tapestry.

Geneva's flat was shabbier than the previous one, with the dispirited atmosphere of a place of temporary stops. The windows had been smashed by bomb blasts and boarded up, and the only means of heating the high-ceilinged room was a small gas fire standing on the grate. When he lit it, a concealed light bulb caused a red glow to flicker on a reflective screen behind the gas mantles to give an illusion of flames. He dropped into a chair, feeling letdown and depressed, and studied the imitation fire. Was it all an illusion? Was the great love of his life nothing more than the flickering image of verity, without form and substance except in his mind?

He had been looking forward to a triumphant return to Geneva for so long that he supposed the reality hadn't a hope of matching the dream. By the time she returned, late that evening, he was ready for his questions to be answered honestly and was in no mood for evasion. "Gennie, what is it? Something's bothering you. I see your eyes drift away and I know your mind's gone too."

She turned to him and went into his arms. He could feel her fingernails on his back and they conveyed more terror than passion. She was trembling but said only, "I'm cold. Hold me. It's been a nerve-racking winter and we're only halfway through it."

"No, Gennie. That isn't good enough. If you can't trust me enough to tell me what's really eating at you, then I don't know what I'm going to do. I can't stand it when you shut me out."

"Oh, Matt! I'm sorry. I didn't want to put more of a damper on things than is already there. I'm desperately worried about my father. I spent the afternoon trying to find a certain army officer." She told him of her conversation with Huw and added, "After the abbey was bombed, Jefferson and the other officers were sent somewhere. I haven't been able to find out where. I've tried to reach Huw, but his grandfather says he left rather abruptly the same evening he had dinner with us."

"And if you run down this Captain Jefferson, what then?"

"Matt, the man they want to contact in France is named Andre Thibault."

"Thibault," he repeated. "Celine Thibault. You think he's related to you? Good God! You think your father found him on that trip he took—and didn't tell you? Why, for pity's sake?"

"I think perhaps because he learned who my father is, or was, and didn't want me to know."

Matt's breath left him slowly. "Then your father was *not* my father. If he were, we'd have been told. I'm sure Ian would have rushed home and told you that we're half-brother and sister. He's perceptive enough to know how we feel about each other."

There was something in her eyes—denial? An undercurrent that had nothing to do with what she said. Or was it that she really wanted them to be brother and sister? To be safe from a total commitment to him?

She said, "At the moment I'm afraid I'm more concerned with what my father may be doing. If he's in danger—"

"Gennie, has it occurred to you that perhaps those stories about Huw may be true? If he's a German agent, it's possible he's already betrayed Thibault to the Nazis and wants to save your father because of some remnant of loyalty to Terry and you."

She bit her lip. "I can't believe that of Huw. But in any case, I can't find Jefferson—or anyone who will admit there *is* such a group as the SOE."

"We'll try again first thing tomorrow. Now let's eat; neither of us have had a bite since early this morning."

They opened the hamper they had brought, which contained cold chicken and wheat bread and a jar of pickled cabbage. They both pretended that the simple meal was as intimate and carefree as the first time they dined alone, but they were playacting and both knew it.

"I suppose your friends in the States feted you as a hero," Geneva said.

"Well . . . resurrected, anyway."

"The new year will soon be here, Matt. What will 1941 bring, do you think?"

Somehow I can't feel it will bring us together, Matt thought despairingly. Aloud he replied, "Well, I figure England is over the hump. Hitler won't invade now; he's lost the opportunity. And the blitz isn't beating you to your knees either."

"We probably won't lose the war. But can we win it alone?"

Matt stood up. "Quit talking about it and come here. I expect any minute you'll find an excuse to go rushing off somewhere, and I need to hold you first."

They lay on the hard double bed under blankets that smelled of camphor, and Matt kissed her and stroked her cool bare flesh, but she was still tense and unyielding.

"Matt, do you ever worry about having to pay for pleasure
. . . with later pain? That there's bound to be retribution?"

"No," he said, pulling her closer to the warmth of his body.
"And if that's what's bothering you, how about reversing the
order of things? Telling yourself that maybe you deserve a
little happiness now. God knows you've suffered enough for
it."

"It isn't that I fear what will happen to me personally, but I
couldn't bear it if any harm came to those I love."

"You're really down tonight, aren't you? It's understand-
able. Apart from the worry about your father, you must have
seen some pretty gruesome sights, driving that ambulance.
That's hard for a woman to take."

"What about a man? Isn't it hard for a man to take too?
Aren't you repelled by injuries? Deformities? Missing
parts?"

"Why yes, of course, but—" He stopped, staring at her.
There was something in her expression. A desperate appeal—
for what? Was she referring to Dulcie, to a missing mind
perhaps? The silence between them lengthened as he strove
to think of the right thing to say so that she would tell him
what brought that terrible pain-racked wariness to her eyes.
But before he could speak there was a knock at the door.

Matt pulled on his trousers as Geneva went to the door.
Standing outside was an older woman wearing a dark blue
police uniform. Matt took one look at the woman's grim
expression and moved swiftly to Geneva's side, putting his
arm around her.

"Mrs. Terrence Saxon? Of Saxon Hall, near Saxon Quarry?"

Geneva nodded silently, her lips white and compressed.

"Could we go inside—sit down?"

"Is it my father?" Geneva's voice cracked before she could
finish the question. Matt's fingers dug into her shoulder.

"No, I'm sure he's quite all right. I'm afraid it's your little
girl, Dulcie. She's been kidnapped. Now wait, don't take on.
We know who took her. We'll get her back. Your nursemaid
caught the man in the nursery and he knocked her unconscious, but she picked his picture from local police files. A
man named Charles Dutton."

Matt caught Geneva as her knees buckled.

Charlie Dutton sat in the back seat of the car with Millie
and the baby. Coby was in the chauffeur's seat, in uniform.

The car was for use by a Member of Parliament, on official business only, according to its markings. It was filled with black market petrol.

"Ain't she pretty, Mil?" Charlie said again, his finger touching Dulcie's silken cheek. The baby was examining a heavy gold ring he wore on his other hand, her little fingers curling around his as gently as the petals of a flower. For the first time since Josie died, Charlie felt he could breathe again.

Millie ignored him, her eyes fixed on the road ahead. "I just hope Coby don't run into nothing. He's too little to handle such a big flamin' car. What about when we get to a town with the traffic?"

"Well, there's not much of that nowadays, is there? Except for the army and the fire brigade and—" He stopped before he added "police" because old Millie was nervous enough without reminding her that the scuffers were probably after them by now. Pity that nanny had caught him lifting Dulcie out of her cot and he'd had to belt her. He'd been careful not to hit her too hard. After all, she'd been taking care of his kid. He still thought it had been a good idea to grab her over Christmas, when everyone's minds was on presents and food and booze. The blackout helped too, with the long winter nights. Coby had hid in the woods, watching the Hall for a couple of days to see who was there, and had seen Geneva leave with the Yank sailor, leaving only the nursemaid, the old gardener, and Cook and a couple of girls. All the Land Army girls were home for the holidays.

Dulcie cooed and smiled as he tickled her under the chin. She was worth it. She was his, his very own flesh and blood. In a way Millie, and even Josie, never were. He was amazed by his own feelings. And the baby seemed to know it too; she wasn't the least bit afraid of him. A rosy picture of the years ahead stretched out before him.

Millie was muttering, "I don't like the idea of going through London. They've been catching it in the daytime too. What if there's a raid and we're on the streets? You can't take the kid into a shelter."

"We're only going through the outskirts of London, Mil," Charlie lied. "We'll get my daughter home quick as we can. Ain't good for a baby to be in a car for a long time." His chest puffed out when he said "my daughter," and a sense of wonderment dispelled even Millie's perpetual gloom.

"Well, I don't like it," she went on nattering, but Charlie shut her out.

The road had narrowed to a lane, running through winter-bare fields under a gray sky. Millie had wanted him to grab the kid before the winter set in, but he had to get the cottage fixed up first. Besides, the long winter nights would have meant they'd be well on their way before Dulcie was missed—if it hadn't been for that nanny.

"Charlie," Coby said from the front seat, "I'm going to have to stop for a Jennie Riddle." Coby sometimes lapsed into Cockney rhyming slang, despite the fact he wasn't London born.

"Oh, Christ, can't you hold it?" Charlie grumbled. "All right, pull over to the side and hop behind them bushes. And hurry up, I want to get there before dark."

While Coby went to answer the call of nature, Charlie picked up Dulcie and walked her up and down the lane. She felt plump and solid in his arms, and her little body curved against him as though it belonged there. She'd be well made, like Josie was, when she was grown. The air was cold but bracing. Charlie felt ridiculously, wonderfully at peace.

"She's pretty big not to be walking," Millie sniffed when they got back into the car and Coby started the engine again. "I don't know if my back's up to carrying her around. I think our Josie could walk by this age. She's nearly two, isn't she? And not toilet-trained either, and can't feed herself. Hell's bells, what've I let meself in for?"

"Oh, shut your gob," Charlie said. "I'll look after her. She's just a bit slow, that's all. She's not Mongoloid like Josie. She'll soon be walking and talking and everything. You'll see. Them bloody Saxons probably kept her like this just to spite me."

Millie glanced at her brother out of the corner of her eye and if she wondered at that particular rationale, she made no comment.

They reached the outskirts of London shortly after two that afternoon. Charlie had not told Millie they had to return the borrowed car and go the rest of the way by train, or that there was a shipment of black market goods he was to receive payment for, if the spiv who bought them had come up with the cash, and by Christ he'd better have if he didn't want his bones broke. It wouldn't take long, and with a bit of luck there wouldn't be an air raid this afternoon. Jerry had been pounding the city all over Christmas, and a lot of his planes had been shot down by the Spitfires and Hurricanes. Like everyone else, Charlie was becoming accustomed to the routine of life under bombardment. "If your name's on a bomb, you'll get it, and if it's not, why worry?" was the creed.

"Coby's going to take you to a cafe for a spot of grub, Mil," he said. "I've a bit of business to see to."

"Oh, no you don't, Charlie boy," Millie snapped. "You don't go off and leave the kid with me. You got somewhere to go, you take her along too. I'm not going to the jug for grabbing her."

Charlie shrugged and hoisted the baby to his shoulder. She was such a good little thing, never a whimper out of her. They'd fed her some milk and a bit of pureed stew Millie had prepared ahead of time, and now Dulcie blinked and rubbed her eyes and was ready for a nap. She'd be no trouble. She put her face down in the hollow of his neck and he could feel her breath, warm against his skin. It made little nerves jump down his back, just the feel of her.

He liked the way everyone gawked at them as he walked down the street after Coby dropped them off a block from where the spiv lived. Charlie knew that despite growing his hair out and shaving the mustache and goatee, his size was still impressive. He supposed they stared because he was so big and strong looking to be taking care of a little baby. One boozy old woman came staggering out of a pub, took one look at him, and burst into tears. "Lost your wife, ducks?" she sniffed. "Sod the bloody Germans and their bombs." She shook her fist at the sky.

"That's right, Ma, give 'em hell," Charlie said, turning into the entrance to a three-story block of flats.

The spiv lived on the ground floor and Charlie kicked the door impatiently. A moment later a weasel face peered at him through an inch opening before swinging the door open to admit him. "Wot the 'ell did you bring a kid for?"

"She's my little girl. Dulcie," Charlie said proudly. "She's come to live with her dad." He picked his way through a room filled with packing cases and cardboard boxes, found a sofa, and dropped into it. Dulcie was asleep against his shoulder. "Now then, Bert, where's my lucre?"

Bert was dressed in the flamboyant style of suit adopted by the recently emerged Cockney "wide boy," with draped trousers and excessively padded shoulders. He opened his checkered coat to look at a gold watch hanging from a chain across the waistcoat he wore. "I'll have it for you in an hour,

Charlie, for sure. Bloke's bringing it over, see. He'd have been here before this, but he had to go and pick up some Yank stockings some merchant navy blokes brought in. The Yanks 'ave this new artificial silk, they call it nylon. The women's going crazy for nylon stockings, after them shitty lisle 'utility' ones they've had to wear."

"Never mind stockings, I've got me sister waiting in a cafe," Charlie growled. "You get the 'ell out of here and get that cash back here before she finishes eating, or else I'm going to pull your arms and legs off your body, see?"

Bert smiled weakly. "All right, Charlie. I'm only short a few quid. I can borrow it from one of my mates. You and the kid stay here; I'll be back in a sec." He darted out of the room, negotiating the clutter of black market goods like a maze-trained mouse, and disappeared through the front door.

Charlie eased the sleeping baby to the sofa cushion beside him so that he could remove his overcoat. The place was like an oven, considering it was heated by a coal fire and coal was rationed.

Coal . . . it had been a long time since he was down a pit. He thought of his father, those last days before he died of the black lung. Sitting ever so still because even the slightest movement brought that terrible gasping for breath and up would come the vile black spittle. Well, Charlie wouldn't ever get black lung. He drew several deep breaths and looked at Dulcie again. She was like a perfect little china doll, lying there asleep, so pretty and contented.

She'd never nag him, drive him to his death the way Ma had driven his dad to his. "Try to work a double shift—we need the money." "Can't you work the screening shed too?" The old bitch should have tried hacking away at a coal face for twelve hours. Bloody women got off easy.

He leaned back against the dusty upholstery, which stank of tobacco smoke. It had been a long ride and he'd been up all last night. His eyelids drooped. Might as well catch forty winks. Bert would wake him up when he came back.

Dreams came quickly; fleeting, fragmented, all mixed up the way dreams were. He was playing with the baby, fondling her, and all at once it wasn't Dulcie he was tickling, it was Josie.

He drifted to the surface of consciousness, looked at the unfamiliar surroundings in bewilderment. His dream of Josie had been so real. What hijinx they used to get up to when Ma's and Millie's backs were turned! It had begun when they were both little kids. Of course, at first it was no more than tickling and wrestling about and playing house. They'd wait until Ma and Millie went down to the shops, and then they'd crawl under the sheet in the big brass bed Ma and Dad slept in and lie all fitted together like two spoons, and he'd poke Josie a bit with his thing and try to get it between her legs.

The packing-case clutter of Bert's flat came into focus and Charlie remembered what had happened before they got here. He looked around and saw the baby lying beside him on the couch. He stroked back a golden curl of gossamer-soft hair, trying to remember how old Josie had been when it first began with her. But he was still half asleep and was soon dozing again, only to be caught in a different dream. This time it was more of a nightmare. He was back down the pit, choking on the coal dust, and he was glad when a distant sound intruded, waking him up . . . was it Millie screaming?

His eyes flew open. The air was filled with the whistle of falling bombs and the crack of antiaircraft guns. There was an explosion nearby that flung the baby from the sofa and she awoke, crying with fright.

Charlie dropped to his knees to pick her up, still half asleep and trying to gather his wits. He hadn't even heard the sirens. The blast from another stick of bombs sent a cloud of soot and smoke billowing from the chimney. It was all happening so fast. He groped among the packing cases for Dulcie, his hand finding a small foot.

His ears almost burst with the pain of an explosion. It must have been directly overhead. He had just enough time to fling himself over Dulcie as the ceiling came down, bringing with it all the furniture from the flat above and walls and bricks and unbearable, crushing pain. It pressed heavily on his back, mangled his legs.

He felt his lungs slowly collapsing and he gasped for air, sucking at the tiny space in front of his mouth, crying and sobbing as he felt the blackness surround him and entomb him. Under him Dulcie was quiet, unmoving. There were two other floors above them and the raid had only just begun. No one would come to dig them out, not for ages.

What was that . . . wet and sticky in the choking darkness?

Oh, Jesus, it was his own blood. Where was it coming from? His mouth opened and closed like a goldfish, trying to find air. But there was no air, there was just smoke and dust. The debris shifted, coming down over his mouth and nose. Charlie screamed, silently begging someone to come and give him air to breathe.

Chapter 35

Matt paced back and forth across the marble floor, occasionally stopping to glance upward through the carved balustrade of the staircase. The pall of gloom hanging over Saxon Hall was intensified by the dark winter day and the continual sobbing of the young nursemaid, who sat by the front door on her suitcases, waiting for the taxi to come and take her to the station.

Dr. Evans appeared on the landing and started stiffly down the stairs. Matt ran up to meet him. "How is she?"

"Hysterical with grief," the doctor answered testily. "I've given her a sedative. There's nothing else I can do. She'll have to deal with it. At the moment she's denying it, refusing to believe her child is dead."

"Is there any chance there was a mistake?"

"None. The police picked up Dutton's sister and his manager, and they confirmed Charlie took the baby to the flat. The owner of the flat said the baby was there when he left. The Germans have begun to use larger bombs—that was a land mine that hit. There were no survivors in the building. We'll be informed when all of the bodies have been dug out, but there's absolutely no reason to hope."

Matt offered his hand to help the elderly doctor negotiate the turn in the stairs, but was ignored. "Will she see me yet?"

"No. She said you are to go home and leave her alone. She said you knew why."

Matt knew that all the way from Liverpool to Saxon Hall, Geneva had repeated over and over that if anything happened to Dulcie it would be her punishment for having an affair with Matt.

"I suggest," Dr. Evans said curtly, "that you abide by Mrs. Saxon's wishes. She is delicately balanced on the edge of a breakdown. If she's blaming you in some way for the tragedy, your presence here certainly won't help her." At the foot of the stairs he paused and added under his breath, "Ironic, the whole thing, from beginning to end."

"I beg your pardon?"

"Nothing, nothing."

"What about her father? Can't you use your influence with the army to bring him home? God knows she needs him."

"I'm a doctor, Mr. Lauren. I've been retired for years and I don't particularly enjoy being put back into harness. I've enough to do getting my rheumaticky old bones from one patient to another, without worrying about anything else."

Matt watched the old doctor cross the hall and whisper to the nursemaid. Matt assumed the girl had been offered a lift in the doctor's car. When they were out of sight, Matt went up the stairs and began opening doors until he found Geneva's room.

She lay in a four-poster bed, her dark hair spread across the pillow, her eyes wide open but unseeing. He approached silently, picked up an ice-cold hand, and held it to his heart. "Gennie, don't send me away. Please. Not now. I can't bring Dulcie back, but let me stay with you, comfort you."

Her voice was husky, drugged. "Go home, Matt. It's all over between us. We have to pay—sooner or later we have to pay. We've got to stop now, before something really terrible happens to Dulcie. Oh, they'll find her soon and bring her home. But don't you see? This is my warning . . . what we've been doing is wrong."

Helplessly he brought her hand to his lips, searching for the right words to say, afraid of the blankness in her eyes. "Let go of me—leave me alone," her voice rose, close to hysteria.

A quiet voice behind him said, "Lad, you'd best do as she says."

He turned to see a middle-aged woman with soft brown hair and expressive eyes, with that faded-rose look that comes to women who have been beautiful in their youth. She moved hesitantly toward the bed. "Gennie, love, ah, love, I'm so very sorry. Oh, lass, what can I say?"

"Nancy!" Geneva breathed the name like a cry for help. "Nancy, I'm so glad you came."

As Matt went through the door he saw the older woman gather Geneva into her arms. They were both crying.

Nancy stayed on at the Hall, a quiet presence through the agonizing stages of Geneva's bereavement. All attempts to locate and bring Ian home failed as everyone close to the family ran into maddening tangles of red tape. Huw Wakefield had evidently lost his job as interpreter and had disappeared.

Geneva stayed in her room, refusing to do anything but stare out of the window. Her food trays remained untouched unless Nancy remained with her and insisted she eat.

Geneva was scarcely aware of the passing of time. She relived every moment of Dulcie's brief life, searching for a clue that should have warned her of its sudden and violent ending. Then she would imagine the pain and terror of her child at the moment the bomb exploded, and she would bite her knuckles to keep from screaming in anguish.

Days and nights blurred into periods of nightmares and intervals of bitter regret and self-recrimination. She shouldn't have gone to Liverpool to join St. John's; she should have stayed home where she belonged. With her child. She shouldn't have gone away with Matt. She should have stayed and protected Dulcie. She was being punished. For her infidelity, for wanting to end her pregnancy—hadn't she wished Dulcie dead before she was born? It was all her fault. She was guilty of her baby's murder.

Nancy would come to her and hold her and Geneva would realize she had been shrieking, not in her head, but aloud. One evening, when she hadn't eaten all day, Nancy entered her room to find her doubled over, clutching her stomach to quiet her hunger cramps.

"Is it your period, Gennie?" Nancy asked gently. "Shall I fetch you a sanitary napkin?"

Geneva straightened up and gazed at her incredulously, then burst into hysterical laughter.

Later, when she calmed down, Nancy said, "Gennie, you've got to stop blaming yourself. You're making yourself ill. You must accept it now. Nothing can bring her back. She's at peace; nothing can ever hurt her again. You must accept it. You're pretending it hasn't happened, lass. But it has."

Late that night Geneva paced her room, thinking that Nancy was right. It had been easier to tell herself it was all a mistake, they'd bring her baby back to her any minute. Some pain was too great to be borne and the mind had to slide a shield into place, block it out. While she punished herself for her own weaknesses, it was possible to hope that if only she truly repented, then somehow it would have just been a warning, a premonitory dream, and Dulcie would be restored to life.

The denial was replaced by anger. She ranted about the war, the bombings, the existence of monsters like Charlie Dutton. Nancy listened quietly, nodding her head.

"We were pacifists, you know, Nancy. Father and I—like Neville Chamberlain. We thought we could talk the Germans out of attacking. My God! They're not human. How can they kill innocent babies? Nancy, I must make them pay. They have to be punished."

Nancy held her and whispered, "It will pass. The grief will pass in time."

"I don't want it to pass!" Geneva screamed. "Not until I've made the Germans pay for killing my only child."

The first evening Geneva left her room following Dulcie's death, she found Nancy sitting in her father's study, running her hand back and forth over the smooth leather of his armchair.

Still shaky on her legs, Geneva paused in the doorway. There was a tight band around her temples and a gaping void around her heart. Her grief was a sharp pain when she tried to swallow or blink or breathe. There were periods of disorientation, small holes in her memory that she supposed were due to prolonged periods without sleep. Seeing Nancy in her father's study was a shock. She was framed by all of his things, this woman who had been a part of her father's life, yet not a part. Some tiny connection, linking one emotion to another, snapped in the back of Geneva's mind.

Nancy was speaking to her. "Gennie, I'm glad you got up, lass. Moping in bed won't do you no good. Listen, I've been thinking, I should get on home. What will folks say, me stopping here. There'll be such gossip in the village."

Geneva walked across the room, having no idea she was

going to do it. The intricate system of control between thought and action was lost, and her hand flew through the air before she could stop it. She slapped Nancy's face.

The sound of the slap hung in the air accusingly. Nancy looked up, shock bringing tears to her eyes. Geneva stood perfectly still, appalled by what she had done. Yet she wanted to do it. The words burst from her, as though the slap was a cork that had held them back.

"Damn you, Nancy Whitaker, you could have made my father's life happier. You could have lived with him, married him, supported him when he needed someone to lean on . . . but for your damn rotten pride; your stupid low-class bigotry. What the hell did you prove with it all? Damn you, you kept my father from finding someone else, yet you wouldn't give him all of yourself. You were a dog in the manger, Nancy Whitaker. You didn't want all of him, all that sharing his life would have entailed. But you wouldn't let go and let someone else have him either. I hate you for what you've done to my father. Go on, go back to your miserable little house and pull the walls in around you. I don't give a damn what you do."

Nancy came up slowly from the chair, a diver rising from some remote ocean, her hand on the cheek Geneva had slapped. "Ee, lass, tha' talks as if he's dead. He's not dead, Gennie. Your baby is dead, not your father. It's all right, don't cry, love, I understand. You're hurting so much, you poor child, you want to hurt someone else. It's the shock of your baby being killed."

Geneva turned and stumbled from the room, ran across the hall and up the stairs. She couldn't believe what she had said, nor guess at the reason for the outburst. Nancy had stayed with her, been so kind.

Upstairs in the deserted nursery Geneva stood beside the empty cot in the darkness, the echo of her accusation ringing in her head. Who was it who said what we hate most in others are our own faults? What she had said about Nancy holding on to her father also applied to her own attachment to Matt. She should have released him completely before she sent him away. He had gone home to America, but he'd return, she knew he would, as long as she'd left him with one scrap of hope. She hadn't told him the whole truth, because she simply hadn't faced it herself, hoping for some miracle to put it all right again.

The telephone rang somewhere. She ignored it. A minute

later she heard Nancy's voice, excited. "Gennie! Come quick!"

Afterward Geneva was never sure who called or what they said exactly. But the fact was, Terry had escaped from POW camp, had been shuffled across the continent by the underground, was home, safe. He was in London and would be at Saxon Hall within days.

Sometimes, in the confusion of waking, Geneva would think that somehow her father had gone to France and helped Terry escape. But, of course, there was no connection. She was glad Terry was coming home; his impending arrival helped distract her mind from the need for both penance for herself and vengeance against her child's murderers. Dutton was dead and she couldn't kill him, but there were millions of Germans yet to be punished. Geneva would awaken in the night, heart pounding, hands tearing at the imprisoning sheets, burning with a need so terrible it had no name. She dreamed of standing over a German bomber pilot, a gun in her hand, and awoke knowing a fearful resolution had been made and sealed with blood.

Then, one drizzly afternoon, Terry was at the door, gaunt and pale, but his amber eyes lit up when he saw her. He wrapped thin arms around her and held her close. "Gen, oh God, it's wonderful to see you, hold you." He pulled away for a moment, searched her face. "They told me about Dulcie. Oh, lord, what you must have suffered. I should have killed Dutton years ago."

Her fingers went to his lips to silence him. "I'm all right now, really. I'm so glad you're home. I've been worried to death about you."

"If I could have been here, perhaps—"

"Terry, I've had a lot of calls from friends and relatives all wanting to come and welcome you home. I know you've only just learned about . . . about Dulcie . . . but everyone else has sort of had time to get used to it. I know you loved her, but your homecoming means a great deal to so many people."

Terry appeared taken aback by her composure and studied her silently for a moment. *No,* Geneva thought, *I'm not the woman you left behind. There are times when I don't feel like a woman at all, but some sexless avenger with a bloody quest that keeps beckoning me, if only I could see which way to go.*

Slipping his arm around her shoulder, Terry said, "I understand. Don't worry, I won't talk about Dulcie until we're alone." They crossed the marble floor and he added, "I heard about Uncle Dee Dee and Meredith too. I think perhaps the civilians are faring worse than the services."

He glanced about the hall, finding familiar objects. "Something's different—missing. Grandmother's ghastly old clock! Thank the lord. Did you get rid of it? Where's Ian, by the way?"

"The clock was also an air raid casualty," Geneva replied. "And as for father—"

"Yes?"

She had time to tell him briefly what Huw had told her in the minutes before the first of a solid stream of callers arrived to welcome Terry home. By evening the house was full of friends and neighbors, every serviceman home on leave, Ted Corwin. Huw had mysteriously reappeared and came over with his grandfather. Saxon relatives who lived in the south began to arrive. Nancy stayed too and helped in the kitchen, as though she had always lived at the Hall. No one commented on her presence and everyone acted as though she were a member of the family.

Terry hid his grief over Dulcie and regaled everyone with stories of his imprisonment and escape. They were of a light-hearted vein but did not deceive anyone about the true nature of his ordeal. He had been hidden under the noses of the Germans after escaping from a prison hospital. On one point he was adamant: The German surgeons had saved his leg; their medical treatment had been swift and exemplary.

"I actually felt like a bit of a rotter afterward, pretending I couldn't walk without crutches. But that kept me in minimum security quarters so I could escape. It also kept me in northern France. I understand some of our blokes escaped by going south, crossing the mountains into Spain."

"How did you actually get out?" Ted asked.

"A tunnel. We were very soon organized. Escape committee, team to make civilian clothes, identity cards and so on. Luckily I never had to use my phony ID. We had an RAF pilot in sickbay who'd been picked up by the French underground briefly before he was caught trying to board a train. Anyway, he knew of several safehouses. By the time I escaped, the French had a chain of them going. Although I'm not sure about the 'safe' part—since the ones I stayed in were all *maisons de passe.*"

There were appreciative grins from the other men, and Geneva looked at them blankly.

Terry explained, "The Germans didn't close the brothels in the occupied zone. And they put the *maisons de passe* in the same category, so left them alone too. They're scruffy hotels where a man and woman can go for a couple of hours at any time of the day or night, no questions asked or IDs required. Visitors are never asked to sign registers, and a man alone merely says he's expecting a lady visitor. It's an old French custom, and searches would be impractical."

"But how did you get across the Channel?" Ted asked.

Terry grinned. "I could hardly believe it. A Lizzie came for us—me and a couple of agents who were—"

"Terry." Colonel Wakefield interrupted so swiftly that it was a moment before Geneva noticed how everyone had tensed at Ted's question, casting strained glances in Huw's direction and signaling Terry with their eyes. The colonel said, "Perhaps the details are not for common knowledge? Didn't they haul you in for debriefing in London, swear you to secrecy?" He avoided looking at his grandson, but Geneva saw a slow flush spread over Huw's olive features and his eyes darken with anger.

"Well, yes," Terry said. "But good lor' I'm among friends—"

Huw sprang to his feet. "I have to go, Terry. I'll see you tomorrow." He strode to the door without looking back. His grandfather got up more slowly and followed.

Terry was half out of his chair, but Geneva restrained him with a hand on his arm. "Let them go," she whispered. "I'll explain later."

For a moment no one spoke, then Ted steered the conversation tactfully toward catching Terry up with current news.

Long after midnight, when the visitors had left and guest rooms were opened for relatives staying overnight, Geneva and Terry went wearily up the stairs. "What's a Lizzie?" Geneva asked.

"A Lysander—a light plane. It landed in a field and picked us up. Though I believe the two British agents were the reason for the deluxe treatment, not me. One of the agents was a slip of a girl, incidentally. But tell me what precipitated the sudden departure of the Wakefields."

Geneva told him about the night the German plane bombed the area. "One of the agents was a slip of a girl" echoed in her mind.

"Damn them all to hell," Terry exploded with anger. "Huw isn't a traitor."

"He's your friend, Terry, and I don't believe you could give your love and loyalty to someone so two-faced, so I agree with you. I have faith in him too. But it seems even his own grandfather isn't sure of him. You saw how the colonel stopped you from giving details of your escape in front of Huw."

"But Huw told me that until recently he'd been working with MI—that the only reason he lost the job was because the group he worked with had been disbanded. Surely if he were suspect, they wouldn't have kept him on after the bombing? God, it's damnable to be condemned by gossip and hearsay."

"I'm not sure how secret his work was. He was employed as an interpreter originally. But he did know about Father." She had not had time to fully discuss with Terry what Huw had told her about her father's possible connection with the SOE.

"He told me earlier this evening, that he'd been forging identification papers in German, but that just before they let him go he'd been switched to translating German radio broadcasts. Gen, don't worry about Ian. It's possible all they want him to do is talk to this Andre Thibault on the radio. After all, he's a bit old for cloak-and-dagger stuff. I'm a little surprised at Huw for telling you . . . but I still feel it's no reflection on his loyalty. Sometimes personal loyalties outweigh patriotism. If it's a case of saving your family or saving your country—"

He stopped, realizing they had been so engrossed in their conversation that they had walked without thinking to the room they had once shared. Now they looked at each other, embarrassed. Terry's hand found her arm, tentatively. "Gen, let me sleep in your arms tonight."

She couldn't deny him. Nor did she stop him when he began to kiss her. She closed her eyes and tried to shut out the image of Matt. But the months of imprisonment had left Terry, at least temporarily, impotent. After a while she just lay in his arms and they talked until dawn.

Huw came over to see them the following afternoon. He was alone. Nancy had gone home, insisting her house had been too long neglected, and Geneva and Terry were strolling together through the plowed-up grounds when the Wakefields' favorite black mare came cantering up the driveway, Huw astride her.

Watching his friend approach, Terry said, "God, he's a magnificent-looking scoundrel, isn't he? Every time I see him on horseback, I expect to see ten thousand warriors come riding over the crest of the hill behind him."

Geneva's hand tightened on Terry's arm, she was unsure if in warning that they should not be blinded by the familiarity of knowing Huw for years, or by his dashing good-looks, or if a sense of premonition arrived with him. Huw was sliding down from his horse, his dark eyes implacable.

"Where've you been all day?" Terry demanded with mock petulance. "I haven't had a moment alone with my best friend."

"Then I'd better run along and let you two talk," Geneva said lightly, avoiding looking at Huw's unsmiling face.

"No, please stay. Could we talk for a minute out here?" Huw said quickly. His olive skin and black hair looked more exotically foreign than ever in the pale winter light.

"Of course," Terry said. "But you must stay to dinner too."

"I can't, I'm sorry. I'll be leaving this afternoon. I'm going down south. I'll come and visit Grandfather occasionally, but no doubt the army will have sent you God-knows-where by then, Terry."

"I say, Huw, isn't your grandfather getting along a bit in years to be left alone? Old boy must be nearly eighty."

Huw held the mare's reins loosely and began to walk her. They fell into step with him. Huw said, "He's got Higgins to take care of him. He's never needed me."

Geneva said, "He's very proud of you, Huw. How could he not be? You're always the very best in everything you do. Why, every sport you ever—" She broke off, remembering his professed heart trouble.

Huw's pace quickened slightly. "I suppose you've heard all the rumors about me by now, Terry? There'll be more after today. They'll say my grandfather threw me out of the house."

"And I won't believe a bloody word of it," Terry said angrily. "You know better than that, Huw, dash it."

"Yes," Huw answered softly, turning to look at him. "Yes, I do. Yet if I were in your place, I wouldn't be able to keep faith. The evidence against me is overwhelming. Heidelberg, my German friends from student days, my Eurasian blood. You know that my mother killed herself because my father died in one of Grandfather's programmed explosions. But how can you—who has no concept of the prejudice on both sides against mixed marriages, half-caste children—how can you really understand how I feel? Was my father's death really an accident? Would my mother have killed herself in any event because she could no longer stand to be shunned? And would everything have been all right again, afterward, if it had not been for my existence? I was there, you see, with my Anglo-Indian blood, to forever remind them that my parents had flaunted their taboos. My maternal grandfather no doubt settled a fortune on me in return for my paternal grandfather taking me far away. A bargain to dispose of the evidence."

"Huw," Terry said, "I think you're misjudging your grandfather. You're understandably upset at these ghastly rumors, but he obviously doesn't believe them."

"No? He hasn't spoken to me, except in public, since the night the plane bombed the abbey."

"Oh, Huw," Geneva said. During his recital of his own pain she had wanted to interrupt, to tell him that Terry's ordeal, Terry's losses due to bereavement, were more important than his personal anguish, and that this wasn't the time to pile his own misery on his friend. But she saw now that Huw had probably missed Terry's companionship even more than she had. There was no one else on earth in whom he could have confided. Terry wordlessly threw his arm across his friend's shoulders.

"Terry, Geneva . . . it's asking a great deal, but I need to know you two, at least, haven't turned against me. I can't explain any of my actions to you. I can't assure you that I'm a loyal British subject. I can only tell you that I am, and always will be, loyal to our personal friendship. That I would gladly die for either of you. I always knew that it would have been the same here without your friendship. I would have suffered that same prejudice. Oh, it would have been polite prejudice, but it would have been there. You made them accept me, because I was part and parcel of their knowing you. And you, Terry, my friend, have always been one of those golden people whose popularity is guaranteed by the gods."

"I say, cut it out. You're embarrassing me."

"Terry," Geneva interrupted, "I think Huw is leading up to something." Her sense of uneasiness was growing. She noted that Huw was striding impatiently now, his hands tight on the reins.

He said, "Your wife is right, Terry. I came to tell you both something a great deal more important. It's just that I may not see you again for a while and I wanted you to know

. . . how much your friendship has meant to me. How much I value your loyalty."

"Huw, is it something about the group you worked for?" Geneva asked. "Do you have news of Father?"

"I spent the entire night and most of this morning sneaking about in places I wasn't supposed to be. I thought the least the SOE could do was to tell you what had become of him."

Terry's arm went around Geneva. They stopped and waited. Huw's dark eyes were fixed on Geneva. She felt his stare pin her to the spot, drive away all sensory perception except the sound of his voice.

"He was sent to a special training center in the south. His code name is *Grand-père*. I suppose at age forty-four he was by far the oldest man in the SOE group. The whole operation was so secret that no communication in or out was allowed. Ian's mission was to deliver a message, and plastic explosives, to Andre Thibault."

Geneva's voice was a whisper. "Where is he now, Huw? Did you find out?"

"He was dropped into the occupied zone of France two days ago."

suggested she wait in the kitchen, but she done insisted on going in the library." His voice quivered with outrage.

"Thanks, Nathan. I'll go right in," Matt said, bemused. Whoever his unexpected visitor was, it was clear Nathan believed her to be of the servant or tradesman class.

Matt was not prepared for the young woman who was curled up on the couch, engrossed in a book. She raised enormous dark gold eyes ringed with thick black lashes that lay on café au lait cheeks. The high cheekbones were emphasized by flaring nostrils and full lips. Her hair was completely covered by a white silk turban that matched a simple white shirtwaist dress. No wonder Nathan had been outraged. She was a mulatto and he had the full-blooded African disdain of half-breeds. Still, even Nathan would admit this was one classy looking dame . . . who surely didn't belong in that beat-up Chevy?

"I'm Matthew Lauren. You wanted to see me?" Matt inquired, still mesmerized by the incredibly sensual allure of the woman. She was like a sleek cheetah, all lithe muscle and controlled stamina, stretching almost imperceptibly as he spoke, like an awakening cat. Rising, she gave him the full force of her appraising stare. The cheetah image persisted; she looked as though she were prepared to race after an already doomed prey.

She was smiling, her full lips curving upward to reveal perfect teeth. "You don't remember me, huh? Reckon I changed some since you last saw me."

"Ma'am? I'm sorry, you have me at a disadvantage."

"I was shining shoes in a hick town in Illinois the last time we met. My name's Leah."

For an instant it seemed that all sound, including his own breathing, stopped. Distantly he heard his own voice say, "Specks' daughter . . . Specks and Lottie's daughter."

The years were spinning away, and that other life, those other people who had receded into the shadows, all came rushing back. They had not been lost or forgotten, merely held in abeyance while he moved through other dimensions. "Lottie? How is your mother?"

Leah's gaze was hard, unblinking, almost accusing. "She died. Two years ago. I was supposed to come and tell you—it was the last thing she asked me to do. But I couldn't come then. Your man says I'm lucky to catch you home. That you spend a lot of time at sea. Maybe it was just as well I didn't hurry none." There were echoes of the South in her voice,

overlaid with northern speed and harshness. And something
else. A throaty, sexy rasp that was reminiscent of Lottie.

"I'm glad you came, Leah. I'm sorry about your mother.
Was she ill for long?"

The golden eyes remained fixed on him, as though afraid to
miss the slightest change in his expression. He felt as though
he were being dissected by an invisible knife. "Lottie got
beaten up in a whorehouse. She was in a coma for three days,
then died." She might have been reciting something that had
happened to an acquaintance.

Matt swallowed. "I'm sorry," he said again, inadequately.

"Weren't your fault." She replaced the book she was
holding into its space on the shelf. It was a copy of Somerset
Maugham's *Of Human Bondage*. She saw his eyes follow the
movement of her hand and allowed her fingers to remain on
the book, fingering the title. "I don't read so good. But I like
books. I like the feel of them, the way the printing makes a
pattern on the page. Some day I'm gonna learn how to read
so's it makes sense. Ain't never had the time." She gave him a
sly glance. "Too many other good things to do in this life."

"Will you stay for dinner?" Matt could feel a definite
warmth under his collar. "I'll get Nathan to set another
place."

"In the dining room? With you?" Her eyes were amused
now, watching him squirm.

Matt said, "Of course," and felt like a fool without
knowing why. There was something about her, sexually
magnetic, vaguely threatening, yet exciting in a way that
disturbed him. She was the kind of woman it was possible to
want without loving, but she wouldn't be easy to forget. Once
a man got himself involved with her, look out. His thoughts
made him uncomfortable. Why did he assume, without
knowing her, that she was promiscuous? Because her mother
died in a whorehouse? She was Specks' daughter too.

"Your man Nathan going to stand still for me eating in the
big house with the white massa?" she asked, lowering fringes
of charcoal lashes over her eyes.

"We could eat in the slave quarters, if you prefer."

She laughed then, delicious peeling bells of merriment that
rippled through the room and down his spine. She sat down,
crossing one slim leg over the other, the silk dress riding up
over her knee. She leaned back, still laughing, the thin
material tightening against her breasts. Matt had to turn

swiftly and go to find Nathan before she realized he was aroused by her.

Nathan sent a young housemaid in to serve dinner, after muttering that no low-class half-breed female trash had ever been served in the Greenboughs' dining room and he wasn't going to start now and Mr. Castleton would spin in his grave and it was jes' a blessing that Mr. Matthew was dining alone tonight, for mercy's sake, 'cause the Lord know what folks would think. All of this was addressed to the silverware he was polishing furiously at the kitchen table, and not to Matt.

Properly chastened, Matt went back to take Leah into the dining room and offer her a glass of wine. The housemaid appeared minutes later with shrimp cocktails.

They had a succulent pork roast with dressing and thick gravy, fried okra, yams oozing butter and honey, followed by a pecan pie and ice cream. For the first time since he left England, Matt plowed into the food without remembering with a pang of guilt the meager rations upon which the British in general and Geneva in particular existed. There was something about Leah that made the enjoyment of food sensually exhilarating. She watched him with those limpid eyes, her lips caressing each mouthful of food, and her laughter rang out frequently. A random thought persisted that if he were to pick her up and carry her up to the bedroom, she would make love with the same reckless abandon with which she consumed the food.

He avoided asking her what she did for a living. Her clothes were tasteful and expensive, despite the battered Chevy parked outside. She was immaculately clean, groomed like a racehorse. Inch-long fingernails, dark red, fluttered above the china and crystal like exotic flying beetles.

After dinner they went back into the library, at her request, and she pulled out various books and ran her hands over the binding and flipped through the pages. He watched her, wondering how it would feel to have those fingernails dig into his back. The evening passed astonishingly swiftly.

At eleven o'clock she announced abruptly that she had to leave.

"You have to drive far?" he asked.

She looked up at him again from beneath half-closed eyelids in a way that was uniquely her own and seemed equally a glance of assessment and flirtation. "What's it to you, honey?"

"I just wondered. It's getting late for a long drive and, well, that car looks like it's seen better days."

She laughed again. "I ain't the world's champion driver. I guess I banged it up some. Had a couple of accidents—kept running into trees on the way here, and I hit a couple of parking meters and fire hydrants back where I live."

"Oh, where's that?"

They had stood up and she was inches away. He could smell her perfume. She gave an enigmatic smile. "Up north. But don't worry about me none, I'm staying in town tonight."

"You could stay here if you wish." He tried to make his voice sound casual, but realized with a start that he wanted her to stay very badly. Geneva had not replied to his letters, and his private hell of missing her and wanting her had not lessened as the days went by. It suddenly occurred to him that he had not thought of Geneva all evening. Geneva was a continual aching longing, but Leah was the sudden high of bubbling champagne, blocking out the past, having nothing to do with the future.

She giggled. "And have that old darky butler throw a fit? No, thanks. Come on, walk me out to my car so's I can give you something I brung for you."

The stars were just above their heads, suspended in an infinite sky. Down the river a whippoorwill called. Leah opened the trunk of her car and pulled out a worn leather case. Matt knew immediately what it contained.

"Specks' trumpet," he said softly, holding it in his arms.

"Lottie thought you should have it. She talked about sending it to you, but you know how she was. After you visited us in Maple Ridge she said, 'I should've given him Specks' horn. I reckon that horn and that boy both meant a lot to Specks, only sex is a mighty powerful draw. You know what, Leah, a woman can get almost anything she wants from a man with sex. She can get him to give up his home and his family and just about anything else.'"

"Specks loved your mother," Matt said. "I don't think it was just sex." He noticed again that Leah called her mother Lottie, as though to dismiss the relationship. He placed the leather case down on the hood of the car. The clasp was broken and the case had been fastened with a trouser belt. Unbuckling it, he opened the case and drew out Specks' trumpet. The brass gleamed with a fresh shine, catching the starlight and sending it flashing back to the heavens. Somewhere, far down the river, Matt thought he could hear the strains of "Honeysuckle Rose." He brought the trumpet up to his lips, not blowing, just breathing lightly into the mouthpiece.

When he put it back into the case, he said, "Thank you. Thank you for bringing it to me."

He felt Leah's hand close around his wrist, slip up his arm, drift across his shoulder and around the back of his neck. She pulled his face down and kissed him full on the mouth. Her lips were moist and parted, and as soon as he began to respond her tongue was in his mouth and she pressed close to him. He could feel her body through the thin silk of her dress, warm and sinuous, the hard peaks of her nipples insistent against his chest, her thigh moving against his, sliding her body into a position so intimate that if they hadn't been dressed, he would have been inside her. He felt desire race through him. His hands clutched her roughly, moved to cup her breasts, slip inside the silk and caress the taut flesh underneath. Then his mouth was on her throat, kissing and nibbling, moving downward.

She stopped him as his lips reached her nipple. "Not now." Her voice was a husky whisper. "Not like this. Old Nathan will come flying out and throw a bucket of cold water over us." She shook with suppressed giggles again, exciting him even more.

"Where are you staying? I'll go with you."

She pushed him away and buttoned her dress. "Not tonight, baby. I'll call you tomorrow sometime, maybe in the evening."

"I'm leaving for New York tomorrow, to see a man about a ship. I could leave it until the following morning. Give me a definite yes on tomorrow night. Listen, I want to take you out. I want to eat and drink and dance and go to nightclubs and be in the bright lights . . . have fun—the carefree, uninhibited kind. I don't want to worry about anything but having a good time. You don't know what the hell I'm talking about, do you? Never mind. Tell me where I can pick you up tomorrow, and get dressed for a big night on the town."

Her voice was silken, mocking. "Sure, baby. We'll paint this old town red. Where you gonna take me we won't get thrown out?"

Matt fumbled out of his fog of anticipation to give the question rational thought. "You've got a point. Okay, how'd you like to fly up to New York with me instead?"

"White massa, I thought you'd never ask."

She climbed into the driver's seat and turned the key in the ignition. "I'll call you after I find somebody to drive my car home for me—can't get by without my wheels, baby." The Chevy leaped forward, slick tires screaming, and took off down the drive at breakneck speed, narrowly missing the gateposts as it went through. Matt watched until it was out of sight, hoping that wherever she lived she had only to contend with rural roads. She drove like a racecar driver alone on a track.

In New York, Matt put Captain Chisholm aboard the *Geneva* and sent him on his way with less of a pang than he'd expected. Leah was installed in Delmonico's, having mysteriously produced an impressive array of luggage when she met him at Greenboughs' gates, delivered there by a taxi the day after her arrival in the scarred Chevrolet.

The Great White Way blazed its invitation that first evening in New York, and Matt went to pick her up with plans for an elaborate dinner, champagne, and as many nightclubs as they could cram in before dawn.

She opened the door to him wearing a long wisp of white silk jersey, strapless, defying gravity, her shoulders and throat golden smooth, bare of jewelry, free of any flaw. Her hair was covered by a sequined helmet that dazzled but did not detract from the gleaming promise in her eyes.

He wasn't aware of locking the door, or of taking her into his arms. They just seemed to collide in hard frenzy. A zipper down the back of her dress slid open easily and the white jersey slithered to the floor. She was naked under it, except for high-heeled satin slippers and white silk hose, twisted and knotted on her thighs to keep them up without a garter belt. When he swung her into his arms, she clung to his neck and kissed his face, and her musky breath whispered, "Oh, baby, oh, baby." He stumbled to the bed and placed her down and began to smother her body with his mouth. When he came to the sheer silk of her stockings, he could no longer wait. He swung himself over her and rammed into her so hard and so fast that he was surprised to find she was moist and ready, already whimpering and writhing, her talons digging into his back to bring him deeper inside her.

The first climax came quickly, leaving him physically spent but sensually only just awakening. He was astonished to find he was still dressed. Leah merely laughed and began to unbutton his shirt, remove his tie. Hard red fingernails tantalized as they brushed against his bare skin. He pulled the sequined helmet from her head and her hair sprang about her face, bronze undertones glinting among the dark brown curls. It was soft against his thighs as her lips and tongue brought him back to an almost instant erection.

They didn't leave the room that evening, or most of the following day. They called room service for a champagne brunch sometime in midafternoon. Leah lay under a single sheet, her body outlined in every detail, and watched the waiter stumble over his feet and rattle the ice cubes in the glasses of water and try to avoid looking at her. Matt took pity on him and told him he'd open the champagne bottle himself. Leah's giggles followed the red-faced waiter from the room as Matt, a towel wrapped around his middle, went to the ice bucket and picked up the bottle of champagne.

The cork popped and he filled two glasses and handed her one, raising the other in a toast. "To the wickedest woman I ever met."

She blew bubbles at him as he sat down beside her on the bed, then downed the champagne without a pause and offered him the empty glass. "I'll drink to one powerful-fine lover," she said, "if'n he fills up the glass again." Her long slim arm reached for the silver-covered dishes and the sheet slipped, exposing a perfect caramel-colored breast.

"You know, hungry as I am, I could easily forget the food," he said, one eye on her as he reached again for the bottle.

She laughed. "For a white guy, Matthew Lauren, you got promise. Reckon that some of Specks' raisin' of you penetrated that white hide?"

"I hope so. Black or white, Specks was the best."

"Yeah, you'll do. You'll do jes' fine," she said. She gave another chuckle, deep in her throat, as though enjoying a private joke. She had found a fruit compote in a crystal dish under the chilled silver cover and picked out an apricot with her fingers and offered it to him.

Taking it with his teeth, he nibbled her fingertips, allowed one hand to drop to her bare breast. Some of the juice dripped to the soft flesh he caressed, and he bent and licked it. She smiled and dropped a small bunch of grapes into the hollow between her breasts, pushing aside the sheet completely.

Laughing, Matt chased the slippery grapes downward,

capturing them in the region of her navel. "Emeralds in the navel of the Queen of the Nile," he said triumphantly, bringing the bunch of grapes, in his teeth, to her mouth.

Eyes fixed on each other, they consumed the grapes until their lips met, then tongues. A long breathless moment later Leah said, "Didn't we order strawberries and cream?"

Matt nodded. "And crepes and God-knows-what-all. Who cares?"

She pushed him away, all the way down on his back on the bed, then pulled the towel from his middle and tossed it on the floor. She found the strawberries and dish of thick whipped cream. Her eyes gleamed mischievously as she stood over him with a heaped spoonful of cream.

"What are you going to do with that—oh!" The question ended in a gasp of sensual pleasure as her finger transferred the cream from the spoon to his erection and followed it swiftly with her lips. "Mmmm . . . delicious," she whispered. "Now this is what I call brunch!"

There would never be another meal like it, Matt thought several hours later, after they had eaten all of it, from every part of each other's body, and made love every way it was possible, between courses. They didn't have the strength to go out that night.

When they did go out, he was proud of the way every man gawked at her, and it didn't matter, not too much, that she returned every glance with one even bolder than she received. Under the neon lights she looked more white than she had in Natchez. They were not denied entry anywhere, as they might have been in the South. Matt almost forgot that her father had been a full-blooded African, grandson of a slave.

Two days later Alvin called him to ask petulantly what was keeping him in New York, there was work to be done in Natchez. The *Geneva* wasn't the only ship they owned, and there were the Mississippi barges. Matt told him to go ahead and use the power of attorney he had and not to bother him. Throughout their telephone conversation Leah lay naked against him, playing with him, giggling softly, and Matt was bursting from need and trying not to groan into the receiver.

She was even more insatiable than he, always ready, often the instigator of a wild session of lovemaking that had no equal for sheer sensuality. There were always new tricks up her sleeve, nuances, orchestrations, choreography . . . a realm of the senses that had been explored and perfected by a connoisseur. By the end of the week he could scarcely remember his own name. He was also becoming jealous of the attention of other men and was quick to anger when she openly flirted with them.

One evening as they were dining a well-known Broadway actor stopped at their table. "Leah, darlin', where've you been hiding, you delectable doll-baby?" He bent to kiss her upturned mouth and found himself instead crashing backward into a serving cart laden with chocolate mousse. They were all asked to leave.

Leah laughed about the incident and kissed Matt's bruised knuckles as they went back to the hotel. They made love that night more wildly than ever; rough, frenzied battering, body against body, joined here and there and everywhere and nowhere. But in the morning, when Matt awakened in the tumbled disarray of the bed, she was gone.

Chapter 37

Ian sat in a small cafe in Paris, watching the street through rain-spattered windows. The square outside was almost deserted, and the scene was far removed from his memory of Europe's gayest city. No crowds or traffic jams. Any petrol-driven cars contained Germans—or collaborators. Occasionally an ordinary Frenchman would go by in a strange-looking vehicle with a small furnace at the rear which supplied wood gas to a balloonlike container on the roof, but even these were rare. There were cyclists and *velo* taxis—wickerwork seats pulled by heavy bicycles. There was a forlorn look about the city that even bomb-battered London didn't have.

The tables around him were empty because of rationing. Frenchmen who could afford black market food took it home to cook rather than allowing the restauranteur to add his charges. Ian moved his foot under the table, trying to ease the dull throbbing of his ankle. He had sprained it upon landing and hadn't helped it heal by walking on it. He had been careful not to limp. *Don't do anything to call attention to yourself.* If you're having a cup of coffee in a cafe and the Gestapo walk in, remember, innocent people do not jump up and rush out when confronted by policemen. Stay out of crowded cafes; they'll be full of Gestapo and collaborators. Don't sleep in hotels—an Englishman is liable to wake up and answer a knock on his door in English instead of French.

Of course, Jefferson and the others who had given him his training had never expected most of the rules to be of value to him. They couldn't have anticipated that instead of a quick trip to a country house outside Beauvais, he'd be waiting in Paris, surrounded by Germans, to meet the elusive Andre Thibault.

Ian had been dropped near the Thibault country house and was lucky that Andre's housekeeper, the fluttery, birdlike Marie, remembered him. She ushered him into the entry hall, which was still noisy with the ticking of all the clocks and their unsynchronized chiming.

Marie marveled that he could appear on their doorstep in the middle of the occupation. He quickly established that she was alone in the house, and told her he wanted to recruit Andre Thibault to organize resistance against the Boches.

Marie was now beside herself with excitement, bursting to tell him what she had evidently been dying to tell someone for some time. "But Monsieur Thibault he has already begun to fight the Boches, underground, as you say. How could you guess this? Even his former customers believe he is a collaborator."

She went on to explain that the art gallery and antique shops had been culled by the invaders of the most valuable pieces. The Germans were collecting French art treasures for shipment back to Germany. Andre had suggested to the local garrison that since they had almost put him out of business anyway, perhaps they could use his services as an appraiser and cataloger. In this capacity he was allowed to travel about the country, frequently to Paris, and was able to act as courier between the various safehouses, a network of loyal French citizens who helped downed RAF flyers escape and harassed the Germans in any way they could. Unfortunately this meant that in his own part of the country, Andre Thibault was shunned as a collaborator.

"And when do you expect Monsieur Thibault to return?" Ian asked.

"Oh, not for several weeks. He is doing a big job—cataloging a large collection in Paris," had been the disappointing answer. Ian could not stay more than seven days, at which time a plane would return for him. The Moon Squadron who flew the Lysanders kept a strict schedule, flying only just before and just after the full moon.

"Do you know anyone, anyone at all, who might be aware

of his activities? Or who could be trusted to relay the information I have to him upon his return?"

The housekeeper shook her head. "For his own safety, Monsieur Thibault keeps his work secret. He is more valuable if the Boches believe him to be a collaborator and his own people hate him."

"Then perhaps I must go to Paris."

"Forgive me, monsieur, but I do not think that is wise. Your French is good, but occasionally accented."

"Madame, there is one other possibility. Do you know the location of the nearest safehouse? One where a shot-down pilot or escaping Frenchman has been sheltered?"

Marie was almost weeping in frustration at her inability to help him. No, she did not know where there was a safehouse; she knew nothing of what Andre did or where he went. He had only told her vaguely of his resistance work because she had threatened to leave him if he continued to collaborate with the Germans. Then she clapped her hands and exclaimed, "But, of course. Rascasse! *He* will take you to Paris."

And so Ian met Rascasse. He was distantly related to Marie and had an elderly father he visited in the village from time to time, but Rascasse was presently on the run, hiding from the police. Rascasse was a thief, but his crime was that of stealing from the occupiers—food, blankets, watches, cameras. No loyal Frenchman was going to let the police have him for that. He had been sheltered by several villagers recently but was known to be planning to move on.

Rascasse appeared at the house as soon as it was dark. A pale, thin young man with a fixed stare and a curious habit of swaying slightly from side to side, even when seated. To Marie's distress, Rascasse expressed immediate indignation that London had sent a British agent to contact that scum, Thibault. "You want to go to Paris—see for yourself that Thibault is a traitor?" he asked Ian. "If so, I will take you."

"Thank you," Ian said. "When can we leave?" He studied the young man's small round eyes that rarely blinked, the protruding nose and receding chin. He did indeed look a little like the small fish that was called *rascasse*. He did not offer to divulge his real name and Ian in return introduced himself by his code name, *Grand-père*.

The journey to Paris had not been difficult. They traveled in packed trains, and the only time their forged papers were examined, it was by harassed railway officials who gave a perfunctory glance and turned to the next in line. Although Ian estimated that he must have shown his papers at least six times, he was never challenged. Nor did he see the Gestapo on any of the trains. Rascasse informed him that their only fear would be if the Gestapo had been alerted to search a particular train because it carried an agent.

In Paris they left the train separately after Rascasse instructed him to ride the metro to the address of a French actress, Mignon Cuvier, who was known to have hidden a group of English soldiers after the collapse and later helped them to reach Spain. It was a tenuous hope and Ian was dismayed at being so abruptly abandoned by Rascasse, who claimed urgent business elsewhere. Rascasse left him with hurried reminders not to forget that the Master Race had decreed every other day was a nonalcoholic day, a *jour sans,* in order to conserve wine stocks. "Don't order wine on a *jour sans,* and speak as little as possible; your accent comes through when you are nervous."

"This actress, Mignon Cuvier, you're sure she runs a safehouse?"

Rascasse gave him a fishy stare. "I'm sure, *Grand-père. Au revoir. Vivre libre ou mourir.*" Live in freedom or die.

Madame Mignon Cuvier proved to be an ebullient, generously endowed woman. She was about his own age, with a froth of hennaed curls and an infectious chuckle, low and throaty. She seemed an unlikely candidate for undercover operations, but when Ian arrived at her flat, there was a young British agent there who had actually been picked up by the Gestapo and had escaped by crawling out of a hotel window three stories up. He was preparing to leave that night. "Complete bloody lash-up," he told Ian gloomily. "Our people are parachuting right into Gestapo hands. They've infiltrated the few French resistance groups there are, and can pinpoint a wireless transmitter practically the minute it starts sending messages."

"Our organization is a clumsy child, fumbling in the dark," Ian responded. "We'll get better—organized—as time goes on."

Mignon regarded him with flirtatious delight. "Monsieur—pah, I cannot call you *Grand-père,* you are too young, too handsome," she declared. "What is your name? Give me any name you wish, so long as it is young and lively."

Ian smiled and gave her his real first name, and she soon brought him news of Andre Thibault. "You cannot go to the places Thibault goes to; there will be many Boches around him," Mignon told him two days later. "We will get a message to him and he will—if he chooses—meet you at a cafe known to be safe. But you will be on your own, handsome Ian. No one believes that he is not a collaborator. Your life could be forfeit if you are wrong about him, and *mon dieu,* what a waste that would be."

Thibault had not appeared at the cafe the previous day. Ian waited an hour and then left, walking as casually as he could back to Mignon's flat. Today he had been waiting only minutes when a man entered the cafe, black beret pulled low over his forehead against the rain. But he was not Andre Thibault. He sat in a corner and ordered food.

A young couple who looked like students came in, shaking the rain from their hair, and ordered soft drinks. They chatted and laughed and ignored the two silent men.

The minutes ticked by. Ian glanced at his watch, feeling uneasy. If Andre had received the message, what was keeping him away? Had he gone over to the other side? No, that was impossible. Yet hadn't France's greatest living World War I hero—Pétain of Verdun—become a collaborator? But Andre . . . Andre who cast out his own sister for conceiving a German's child? No, not Andre.

A large black Citroen pulled up in front of the cafe window. Four men got out and walked across the wet pavement. Two of them took positions at either side of the door while the other two moved into the center of the room.

Ian froze. There was no mistaking what they were. Their heavily padded shoulders, their hats, even the way they walked, gave them away. Gestapo.

The conversation of the young couple stopped abruptly. The girl spilled her drink on the front of her coat and was apparently unaware of it. She was staring at Ian with an expression of terror in her eyes.

Ian didn't move as they approached, negotiating their way between the packed tables without regard for the bulk of their bodies and the clutter of the cafe. A chair tipped over and fell to the floor with a stunning crash. He felt more incredulous than frightened. The unthinkable was happening. His thoughts were racing, trying to cope with the situation.

They walked directly toward his table. The heavier of the

two had yellowish skin, folded loosely over flat facial bones like a film of grease on the surface of a lumpy stew. His eyes were almost lost under outsize lids but they took in every detail of Ian's dress and manner. He forced himself to take a sip of his cold coffee as they reached his table.

They continued walking, right past him, to the man in the black beret sitting in the corner. The first to reach him jammed a Schmeisser automatic pistol into the man's chest and said, in German-accented French, "Gestapo. You come with us."

The Frenchman leaped to his feet, evidently too quickly for the German, who smashed his fist into the side of the man's jaw, knocking him down. He lay on the floor, winded and gasping. The two men seized him, hauled him to his feet, and dragged him to the front door. He was bundled into the Citroen and the car moved away. Only minutes had passed.

As soon as the car was out of sight, the door to the rear of the cafe opened. A shadowed figure beckoned to Ian.

Still shocked by the abruptness of the events, Ian followed him into a small kitchen where the French proprietor and his wife were preparing a pot of soup. Neither of them looked up.

"You fool," Andre Thibault said. "Why did you come to Paris?"

Ian glanced at the other two occupants of the kitchen, but Andre said, "They are patriots. What is it you want of me? Your presence here is a danger to all of us. That man the Gestapo just took away is risking his life to divert them from you."

"But—" Ian began. Andre was not yet prepared to let him speak; he went on, "You were seen here yesterday, before I could get to you. There is always a collaborator ready to run to the Gestapo. I was able to delay them, and you had gone by the time they got here. Today we gave them someone who will prove to be the innocent concierge from a rural pensione, in town to meet his mistress. He is playing a dangerous game. He will now have to prove his innocence, because we sent the Gestapo word that the British agent wore a black beret and was a short dark man. Our concierge will probably suffer considerable discomfort to his person because of you. Now I ask you again, what is it you want of me?"

Ian drew a deep breath. "To give you weapons with which to fight the occupiers. Explosives, radio transmitters. To arrange codes and safeguards for regular transmission of intelligence to and from London. We've been unable to establish any wireless contact."

Thibault's eyes gleamed with that same pearlescent glow Geneva's had when she was pleased or excited. He said, "And how will this be accomplished?"

"Air drops. They've designed cylinders to hold small arms, explosives, medicines. They're about six feet long and weigh a hundred pounds when fully loaded. Naturally we don't want to drop them into German hands. We must arrange for your people to be on hand. In addition to parachute drops— probably from Hudsons and perhaps Lancasters—we've prepared a light single-engine plane, the Lysander. It has a rugged undercarriage and can land and take off in about four hundred yards. Fitted with an extra fuel tank and stripped of armament, it has a range of up to four hundred fifty miles. They'll fly supplies—and agents—during the week before and the week after the full moon. Before I return to England, I must find several suitable landing strips, free of mud and ruts. It will be necessary for your people to light flares briefly as the plane approaches. Also for parachute drops."

Thibault nodded, satisfied. "At last. I was afraid London was never going to respond to my pleas."

Ian blinked. "Your pleas? You've been in touch with London—asked for help?"

"A friend who wished to join de Gaulle in England was sent with the message that I have many resistance contacts in a part of the country particularly suitable for air drops."

Ian said, "I don't understand, then, why they sent me . . ." He stopped, his shoulders slumping in realization. "Ah, I see. My real purpose here was unknown, even to me."

"And that is?"

"Your role of collaborator seems to have even your own people convinced of your treachery. I wonder if London wanted me to find out whether or not you are a double agent."

Andre pondered this for a moment, then shrugged. "It does not matter what they believe, so long as they give us what we must have to fight the Boches. Too bad I must leave now for Valenciennes."

"Valenciennes?" Ian asked, several ghosts stirring in memory.

Andre took the soup ladle from the cafe owner and sampled his watery broth, grimacing. "I must stop there

briefly on business. I can't take you with me—all of the
border regions have been annexed by Germany and are
heavily patrolled. The *departements* of Pas-de-Calais and
Nord are annexed to Belgium under the Belgain Occupation
Command. Your papers won't allow you into the Forbidden
Zone. Yet I am reluctant to leave you here. You are too
valuable; you would be picked up by the Gestapo before I
could return." He frowned thoughtfully and took another sip
of soup. "I think perhaps I will take you as far as I can and
then leave you at a safehouse."

"The sooner we leave here, the better," Ian said. "Isn't it
likely that any moment the Gestapo will realize they picked
up the wrong man and come back?"

Andre walked over to a door which opened to a small
pantry. The rear wall was covered with shelves containing
bottles and jars of various spices and herbs. The shelves
concealed an opening that led to the baker's shop next door,
which had an exit on a back alley.

The rain was now heavier, the skies black with clouds, and
Ian was relieved to find that Andre had a car waiting. He was
slightly disappointed when Andre said it would be better not
to return to Mignon's flat. They would leave Paris at once and
head for the country, using seldom-traveled lanes and bypassing towns.

"I take it you have a petrol ration," Ian said, settling into
the front seat as Andre took the wheel.

"For a trip to Valenciennes on Boche business? Of course."
He gave Ian a sidelong glance as they began to move. "It is a
pity I cannot take you there. It would bring back memories
for you, no? Not far from where you met my sister, Celine.
Not far from the convent where she and her child were taken.
Old battlegrounds for you. You would perhaps feel your life
had traveled in a circle."

"I feel that already," Ian answered. He leaned back,
drained from the interview and what had preceded it. His
sleep had been fitful since arriving in France, and fatigue was
beginning to tell on him. The rain was now a cloudburst and
the streets appeared completely deserted. Certainly there
was no car following them. Ian closed his eyes and dozed.

He awakened with a start to see the silhouette of a building
on a wooded hillside that looked exactly like the Sisters of
Mary convent where Geneva had been born. But, of course,
they were miles from there. Still, the shadowed scenes flitting
by the car windows reminded him of some of the battle-

grounds of the First World War. Imagination, he thought, honed by Andre's mention of it. Slipping away again, he was awakened by Andre's rough admonishment, "You talk in your sleep, Englishman, in your own language. A risky practice."

"What did I say?" Ian mumbled, disoriented by the strange surroundings.

"You said you must go and get them off the front-line wire."

Ian shivered and sat bolt upright to keep from falling asleep again. His father and brother . . . hanging on the front-line wire. A chill crept along his veins. He had been thinking about the First World War. A dream about his father and Terence had its origins in that, nothing more. Odd how the memories hammered at his brain as he traveled this strange-familiar country. But, of course, he had been here before, long ago, in a different war. No, not here—north and east of here. *Get a grip on yourself, old man. Are you awake or asleep? Motion of the car . . . soothing. Couldn't tell what time it was . . . past or present. Am I dreaming again?*

"Rauch, Wolfgang, Oberleutnant. The last of our rear guards left . . . the village is empty."

HOSTILITIES WILL CEASE AT 1100 HOURS TODAY, NOVEMBER 11. TROOPS WILL STAND FAST ON THE LINE REACHED AT THAT HOUR.

"What time is it, Corporal?"

"Nearly half past, sir."

Not much longer to go, don't want to precipitate anything.

Andre Thibault's voice sliced into his consciousness. "You didn't answer my question."

"I'm sorry, I was dozing."

"I asked what your daughter's reaction was to the news about Rauch, her father."

"I never told her that I found you. Andre, if anything should go wrong, will you let her know? About me—and about her real father. I should have told her, but . . ."

Andre threw him a curious glance before concentrating again on the dark road ahead. "You never told her that her father was a Boche? Why would you want her to know now, after what the Boches have done? It seems an unnecessary burden for her to bear."

"Actually I believe it will be a great relief to her to know that her father was not the American your sister married. Will you please send the whole story to Geneva, somehow? As you told it to me when we first met?"

"You can tell her yourself. You will be back in England in a day or two." He braked and the car came to a stop.

"Where are we?"

"To your right is a wooded hillside. A small group of men are camped deep in the woods. They are wanted by the Boches for sabotage activities, so they are camping there permanently. They cannot return to their homes; they have no ordinary life. They are former army officers who escaped the Boche dragnet. One day there will be thousands of them. They will help you to find the landing strips you need while I travel on to Valenciennes."

"Why didn't you tell me this was your plan?"

"Because you would have told the Gestapo of their existence had you been picked up."

"I wouldn't have betrayed you."

"I've seen men betray their own mothers—beg to die. One night I was walking past a Gestapo house in Paris when the body of a man crashed through an upper-story window. He had flung himself to his death to escape further torture. I will spare you the details of the condition of his body."

Ian reached for the door handle. A gray and gloomy dawn was breaking along the horizon beneath massed rainclouds. Andre surveyed the skies as he climbed out of his side of the car.

"When it rains, my saboteurs in the hills get wet; their clothes stay wet. They cannot light fires to dry them. Come, we must hurry."

The car was parked on a narrow dirt road bordering a field, partially hidden by trees. Andre led the way across the open field. "There is just one lane to cross. I don't expect any traffic this time of morning."

Ian was less aware of his surroundings and the damp chill of the morning than of the pain in his ankle as Andre set off across the field at a killing pace.

There was a gate leading to the lane, which rose sharply to the crest of a hill. On the other side of the lane, about twenty yards away, was a stone cottage. Ian saw that the cottage was in ruins, very old.

They were halfway across the lane when the motorcycle roared up over the crest of the hill, bearing two uniformed German soldiers, one riding pillion.

"Run!" Andre ordered. "To the cottage."

They sprinted toward the ruins, slid over the rocky earth, and tumbled behind the nearest wall. Andre pulled a revolver from a shoulder holster. Ian had been issued a Colt but had left it behind aboard the Hudson from which he had parachuted into France.

The motorcycle skidded to a stop and the driver yelled to them in German to come out. For answer Andre put a bullet between the eyes of the pillion rider. He went over backward, crashing against the motorcycle and toppling it to the ground, sprayed with blood. The other German dived for the ditch as Andre's second and third shots slammed into the ground beside him. The top of his steel helmet came up, and there were three flashes as he fired his service revolver in rapid succession. Andre ducked behind the stone wall as the German emptied his gun at them.

For a second the pain did not register on Ian's brain. Then he felt as though a red-hot spike had been driven into his knee. He felt a spasm pass through him that arched his spine, and a numb, falling away sensation. He looked down the length of his sprawled body and saw that although his upper torso was safely behind the ruined stone wall, his legs were in the open. The German's last bullet had blown away his kneecap.

Andre was dragging him behind the cover of stones. The agony of his leg blocked out thoughts of danger, realization of where he was and what was happening, as all the forces of his mind and body united to insure survival. Everything in the immediate vicinity blurred for several seconds.

Two more explosions of sound indicated that Andre had again fired at the German, risking raising his head above the wall in the moments it took the German to reload. Ian blinked, trying to bring the Frenchman into focus. He was yanking off the tie he wore, and a second later Ian felt the tightening around his thigh as the tourniquet was applied. A hand slapped his cheek, gently but insistently.

"Don't faint. Do you hear me? We must move at once. They are riding the advance point of a convoy to be sure the road is clear. The other vehicles will catch up any moment. Can you stand up? If we reach the cover of the woods we have a chance."

Ian struggled to a sitting position, blacked out again briefly; forced himself to remain conscious. He left a trail of blood on the ground as he moved. Andre put another couple of shots over the wall and was immediately answered by a bullet that ricocheted, spraying them with rocks. Ian hauled himself up on his good knee, accepted Andre's shoulder under his arm.

The moment he tried to stand, his leg gave way and he fell heavily.

He lay panting, his temples squeezed in a vise that strove to pull him into unconsciousness. Andre's face was a pale blur above him. Ian clutched Andre's lapel as he bent over to help. "Go, you're more important than I am. Leave the revolver. I'll keep him pinned down while you get away."

"If they take you alive, I might as well be dead too."

"Drag me over to the end of the wall, so I can shoot around the corner from a sitting position."

"Other men believed they wouldn't talk—"

"They won't take me alive. Go, for God's sake, before I pass out."

He could hear the distant rumble of lorries moving through the quiet countryside, coming closer. The German yelled at them again to come out with their hands in the air.

Andre grabbed Ian's shoulders and pulled him to the end of the wall, arranged his legs in front of him. Ian leaned back, feeling sweat drip from his face. He tried to breathe deeply and evenly, rested his eyes for a second. The gun was pushed into his hand, a clip of ammunition placed on his lap. Then Andre patted his shoulder and ran, keeping his head low and using the ruined cottage as a shield between him and the German.

Ian peered around the corner, raised the revolver, and squeezed the trigger. The recoil of the gun trembled up his arm. He fired a second and a third bullet, blinking to try to see if Andre had reached the woods.

When he leaned too far out for a fourth shot, a bullet slammed into his shoulder and the revolver slipped from useless fingers.

Time telescoped. It rushed around his head in dizzying eddies and currents; advancing, receding. That distant rumbling was growing louder. The artillery was bad tonight. They'd be going over the top at dawn. He'd have to try to get them off the front-line wire. Couldn't leave them hanging there with swagger sticks clutched in lifeless hands.

He could smell blood, strong and gamy, but the walls of the trenches were obscured by a red fog. He was glad he couldn't see them. Dead hands and feet kept slipping out of the mud walls and had to be chopped off and buried again. Once a head had appeared, eyes wide and accusing. Madness. Utter madness. All of it.

Someone was speaking to him in German. He blinked open

his eyes and saw the shadowy figure moving slowly toward
him. Sunlight pierced the clouds and glinted on the gun in the
German soldier's hand. He was speaking haltingly in French,
groping for the words.

"Do you understand me, Frenchman? The Gestapo will do
unspeakable things to you. You killed my sergeant, but I
cannot tolerate what the Gestapo will do to you. Do you
understand?"

Was he asking for name, rank, and serial number, Ian
wondered, unable to decipher the guttural French. The man
rambled on, and Ian couldn't make any sense of what he
heard. He thought it would be a good joke to reply, "Rauch,
Wolfgang. Oberleutnant. The village is empty. The last of our
rear guards left—"

He never finished the thought. There was a deafening
explosion, a blinding pain in his chest, then oblivion.

Chapter 38

The Arabs called it *khamsin*. A searing wind out of the Sahara that raised desert temperatures thirty-five degrees within hours and sapped the strength of even the hardy Bedouin, whose tribal law permitted a man to kill his wife after the hot wind had blown for five days.

Terry wore goggles to protect his eyes, and his face was swathed in a cloth mask, held in place by his helmet. He sat with his back to the overturned lorry, sucking parched air into protesting lungs. Visibility was zero. Sand particles whirled for hundreds of miles on a ninety-mile-an-hour wind, blotting out the sun.

Several jerry cans of water had fallen from the back of the lorry and were slowly being consumed by drifting sand. The other unauthorized passenger, Glendenning, was still in the hole he'd dug, head and shoulders so thickly coated with sand that he appeared to be buried alive. Terry felt compelled to get up and move about occasionally, as much as the wind allowed, to be sure he had not choked to death.

Already his brief leave in Cairo seemed like a distant dream. If this particular *khamsin* blew for five days they'd be in trouble. The water they carried was the most precious commodity in the desert war, despite the fact that it looked like coffee and tasted like sulfur.

Still, the windstorm would also halt the battle, pin down tanks, ground planes. But he and Glendenning would shortly be absent without leave. Crouching behind the lorry, Terry regretted listening to Glendenning's suggestion that they could gain an extra day in Cairo if they hitched a lift back with the water carrier. Gunga Din, as Glen had dubbed him, lay dead at the wheel, killed when the wind overturned the lorry.

Cairo had been an oasis of luxury. Cool drinks, hot baths, warm women. Terry had explored the teeming streets, stopped to buy souvenirs in the noisy marketplace, and watched Madame Badia's belly dancers. He felt the exhaustion of desert fighting slip away.

He rented a camel and was taken by an Egyptian guide, himself astride a donkey, to the Cheops pyramid. It was here, amid the awe-inspiring majesty of an ancient civilization, that he met Glendenning.

"Smile! Say 'cheese' . . . hey, over here!"

Terry turned in the direction of the schoolmasterish voice and saw a lanky captain in crumpled shorts and battered pith helmet that looked as if it had been present when King Tut's tomb was opened. The decrepit officer was aiming a camera at him and the camel. Terry obliged with a wide grin. The camel snorted.

The unkempt captain sauntered over to him. "Glendenning. Glen, to my friends. If I had any. Who are you? I always like to know who I am immortalizing. Not that you'll get a print, you understand. It will be enough to know that your image has been captured by the Great Glendenning, so that you'll remain forever frozen on the back of that idiot camel through all eternity—never mind that your carcass is rotting out there in the desert somewhere." He gave a melancholy smile that cracked the dust on his face but did not express pleasure or anything else a smile usually conveys.

"Thanks," Terry said, sliding down from the back of the camel, which had been prodded to a sitting position, "for the optimistic forecast. Saxon—Terry to friends and enemies and the undecided." He offered his hand, curious about a fellow officer who scorned both spit and polish and the conventional overtures to a stranger.

Glendenning moved his camera carefully to his other hand and gave a perfunctory handshake. "I've a staff job at GHQ."

"Oh?" Terry inquired, his eye on the battered pith helmet. "Whose army?"

Glendenning made a sound something like the cackle of a rooster, which Terry took to be laughter although there was no smile to go with it. "I'm going to like you, Saxon Terry. How would you like to get away from the flies and grit of Cairo? There's an island in the Nile called Gezira. Polo, cricket, golf. Though you don't look like a golfer."

"Polo. Though I don't mind a spot of cricket, either."

"No need to be apologetic about it, old man. Come on, let's get away from this disgusting beast." He wrinkled his nose at the camel's intolerable odor. It sneered back at him and dribbled saliva.

"So, young Terry, you're on leave and you've sipped aperitifs on the terrace of Shepheard's and dined more sumptuously than ever before in your life. And you've danced at the roof garden of the Continental Hotel. Before I take you to Gezira, would you like to see how the other half live?"

"I get the feeling I've been taken under your wing. No ulterior motives, I trust?" Terry said lightly, watching the captain carefully. Glendenning was probably only in his thirties, but he had that shopworn air of certain professors Terry remembered from university. Sandy coloring, matching hair and mustache and skin—so like the hues of the desert that he appeared to be camouflaged.

Glendenning looked around. There were other British soldiers touring the great pyramid, a few army women. All were in groups or couples. "You and I are the only ones who are alone. Doesn't do to be alone here. Not that you have much to fear from the peddlers and guides—we're fattening their purses too much for them to wish us harm. But a man alone starts thinking, and thinking is the worst hazard of all. Do you think when you're alone, Terry?"

"No. I write long letters to my wife."

"Well, regarding your question about an ulterior motive. Actually, I do have a small one. You're obviously in from the forward positions, I can tell by that wary watchfulness in your eyes . . . among other things. You see, I've decided to give up my nice little desk job and I'll be moving out in a few days. I'd like to find out what I'm in for."

He turned and spoke sharply in Arabic to two peddlers who were plucking at Terry's sleeve. They scurried away. "I did *ask* for the transfer—demanded it, actually, when I was roaring drunk, so I can't very well back down now. Lose face, you know, old boy."

That night Glendenning took him to the Melody Club, where the band was protected from brawling soldiers of lesser rank or refinement by a barbed-wire fence. The highlight of the evening was a belly dancer named Hekmet, who so inflamed Glendenning's senses that afterward Terry found himself sharing a bed with the creased captain and three women he had produced out of thin air. The women giggled and teased and delivered exotic pleasures but spoke no English. Terry was vaguely aware of the hubbly-bubbly emitting the sweet stink of hashish, of Glendenning's foot in the middle of his back, and plump moist skin everywhere in a writhing ballet of sensualism that expanded the boundaries even Dory Gates had opened for him. He couldn't believe he was participating in some of the things he—and they—were doing to each other. Perhaps he wasn't; perhaps it was all a dream. *Am I a man dreaming I am a beast . . . or a beast dreaming I'm a man? Did Glendenning say that, or did I think it?*

The following morning Terry staggered back to the hotel. A Free French officer, supported by crutches, was making his way slowly down the steps. One trouser leg was tucked neatly over a stump of thigh.

Glendenning appeared at lunchtime to reiterate his offer to take Terry to Gezira. They went out onto the terrace to have a drink.

"What did you think of the Melody Club, Terry?"

"Interesting. Almost as interesting as what followed."

Glendenning laughed. The feat of laughing without smiling fascinated Terry. His companion nodded toward the adjacent tables and wicker chairs occupied by both soldiers and civilians. "Half of this lot are Axis spies. This town is a den of intrigue. Full of innuendo and rumor. Communications are rather spotty between here and the desert. When Egypt broke off relations with Germany, it didn't deter her vocal group of Axis supporters."

"Yes, I heard a mob of students chanting 'Press on, Rommel' the first day I was here."

They both became silent, pensive, as the sadly haunting refrain of "Lili Marlene," sung in German, drifted across the crowded terrace from a nearby wireless.

"There are officers in the Egyptian army just waiting for Rommel to arrive," Glendenning said as the last poignant notes faded and conversation around them resumed. "They want our arses out of here. And as for the Desert Fox—he's reported to have an intuition for his enemies' weakness. *Sturm, swung, wucht*—attack, impetus, weight. He's a master of deception; he'll have some surprises in store for us."

Terry said, "He was commander of the Seventh Panzer Division—they called it the Ghost Division when we were retreating across France before Dunkirk. Kept showing up where we least expected it."

"Well," Glendenning said gloomily, "our defenses in eastern Libya have been stripped to the bone so we could send the expedition to Greece. Our western flank is dangerously vulnerable."

Terry glanced about. "Hadn't you better keep your voice down?"

Glendenning snorted. "You think it's a secret? My God, since I knew we were led by asses, why wasn't I content to stay at GHQ? Kismet, I suppose, as the Arabs say. Tell me about the desert fighting. What's it really been like?"

"It's not so bad. Bit of a muddle, that's all. Water is the main problem. You'll learn to take a bath in a teacupful."

"In other words, you don't want to talk about it."

Terry shrugged and smiled. "There are better things to talk about. For instance, who are those two stunning women who just went into the bar?"

Glendenning gave a cursory glance in their direction. "I can introduce you, if you'd rather spend some time with them than go with me to Gezira." He was obviously in a morose mood; perhaps, Terry thought, as a result of the plunge to reality after the reckless debauchery of the previous night.

"Not at all, old chap. Onward to Gezira," Terry responded. "I'll nip up to my room and pack an overnight bag."

"Good. I'll call for you as soon as I've taken care of a couple of things."

When Terry had shaved, bathed, packed, and there was still no sign of Glendenning, he began to regret not pursuing the two women in the bar. At length he opened his writing case and looked at the letter he had been writing to Geneva. It was growing to heroic proportions, since he never seemed able to end it. He had started it shortly after he had persuaded one of the reconnaissance pilots to take him on a flight across the desert, which had ended when they developed engine trouble and had to land miles from anywhere. They had set off on foot and been lucky enough to reach an oasis, near which was a Bedouin encampment. He began to read what he had written.

> . . . and reached the encampment just after sunset. Gaunt men and shriveled children greeted us with extravagant phrases of desert welcome, and slaughtered a sheep for a feast. They set great mounds of rice around the sheep and poured butter over the whole until it ran into the sand. We looked at their starving faces and knew they'd go hungry for days after this lavish show of hospitality. Yet we could not refuse. *Salaam aleikum,* you are a hundred times welcome, they kept telling us.
>
> The Bedouin chief was a black-eyed brigand with a fierce, hawklike face, named Sanfara. He spoke English—*Oxford!*
>
> Hyenas visited the encampment during the night, but we'd left little to eat. The platters had been licked clean; bones were broken open to suck out the marrow. Bodies were anointed with any grease they couldn't get into their mouths. The hyenas ate my shoes instead. Sanfara roared with laughter and said it was Allah's will.
>
> They agreed to take us to the nearest outpost, and we rode until the sun was high, then rested. They propped their robes on sticks to form pockets of shade from the blinding rays of the sun—they're like steel claws descending from a molten sky. The air is so dry it crackles in your throat. We moved on again in the early evening. The sunset was a tapestry of flame and scarlet weaving the sky to the distant dunes. We rode until we fell with exhaustion.
>
> I awoke before dawn to an eerie silence. The stars hung in the sky, near enough to touch—a brilliant Venus—Cassiopeia. The desert sunrise is a mystical litany, reaching from the unadorned rim of the earth to touch some chord in the soul. Geneva, I can't begin to explain how I felt. Like I'd come home, was at peace. Clear silver light illuminated all the subtle variations of the desert landscape, warmed the dust-etched faces of the sleeping Bedouins.
>
> I was caught in the fragile spell of the desert. I didn't even remember why I was there. Even the barren dunes where no living thing grows have a stark and

compelling grandeur. As though the earth were stripped to its bare bones of everything too mortal to survive—

Terry stared at the last words he had written, then crumpled the letter in his hand. He held it for a moment, then tossed it into the wastepaper basket. What the devil was keeping Glendenning? He sat down and picked up his pen and began again.

Had my first experience riding a camel recently. Incredibly uncomfortable. I was tired and began to doze and the miserable animal sensed this and lurched over to nibble some desert grass. I was flung rudely from his back and landed with a jolting thud in a cloud of dust. The Bedouin were highly amused. They'd warned me I was stupid to treat the camel with the "Inglese" excessive kindness, instead of curses and camel-stick prodding to which it was accustomed. My reward was a haughty beast quick to take offense, forever wandering off in search of a tasty morsel and prone to leap to its feet when I was in the act of climbing to its back. It stared at me malevolently, dribbling bright green saliva with an unbelievable stench.

That day a mud-colored cloud on the horizon suddenly separated into three distinct whirlwinds of sand, towering high in the air. The dreaded jinn of the desert—swirling air masses and thunder exploding all around like a host of roaring gods descending from the skies in avenging wrath.

The rain fell in an unbroken deluge for several minutes. The effect was almost sensual. I rolled on my back and tore off my clothes to let the warm water wash over my parched body. The Bedouin told me it had been three years since the last rain.

I looked up to see Sanfara watching me with an amused stare. So I quoted, *". . . how We put water in showers Then split the earth in clefts and cause the grain to grow therein and grapes and green fodder and olive-trees and palm-trees And garden-closes of thick foliage and fruits and grasses: provision for you and your beasts."*

The expression on Sanfara's face changed to surprise. "So, *Inglese*, you have read the Koran." And I replied, "Is that more astonishing than you learning my language?" He shrugged and commented, "We learn what Allah wills."

Terry laid down his pen. In making so much of a two-day encounter with the Badu caravan, would he give Geneva the impression he was on some mystical odyssey, rather than fighting Germans and Italians? And would the censor report that unauthorized flight to forbidden territory? It would be a surprise to Geneva that he had read the Koran. Was she ready to have lighthearted old Terry reveal some of the deeper insights into humanity's soul that he'd pondered since the war began? He supposed all men confronted with the necessity of killing or being killed sought similar answers. What was it Ian used to say—that there were no atheists in the trenches?

Glendenning suddenly pounded on his door, and he slipped the unfinished letter into his pocket.

Gezira was a verdant island, surrounded by the green water of the Nile, basking in sunlight that pierced the heavens like a sword. They had lunch, then Terry joined a polo match while Glendenning watched from the shade. Later Terry followed him while he played a few holes of golf. Glendenning's mood had not improved.

As the sun began to set Glendenning stopped, staring at the sky. "I'm going to die out there in the desert," he said. "Could have spent the war safe and sound in old Farouk's Sodom by the Nile. But no, I had to make the gallant gesture."

"You're a bloody pessimist," Terry said. "And obviously not a professional soldier. What did you do before the war?"

"Historian and linguist. Oxford. That was my downfall— Arabic. They needed interpreters in the forward positions to talk to the nomads."

He swung, missed, and cursed in Arabic. "You know what I think? I think that empty stretch of sand out there will still be nothing but a sweep of deserted desert long after our blood has soaked into it. We certainly won't occupy it after the war. What would be the bloody point? Nor will the Germans or Italians. I mean, no one actually *wants* the sodding place, do they? So why the hell are we all fighting so desperately for it? Twenty years from now it will still be inhabited by a few nomadic tribes, and no doubt another generation of Englishmen—or Germans—or some other poor bastards will be getting ready to have another go at each other over it. I mean, for the love of Christ, it doesn't make sense to die for a piece of barren sand. Or a lush green land, come to think of it. What can be more important than life itself?"

"You're getting melancholy. Let's go and get drunk instead and find some women."

"Drunk *and* melancholy I can be, let me warn you. Or drunk and heroic. Even drunk and philosophical." He held up his golf club and addressed his soliloquy to it. "I put my gear into the storeroom at Shepheard's yesterday. For a couple of pennies a month you can leave your stuff there while you go and meet your fate in the western sands. I doubt I'll be back to claim mine."

"All right, Glendenning. I've had enough. Stay here and cry into your golf bag if you wish. I'm off."

"After I stowed my worldly goods in Shepheard's storeroom, I went outside in time to see an ambulance convoy crawling in from the desert. I think I'd rather get killed than maimed, wouldn't you?"

"Cheerio, Captain. I'm going to the bar. Come and join me if you come out of your depression."

"What do *you* think, Terry Saxon? About life and death?"

"I think," Terry said, considering, "there's a sort of mad splendor to it."

The *khamsin* blew billowing curtains of sand, and Terry silently cursed Glendenning for talking him into riding with Gunga Din, a bleak-tempered Geordie who didn't appreciate the humor of his nickname; forgetting for a moment that Gunga Din would not care much about anything in future.

Crawling to where Glendenning's head protruded from the sand, Terry picked up his helmet and looked under it. Behind dust-coated goggles Glendenning's eyes blinked open and then closed again. Terry settled down again to wait out the wind.

It stopped abruptly the next day. Crystal-clear air and vivid blue skies canopied newly formed dunes. Terry climbed into the back of the lorry and shook sand from one of the jerry cans of water. Glendenning came to his feet like a dusty fossil rising from the earth.

"Still alive, I see, old bean," Terry called cheerfully. Glendenning grunted a reply and staggered to the other side of the lorry to relieve himself.

Terry drank some water, then felt in his pocket for his compass. It was gone. He swore. Must have dropped it in the sand.

Glendenning didn't own a compass, and the other lorries in the convoy were nowhere in sight. Probably weren't even aware they had overturned in the sandstorm.

"Told you so, old boy," Glendenning said when Terry informed him of the situation. "Might as well go back to sleep, we'll never reach Benghazi. This is where we're going to die."

Terry ignored him. "We'll fill as many canteens as we can carry and start walking. If we stay here the lorry will be spotted from the sky and some Jerry pilot will take potshots at us. I can plot a course from the sun. Fortunately we haven't far to go."

Glendenning had to be prodded like a reluctant camel, but they were lucky. They had only marched a couple of hours when they were picked up by a supply convoy. The officer in charge told them that the news of the fighting was confusing and fragmented, but it appeared that Rommel's Afrika Corps was pushing forward and the British forces were falling back.

"Wavell has issued orders to fall back to Benghazi, if El Agheila can't be held," they were told.

When they were alone, bouncing uncomfortably in the back of a lorry, Glendenning said, "Perhaps you should just come to Benghazi with me, rather than going back to El Agheila. Spare yourself another Dunkirk."

Terry was silent, wondering if even Benghazi could be held. He had seen the escarpment to the south and wasn't convinced it was a barrier against tanks. Before his leave in Cairo he had been on patrol, harassing German supply columns bound for the German–Italian outpost at Mareda, ninety miles to the south, and reasoned that Rommel had to maintain that outpost; therefore El Agheila must be attacked soon. Despite this, it was not strongly defended.

"Well?" Glendenning asked. "Are you going to Benghazi or El Agheila?"

"You know where I'm going."

"Yes. To your death. As I go to mine. Bloody fools, both of us. Tell me again what we're dying for."

"King and country and the Honor of the Fleet," Terry answered lightly.

Glendenning glared at him. "Repeat after me: *We are dying for a barren stretch of sand that nobody wants.*"

Terry squirmed into a more comfortable position. "You could have stayed at GHQ in Cairo. Perhaps fulfilled your kismet by dying there—for Farouk and the belly dancers?" Terry grinned at Glendenning's apocalyptic frown.

The lorry was grinding to a halt. "Good-bye, Terry Saxon," Glendenning said. "Do you know why I took that snapshot of you at the pyramid? It was because you seemed to personify the glorious young warrior mankind manages to produce every generation. Handsome, strong, honorable—but not very durable. A perfect sacrifice to the gods of war. I've studied history all of my life and never even come close to understanding why we want to kill off our best—or how we keep managing to persuade them to die. Your photograph is in the storeroom at Shepheard's. If you ever get back to Cairo, go and look at it. But I doubt you will. I should have inscribed it—*Doomed*. Well, there's one consolation, old boy. At least you aren't leaving behind an heir to die in the next one."

They jumped down from the back of the lorry and Terry offered his hand in a farewell handshake, but Glendenning ignored it and instead pulled him into a rough embrace. Embarrassed, Terry pulled away. He said, "Good-bye, Glen. Come and see me after the war."

The day after Terry reached his own company at El Agheila, he was sent out on patrol. Hours later Rommel launched his attack. Tanks and armored cars of Major Irmfried von Wechmar's Third Reconnaissance Battalion thrust forward toward El Agheila, advancing on a thousand-yard front. The vehicles threw up swirling clouds of dust, the density of which indicated numbers of attacking tanks that presented a formidable threat to the poorly defended outpost. The garrison was ordered to fall back to Mersa Brega.

Terry and his patrol found themselves cut off, the advancing Germans between them and their base. They saw the dust raised by the armor miles away and left their vehicles to climb to the crest of an escarpment for a better view. Looking down at the outlines of the German armor within the dust clouds, Terry knew there would be little need to radio El Agheila that they were under attack. The advancing tanks and armored vehicles would be seen for miles. But he ordered his wireless operator to send the message. They were told of the withdrawal and ordered to Mersa Brega.

Terry again raised his binoculars for another look at the

advancing columns. There was something strange about the
last row of tanks and cars coming into view. He had no time
to speculate, for a moment later a pair of Stukas swept out of
the sunlit sky, screeching earthward.

The first bombs hit their ammunition carrier, sending a
pillar of fire upward. The Stukas wheeled aloft and began
another fearful dive. Terry raised his rifle and shot at the
plane as it hurtled toward him. An armored car exploded
beside him, driving red-hot shrapnel into his body and
deafening him.

He pitched to the sand, rolled on the ground in a strange
silent world. There was blood in his mouth. A minute later he
watched in horrified fascination as the wireless operator was
dismembered by an exploding bomb, his arms and legs
literally blown from his torso.

It was all over for their patrol within minutes. As the planes
droned away, Terry dragged himself from one body to
another to make sure they were all dead. His upper body had
been peppered with shrapnel and he'd evidently been hit on
the face, but since he was conscious and able to move, he
assumed none of it had been driven in too deeply. He edged
toward the escarpment, each motion sending stabbing pains
into various parts of him, as though he were crawling on the
back of a hedgehog.

Below on the plain the German panzers continued their
drive toward El Agheila. His hearing had not returned, so
Terry was unsure if the dive bombers were still around. He
couldn't see them. Scanning the sky, he was blinded by the
sunlight. He crawled to the edge of the dunes and slipped
over, unsure what he was doing, or why.

The escarpment was steeper than he realized and he
quickly gained momentum, tumbling over and over in the
fine-grained sand, which stung his eyes and clogged his mouth
and nostrils. Consciousness slipped away before he ended the
fall.

When he opened his eyes, he was lying face up only yards
from a German tank. It was not moving. No sign of life. He
couldn't see any other vehicles. He shook his head, trying to
hear, but utter silence prevailed. He wondered if the explosion had permanently impaired his hearing.

Damn, there was something strange about that tank. What
the hell was it? Perhaps it had mechanical trouble and they'd
abandoned it? He knew only too well how many of their own
tanks had been damaged in transit and were breaking down.

He climbed unsteadily to his feet and lurched toward the German tank.

When he was close enough to touch the side of it, he reached out and felt his hand grasp a sheet of canvas. He blinked and looked again. Then he laughed, or at least he went through the motions of laughing. He couldn't hear if he actually made a sound.

A dummy. A dummy tank. Canvas and cardboard mounted on a Volkswagen chassis. Incapable of firing a shot. But capable of sending up columns of dust, creating the illusion of a superior force advancing on a poorly defended garrison. That last line of armor—and how many in the center?—had all been dummies; only the vehicles in the front ranks and on the flanks had been real. In the swirling sand the outline would have been enough to convince the garrison that they were being engulfed by an overwhelming force. They had withdrawn from El Aghelia, run from a cardboard division, bamboozled by a master of deception. Score one for Rommel.

A face appeared around the canvas turret so suddenly and unexpectedly that Terry had only the briefest glimpse of cold blue eyes and the glint of the revolver. He didn't hear the sound of the bullet that smashed into his face, tearing through his skull and emptying his brains down the canvas side of the dummy tank.

Chapter 39

Geneva had not received any letters from her father, but cryptic notes came regularly from Captain Jefferson assuring her that "the last I heard, he was well."

With the long hours of daylight of midsummer, the air raids in the north had eased somewhat. Now there were only a couple of hours of darkness as the twilight lingered until after eleven at night and dawn began to break soon after two. When the German bombers came, they came in over the Irish Sea, from Eire, to avoid flying over England in daylight and being shot down by fighter pilots or antiaircraft batteries.

Geneva decided to close down Saxon Hall and join one of the women's services. She was filled with a restless anger and a need for personal danger. Her growing hatred of the Germans was not assuaged by driving their victims to the hospital. She wanted a more active part in the war. Perhaps it would ease her heart-numbing grief over Dulcie's death.

She was persuaded to stay with the St. John's Ambulance Brigade until a replacement driver could be found and then was released from her duties. She had been home only a few days when, on June 22, Hitler attacked the Soviet Union, and England gained an unlikely ally.

Churchill's views on communism were well known. It was also well known that he would make an alliance with the Devil himself in order to defeat the Nazis. There was a surge of hope in England that in stabbing his old nonaggression pact partner in the back, Hitler—like Napoleon before him—had now bitten off an undigestible chunk of icy continent that even his undefeated panzers would be unable to chew.

And on the same day Geneva received a telegram telling her that Terry had been killed in action in the Libyan desert.

Nancy and the minister from St. Agnes' parish came to her immediately. She was glad she was home. It would be easier to accept as final, here at the Hall. There would have been that sense of unreality had they come to her Liverpool flat with the news. Of it all happening to someone else.

She listened as they said all the usual things, none of which helped the aching sense of loss. Perhaps she had known, the last time she saw him walking away from her, that she would never see him again. After a while she excused herself and went outside. She was too numb to do anything but walk across the grounds, with their bountiful crop of vegetables, into the woods and along the riverbank. She walked for hours, wondering if and when she would give in to an outburst of grief, wishing she could feel something, anything; because she was afraid that even death itself no longer had any meaning for her. *Do we become immune to the point that we cease to care?* She asked the question as she tried to force tears from dry eyes.

Hours later, when she returned home, she found Nancy waiting for her, the kettle simmering ready for tea. Wordlessly Nancy wrapped her arms around Geneva and held her.

Later she helped cover furniture with dust sheets, pack away valuables. She asked, "What about you, lass, where will you go? Back to your flat in Liverpool until your dad gets back?"

"No. I've decided to join the army. I'm not feeling too coherent, so this probably won't make much sense to you, but somehow driving an ambulance is a sort of passive participation. I want to do more."

Nancy was just leaving to return to her own house when the front doorbell chimed. She left Geneva in her father's study and went to answer it, returning a moment later to whisper, "It's Huw Wakefield, Gennie. Do you want to see him?"

"Not really, but I will. He's probably heard about Terry. I haven't seen Huw for months. I thought he was still in the south somewhere."

She went with Nancy to the door, bade her good night, and gestured for Huw to come in. She took him into the drawing room and they sat amid the white-shrouded furniture, aware of the feeling of being surrounded by ghosts.

"I'll miss him for the rest of my life," Huw said.

She nodded, knowing he meant it. She waved her hand in a despairing gesture, feeling a lump form at last in her throat. She would be able to cry after he left.

"My grandfather refused to see me again. I heard about Terry in the village. Geneva, I'll be leaving first thing in the morning, and God knows this isn't the time to add to your burden of grief, but . . ."

"Huw, I've lost my child and my husband. What else could you tell me—" She broke off, an icy chill settling in the pit of her stomach at the expression on his face. "Oh, dear God no, Huw . . . please, no!"

"I'm sorry, Geneva. I'm sorry it has to be me who tells you, but damn it, I don't think anyone else is going to. There have been agents they've *known* have been dead for months —absolutely confirmed dead, and their families haven't been notified either. There's no chance they'll let you know about your father because they aren't a hundred percent sure what happened to him. They only know he didn't keep a rendez-vous to be picked up and brought back."

"But you . . . you know he's dead? How can you know? How can you be sure? Unless—"

"Unless I'm a German agent? Geneva, listen to me. Your father parachuted into France and vanished into thin air. The last man to see him alive was Andre Thibault, your uncle. They sacrificed your father, Geneva. His death served no other purpose than to establish that your uncle is a German collaborator. So that the next agent sent in could approach someone else to help him form a resistance group."

"No, Huw. Please don't say that. I couldn't bear it if it were true. No one would toss aside a life so carelessly. Not even the army, or whoever it is my father was working for—*is* working for," she corrected herself. "I refuse to believe it."

"What? That your father died needlessly? Or that your uncle is a collaborator? Does it matter? Don't you feel any loyalty to Germany? You're half German, Geneva. Your father was a young officer named Wolfgang Rauch, whom your mother's family refused to allow her to marry. You've been denied your heritage all your life, as I was denied mine, because the English believe that to be English is all that anyone needs or wants."

"How do you know this?" she whispered, feeling less surprise at the revelation than a sense of inevitability, as though the truth had always been available to her, had she striven hard enough to acquire it.

"Does it matter how I know? It's more important right now for you to understand that the man you called Father was not killed by the Germans—he was sent to his death by the English and betrayed by your French uncle."

"No!" Geneva turned on him, her eyes blazing. "I don't believe my father would have risked his life to go to France if he hadn't believed implicitly in my uncle. And as far as I'm concerned, it's as though my German father never existed. How can I feel loyalty to a country I've never seen? To a regime that is warlike and cruel? I think you'd better leave."

Huw shrugged indifferently. "Very well. We probably won't meet again. My grandfather has told me never to come home again." He pulled a slip of paper from his pocket and placed it atop a shrouded table. "This is the address of a country house in the south where you'll find Captain Jefferson. If I were you, I'd just go—unannounced. The actual headquarters of the SOE group is in Baker Street in London, but you won't be able to get in there so easily. I suggest you go and confront Jefferson, face to face, and demand that he tell you what happened to your father."

He offered his hand, but she was too upset to take it. She strode to the door and flung it open for him to pass through, wanting him to be gone. They had all been right, he was a traitor. Perhaps she should call someone and tell them? In the morning, perhaps. He couldn't get very far in a few hours, and she was too incoherent to be able to convince anyone of anything at this moment. As Huw went past her he looked at her with an odd mixture of regret and respect in his eyes. She was too angry to try to analyze what he might be feeling.

After he was gone, she went into her father's study. It was the only room not already prepared for the closing of the house. His desk and chair and bookshelves were as he had left them. It would have been easy to imagine him seated at the desk, quietly and painstakingly dealing with all the myriad details of the colliery and the farms and the Hall and their people.

She sat for a long time in the dark, then prowled the house restlessly, trying to capture images, wanting to conjure herself and Terry as children running to the gentle silver-haired man whose arms and heart was always open to them. At last she went back to the drawing room and picked up the paper bearing Jefferson's address.

The house was a rather shabby looking mansion in the south of England. An army clerk seated at a small desk in the entry hall summoned an orderly, who conducted her to a room bare of furniture but for three chairs and a long table. They didn't seem particularly surprised to see her, or by her demand that she be taken to Captain Jefferson. She was merely corrected as to his rank. He was now a major.

Minutes later he entered the room. She remembered Jefferson from their previous brief meeting. He gestured for her to take a chair but remained standing himself. He was a bony, pointed man whose sharp angles were hidden under an impeccably pressed uniform that managed to disguise the fact that there was any flesh or bone beneath the smooth khaki material.

"I'm sorry there's been no direct communication from your father, Geneva," he said. "But the last I heard—"

"Please. I know that my father went to France to contact my uncle, Andre Thibault. I know he hasn't been heard from since. You sent my father to his death. You believe my uncle is a collaborator—that my father's death proved it. But you are wrong. I came here to volunteer to go to France to try to find out what happened."

His face registered no surprise. For a split second it seemed to Geneva that there had been impatience in his eyes, as though the two of them were rehearsing the preliminary lines to a play and he was anxious to get on with the next act. He asked in French, "What makes you think you are qualified for such a mission?"

She replied in rapid and fluent French, "I speak the language well, better than my father. I've studied French customs, culture, geography. I'm young, healthy. I have no ties. You can train me, as you trained my father."

"If I were to tell you that we're reasonably certain your father is dead, and that your uncle *is* a collaborator, what then? Would you still want to go to France?"

She almost screamed her answer, "Yes!"

"Why? To avenge your father? To punish your uncle? What for?"

She was on her feet. "For me! I want to do it for *me*. I don't want to just *be* here. I want my life to mean something.

Nothing I've done so far has been of my own true choice. Things happened *to* me. I want to *make* things happen." *I want to hurt Germans. For Dulcie and Terry and perhaps my father. I want revenge, God forgive me.*

His face remained impassive, but there was a gleam in his eyes that hadn't been there before. He said, "Your French is excellent. You even have a Parisienne accent. But this isn't the time to talk, not while you're still in an emotional upheaval over your husband's death. I'll be in touch later. Go home and wait."

She supposed he was giving her time to change her mind. In the interim she read everything she could find about the current situation, as far as it was known, in France. She studied the Occupied Zone, Vichy France, the forbidden zones, the annexed zones, making herself aware of boundaries that would be familiar to Frenchmen who had lived under the occupation for over a year. She read the texts of all of General de Gaulle's broadcasts to his fellow countrymen. DeGaulle had arrived in England while the remnants of the French army joined the panicked citizens clogging the dusty roads south of Paris, fleeing from the Nazi invaders.

Several weeks passed before an army staff car, chauffeured by a tight-lipped sergeant, came for her. She was taken to a remote country house, screened by miles of woodland. There were other women in Geneva's preliminary training group. They were mostly members of the Women's Transport Service, First Aid Nursing Yeomanry, or FANY with a sprinkling of WAAF—the Women's Auxiliary Air Force. Geneva was also issued an FANY uniform. Later they would be dispersed into smaller groups and eventually would go to Scotland, they were promised, for a "toughening-up" course. First names only were used.

At an orientation session a Frenchman named Jacques paced back and forth in front of a bare blackboard. "Let me tell you what it was like after the first confusion and panic ended. My people found that the Germans were not quite the ogres they had expected. The occupying army seemed decent, polite. They opened soup kitchens, paid for goods they purchased in shops. So the terror was dispelled. I saw Boches and Frenchmen drinking together in cafes, the Comédie Française and the opera played to packed houses of officers in dress uniforms. The Germans refused to be baited by the few; they continued to mollify the population up until last autumn,

when I left the country. But signs of resistance were beginning, even then. Graffiti appeared on walls—*Vive de Gaulle,*
the Cross of Lorraine—once even on a German staff car as it
was stopped for a traffic light. There were isolated acts of
courage. Someone destroys a segment of railway line; an old
lady directs a German soldier to the wrong destination. Then
the underground newspapers began to appear."

He paused and passed a pamphlet around for them to read.
"The first of the subversive voices. Study it carefully."

Geneva read the heading, "Advice to the Occupied." It
contained thirty-three counsels on how to behave toward the
Germans. "Have no illusions. They are not tourists, they are
conquerors . . ."

Jacques went on, "Soon military telephone cables were
being cut. Posters appeared; British and French flags were
flown. Pathetically little, but a beginning. But then the first
German soldiers were killed—and the occupiers showed their
true colors. Executions, torture . . .

"Our task, ladies and gentlemen, is to link all of the
separate elements of resistance and give them the tools they
need to be effective against the Boches. They have the
will—we must give them the way."

Geneva did not see Jacques again after that first encounter.
She learned that the SOE had been divided into two sections,
one British and one French, at de Gaulle's insistence. She
convinced herself that her father was alive, caught in the
mismanaged and misdirected labyrinth of those first SOE
agents, perhaps waiting in vain to be brought back from
France—condemned to stay there because the SOE believed
Andre Thibault to be a collaborator. Wireless operators were
in critical demand, and none of the first to be dropped into
the occupied countries had survived for long. Knowing she
would need radio contact in order to get her father home—
particularly if he was ill or wounded—and since women were
considered suitable for wireless training, she volunteered to
become an operator.

She went to a special school to learn Morse code and how
to transport and assemble a transmitter. When she was
proficient, the "toughening-up" part of the course took place
in Scotland, on the western coast of Inverness in wild and
ruggedly beautiful country safe from inquisitive eyes. Here
she learned about pistols and submachine guns, map reading,
fieldcraft, demolition. She was spared the "silent killing"
techniques taught to the male agents, but there was hard

cross-country work and living from the land. She listened with some dismay to instructions on how to cook a hedgehog in clay, if the need arose.

One quiet and bewildered-looking young woman who went through the course with her asked her, "What *are* we being trained for? I answered an advertisement for a bilingual secretary."

The young woman's questions were answered by the next instructor. "Cyclonite mixed with a plasticizing medium—one of the safest explosives we know. Won't detonate if struck by a rifle bullet or ordinary shocks of transit. It requires a detonator imbedded well into the mass of explosive. You're going to learn how to handle it like butter."

Eventually Geneva moved on to a school in the southern New Forest. Not all of the other trainees graduated to this part of the course. She was taught the elements of clandestine techniques and security, how to spot a follower, how to conceal a personality. She was taught, "He that has a secret should not only hide it, but hide that he has it to hide."

When she had completed the intelligence training, the coding and ciphering and counterespionage and propaganda, she was sure there was absolutely nothing left they could teach her.

Captain Jefferson visited her and took her out to dinner for the first time since her training began. He even provided champagne.

"I take it I'm now ready to leave?" she asked, sipping the rare luxury.

He watched her with a speculative appraisal that made her uneasy. "Not quite. You still have to go to finishing school."

"Finishing school?"

"We must be sure our recruits have no illusions about what they face. They must fully realize that if they're caught they have only a slender chance of staying alive. We expect half of the agents we send into occupied territory will be caught. The finishing school to which you will now go will put you through simulated Gestapo interrogation."

Chapter 40

August 19, 1941
Saxon Hall, Lancs., England

Dear Matt:

No, I have not forgotten you. How could I? Yes, all of your letters reached me. I'm sorry I haven't replied until now. I must tell you as quickly as I can—because to linger over the details would open wounds I have tried to anesthetize, if not close—that Terry was killed on active duty and there is only a slender chance that my father is still alive.

I have closed Saxon Hall. If my father doesn't return I will sell the entire estate later on. I could never live there happily again and Terry did not have an heir, so the Saxon line is gone forever. How important it is to us that our bloodline continues down the generations. Our immortality, I suppose. Is that the reason I could never bring myself to tell you why we could never marry, you and I? Perhaps. But before I get to that painful revelation, I must tell you that you were right in assuming that my father did learn that I am not the daughter of the marriage between your father and my mother. My father was a German officer named Wolfgang Rauch. My mother was not permitted to marry him and was in fact driven from her home because she carried me. Apparently she met your father shortly after this . . . what a wonderful man he must have been, to love her and marry her even though she carried another man's child. But no more wonderful than you are, dear Matt. I understand why my father— my real father, as far as I'm concerned—didn't want me to know. But he was wrong to keep it secret. I feel no divided loyalties. I love my family, my home, England, in that order—but, of course, I no longer have a family if my father is dead. The Saxons are gone forever. What do I know of the Rauch family, the Thibaults? They did not make me what I am. Yet blood ties are important; I don't mean to diminish them, because to do so would be yet another evasion on my part.

I suppose my greatest weakness is that I couldn't acknowledge life's sterner blows and would simply pretend they hadn't happened. But you saw that when I lost Dulcie. Perhaps it all began with Charlie Dutton. What he did to me was so ghastly that I would have gone mad if I hadn't pretended I didn't remember all of the details. Then on the night Dulcie was born, I was plunged into another nightmare because of Dutton. While his first assault left me pregnant, his second left me unable to ever again bear a child.

And this, my dear, is the reason I'm writing to tell you that I release you from all promises to me, as I beg you to release me. Please find someone to love, who will love you. I don't want you to forget me, as I could never forget you, but I want you to be happy without me. If we were of different temperaments perhaps one day we could be friends, but we both know that's not possible for us. So it's better that we don't meet again.

I know I should have told you long ago that I can't have children. It was unfair of me to let you think other reasons were all-important in precluding our marrying . . . the possibility we were blood-related, my wish to spare Terry hurt . . . Dulcie, my father. Perhaps I even rationalized to myself that these reasons were strong enough to keep me from your arms. But I know they were not. Now that we are certain we aren't brother and sister, now that I am a widow, now there is nothing left but the truth.

So there it is, Matt, unvarnished. You wrote to ask

me when you could return to me. The answer is, forgive
me, my darling, never. Don't come back to look for
me, because I've joined the womens' services and am
leaving shortly for overseas duty.

Be happy, have a good life my darling.

Always,
Gennie

Matt replaced the letter in the envelope for the tenth time
and slipped it into his pocket. He leaned back in his chair,
surveying his littered desk. In the outer office he could hear
Alvin wheezing a reprimand to a young stenographer who
had made an error on a consular invoice. The early September
air hung heavy and still, the humidity a sodden cloak that
numbed his brain and left the stack of letters awaiting his
signature still curled into the shape of the typewriter platen.

His mind groped sluggishly for answers to questions that
had no answers, holding a postmortem on the past, wishing
for what might have been, searching for a lost dream.

Sometimes, when he saw a woman walk by with a particularly graceful carriage, or an inclination of the head that
suggested fragility and courage at the same time, he would
think of Geneva. But there were other times when he heard a
woman laugh or murmur in a certain pitch, or move across a
room like a lioness stalking her prey, and he would remember
Leah and the brief heady madness of his affair with her.

He had never been able to find Leah again although he'd
tried. There had been bartenders and maitre d's and waiters
who had recognized her, doormen who addressed her by
name. But like himself, none of them knew where she came
from or where she went. Apparently it had been her practice
to come into town briefly, then disappear for months. Some
said she made New Orleans her home, others said she went to
Chicago or St. Louis. He considered hiring a private detective
to find her but then decided he didn't really want to.

Leah had been a high fever, a third-degree burn, but when
she was gone it was possible to go back to the routine of work
and gentler social pursuits with almost a sigh of relief,
knowing that kind of intense passion was self-consuming. It
wouldn't have lasted.

A ceiling fan whirled overhead, stirring up the muggy air,
and his office door was ajar to catch any cross-ventilation
from the outer office. Alvin's wizened face peered around the

opening. "Matt? You sign that mail yet? We've got to get those cargoes moving to the dock."

Matt picked up his pen. "Any word from New York yet about the *Geneva*?" He scrawled his signature on the top letter of the pile.

"Not yet. But she's not due in until today. And you know what an old woman Chisholm is. He won't push her."

"I'm taking her out myself, next trip. I want a cargo for England. How about lend-lease goods?"

"Matt, it's none of my business—"

"That's right." Matt finished signing the letters and pushed them across the desk. He looked up into Alvin's worried expression and added, less brusquely, "I want to be there for Gennie's birthday—November eleventh. It's weeks away, I know, but it may take me a while to find her." His eyes looked through Alvin to some invisible place in his own mind. "She always hated her birthday. Armistice Day, you know. Don't suppose this one will be over by then, so I doubt there'll be that two-minute silence she used to dread so much."

"Not much chance," Alvin said. "Who'd have thought the limeys would have lasted all alone for two years?"

"She lost her husband, maybe her father too. I guess he must be missing in action.

"I wondered about that letter you kept reading over and over."

"She joined the Women's Army. I don't know how I'll find her. But I will, somehow. I may send the *Geneva* home with a strange skipper. Don't be surprised."

Alvin wheezed a small chuckle. "I'm never surprised by anything you do, Matt."

The telephone rang in the outer office, and a moment later the stenographer pushed his intercom button. Matt picked up the receiver.

"Mister Matthew? It's Della, at the house. Sir, I figured I'd best call you right away. It's Nathan. He's took mighty sick, Mr. Matthew."

"You call a doctor? Okay, I'll be right there." He slammed the phone down. "I'm going home. Nathan's ill."

Matt drove back to Greenboughs at breakneck pace, expecting to pick up a police escort and a speeding ticket all the way home, but he was lucky.

Della, the housemaid, was waiting for him, her face

tear-streaked. "I got him into bed and the doctor is with him now."

Matt collided with the doctor as he left Nathan's room. He shook his head, his face grave. "He's a very old man, Mr. Lauren. It was a stroke—a small one, but I suspect there'll be more. I'll get an ambulance over here to take him to the hospital."

"No," Matt said. "Get a nurse over here and any equipment you need. Nathan's not going to die in a hospital."

"There isn't much we can do at his age. He's comfortable now; you're wise not to move him."

"Can he talk?"

"Yes, it didn't affect his speech much. But as I said, this could be the first of a series of small strokes. He may lose more of his faculties with each succeeding one. He's had a good run, Mr. Lauren. Outlived your grandfather by quite a spell."

Matt went into the room. Nathan's face seemed suddenly shriveled and gray. The tired eyes blinked open. "Mr. Matthew, seems like we done went through this scene once before."

Matt patted the old man's hand gently; the skin felt dry and brittle. "Take it easy, old-timer, you're going to be fine."

"Not this time. This time I is going to meet my Maker."

"You thought that last time, Nathan. You'll be up bossing us all around again before you know it. Don't go making any more deathbed confessions, hear? You'll probably live to regret them."

"Mr. Matthew, this old sinner got to tell you what he did. I didn't have no right—"

"You rest now. You told me about Specks a long time ago, remember?"

"That young woman . . . Leah. She was here. Two, maybe three weeks ago. While you was in New Orleans with Mr. Dooley. I sent her away. Told her you done went abroad."

Matt digested this news silently, unsure if he was perturbed or grateful. Another wild spin with Leah was not in his immediate plans. Looking back from a more rational standpoint, he knew Leah could become an addiction that would bring more pain than joy. He said, "That's all right, Nathan. You did the right thing."

"Trashy female. That's all she was. A trashy young—"

"I said it was okay, Nathan. Don't worry about it."

"She think I'm an old fool. She think you is a young fool.

Maybe she think we can't count? It weren't no more'n seven months ago, she come driving up here in that old Chevy, sending the gravel flying every which way, skidding all over the place 'cause she driving too fast. All decked out like she was some high-falutin' society lady. Jes' another high-yella whore . . . beggin' your pardon, Mr. Matthew. I done told her it weren't your baby and if'n she went 'round telling folks it was, we'd sure enough—"

Matt caught the gnarled fingers in his, shook them slightly. "Baby, Nathan? What baby?"

"She had a baby boy, Mr. Matthew. Jes' two weeks old. I didn't know what was going to happen. I reckon I never would have sent her away like that, if'n I knowed."

Matt drew a deep breath. "Leah said it was my baby?"

Nathan nodded. There were tears in the corner of his eyes; they bubbled up and slipped over the edge, running down the still and sunken cheeks.

"Where are they now, Nathan? Did she say where she was going?"

"No, sir, she didn't. But there was a call from a hospital in New York City. They found your name and address in her pocketbook. They was in a car accident, Mr. Matthew. Leah was driving, she was killed outright, but the baby was thrown clear. I told the hospital she was jes' a maid who worked for you . . ."

"The hospital, Nathan, what was the name of the hospital?" Matt's voice shook. Somewhere in a whirling mass of images in his mind were the answers he was seeking.

Chapter 41

The cold metal floor of the plane vibrated under her and the noise of the engines buzzed in her ears. Geneva felt like a trussed chicken in her parachute harness. She tried to stifle pinpricks of dread by thinking of the slogan so beloved of England's wartime comedians: "Is your journey really necessary?"

Beside her the other two passengers slept, unconcerned, or pretending to be. A hard-faced army major and a young man who looked too French to be the Shropshire man he actually was. The three of them lay amidships, wedged between the strange shapes of the objects to be dropped into France with them.

Geneva had made four parachute jumps over Ringway, all without difficulty except for bruising her foot the first time. But she had witnessed sandbags dropped by parachute that burst upon landing, the chute having failed to open. The hollow core of the Hudson was illuminated only by a ghostly green light, and she studied the cheerfully sinister face of the dispatcher as he negotiated the clutter to wake the two men. "We'll be over the drop zone in a few minutes," he informed them in the same breezy manner adopted by all of the RAF personnel who had handled them.

Geneva cautiously uncoiled arms and legs, wishing she felt as lighthearted. *This isn't happening to me*, she thought. *It's happening to someone else.* The reality of the plane, the parachute, the changes wrought in her own physical condition and personality by her training, were surface manifestations. She still felt attached by a slender thread to that other Geneva, creature of a vastly different environment. Jefferson had told her, just before she left, "None of us know our inner strengths, not until we're tested."

She had wanted to reply, "There isn't anything else I fear. The worst has already happened to me." Now she flexed numbed muscles and felt the pounding of fear in her throat, in her chest. The question "What am I doing here?" kept swimming into her mind. *We get swept along*, she thought, *by events, by our own emotions, until we find ourselves hurtling down some unexpected path without knowing how we came to be on that particular journey.* She told herself firmly, *I'm going to find out what happened to my father.*

She rose stiffly, and the dispatcher hooked her parachute onto the static line. She was cold and it was difficult to move. The dispatcher was opening the hatch.

She could see moonlit fields and woods less than a thousand feet below. The plane circled, searching for signal lights from the ground.

Please let there be a signal, she thought. *I couldn't stand this tension again. Let's get it over and done this trip. One flash of light down there, please.* The starboard wing lifted as the Hudson circled back for another look at the DZ.

There! A light flickered on, then another and another. One tiny light was flashing the letter L in Morse, answering the plane's signal. They were ready for the drop on the ground, ready to rush out and hide parachutes, pick up baggage, guide the three agents.

Over the intercom came a confused babble of sound, conversation between pilot and dispatcher, then the green light flashed and the dispatcher shouted, "Go!" and the Shropshire man vanished from sight.

Her pulse quickened. *What do I have to lose? Better me than some woman with a husband and family—or one capable of bearing future children. Was everything stripped away from me for this? For one selfless act?* She heard the dispatcher's next "Go!" and, inwardly shrinking, dropped into the black void.

Instantly she was caught in the slipstream of the plane and shaken violently. There was an overpowering sensation of panic as she fought to be free of the turbulence, striving to get away from the plane. Then her parachute opened and the vibration stopped.

She felt suddenly warm and safe, drifting earthward toward the tiny flickering lights below. She began to breathe deeply and evenly. With luck she would drop fairly close to the signal lights. Her moments of peace were short-lived as her arms soon grew achingly tired from the strain of tugging the guide ropes to check the parachute's oscillation.

As the dark ground rushed up to meet her, she saw trees and twisted to avoid them. Two fiber suitcases containing her wireless equipment and clothes should also be floating down by now. A comfortingly large bundle of francs was tucked into the small of her back, inside the trousers she wore over a dress. She had been astonished by the amount of money the RAF cashier casually handed her before she boarded the Hudson. "All right, ducks, now empty your bag and your pockets again. Don't want no bus tickets to Baker Street in there, do we now? Looks like you'll have to hang your bag around your neck, love. Here, we'll shove the money into your trousers, see. Can you walk?"

The other items were not mentioned by name; they lay on a table and she caught sight of them as someone put a protective rubber helmet on her head. Her wireless crystals, a loaded Colt revolver which would fit into the hollowed-out core of a book . . . and her lethal tablet. She had been tempted to say, no, I don't want to take the lethal capsule with me, but she hadn't.

She landed, hardly jarred by the impact, and went sprawling on her face on the soft earth, loving the smell and feel of it. She was on her feet, pulling in her parachute, when the three men materialized out of the shadows. Quickly, efficiently, and silently they helped her out of the harness. Two of them scooped up the yards of nylon while a third took her arm and propelled her from the landing field.

Neither of them spoke as they hurried through the night's stillness, crossing the field, along a narrow lane, over another meadow. She felt no sense of danger as they traveled through a wooded area and emerged beside a field with a cluster of sleeping cattle in one corner. She could see the dark shape of a farmhouse at the end of the lane.

The moonlit countryside was disturbingly like England and made her think that nature's subtle differences from one country to another were not in proportion to the magnitude of the cultural and ideological differences of their inhabitants.

Why did people strive for dissimilitude? Had her father died here in these almost familiar surroundings? She could accept more readily that Terry had died in the searing heat of the desert, an alien environment.

As they approached, the farmhouse door opened. They entered a darkened room. The door closed behind them and a light went on, illuminating a large kitchen. A plump woman with sun-coarsened skin approached her with outstretched hands. As Geneva accepted the warm handclasp, she noticed a young man seated beside the stone fireplace. He gave her an unblinking stare and his body undulated slightly toward her to acknowledge her arrival, although he did not rise. The man who had brought her from the plane had disappeared.

The woman said, "You are Celeste?" Geneva nodded, now thoroughly accustomed to the code name she had been given early in her training.

"I am Jeanne. Over there is Rascasse." The young man with the fishy stare nodded to her.

Geneva said, "What about my luggage? There are two cases."

"They will bring it here as soon as they can."

Geneva slipped her bag from her neck to her shoulder, hoping her crystals were still intact. She had wrapped them carefully in several silk scarves.

Jeanne was studying her clothes. "They dressed you less conspicuously than the last woman they sent."

"A small factory has been opened now. Refugees from the continent are making our clothes for us. Mine even have genuine labels taken from the clothes of foreigners arriving from abroad."

"You speak better French than your father," Rascasse said. "I had to tell people he was a Belgian."

"You knew my father?" Geneva asked, a pulse quickening.

"It was I who took him to Paris. Delivered him to that swine Thibault. Ma'mselle, if it could be undone . . . . We found it hard to believe that London wants to recruit him. I will take you to Thibault, but this time I will be nearby. Thibault joins the Resistance or he dies by the garrot."

Geneva's hands went into her pockets to hide the slight tremor. She felt as though she were clenching every muscle in her body. "Then my father is dead?"

"You will have to ask Thibault that question."

"When will I meet him?"

"Tomorrow morning. He lives just outside the village. We

cannot risk being out during curfew hours. His housekeeper is my aunt—almost my aunt. Her name is Marie Bouchard and she will get a message to me if you are in trouble. You can trust her."

"Where will you hide my transmitter? Will it be safe? I must keep to a rigid schedule of transmissions—the first in two days. London is concerned that none of the wireless operators they have sent have avoided capture. We had only one operator transmitting from the Occupied Zone—from Le Mans—and he has not been heard from since November."

Jeanne said, "We put your transmitter up there." She pointed to a small square trapdoor in the ceiling that would have been the first place Geneva would have searched, had she been Gestapo.

Reading the glance, Jeanne added, "There is a steep roof and beneath it is a false roof. A small space only big enough to lie down—and hide the transmitter. Are you hungry?"

Geneva shook her head. "The flight is short. They fed me before I left. I would like a glass of water, please."

Jeanne gestured for her to be seated while she brought the water. Geneva sat opposite to the fish-eyed Rascasse, who never took his eyes from her. A few minutes later there was a distinctly programmed knock on the door, the lights were extinguished again, and when they went back on Jeanne was puffing as she carried a heavy case to the table. Geneva went quickly to open it and check the contents. It contained her B Mark II shortwave Morse transceiver, apparently undamaged.

"What about the other case? Where is it? It contains my clothes and the aerial I need."

"They will bring it as soon as they find it. Probably it landed in a ditch or some bushes. Don't worry."

But Geneva did worry. She worried that it had not been found by the time she fell into exhausted sleep, and she worried that it still had not arrived when she and Rascasse set off for her uncle's house the following morning.

Rascasse faded into the beautifully kept shrubbery after depositing her on the doorstep of Andre Thibault's country house just outside a picturesque village set in a thickly wooded valley. The house was enclosed by extensive grounds that appeared to be undisturbed by war. Despite severe rationing, the rose gardens and formal lawns and shrubberies had not been uprooted to plant vegetables as at Saxon Hall. There was, however, a fruit orchard to the side of the house. The leaves on the trees were exploding into autumn hues.

As she waited for a response to the door chimes, Geneva mentally compared the Thibault house to Saxon Hall. The Thibault mansion was a graceful structure, with extravagantly tall windows that made her wonder how they would keep the glass from shattering should a bomber stray this way. She glanced over her shoulder to be sure Rascasse was gone. She hoped he would heed her plea that he not jeopardize either her credibility with her uncle, or the safety of the others, by keeping too conspicuous a vigil on the house.

The door opened and a jovial looking woman who reminded her a little of Meredith stood on the threshold. Her polite smile of welcome fell from her face. She stared at Geneva, her mouth gaping.

"May I see Monsieur Thibault? I am his niece." It had been decided that "Celeste" would be Andre's estranged niece who had been living in the south of France.

"Celine's daughter? After all these years . . . come in, come in. I am Marie Bouchard. I have kept house for your uncle since his wife died, but I knew the family. Your mother and I grew up in the same village."

Geneva stepped into a cluttered entry hall, blinking from the sudden dimness after the bright sunlight. Various shapes came into focus. Clocks. At least a dozen of them.

Marie had disappeared but returned almost immediately, followed by a dark-haired, wiry man whose quick movements suggested a younger man than the deeply etched lines on his face indicated. His eyes were pearl gray, like her own, perhaps more intense, filled with more experience than hers had yet acquired. He too stared, transfixed. A moment later he enveloped her in an embrace. When he spoke, his voice shook. "My dear child, forgive me, I am overcome. You are so like your mother. For a moment I thought Celine had returned—looking as she did that last summer before . . ."

He took his handkerchief from his pocket and blew his nose. Marie herded them into a sitting room and withdrew, closing the door behind her after promising to return with refreshments.

Geneva stood on a sun-dappled carpet regarding her uncle, her mother's brother, trying to feel kinship, but experiencing only that same curiosity an interesting stranger generates. She was much more anxious to learn what had become of her father. She listened politely as Andre chided her on the danger of being here, then spoke of her mother, of the terrible days of the First World War. He did not ask her either to forgive or to understand why he had found it necessary to cast Celine out of her home at a time when she most needed her family. Geneva knew that if she thought about this she would risk giving in to a bitter anger that would be purposeless, because nothing could be undone. When at last Andre allowed her to speak, she asked simply, "Where is my father?"

Andre's eyes were shocked. "They did not tell you in London? *Mon dieu!* Must I break that news to you also?" His face was stricken; there was no need for him to confirm what she saw there. She said, "He's dead, isn't he? They told me they thought he was. What happened to him?" Her voice was calm. It was as though a mantle of ice had enclosed her, so that although she was aware of everything around her, she saw and heard through a tough cold shield, mind and body protected, almost immune to feeling.

"He was a brave man, your *père anglais*. We were almost caught by the Boches, he and I. And not far away were a group of saboteurs, hiding in the woods, who might also have been picked up in a dragnet of the area. Your father was wounded in the leg and could not walk. He kept the Boches pinned down while I escaped and warned the others. We were gone before they had time to search the woods. I sent word of this to London."

"But you don't know for certain he was killed?" Geneva persisted, clinging to any fragment of hope left.

"I learned later that he was killed. He died quickly, without suffering. Of this I'm sure. He died there beside the ruined cottage, not at the hands of the Gestapo. I do assure you."

"How . . . how can you know this?" Geneva tried to keep the suspicion from her voice, but his expression said he knew it was there.

"Because I move in Nazi circles. There is a high-ranking officer in those circles who knows what I am, as I know what he is. It's better you do not know more than this, for all of our sakes. The fewer names you know, the fewer you can betray if you are caught. Your father's body was taken away. The Gestapo hoped someone would try to find out what happened to him. Your people have played into their hands by sending you here."

She had sat down on a graceful but uncomfortable sofa and she moved her body over its uncompromising hardness. "That wasn't the only reason I came to France. I came to ask you—as my father must have asked you—to organize some of the scattered pockets of resistance into a more effective force. With your freedom to move about the country, and your connection with Nazi officials and French police—"

He made a pyramid with his fingers and regarded her over its peak. "I suppose British Intelligence decided that even if I am a collaborator, it is unlikely I will deliver you—the daughter of my dead sister—to the SS. What did they tell you about me? Did they tell you that money is my god and I worship it above and beyond patriotism? Therefore, offer him more—if he is a collaborator, or a German agent, try to convert him to our side—or convince him to become a double agent. Any man can be bought; offer him more money."

Geneva ignored the question, uncomfortably aware of the large bundle of francs that were now tucked inside the overnight bag Jeanne had loaned her. Perhaps another line of questioning would be better now, giving her more time to study this man before reaching conclusions about him.

She said, "We don't wish to recruit anyone who does not wish to join us. Since I'm here, perhaps you could tell me more about my parents . . . about my real father."

"Ah! So now you question your own loyalty?"

"Not at all. I question my origins. The why of events over which I had no control."

"Your English father never told you anything—not even after he came to see me that first time?"

She shook her head. "He tried to give me a French heritage. I see now that he was trying to fabricate it for me, because he knew nothing about my mother."

Andre nodded, as though understanding. "I didn't question him much about you either. I was bewildered, perhaps angry all over again. Later, when he was gone, I regretted not making more inquiries. Then, when he came to me a second time"—he paused, slapping his forehead with the palm of his hand—*"mon dieu!* I'll never forget him sitting there in a cafe, unperturbed, with that icy calmness the English have that seems even more stoic under duress. . . . What was I about to say? Ah, yes. On his second visit he told me about your husband and your child. Why do you risk your life to come to me? Is your life not precious to those who love you?"

"They're dead. Both of them," Geneva said. Odd how the more times she said the words aloud, the easier it became, not only to say it, but to accept it. "My husband was killed in action in North Africa. My child in an air raid."

His condolences seemed genuinely offered, but the words drifted toward her overshadowed by his penetrating stare. *He's summing me up, trying to decide if I am cold, unfeeling. I'm an unknown quantity to him, as he is to me. We have to exchange more of ourselves before either of us will know, for sure, it's safe to proceed. I'll give a little piece of myself, then so will he. If I allow myself to think of my father's death, I'll go mad.*

"Is there no young man in your life? No lover to keep you from such foolishness as this clandestine activity?"

"I told you—I'm a recent war widow."

"That is not an answer. I asked was there not someone you love."

"Love? What is love? We choose objects upon which to focus our affection, then we invest them with all the admirable qualities we wish we had ourselves. We orchestrate our own feelings—and theirs—to what we believe love should be. Then we wonder why we suffer pain and disillusionment."

"Ah, I see. You *are* in love. But your lover disappointed you."

"It is I who don't measure up to his expectations, I'm afraid. But I came here to talk about you, not myself."

"I am as much of a patriot now as I ever was, but now I temper patriotism with realism. Although it grieves me that I am known as a collaborator, I must outweigh the surface disgrace with the advantages. When your father came to me, I had already established contact with others who wanted to strike back at the Boches—former army officers, civilians, local officials. We did what we could, even without weapons. A network of safehouses to aid escaping prisoners, English flyers, was established. At first we sent them south, then over the mountains into Spain, until your people began to send agents here, and there were pickups from deserted beaches by submarine. But we quickly learned that one man with a list of names is a walking time bomb—he is picked up and takes a dozen others to their deaths with him. Even if he does not talk under torture, eventually he dies and our small numbers are depleted. None of those early *resistants* are still alive. I learned it was better to have few contacts, widely scattered across the country."

"And when my father came to you?"

"Did they tell you in London of the comedy of errors being performed in France, my niece? Of a newly arrived agent arrested with the address of a safehouse in his pocket, so that a string of agents knocked on that door and were promptly arrested . . . a *souricière*—a mousetrap for catching visiting British agents."

"Wireless communication hasn't been good so far."

"The Gestapo direction-finding teams are most efficient in tracking a transmitter. But you did not let me finish my recital of blunders. There are French agents and British agents both coming from London with conflicting orders and goals, sometimes unaware of the presence of the other. We have an unconfirmed report that the Abwehr sent back to London a triple agent—obligingly picked up by the Royal Navy from a Breton beach."

Geneva squirmed uncomfortably. "Any embryonic group such as ours must suffer growing pains. I admit there has been some friction between the Free French and the British. That's why we so desperately need men who can coordinate both sides—move about freely, socialize with the Germans—who can tell us who we can trust. Someone like you."

"At present only a handful of men know I am working for the Resistance. I do not intend to jeopardize my position by broadcasting it to London."

"You don't have to. You meet high-ranking Nazi officials; you must be able to gather intelligence from them. I am a trained wireless operator. I will be your contact—your only contact. I will send your intelligence back to London."

Andre stood up abruptly and began to pace about the room. "I suppose you're aware that Vichy payments of the occupation costs to the Boches are being used, in part, to buy our old masters? Ironic, isn't it, that they buy our art treasures with our own money? And I have to catalog and appraise them. Yes, I could gather intelligence for you to pass along—and possibly end up like some of your other agents in this absurd venture. Or I could continue to fight the Boches in my own way, with a small group of *resistants* I can trust—blow up a railway track here, cut a telephone cable there, kill a German when we can. If I give you information for London, what do they offer in return?"

"Regular air drops of weapons, medicine, whatever you need. The SOE is working on a number of devices. Hollowed-out matchsticks to hold microfilm, mines disguised as horse droppings. We are much more advanced now than when my father came to you last winter. Look." She slipped her hand into her purse and pulled out a mechanical pencil. Wrapped around the lead was a square of sheer silk that opened to reveal a detailed map of the area of the drop zone. "My compass is concealed in the back of a miniature hairbrush in my purse—a precaution in case my parachute drifted away from the DZ. You spoke of blowing up railway tracks. We can give you plastic explosives to use."

He frowned. "I don't like the idea of your staying here. I have borne a lifetime of guilt about your mother. I do not want that guilt compounded by your death. I often thought that my punishment for throwing her out of the house when she was pregnant was that my own dear wife and I could never have children."

"I'm sorry, Uncle Andre. I must stay. At least until London is satisfied that you aren't a collaborator." She had called him uncle, she realized. She added, "When I am sure of your loyalty, then I will go home. You can choose one of your own people to take my place."

"If you are sure of your own loyalty, then be sure of mine," he snapped back. "We are of the same blood."

"My husband had a very dear friend. We both believed implicitly in his loyalty too. But we were wrong."

"We shall have to think of a story to explain your presence here."

"I'm your long-lost niece from the south, come to stay with you because my mother recently died. I have papers to prove it—my identity papers, ration card, her death certificate."

"Quite efficient, your SOE, in some respects."

"Yes. Now shall we open the door and let Marie in? She's wondering how to knock with a tray of cups—or glasses—in her hands."

Andre had to leave for Paris the following day, and Marie went to a nearby farm to try to buy some eggs. They had decided to keep to their usual routine. Geneva spent the day alone, which gave her time to reflect upon her mother's tragic life and death and to think about Andre's avenging cruelty. She wondered how she had managed to be civil to him. She dared not think about her father's death, or Andre's part in that too, because to do so would be to give in to tears, which once begun would not stop.

Here I am, she thought, *fulfilling some dictate of destiny without an inkling as to the reason. The interlocking pieces of my life, and my mother's life, are they all going to come together for me now, so that I can go forward without feeling the pull of the past? Yet how can I go forward without Matt? He can't love me now. Not now that he knows I'm just an illusion. A hollow shell. If we can't reproduce our own kind, what purpose do we serve? Andre's wife was barren—my mother died giving birth to me. The end of their line. The Saxon line ended too, with Terry. If I marry Matt, then his line will end. There has to be continuity for*

Matt, because I love him enough to sacrifice my happiness for his. Yet the thought of life without him is unbearable. Is that it, really? Is that why I'm here? Would I rather die than live without him? But I haven't the courage to kill myself. Was that why I was so afraid of carrying their lethal capsule? Because the temptation to use it would be so strong? Do we invite our own fate? Am I here to die at the hands of some unknown someone from the same race who gave me life? Am I expecting to die?

She pressed her fingers to her temples, trying to drive away the melancholy thoughts. She was glad when Marie returned.

"I saw Boches going toward the village," Marie said breathlessly, dropping a bag of potatoes on the table. "Perhaps they are just going through on the way to Paris. Come, I will make supper and then you can have a nice warm bath and go to bed. Monsieur says you must get plenty of rest tonight."

They had a light meal and Geneva retired to bed, thinking that this time tomorrow night she would have to make her first transmission to England. She hoped her uncle would bring back something she could relay. But the ghosts of the past would not let her rest; she drifted in and out of troubled sleep, wishing she did not have to wake up to the memory of all the people who were dear to her that she had lost, especially her mother, whom she had never known in the first place.

A hand on her mouth awakened her. The moonlight painted a silver outline around the window shutter, now slightly open. She struggled as a silhouetted head bent over her and hissed in her ear, "Rascasse. No noise."

The hand left her mouth and she looked into his fishy stare. "I came to see you are all right. I did not want Marie to know I came. I saw Thibault leave this morning. What if he brings the Gestapo back with him?"

"I shall be safe here. I'm sure of it."

"You did not hear me come in through your window."

"You're very skillful. I hope more so than the SS."

"I was a cat burglar." His teeth flashed in the darkness in a cheeky grin. "I still am, when the opportunity presents itself. You, ma'mselle, remind me of your English father. Oh, not so much in looks, you understand, but in that manner. Imperturbable. Did you learn that from the English? Are you not afraid?"

She supposed he had other things on his mind anyway, but she wasn't happy about having him on her bed. When in doubt, talk your way out. "Yes, I suppose we could all be killed. But do any of us really fear death? We fear dying. I don't fear dying because I have the means—quick and painless. It was issued to me along with my phony papers and authentic French country clothes. You'd be surprised at what your mind learns to accept. A lethal capsule becomes an indispensable accessory I carry everywhere—as I used to carry a vial of perfume to sprinkle on my handkerchief to ward off unpleasant odors. That was a little trick my grandmother taught me."

"And you would use your poison capsule? Are you sure? Would you commit the mortal sin of suicide?"

"Oh, yes. If I had to. I've rehearsed it in my mind. We were put through simulated Gestapo interrogation. I'd use it, never fear."

"You sound like a woman who has decided her life is over."

Geneva was silent, thinking about Dulcie and Terry and her father. Did some part of her secretly want to join them? Was that the only real antidote to the pain of bereavement?

"I'm talking too much, Rascasse. What about my other suitcase? Is it safe in the attic with the transceiver?"

He got up. "That wasn't my job. I'll come for you tomorrow night, take you back to the farm to make your transmission." He went to the casement window, slithered over the sill, and disappeared.

Geneva lay in bed, wide awake. Rascasse had reminded her of her own earlier doubts. She wondered again if she would kill herself if she were caught by the Gestapo.

A vision of Matt's face flashed into her mind. She could see his dark eyes looking at her in that all-consuming way that was uniquely his. If only she could know how he felt about the revelation in her letter. That she was incomplete, less than a woman—perhaps not a woman at all? Now that he knew, she couldn't bear to see him again. It would hurt too much. Better to remember him loving her, wanting her . . . not pitying her.

Yes, perhaps she would take the lethal capsule after all, if they picked her up. Then she could live on in Matt's memory as he last remembered her—an unblemished, if lost, love. She would never have to face him and hear him lie to her that it didn't matter that her very essence as a woman had been taken from her. It was a long time before she went back to sleep.

The sun was high when she opened her eyes to the sound of a car approaching, churning the gravel of the driveway in front of the house. A petrol-driven car, property of a German or a French collaborator.

She slipped out of bed and went to the window. Coming to a halt at the front door was a black Mercedes. Her uncle and a uniformed Nazi officer got out of the car.

Chapter 42

Geneva dressed quickly. In the outside pocket of her handbag was a book, a popular novel published in France just before the war. She withdrew the revolver from the hollowed-out center of the book, sat down at the dressing table with the gun on her knee, under the open drawer. She had just raised a hairbrush to her head with her left hand when there was a knock on the door.

She called *"Entre,"* keeping her eyes fixed on the dresser mirror so that when the door opened, she saw instantly that it was Marie and she was alone.

Marie carried a breakfast tray. She whispered, "Boche—don't worry. He has been buying all of the paintings of a young artist, one of Monsieur Thibault's starving unknowns. The Boche knows you are staying here; we said you were feeling ill. However, your uncle says if we do not get rid of him soon, you'll have to come downstairs. We don't want him to get suspicious. His name is Karl Stolper, which is all I know about him."

"I was hoping to visit the farmhouse where Rascasse is staying this morning. Can I get out of the house without being seen?" Geneva asked. Surely by now they had found the second suitcase and its parachute. And if they hadn't, all three agents would be in trouble if it was found by the Germans. She had to know.

"No! Impossible."

"The case containing my clothes wasn't picked up. I have this one wrinkled dress only. How do I explain that to my uncle's German visitor?"

Marie smiled indulgently, understanding a woman's concern for her clothes. "Don't worry, *chérie*. If you have to go downstairs, I'll show you what you can wear."

She went to the armoire standing against one wall of the room. It contained dresses, coats, suits, blouses. Marie pulled out a dress and held it in front of her plump body. "They belonged to Madame Thibault." She sighed. "He could never bring himself to dispose of her things. She's been gone many years. What a pity there were no children. Such a disappointment to them both."

And judgment on him, for what he did to my mother, and he knows it, Geneva thought. The clothes were hopelessly out of style, but perhaps the more tailored ones, or the evening dress with classic lines, would be wearable. Clothes were scarce, rationed; she was sure that in France, as in England, many attics had been turned out to retrieve discarded clothing.

I'm thinking like an SOE agent again. Their training was more thorough than I realized. The catharsis from what I was before, to what I am now, more deeply ingrained than I'd believed. If they can change me so, why can't I change myself?

Marie was speaking of her deceased mistress, and Geneva murmured sounds of agreement. Odd how at times of greatest stress the mind worked at fever pitch, as though thoughts must keep pace with actions to keep everything in concert.

Marie left and Geneva hid her hollowed-out book with its concealed addition beneath the mattress on her bed. A somewhat obvious place, but she wanted it close at hand. Then she ate two rolls and drank ersatz coffee.

She studied her reflection in the mirror, trying to decide if she should wear the wrinkled dress or change into one of Madame Thibault's old-fashioned gowns. The dress she had brought from England was, they had assured her, authentically French—just a couple of years out of style with appropriate wear; a little looseness here, a seam puckered there. It had a high neck and small collar that made her look more schoolgirlish than sophisticated. They had cut her hair before she left, insisting that in wartime no one wore their hair long. Besides, it was against the regulations of the Womens' Services to wear one's hair below a uniform collar, whether she was to wear a uniform or not. Her head felt naked but free. She ran her hand through the soft waves and wondered fleetingly what Matt, who had loved her long hair, would have thought.

Two hours passed nerve-rackingly. She changed into one of Madame Thibault's tailored serge skirts and a plain blouse. It was almost noon when there was another tap on the door and Marie came in. "He wants you to come down for lunch. And I stopped by to see Rascasse and inquire about your clothes while I was out shopping."

"Did they find the case?"

"Rascasse says not to worry. They have searched thoroughly. If they cannot find it, the Boches cannot find it either. Perhaps it was not dropped from the airplane?"

Geneva was silent, quite sure it was dropped with her.

"There's a bottle of wine for lunch," Marie said helpfully as Geneva nervously pushed her hair into place with her fingers.

"Good. I'm going to need it to bolster my courage."

"You look pale, but that is good. It will bear out what we said about you feeling ill. You look lovely in those clothes. Like an old photograph stepped from its frame."

Geneva followed Marie down the stairs. Halfway down she could see the open door of the sitting room and the Nazi officer standing in front of the fireplace, his back to her, studying a picture hanging above the mantelpiece. Her uncle was speaking of the artist, telling the German that the man was brilliant but lazy, working only when the mood was upon him and living in poverty in a village somewhat remote and not on Andre's traveling circuit. "Still, I will go and see if he has any others," Andre concluded, "At least he will not cheapen his work by flooding the market, eh? I'll go in a day or two; there isn't a telephone in that whole village—" He broke off as Geneva entered the room. "Ah, here she is. Herr Stolper, may I present my niece, Celeste."

The German turned, clicking his heels. He was about thirty, with that Aryan blondness and balance of features so prized by his leader. Geneva saw the lightning-flash insignia on his shoulder instantly. He was an SS officer. "*Enchanté,* ma'mselle," he said, bowing. "But please, Andre, let us not stand on ceremony. My name is Karl. Surely we can be friends as well as business acquaintances?"

His French was good, although gutturally accented. Geneva felt confident as she murmured a greeting and responded to her uncle's inquiry as to whether she was not feeling better.

She said, "A little, thank you, Uncle." Turning to the German, she added, "Just a case of travel fatigue—the long journey from the south, not made easier by all of your security checkpoints."

Karl Stolper apologized for any inconvenience. Geneva's tension began to vanish. He seemed polite, civilized. The German's eyes never left her, but she recognized that look. He was more admiring than suspicious.

Marie announced that lunch was ready, and they went into the dining room to sparkling wine, crusty bread, and home-churned butter, with a meat pâté that was delicious. Geneva thought that either the French were not as bad off for food as she'd been led to believe, or her uncle's masquerade as a collaborator brought him black market side benefits.

When she was asked about her home in the south, Geneva unhesitatingly described the Riviera resort where she and Ian had spent so many happy holidays. Karl Stolper had been stationed in Paris and here she was on shakier ground, being unaware of all the changes in the city since the occupation, but he was evidently attempting to impress her with his love for French art and was soon doing most of the talking. Andre sat back and observed them with alert eyes, as though witnessing a duel he had arranged for his own amusement.

After two glasses of the excellent wine Geneva felt bold enough to inquire, "And are you stationed nearby, Karl?"

The vivid blue eyes flickered from her to Andre. "Temporarily. We have some investigative work to do in the area, so we have moved into a house in the village."

"This is a beautiful part of the countryside. You're lucky you haven't been assigned to the Russian front," Geneva said with malicious pleasure.

"Should my Führer wish me to fight in Russia, I would go gladly. I was sent here because of my mastery of the language."

Me too, Geneva thought, smiling at him. She felt like an actress, speaking lines written for her, curiously indifferent to the other player's responses. At the same time she was aware of a vague sense of relief that she was able to move away from her own personal turmoil, occupying her mind with the more immediate cat-and-mouse repartee.

"The war is small pieces of a great whole, ma'mselle," he went on. "At this moment there is indeed heavy fighting on the Russian front and in North Africa. There are sea battles, air raids. But for us there is this moment in a quiet country setting. Still, the war exists, even here."

"Oh?" Geneva glanced questioningly out of the window at the tranquil garden.

The German's voice was low, smooth. "We picked up a British agent early this morning only a few kilometers from here."

Geneva felt her smile freeze on her face. Who? The army major or the Shropshire man? Would he give away the presence of the other two agents who had parachuted in with him? *Would he swallow his lethal tablet?* No, don't think about that now, say something appropriate, quickly. She said, "Good heavens! What would a British agent be doing in this quiet spot?"

Stolper smiled faintly. "I have no doubt we shall find out . . . eventually."

The wine had suddenly turned to icewater in her throat. She swallowed. "Is that why you're here? To interrogate the man the police picked up?"

"Man? I did not say the agent was a man. The British and the Gaullists are using women as well as men."

"I just assumed . . ." Geneva shrugged, feeling a flush creep upward over her face. Careful! Don't get rattled.

"I am here to purchase a painting from your uncle."

"Of course, but I couldn't help noticing your insignia. It seemed to indicate a connection with the investigative work you mentioned. I'd forgotten about the painting."

She was rewarded with a calculated smile. "A beautiful woman can be forgiven for forgetfulness—or anything else."

Andre, who had been silent until now, leaned forward, his glass raised in a toast. "To my beautiful, forgetful niece, and to the sale of one of my budding genius's paintings to my most discriminating buyer, Herr Stolper."

Marie appeared with a delicate souffle and Geneva was grateful that her uncle monopolized the conversation for the remainder of the time they were at the table. He suggested that she rest, in view of her earlier faintness. Karl Stolper rose, expressing regret that he was to be deprived of her company. Then he said, suddenly and unexpectedly, "So you have only just arrived at your uncle's house, ma'mselle? Last night? Early this morning? How did you avoid being out during curfew hours?"

"Curfew?" Geneva repeated. "Oh, I wasn't out during

curfew." She was getting more jumpy. What had her uncle told him? How long was she *supposed* to have been here? She fought rising panic.

Stolper said, "You chided me for having been subjected to our security checks on your journey. And said this was the reason for your illness. Surely this indicates you have just arrived?"

"Oh, yes, of course."

"You didn't say *when* you arrived."

She blinked and turned to Andre. "What day is this, Uncle? Is it my third or fourth day here? How long was I in bed?"

"My dear, it's been almost a week. You really were quite ill when you arrived. I'm not surprised you've lost track of time. But Herr Stolper—Karl—I told you my niece arrived last week."

Stolper bowed slightly. "I trust I will see you again soon, ma'mselle? Perhaps you and your uncle could join me for dinner tonight?"

"Why, we would be delighted," Andre said at once, despite the pleading glance she flashed in his direction. "And perhaps in return you could see about some extra gasoline so that I can drive down to visit your favorite artist?"

Stolper frowned. "I know that village; there is good rail service. I am not one of your friends in Der Kommandant von Gross-Paris, with the power to issue gasoline for nonessential trips."

Geneva seized the opportunity to make her escape, walking unsteadily from the room and up the stairs. *No more wine,* she thought. *Must keep my wits about me.* Looking back on the encounter, she realized with surprise that she had been acutely aware of the danger she was in—and, more than that, had experienced an intense desire to survive. Despite all of her fears that she was in a self-destructive frame of mind, her will to live had evidently triumphed. She felt suddenly stronger, more alive, than she had for months, perhaps years.

Back in her room she paced nervously until she heard voices under her window. Her uncle was getting into the Mercedes with Stolper, placing the painting on the back seat. When the car disappeared from view, Geneva ran downstairs again.

Marie was washing the dishes in the kitchen when Geneva burst into the room. "You didn't tell me the Germans had picked up one of the other agents."

Marie looked at her with frightened eyes. "Rascasse said it was better you didn't know, at least while Stolper was here."

"Did the Germans also get my case of clothes?"

Marie nodded, biting her lip.

"So they know a woman was dropped last night." Geneva's mind was racing. Did Stolper suspect? What about her uncle? Why had he brought an SS officer here today, of all days? The time of her first transmission to London was still hours away. Besides, she had no aerial—she needed at least seventy feet of aerial, well spread out. Perhaps Rascasse could get it for her from somewhere.

"Rascasse and Jeanne had to leave the farm," Marie said. "The Germans are questioning everybody."

"Did Rascasse tell you how or when the other agent was arrested? Who it was?"

"He and Jeanne were burning papers, packing their things, when I got there. They had time only to tell me the agent had been caught trying to board a train. He was picked up because his papers weren't in order, then turned over to the Gestapo. Rascasse said the Boches are going over the whole valley with a fine-tooth comb. He said they would leave your other case where you saw them put it."

In the hiding place under the roof, Geneva thought. *But I need the aerial to transmit. And how good are my forged papers? Probably the fact that Andre Thibault is a collaborator saved me from being taken in for questioning by Stolper.* Her uncle must surely have been playing for time in accepting the dinner invitation.

"Marie, I'm going back to the farmhouse—now, before the Germans get there."

"No! You must not leave until Monsieur returns."

"I'm leaving now." Geneva uncurled her sheer silk map to check the way back to the farm.

The afternoon sun was warm, mellow; summer lingering into days reserved for autumn. Geneva saw no one as she walked quickly across harvested fields, staying near bordering hedges. She had just reached a copse of trees close to the house when she heard the throb of motorcycles. She flung herself to the ground as two motorcycles with sidecars went hurtling toward the farmhouse along a dirt road only feet from where she lay.

Geneva stayed on the ground, inching forward to a small rise where she could observe the front of the farmhouse from

behind closely grown saplings. The two motorcycles were
parked outside. The German drivers—or were they French?
—had disappeared inside.

Minutes later a uniformed German soldier came out of the
house carrying the fiber case that contained her transceiver.
He had not had time to thoroughly search the sprawling
house. He must have gone directly to where it was hidden.
Geneva crawled away, jumped to her feet, and began to run.

She was panicked and she knew it. She ran regardless of
whether she was in the open or could be seen, caring little
about the sobbing breaths she took or the fallen branches that
snapped with resonant crackles under her feet. All of the
nerves down her spine tingled with expectation, waiting for
restraining hands to grab her. But none did. She reached the
far side of the field where the grass was long, mixed with blue
flowers that looked like English cornflowers. She rolled
breathlessly into the grass, gasping, a stitch stabbing at her
side.

After several seconds she cautiously raised her head. The
field lay serene in the sunlight, its harvested stubble un-
marked by her mad dash. A bird twittered, scolding, somewhere in the tangled hedge.

Her heartbeats gradually slowed. She dug her fingernails
into the earth, seeking its eternal solace. Inches away from
her face a tiny iridescent insect with gossamer wings made its
way slowly up a blade of grass, intent upon reaching the
pinnacle, oblivious of everything but its own miniature world.

What am I doing, she wondered with a sudden sense of the
ridiculous, *scrabbling in the grass like a child engrossed in a
game, frightened by its own imagination. Dread is always
worse than the realization of that which is dreaded, isn't it?
Anticipation more tantalizing than realization?*

The inner voices were a babble; thoughts were pictures,
images, as well as words. For a few minutes everything was
compressed, condensed; all that had been and would be,
flashed, lightning-fast, in and out of her mind, like a dissect-
ing scalpel wielded by a demented surgeon. All of her life
seemed like the interlocking jaws of a trap, clicking into place
to pull her deeper into its inescapable core. If Ian Saxon had
not found her mother on the battlefield, he would not have
taken home an orphan baby who would be used as the
instrument of his own punishment by Charlie Dutton . . . .
But wait, her father had never known what Dutton did to her
in the name of revenge. That had been Geneva's obligation to

her father. And if Matt's father had not abandoned his son, then she and Matt would never have been bonded together in that mysterious way. If, if, if . . . if there were no wars, if there really was a brotherhood of man, if there was hope . . . somewhere. She remembered her father telling her he had hoped to enter the Church, but that after he returned from the trenches of the first war, he knew it was no longer possible—not, as his mother had believed, because of duty to the Saxon estate, but simply because his own faith had been lost.

She lay on the ground, knowing she had not yet submerged the she that used to be, and she wished passionately, prayed desperately, for a resurrection of hope. The tiny insect was still moving up the blade of grass with stately precision toward some unseen goal, secure in its own world, unaware of the terror of hers. The roar of the motorcycles shattered the silence, but they were going away from her.

Drained, she stood up and began to walk back to her uncle's house.

Andre was waiting for her. He flung open the door and grabbed her arm to yank her inside. "You little fool. Do you know how close you came to being picked up?"

"I don't know who to trust," Geneva flared back. "You brought an SS man here. Someone must have betrayed the British agent who was arrested. How do I know it wasn't you? They've just found the wireless I left at the farmhouse. I'm stranded here."

Andre released her so abruptly that she almost fell. "Come with me," he ordered. He strode toward a door that opened to reveal a flight of stairs descending to a cellar. Geneva waited until he found the light switch, then followed him to what had once been a wine cellar but was now bereft of anything but empty racks, cobwebs, and several broken clocks. He went to a large wooden keg, pulled out what appeared to be a wall clock with a missing face. A moment later he triumphantly laid a smaller box at her feet and lifted the lid. "Do you see what it is?"

She stared disbelievingly. "It's the smallest transceiver made. An A Mark III. Where did you get it?"

"I have crystals also—the kind needed for night transmission. Several, so you can change frequency often. And aerial, plenty of it. Can you use it?"

"Yes, of course."

"I know the house in the village that the SS are using. We

can set the aerial out on the roof—put the transmitter into the attic, it's easily accessible. When we dine there tonight, you will send your message to London—under the noses of the Boches."

"Are you mad? They'll catch me."

"They're more likely to catch you at some remote farmhouse. Listen to me, the Germans play *funkspeil*—literally, a radio game, with the British. The Germans are clever and quick to trace a transmitter; this is why there has been no regular contact with London. The Boches have direction-finding teams who travel disguised as ambulances or repair trucks, pinpointing the location of a transmitter within minutes. And if that doesn't work, they simply cut off current, subdistrict by subdistrict, until transmission is interrupted. But they aren't likely to cut off current in their own headquarters—nor believe an operator is working under their noses. They are not a race with an appreciation for such irony. By the time they realize where you are, you will be finished. You can get away with it, if you are careful to transmit for only two or three minutes at a time."

Geneva fingered the transmitter key. "Do you have anything I can give to London?"

"I have the name of an officer in the High Command who is planning to try to assassinate Hitler."

"And he might need some help? Who is he?"

"You'll know later, when the time comes. I want you also to tell your SOE you are in grave danger and must be picked up and taken home immediately."

"Stolper?"

"Possibly. He gave no indication he disbelieved me, but he must tread warily. He knows I have assisted his Kommandant with a large collection to be shipped back to Germany. Stolper will not make any move until he is absolutely sure. He is insisting that I travel to the home of that young artist immediately, which makes me suspicious, because that is where my group of saboteurs are hiding. The artist is one of them—and not a good enough craftsman to warrant Stolper's interest."

Geneva regarded the transceiver. "I could try to send a message now—someone might pick it up. Give me the name of the traitor in Hitler's High Command."

"No. Tonight. It's too risky now. There is a direction-finding van patrolling the village. If you are caught it is the end of me too. You must get back to London and convince them to send me the tools I need—plastic explosives, weapons. Not English agents who are more trouble than they're worth."

"English agents who risk their lives to help you."

"I'm not denying that. I'm saying they can best help by letting us organize our own underground army."

"You sound like de Gaulle. We *are* sending equipment. But the pockets of French resistance are so scattered and disorganized that we must send agents to try to link together the various groups. That's why you who can travel freely are so valuable. If you would take orders from London, I can arrange air drops to wherever you say, of whatever you want, immediately."

"I will take orders from no one but de Gaulle."

"Very well. There is a French section—SOE R/F—for Resistance France. It consists exclusively of Free French. But you understand that funds and equipment—everything—comes from the British? De Gaulle himself told Anthony Eden that he is too poor to beg, too weak to bow."

"Why have there been no air drops for the Gaullists here? It is this fact that makes me suspicious of your British SOE."

"I promise you there will be."

"Come then, I'll draw a diagram of the house the Gestapo are using. You won't have any trouble finding the attic."

Geneva followed him up the cellar steps. At the top he turned and looked at her with that peculiarly searching look he had. "You realize that Stolper is attracted to you? He will try to get you alone—and you must let him. He is not an accomplished drinker; he will quickly pass out. His room is on the third floor, only a short flight of stairs away from the attic where I will place the transmitter. Once you are in Stolper's room, no one will bother you."

"Only Stolper," Geneva said. "What if he doesn't pass out?"

"He will sleep . . . eventually."

"I take it his men are accustomed to him taking a French-woman to bed with him?"

"He has occasionally. But you will have an advantage they didn't have. Two bottles of my very best champagne. Make sure he drinks the lion's share of it. Geneva—Celeste—it is a small thing to allow the German the use of your body for a little while—he is young, good looking, healthy."

Geneva regarded him with her feelings carefully masked. "You're asking me to do what you cast my mother out of her home for doing, even though she did it for *love* of a German."

He evaded her eyes. "These are different times. We must survive. France must survive."

She stumbled past him, feeling revulsion, wondering if she would ever understand the duplicity of some men's morals. At the foot of the stairs the grandfather clock made its malevolent presence felt. She said, "I'll go upstairs and dress, it's getting late."

"Wear my late wife's rose-colored evening gown," he called after her. "The color will set off your hair and eyes."

The dress was slightly too short, ending just above her ankles; otherwise it fit almost too well. The bias-cut material clung to her figure, revealing every curve. There was no way she could hide her revolver on her body. She doubted that even her wireless crystals would pass unnoticed, but she wanted them with her rather than risk them getting carelessly broken. She would have to carry gun and crystals in a purse.

Marie found a black silk evening bag that was gathered like a small duffel bag and would hang from her arm. It was large enough to take the gun and crystals, wrapped in handkerchiefs. She pulled the drawstrings tight and was relieved to see that the shape of the gun did not show amid the gathers of the lined silk. Marie also brought her a fox fur, since the evening was cool and damp. The fox's eyes stared sadly as Marie arranged the tails in back and snapped the fastener closed on Geneva's left shoulder.

It was not quite dark when they set off for the village. "Stolper wanted to send his Mercedes for us, but I talked him out of it," Andre said, placing a leather case containing the transceiver in the trunk of his car and covering it with a raincoat. He slid into the driver's seat and glanced at her. "Don't worry, my niece. This isn't quite the reckless venture I let you believe. We'll have help."

She looked at him questioningly.

"Paris HQ are sending a senior officer—Stolper's superior. He'll probably arrive late. Note his name well. He's one of several high-ranking German officers who want to remove Hitler from power. However, unknown to his co-conspirators, he is also a double agent, with a contact in England. Which makes him both doubly valuable and doubly dangerous, perhaps, to us. How much will he give one side in return for information from the other? Whom will he sacrifice in order to ensure that the coup de grace is not thwarted? Two pawns for a rook? His knight for our bishop?"

Geneva leaned back against the cold upholstery of the car, tension ebbing slightly. So that was how he proposed to get the transceiver into the house, with a German accomplice.

Several houses flitted past the car windows as they came to the outskirts of the village, then a row of shops. They turned a corner and were in a pleasant square. A large swastika flew from an upper window at the far side of the square.

"The *croix gammée*," Andre muttered. "The twisted cross marks the house. *Mon dieu!*" He drew in his breath sharply, slamming on the brakes so violently that Geneva was flung forward.

She looked out of the windshield, pressed now to her face, and saw what had startled him. Dangling from a lamppost in front of the Gestapo-occupied house, his eyes bulging like a dead mackerel's, was Rascasse.

Chapter 43

Karl Stolper greeted them cordially at the front door and did not even glance in the direction of the murdered Rascasse. They were conducted to a formal dining room where a table was set for six.

Geneva could feel herself trembling as Stolper's hands touched her when he helped her remove the fox fur. She was aware of conversation around her, German and French, and marveled at her uncle's composure. No one mentioned the dead body hanging in the square.

Stolper was explaining that they were to dine with two junior officers who did not speak French, and a senior officer was expected shortly. He was traveling from Paris.

Smiling and nodding, Geneva knew her eyes must be staring too fixedly and her smile was only painted on her face. A throbbing had begun in one temple. Stolper did not appear to notice. He was wrestling with the champagne her uncle had brought. Andre had offered one bottle openly but placed a paper bag containing two more bottles discreetly in the hall after whispering in Stolper's ear that they were for his private use.

The cork popped from the champagne to the accompaniment of a murmur of approval. "Do you realize what this would bring on the black market?" Stolper asked, offering her a glass.

"I don't deal with the black market," Geneva said, taking the glass and raising it in a silent toast. *To you, Rascasse, I hope you died without betraying me.*

The German laughed. "Then you go hungry, ma'mselle." His eyes went over her insinuatingly. "You are a little slender perhaps. No matter, your uncle will soon fatten you up on his black market food. You look lovely, nevertheless. Your gown is so . . . Parisienne. You French have such a flair for dress. Come, let me escort you to your place beside me at the table."

As he pulled out her chair he whispered, "I'm anxious to finish the meal so I can enjoy your company without the bother of these others."

"But I understood you are one guest short? Won't you wait for the officer who is coming from Paris?"

Stolper shrugged. "Who knows what time he will arrive?"

No, Geneva thought, *don't start without him. I don't want to go up to your room with you until I'm sure the transceiver is in the attic.* The small set, measuring ten by seven by five inches, was still too large to be concealed on Andre's person and stayed in the attache case in the car when they entered the house. She pushed aside the tortured face of Rascasse that kept intruding into her mind and surreptitiously exchanged her almost full glass for an empty one at the next place setting as Stolper's attention was taken by her uncle.

Andre said, "Our friends have adopted the custom of a leisurely meal, Celeste. The other guest will arrive to find we are still at the table—a couple of hours from now." He added to Stolper, "My niece has not had much to do with the occupying forces, having lived until now in Vichy France, you understand. She believes you Germans devour your food with the same efficiency you devour countries." Andre's gray eyes were guileless, but Geneva held her breath in case Stolper took offense.

He sat down, ignoring Andre's attempt at humor, and rang a dinner bell. Geneva thought that her uncle was exhibiting reckless bravado, despite the hidden advantage he possessed. She wished he would have given her the name of the senior officer in advance. What if they weren't introduced? She wished Andre had taken her more into his confidence. She couldn't help but feel like a lamb going meekly to the slaughter.

Evidently her manner did not betray this fact, for Stolper

said, "You have the same extraordinary gray eyes of your uncle. There is no doubt you are blood-related."

Is that the reason you haven't arrested me? Geneva wondered. She took a small sip of champagne from her now refilled glass. It tasted sour and her body felt like ice. She looked around at their immaculate uniforms, their scrubbed handsomeness and smiling mouths, and wondered what their souls looked like, or their consciences—they would have to be ugly, filthy, putrid with decay, that they could laugh and talk and sip champagne with the hanged body of their torture victim outside.

"And like your uncle," Stolper continued, "you have that devastating air of hidden turbulence beneath an air of calmness like an arctic sea. One would imagine you were Swiss instead of French. Have you ever noticed how politely cold the Swiss are? Perhaps that's the reason they've lived at peace for seven hundred years. They are too unemotional to go to war, *ja?*"

"I've never been to Switzerland," Geneva said.

Andre put in, "And look what their seven hundred years of peace has produced—the cuckoo clock!"

Stolper smiled. "I once spent a holiday on the northeastern shore of Lake Geneva."

Geneva held her breath, but he paused for only a fraction of a second before adding, "It was in 1935. I was surprised to find the Swiss had erected a statue and named cafes after your poet, Byron, despite the fact that he insulted them by saying their country was swinish and selfish."

"Our poet?" Geneva asked quickly. "Surely you mean the English poet? Byron was English."

"Of course. As I was saying—the lake is beautiful. Sometimes it is the color of your eyes. Of course, it is also noted for sudden squalls that catch sailors unawares. But perhaps without that . . . unpredictability . . . we would not appreciate beauty so intensely?"

Geneva inclined her head, as though in agreement, and resisted the urge to glance at her wristwatch. A white-jacketed servant entered the room carrying a soup tureen, which he placed on the sideboard and began ladling soup into bowls.

Stolper addressed the other officers in German and they responded with smiles and sly glances at Geneva. Her uncle was looking at his watch, she noticed. She took a small sip of soup, hoping it would warm her. She was afraid she would begin to shiver noticeably. The throbbing in her temple was becoming a full-fledged headache.

At last she could stand the tension no longer. She burst out, "Why is there a body hanging from the lamppost outside? Why does no one mention it?"

Andre stared into his soup bowl. The other Germans looked at her questioningly, not understanding. Stolper turned to her with an unreadable expression on his face and said, "The man was a common thief who compounded his villainy by aiding the British agent we caught. His body will remain in the square to teach the villagers the lesson they must learn. We will not tolerate espionage. Anyone caught aiding the British will be executed."

Before Geneva could respond, her uncle interrupted, "This consomme is exquisite. I must compliment your chef. What is that delicate flavor I cannot identify?"

"Blood?" Geneva suggested, her head pounding.

There was a pause, then Stolper laughed and squeezed her bare arm. "You have a macabre sense of humor."

Geneva fixed her gaze on the long row of silver cutlery extending from her plate, knowing she could not and must not give in to anger or grief, or even speculation, about Rascasse. She had known him only briefly, and she had seen many dead bodies, but none with the expression of horror on their faces that was on his.

The dining room was at the back of the house, and the sixth guest's arrival came without any forewarning. The doors to the room were flung open and a German officer stood surveying the scene. He was tall, his long legs emphasized by black boots with a mirror shine, his overcoat slung capelike across his shoulders, leather gauntlets still in his hands. Blond, eyes bluer even than Stolper's, a small C-shaped scar on one cheek.

Stolper and the other two Germans were on their feet instantly, arms raised in salute to the Führer. Andre rose also, but Geneva remained seated. *"Heil Hitler,"* the newly arrived officer responded. He was an SS colonel. He glanced at Geneva, then spoke rapidly to Stolper in German. Stolper gestured toward the dining table with his hand, indicating the empty chair and place setting, but the colonel shook his head imperiously and turned on his heel.

"Colonel von Hegel," Andre called after him. "It is good to see you again. Thibault—we met in Paris during Herr Goering's visit."

The aristocratic-looking officer said, "I'm sorry. I don't remember you," and turned his back on them, closing the door.

There was a prolonged silence following his departure that was broken when the white-coated servant appeared with the next course. Stolper said lightly, "The colonel has already dined."

"Old-guard Prussian, complete with Heidelberg dueling scar," Andre commented. "Probably feels we are not his social equals, eh, Karl?"

Stolper gave him a glance of silent reprimand and snapped his fingers at the servant to hurry with the fish.

The food kept coming in dismayingly large portions and Geneva forced her dry throat to swallow. There was wine with each course, in addition to Andre's champagne. Toward the end of the meal each of the men, at one time or another, got up and excused themselves to leave the room. The dinner had been progressing, Geneva estimated, for at least two hours. That would mean another hour and a half until she was due to transmit.

Just after dessert was served, a rather heavy pastry smothered with whipped cream, the two junior officers disappeared and did not return. Andre had begun to yawn. She tried to send him a telepathic message that it was still too early to transmit.

Stolper seemed as alert as ever. He shook his head to the offered dessert and, fearing she would vomit, Geneva followed suit. Andre rose unsteadily and said, "Forgive me. I must be getting old. I hate to break up the party, but if you want me to run down that artist for you in the morning, Karl, I must get my sleep. Perhaps you would bring my niece home?"

It was their prearranged signal that the transmitter was in place in the attic. The SS officer with the dueling scar, von Hegel, must have transported the wireless from the car to the house. Only a German would have been able to get it past the guards, perhaps disguised as luggage. But what if von Hegel decided he would ingratiate himself more with his superiors by turning over a British agent . . . rather than with the enemy whose help he sought only for his own planned coup?

Geneva felt a pulse beat in her throat in cadence with her headache. Superimposed over Stolper's leering face was a sudden image of Charlie Dutton.

Andre left and Stolper conducted her, chatting amiably,

from the room. They crossed the hall, where two stone-faced sentries were posted inside the front door, and went up two flights of stairs. She saw the short flight of stairs at the end of the upper landing that led to the attic.

The bedroom was large and, as Andre had indicated, did not have an adjoining bathroom. The bathroom was down the landing, just before the stairs to the attic. The other two bottles of champagne were in an ice bucket on a table near the bed. Two glasses stood on a silver tray.

In a desperate attempt to sound flirtatious, Geneva went to the table and exclaimed, "Let's have some more champagne."

Stolper came up behind her and slipped his hand around her waist, turning her to face him. His eyes were glazed and he was breathing short, irregular breaths. He had unfastened the buttons on his uniform. He muttered something in German and pulled her close so that the buttons bit into her flesh. She held her evening purse away from him as his mouth took hers in a hard bruising kiss that was without subtlety or finesse. It was an impatient preliminary to intercourse, aided and abetted by rough hands on her breasts, kneading and hurting.

She felt him push her backward and her legs connected with the side of the bed; then she was down on her back and he came down on top of her, tugging her gown down over her shoulders, baring her breasts. The evening bag lay beside her on the bed.

He raised his head, releasing her lips, his tongue leaving sour saliva in her mouth. She whispered, "Karl, please, I must use the bathroom first. I was too embarrassed to ask where it was in front of the others. You wouldn't want me to have an accident, would you?" She gave a breathless little laugh and tried to make her eyes promise him what he wanted.

Reluctantly he climbed off her and stood up, discarding his jacket as he did so. "It's down the hall. Hurry."

"Why don't you open a bottle of champagne while I'm gone?" she suggested, her fingers sliding the strings of the evening bag up her arm. Mercifully the contents had not spilled onto the bed.

Stolper grinned and walked around the bed to the ice bucket. Geneva forced herself to walk slowly to the door, turn, and smile at him. Outside his room the landing was still deserted. She ran to the bathroom, turned on the water in the basin, then closed the door and went quickly up the stairs to the attic.

The pencil-sized torch in her evening bag illuminated a room with a steeply sloping roof. There were packing cases and several steamer trunks, but the most welcome sight of all was the small transceiver, laid out on top of one of the boxes.

She fumbled in her purse for her crystals. The first two she unwrapped had broken in the struggle with Stolper. Her heart sank; she had only two more and had hoped to use all four so that she could change frequencies during transmission. The other two were unbroken, and she decided she must risk using only two frequencies. The small transmitter's signal would be weak and perhaps she was taking this risk for nothing. Even if her message was received, the whole tangle of encoding and enciphering wireless traffic with the field was still so highly complicated and was handled by different departments, who occasionally worked against each other, that it would be some time before she could hope to be picked up. Fortunately she would not have to wait for a reply, as since the previous summer a system had been worked out to get messages to agents by means of the BBC Foreign Programme, which broadcast so-called "family greetings"—coded instructions and times of air drops or pickups.

Now, what was that officer's name? Von Hegel, Colonel. It was a little early for transmission, but perhaps someone was standing by. Two-minute transmission for this first try, she decided. She had a personal code that she had memorized; a string of numbers, followed by a more elaborate "worked-out key" which in her case was a line from a poem, chosen because it was easy to remember and more difficult to break than other ciphers. The line was, "Out on the winds of time."

After this came her system of security checks, to assure the receiving station that she had not fallen into enemy hands and was broadcasting at their direction. Hers consisted of certain spelling errors.

Her fingers flew over the Morse key:

FELLOW PASSENGER ARRESTED STOP UNSURE WHICH STOP
GESTAPO ALSO HAVE MY LUGGAGE STOP UNCLE WILL
COOPERATE STOP FRIEND IN HIGH PLACES VON HEGEL
COLONEL STOP NEED IMMEDIATE PICKUP—

She broke off, realizing she had forgotten to include the spelling mistakes. Not daring to take time to repeat the message, she left the crystals with the set, picked up her bag, and raced back down the stairs.

By this time she really did need to use the bathroom. She had barely finished when she heard Stolper's voice outside, demanding to know if she had fallen in and complaining that the champagne was going flat. He laughed drunkenly.

Geneva rinsed her hands quickly and went out to him, patting her hair into place as though she had been primping. He was stark naked, but she was glad to see he had lost his erection. They went back to the bedroom, and he emptied another glass of champagne while she placed hers to her lips without swallowing.

His hand snaked out to pull the shoulder of her dress down again, then plucked impatiently at her brassiere.

"Wait, Karl. You Germans are so impatient. I can see we French have a lot to teach you. The act of love is not meant to be hurried; it should be savored, lingered over." Playfully she pushed him into a sitting position on the bed and backed away, moving her arms and body in a slow and seductive dance. "See . . . first I will undress for you . . . slowly, tantalizingly."

She put her evening bag down on top of the bedside table, next to the ice bucket, then waltzed away from his outstretched hands, swaying her hips as she wriggled out of her dress. Under it she wore black silk panties and stockings held up by garters with rosettes of red ribbon. She continued to dance as she reached behind her to unhook her lace brassiere. As it fell to the floor she thought all at once of Dory Gates attracting Terry as she danced in the chorus line. A surge of both recognition and anger manifested itself in suddenly jerky movements. Sisters under the skin, she thought grimly, flinging the panties across the room.

Stolper was not to be put off any further. He was ready and on his feet and coming toward her, his speech thick and his eyes bloodshot. When he grabbed her and flung her to the bed, she closed her eyes, steeling herself for the assault, telling herself she would endure it, that it meant nothing. She didn't even have to worry about him impregnating her, as her mother had been impregnated by her German lover.

Perhaps it was the thought of her mother, or perhaps it was Stolper's frenzy; Geneva wasn't sure. She only knew that she was not going to allow him entry. He was panting and sweating over her, pressing against her thighs, his semen dribbling on her flesh, scalding her. She looked up at his swollen mouth, again about to come down over hers, and realized she was still wearing her stockings and high-heeled shoes.

She squirmed under him. "Wait, my shoe is caught in the bedspread."

He rolled to one side, his hand still cupped over her breast, as she drew up her knee and pulled off her shoe. She rammed the stiletto heel into his ear as hard as she could. His face contorted with pain and he jerked away from her, clutching the side of his head. "Englander bitch!"

She brought up the shoe and smashed it down on the base of his skull before the significance of his words had completely registered. *He knew*—he'd known all along. He pitched forward on the bed, a trickle of blood crawling down his neck.

Scooping up her dress and purse, she ran.

In the attic she didn't waste time going through all of the preliminaries. She tapped out the message:

> BLUFF CHECK OMITTED   TRUE CHECK OMITTED
> ARREST IMINENT STOP NEED IMMEDIATE TRANSPORT

She was sure there were unplanned errors in her transmission, but hoped they would compare the message with the dummy transmission she, in common with all operators, had made before she left England. This dummy transmission graphically recorded each operator's personal style of sending, which was as varied as handwriting.

The door flew open and Stolper, swaying slightly on his feet, his naked body glistening with sweat, stood framed in the light from the landing behind him.

She didn't hesitate. The gun was in her hand and she aimed for his chest and squeezed the trigger. The roar of the explosion seemed to fill the house, and as she stepped over his body she wondered why she hadn't been issued a silencer. She skidded down the stairs, pulling her dress over her head.

There was the sound of boots running up the next flight of stairs and she ran toward them, screaming hysterically. The first German to reach her tried to run past her to Stolper's bedroom, but she shrieked again and clutched at his uniform, babbling in French that two men had climbed into their room through the window. She mimed a man with a gun and pointed toward the bedroom. The German moved cautiously toward the door as two other guards joined him on the landing. Geneva, sobbing, leaned against the wall in her bloodstained dress.

As the first man kicked open the bedroom door and sprang into the room, Geneva turned and ran down the stairs. The two sentries were still at their posts at the front door, rifles now at the ready. She screamed again, pointing up the staircase, but they didn't move. Geneva clapped her hand over her mouth as though to vomit and turned and ran the other way.

At the far end of the hall a door led to the kitchen. She went past a silent chef who made no move to stop her. A Frenchman, she thought, clutching her purse and hoping she wouldn't have to shoot him.

There was a back door that opened to a small garden. Leaning against the wall was the chef's bicycle. She yanked her dress up over her knees to climb over the crossbar and set off down a deserted alley, exhilarated by the sense of freedom. There was no sound behind her, no cries for her to stop or running feet. She pedaled as fast as she could, turned the corner, and found herself on the square only a short distance from Rascasse's body. No one else about—long after curfew, of course. The bicycle wheels bumped down over the curb, and she pedaled furiously across the square.

She had reached the lane leading out of the village when she heard the car's engine, purring softly, almost leisurely, behind her. She pedaled faster. The car speeded up, caught up with her, slammed into the rear of the bicycle.

Everything spiraled. She sprawled on her hands and knees, grazing the skin. Her purse went spinning away and landed with the revolver's muzzle protruding from between the silk ties. She reached for it as hands grabbed her, twisting her arms behind her back. She felt handcuffs snap coldly around her wrists.

Chapter 44

She spent the night locked in an empty storeroom. There was a board to sleep on, had she been able to sleep. The next morning, still wearing her bloodstained evening gown, she was bundled into the back seat of a Citroen between two burly men in black uniforms.

Gestapo headquarters in Paris, she thought as they came to the outskirts of the city. The car slowed for a traffic signal and an old lady peered through the window and shrieked at her, "Whore!"

At the end of the journey she walked between the two men, recalling her simulated interrogation. They will push you, try to make you fall, then kick you so you can't get up. This will be to teach you, immediately, the lesson that no matter what, you will do what they want you to do.

When one of the men shoved her, she quickened her pace and kept on her feet. Inside the building the corridor was light and airy. Loudspeakers filled the air with the music of Bach. They marched to the beat, and Geneva had a sudden urge to laugh at the incongruity of it all.

She was taken into a handsomely furnished room. Persian rugs on the polished floor, an inlaid desk with oversize leather chair, softly draped windows, lamps. Her handcuffs were removed.

Behind the desk was a little ferret of a man wearing civilian clothes. He peered at her through round eyeglasses, cadaver-gray skin stretching over skeleton jaw as he spoke in passable French. He was polite, addressing her as mademoiselle and at the same time offering her a cigarette.

"Very regrettable, this mess you've got yourself into. So young, so pretty too. Of course, we realize that you did not do this thing on your own. It's the old story, isn't it, mademoiselle? A man who gets you to do his dirty work for him." He nodded toward a chair and she sank into it, accepting a light for the cigarette. She had never smoked but thought perhaps the cigarette would be something to hold on to, stopping her hands from shaking.

"We must know who the man is, of course, you realize that. If you do not talk now, give me the whole story, you will be interrogated in any manner needed to get the information. Then you will be shot. It is as simple as that, mademoiselle."

Geneva took a puff of the cigarette. Turkish, she thought, as the smoke burned her throat and made the room spin out of focus. She had been given nothing to eat or drink since her arrest.

The man behind the desk went on, "We know you could not have taken the transmitter into the house yourself. The only people capable of setting it up for you were the two French servants, or the chef . . . or your so-called uncle, Andre Thibault. We mean to have the name of your accomplice, sooner or later. It's up to you. I can assure you we will learn his name."

Geneva shrugged. "You're going to kill me no matter what I say. I had no accomplice. I smuggled the small set into the house under my dress." ·

His small fist came down on the desk surface with unexpected ferocity, considering his diminutive size. "Impossible! It could not be concealed on your person. I shan't waste my time with you if you refuse to cooperate." He banged on a bell on his desk, and the two black-uniformed guards reappeared and again handcuffed her.

They took her up to the next floor, and as soon as the heavy doors were opened she knew these were the interrogating rooms. Screams and moans came from every direction, accompanied by curses and thuds. She was paraded slowly from door to door, forced to look into each room.

The victims were scarcely recognizable as human beings,

but still the torturers kept hitting and kicking them. In one room a very young girl sat with her arms tied to the back of a wooden chair, her face lolling on her chest, her jaw broken.

Geneva felt the bile in her throat; her eyes blurred with tears. Don't try to invent a story, your questioners will be professionals who will spot any inconsistency and trap you into making all sorts of revelations. Better to just tell them you know nothing. This is the only way to resist. You know nothing. But how could she say she knew nothing when she had been caught with a wireless transmitter, her gun still warm from killing a German officer?

She was pushed violently into an empty room and crashed to the floor. They dragged her to her feet, removed the handcuffs. One of the men ordered her to take off her clothes. Still dazed from the fall, she hesitated, looking down at her bloodstained dress. He hit her twice, hard. She pulled the dress down. She hadn't had time to replace her underwear during her brief flight, but the black silk stockings, torn and streaked with bicycle oil, still clung to her legs. She rolled them down, stepped out of them. Her hands were pulled behind her and she was handcuffed again.

Another man entered the room. He was carrying a rubber hose. He said, "Do you really want to go through with this? Why don't you just tell us who your accomplice was and be done with it?"

She said, "I had no accomplice." The hose smashed against the side of her jaw. She stumbled out of his reach, trying to evade the blows. He followed, hitting her again. He shouted, "Terrorist! Communist!" his voice growing in volume as the blows became harder. She screamed, flung herself down on her knees, and crawled to the corner of the room, bowing her head to try to escape. He beat her on top of the head and the blood flowed down her face, blinding her. She felt the hose strike her back, then ram against her kidneys. She passed out.

She came to her senses in a dark cell only minutes before the interrogators returned. This time she was taken to a bathroom. There was an ordinary looking bathtub, three-quarters filled with water.

In the split second before anything happened, she thought dimly that the five inches of water in the tub apparently didn't apply here. Then she was shoved, face forward, into the icy water. Her head was held under until she was choking and gasping and water was rushing into her lungs. The sense of panic was overwhelming. She was convinced she was drowning. She fought the restraining hands with all of her strength, but they held her down until her body went limp.

They revived her and repeated the process twice. The next time she came to, she was back in her darkened cell. Someone was moaning nearby and a thin voice wailed, over and over, *"Je ne sais rien. Je ne sais rien."* I know nothing, I know nothing.

Geneva rolled over on the hard boards, seeking a position that was less punishing; but it was no use, she was bruised and battered all over her body. As though from deep inside an empty cave, she heard a voice whisper, "Do you hear me? Wake up."

She looked up to see the figure of a man bending over her, and instinctively she cringed away from him. In the darkness she could not be sure, but he seemed vaguely familiar. Behind him her cell door was open and a faint light showed a tall lean man, not one of the burly interrogators. He had brought her a bowl of soup. She sipped it through split lips, feeling it warm her.

Silently he motioned her to get up and follow him. Every part of her body screamed in outrage as she tried to stand up. When she was on her feet, her knees buckled and he caught her and helped her out into the corridor.

There was a light on the wall outside her cell door, a low-wattage bulb but enough so that she recognized him. He was the SS colonel—von Hegel—who had appeared briefly at Stolper's dinner party. Weakness washed over her again. What else should she remember about him? Her mind was a blank.

"There are microphones in the cells," he whispered to her in English. The sound of her own language almost completely devastated her. She wanted to cry and beg him to help her, but a warning voice insisted, *It's a trick, a Gestapo trick.*

"Listen to me, Geneva," he said. "I'm going to help you, but you must do exactly as I say."

Help me find my lethal capsule, she wanted to say. *I need it now. I know I still have it, but they beat me and I can't remember where it is.* Wait . . . he had called her by her real name. No, it wasn't possible. How could he know?

"You must tell me who helped you set up the transmitter. It is essential that I get in touch with the Resistance. I am one of a small group who are working from within the Third Reich to depose Hitler and his gangsters. Just before the war I went to England to visit a friend from my student days—someone you know well. Huw Wakefield.''

Geneva tried to sort her thoughts into logical sequences. Of course, this was a trick. What von Hegel didn't know was that Huw had already been unmasked as a German agent. She said, "Please believe me, I had no accomplice."

"Geneva, they will fasten electrodes to your body on your next trip to the bathroom. Painful electric shocks will slam into you and each contact will make a deep burn on your skin."

"I can't tell you something I don't know. I was alone. No one helped me."

"You were parachuted in with two other agents. One of them was picked up immediately, the other is still at large. You were to approach your uncle, try to enlist him in the Resistance, despite the fact that he was doing business with the occupiers. Huw Wakefield is a double agent. He is my contact in England, as I am his here. Thibault was suspected of being a saboteur by Stolper—who luckily confided in me. I advised him to get evidence before making an accusation. But Stolper is dead and it is imperative that I know whether or not I can trust Thibault. Who betrayed you? Was it your uncle? How did Stolper know you were a British agent?"

"I suppose it must have been the other agent—the one who was arrested. Or perhaps the dead Frenchman—Rascasse."

"No. Neither of them. Stolper told me they both died without talking."

"My clothes—he found my suitcase then, with the parachute still attached."

"That told him only that a woman had been dropped. Stolper must have been more clever than I thought. What about Thibault? Did he agree to work with you? I mean apart from the attempt to radio London—that could merely have been to arrange to have you picked up. Did Thibault agree to organize French resistance? Geneva, there is to be an attempt on Hitler's life. Your uncle's help would be invaluable—he is to supervise the shipment of a large consignment of artworks back to Germany for the Führer's personal collection. You must tell me if I can trust Thibault."

No, Geneva thought weakly, *it's a trick. It's a Gestapo trick, just as I was warned about. First he threatens me with electric shocks, then he tells me this farfetched story about wanting to kill Hitler.*

Von Hegel had turned his head, and the C-shaped scar on his cheek was thrown into sharp relief by the play of light and shadow. She wondered dully if he was enjoying this game as much as he enjoyed fencing at Heidelberg. She said, "I didn't have an accomplice. I was alone."

"You had two accomplices, Geneva. Your uncle and myself. I placed the transmitter in the attic for you. Your uncle arranged your meeting with Stolper so that you could be there to use it. My question is—did Thibault betray both of us to Stolper? And did you kill Stolper in time to prevent him passing on the information to someone else? Think—did your uncle tell you anything of value to your people in London—something that tells us, for certain, he can be trusted."

"Why don't you just ask my uncle yourself?" Geneva said wearily.

"He disappeared—the morning you were brought here. I haven't been able to learn what happened to him." He paused, waiting for her reaction, and when she remained silent he said, "Very well, Geneva. I can't get you out of here now. You will have to submit to the electric shocks tomorrow. When they are finished with you—if you are still alive—I'll try to have you transferred immediately to the prison where you will await your execution, rather than letting them keep you here any longer. That's the best I can do. I wish I could convince you to trust me. If you give your uncle's name to them, then he will be useless to me too." He led her back into her cell and helped her down onto the board. Consciousness swam away from her before he had locked the cell door.

She came to her senses briefly some time later and tried to fit the pieces together. Andre Thibault and von Hegel . . . Huw Wakefield? Yes, of course. Hadn't Huw, in effect, recruited her for this mission? Fed her anxiety about her father, encouraged her sense of outrage? Played on her patriotism by using the old psychological ploy of condemning the English and French—pointing out that she also had a German heritage. But he hadn't wanted to recruit her to the German side—quite the opposite. Von Hegel had said he visited Huw before the war. Was that how he convinced Huw to be loyal to England? By attacking the English—perhaps playing up Huw's Eurasian blood?

But something was missing from her memory. Hadn't Huw done something that proved this was not the case, that he was in fact a German agent? The agony of her body vied for attention, and weakness again sent her below the surface of consciousness before she could untangle the problem.

Some time in the night they came for her again. She was again beaten with the rubber hose and then dragged back to her cell. It took hours for her to become accustomed to the new pains. Just before dawn she was carried back to the bathroom because she could no longer walk.

She saw the electrodes immediately and fear churned through her stomach, rose in her throat, numbed her mind; but there was no physical strength left to resist as they fastened them to her naked back and thighs.

To survive torture, there must be one unshakable reality to cling to. One thought for the bloodied brain to turn to to reassure itself it can survive. One undestroyable talisman.

"I had no accomplice. I was alone. I had no accomplice. I am alone." She repeated it until she believed it, until there was no name for her to give them. "I have no accomplice. I was alone. I am alone." She clung tenaciously to the thought as the electricity tore through her body.

. . . *One unshakable reality to cling to.* One undestroyable talisman. To survive. . . . *I must remember that once there was love and hope. No, that wasn't what I was supposed to remember. I'm thinking of life . . . I'm trying to survive life itself. I'm confusing this agony . . . with that other torment. Oh, God, oh God, help me!*

Merciful blackness returned but did not quite obliterate the pain. Then an unbearable agony seized her wrists. She was back in her cell, hands handcuffed behind her, and she had rolled onto her back, causing the handcuffs to click a notch tighter. She managed to perch on the edge of the board, her back to the wall, to keep from lying on the handcuffs and adding to her own torture.

Bright light flooded her face, awakening her. She had no idea how long she had been in the cell. Her body flinched and shook; tears sprang to her eyes. Someone was removing the handcuffs, dragging her to her feet, thrusting clothing into her hands. Her own clothes, from the missing suitcase. "Put them on. Hurry up."

Bending was exquisite agony, raising her hands above her head nearly impossible. She blacked out again, opened her eyes to find she was dressed and her arms in the grip of two men who propelled her down the same light corridor, filled with the joyful strains of Bach, out into the sunshine, to a black car waiting at the curb. She was pushed roughly into the back seat and found herself falling against the impeccably pressed uniform of Colonel von Hegel.

She couldn't speak; her lips were too swollen. Nor did he say anything as he tapped on the window dividing the passenger seat from the driver. The car slid smoothly away, the motion almost soothing. *I'm going to my execution,* she thought, not really caring.

Waves of nausea and weakness caused her to black out several times, and she was unsure how long they were in the car or at what point they transferred from the chauffeur-driven car to one with only von Hegel at the wheel. Eventually they stopped at what appeared to be a private house and he helped her inside, then up a narrow flight of stairs to a small sitting room with a couch and table and an ordinary wireless set on a wooden stand. Von Hegel flipped on a switch and the room was filled with music; then an impersonal voice announced that they were listening to the BBC Foreign Programme.

Von Hegel said, "You remember what your code is? Will you recognize the message that is for you? Try to concentrate. I have no idea what your personal message is—I know only that the BBC uses this means to contact agents in the field."

Somewhere in the back of her mind hope began to build. He meant it. He was going to help her escape. She cleared her fogged brain and listened to the voice of the BBC announcer.

"When?" von Hegel asked when the messages were finished.

"The night of the full moon. Three torches must be arranged in an inverted L shape, with the crossbar at the upwind end. The same place where I was dropped."

She wondered, with excruciating weariness, if she had just given the Gestapo the pilot and Lysander that was coming for her, but she couldn't endure any more. She hadn't told them about Andre Thibault. They couldn't expect any more of her.

He took her back down to the car. It was now dark. She fell asleep immediately—or perhaps she was unconscious; she wasn't sure. She was aware only of the agony of her body and the same thought hammering away at her brain. "I have no accomplice. I was alone. I have no one. I am alone."

She awoke to the realization that she was being carried in someone's arms. Overhead the moonlight sent pale tentative fingers of light through the branches of trees. She was surprised to see they had lost their leaves. Autumn again, so soon. Then the sky was an inky canopy as a cloud drifted languidly across the moon. She looked up at the man carrying her but did not recognize him.

There was no sign of von Hegel. No one but the silent man who carried her so carefully and laid her down on the ground as the moon slid into view and flooded the field with light. She struggled to a sitting position, clutched his shirt to pull him closer. "Three torches—you will have to light them all, if you are alone. Give one to me; I will flash the Morse signal when we hear the plane." Her mind had cleared, almost as though a curtain had been raised. The price she paid for the clarity of thought was almost unbearable pain throughout her entire body. She went on quickly, "We must wait at the downwind light. The Lysander will taxi in a right-handed turn, 'round the other two, back to the first so that it is turned upwind." Her voice was hoarse; it hurt her throat to speak.

He nodded and she felt the cold metal of an electric torch slipped into her stiff fingers. She fumbled with her thumb to find the switch.

The Lysander came in low over the treetops, skimming the hedge. Geneva's torch blinked its Morse message, and minutes later the plane's wheels bumped lightly to the ground and it taxied past her. The man who had carried her now ran back to assist her. As he lifted her into the plane he whispered, "Don't forget the name—Wilhelm von Hegel. Without Huw's friend Willi, you would be facing a firing squad now."

Chapter 45

Upon awakening in the hospital, the first face Geneva saw belonged to Huw Wakefield. He perched stiffly on the edge of a chair at her bedside and she saw him from beneath a fringe of eyelashes. Her face felt rubbery and numbed. There was a cage over her lower body to keep the sheets from touching her. When she tried to move her legs, she understood why.

Huw said, "How do you feel?"

The question seemed ridiculous in the extreme. She moved her lips but no sound came. He picked up a tumbler with a twisted glass straw that enabled her to drink from a prone position. She sipped the water, coughed, and blinked her eyes fully open. Her mind was curiously blank.

"Can you answer a few questions, Geneva?" The voice came from the opposite side of the bed, and Geneva slowly rolled her head to see Major Jefferson seated there. She moved her lips again, "Huw—Huw—"

"He is working for us, Geneva," Jefferson said.

Huw said, "I'm a double agent. I've been working for both the Germans and the British. I did spot that plane that destroyed the abbey and the landing field. It was a small gesture to endear me to the Germans. You'll remember that although the damage was heavy, no one was killed. I arranged for my grandfather to be away, and the SOE people were in an underground shelter. That landing field was a dummy anyway. You'll recall you trained for your own parachute jumping at Ringway."

Geneva fixed her gaze on him, trying to make sense of what he was telling her. He went on, "You see, Willi von Hegel came to see me shortly before the war. He traveled a winding road to find out what my feelings would be about a possible war between our countries, and where my loyalties lay. He and some of the other Prussian officers feared that Hitler would lead Germany to another *Gotterdamerung*. Willi wanted a friend in England who would help him when the time came to try to remove Hitler from power."

She closed her eyes again, giving in to the ache and throb of her body, allowing her mind to concentrate on each separate pain. It was easier than trying to cope with the game of war. War was a mad, gruesome charade that debased and dehumanized. How could anyone say it was a noble experience?

Huw said, "My grandfather died recently, Geneva. In his bed, of old age. My only regret is that he never knew of my work."

Jefferson's voice came to her, as though from far away. "Anything you can tell us of the conditions you encountered in France will be helpful. Curfews, bicycle regulations, changes in rationing, living conditions." He paused. "We're especially interested in your interrogation."

Fog banks kept obscuring her train of thought. Just as she thought all was clear, an image would vanish. She said, "I had no accomplice. I was alone."

"You didn't betray Andre Thibault. We're proud of you."

"He said—said he would only take orders from de Gaulle." The words came slowly, distorted, like a gramophone in need of winding.

"Geneva!" That was Huw's voice, startling her as it cracked like a whip. Her eyes flew open and she looked at him. His skin seemed darker than ever against the whiteness of the hospital. He had his mouth open as though about to say something, but he was staring not at her but across the bed at Jefferson. "Tell her, Major." His voice was angry, commanding. "Tell her now."

The motion of turning her head toward Jefferson again caused her jaw to throb and sent shooting pains from ears to eyes. Jefferson's face was expressionless. "There's no need, at this time."

"Your uncle is dead, Geneva," Huw said. "We received word from Willi today."

"Then . . . then it was all for nothing." She thought perhaps she wanted to laugh, but could not force her mouth and vocal cords to obey the impulse. The only sound that escaped was a small sigh. She closed her eyes to make the two men disappear. She heard them talking to her for several minutes, but eventually their voices ran together and formed an unintelligible droning noise that lulled her back to sleep.

Occasionally sights and sounds and sensations, mostly painful, broke the long periods of sleep. She lived in a twilit world of white ghosts who came and touched her and gave her water and attached bottles to her arm and changed dressings and pricked her skin with injections. There were nightmares too, of course, and once she awakened to find herself being restrained by two breathless nurses as she cried out repeatedly, "I have no accomplice. I am alone."

Then the nightmares gave way to strange, disturbing dreams. She was in a huge auditorium and there was an orchestra playing on stage, but she couldn't hear the music. There was no audience either; she was all alone. She was thinking, *It's all right, I can't hear them because this is just a rehearsal.*

One morning she opened her eyes and asked if she could please have something to eat. The nurse seemed almost excessively delighted by the request. Geneva thought perhaps she had been in the hospital a week or two and was shocked when the nurse told her it had been over a month. Then she asked if there was anyone they could send for. Major Jefferson said it would be all right.

"Yes," Geneva said. "Will you get in touch with Miss Whitaker—Saxon Quarry, Lancashire. And nurse, please, I'd like to go to the bathroom."

The nurse said she would see, and scurried away excitedly. She returned with a doctor, who said Geneva could try to move. The hospital gown gaped open in the back and she held it closed as she slid her feet over the edge of the bed and stood up, the coolly efficient faces of doctor and nurse receding for a moment as the room lazily revolved around her.

Her ribs hurt and a jarring pain traveled up her legs and spine as she took a couple of shaky steps. The pain was altogether different from the oozing, moist feel of the burns. This was a dry, bone-deep crackling pain. Her body felt battered, her skin flailed. Before she was halfway across the small room, beads of perspiration sprang from her forehead.

She stopped, unsure where she was going. Behind her a

voice spoke in a monotone. "You may suffer memory lapses
as a result of the electric shocks, but it should be only
temporary. You were fortunate you were in their hands for
such a short time."

Geneva turned and looked into the doctor's bland expression and uninvolved eyes. "Oh, yes," she said. "I was
frightfully fortunate. Now will you please tell me where I was
going?"

The nurse moved to her side and slipped an arm around
her. "There's a bathroom through that door. I'll help you."

In the bathroom the mirror had been removed from above
the washbasin. It didn't matter; Geneva fainted before she
could use the toilet.

But she was recovering, she thought, because the cage was
gone from her legs and she was regaining control of her facial
muscles. She no longer cried with the pain when they came to
change the dressings on the burns. She was still having the
dreams, and her memory seemed fragmented.

The second time Huw Wakefield came to see her, he was
alone. He brought a bunch of red and white carnations,
trailing a tracery of delicate green fern, and she wanted to cry
because it was so beautiful; then she was amazed that she had
never before truly pondered the fact that men grew flowers,
tended fragrant gardens, painted pictures, composed music—
and those same men, on sight, could not be distinguished
from bestial monsters who tortured and maimed and killed.
Why didn't it show in their faces?

After several minutes of small talk Geneva asked, "Will
you tell me what happened to Andre Thibault?"

Huw looked at the floor. "There was a small village—the
French Resistance there killed a German officer. The Germans immediately rounded up fifty hostages and executed
them. It had nothing to do with our operation—the Germans
didn't even know who your uncle was. He was visiting an
artist he knew."

Geneva nodded. Andre must have left early the following
morning, not knowing she had killed Stolper—and he, having
sent Andre to the artist, had ensured revenge for his own
death. But of course that didn't make sense. Her mind was
playing tricks again.

Huw continued, "The German High Command issued
orders that hostages are to be shot immediately—no imprisonment or trial. Hostages are not even allowed to contact
family or friends; otherwise Thibault no doubt could have had

one of his German friends intercede. Your uncle was just in the wrong place at the wrong time."

"Yes. I think perhaps that happens to many of us. We should all strive for the safety of the whole, so we don't become the missing fragment."

"I beg your pardon?"

There was a long silence and Geneva tried to think of something to say. "I didn't know—not for sure—whether he was on our side or not. He took the transmitter into the house for me, but he also delivered me to the bedroom of an SS officer." She gave a small laugh that tasted bitter on her tongue. "But then, I'm still not sure about you either, Huw. You tell me you are a double agent. I interpret that to mean you work for both sides, as von Hegel works for both sides. Therefore, why even bother to *have* sides?"

She was quiet again, searching in her mind for the missing piece that kept all of the other elements from fitting together. Without it, nothing made any sense, neither her suffering nor her life.

The nurse's head appeared around the door. "You've another visitor, Mrs. Saxon. There's a Miss Whitaker to see you."

"Nancy! Oh, please send her in right away."

Huw stood up. "You'll have a lot to talk about, I'm sure. I'll come and see you later."

Nancy came hesitantly through the doorway, carrying a small bunch of roses and a brown paper wrapped parcel. Although she started toward the bed with a travesty of a smile on her face, it had crumpled to tears before she put the flowers down and reached for Geneva's outstretched hand. "Oh, lass, oh, my poor lass, what have they done to you?"

A nurse bustled in and said sharply, "Now, Miss Whitaker, there's no need for that. Mrs. Saxon's coming along nicely. You'll have to talk to her while I change her dressings." She was already reaching for the curtained screen. Nancy stood aside, her face tear-streaked.

"Must you do it now?" Geneva asked.

"Sorry. We have to keep to our schedule."

Nancy's voice came to her from behind the white curtain. "It's all right, Gennie. I've taken a room not far from here. I'm going to stay near until I can take you home."

They tried to make small talk while Geneva's burns were dressed, and she gritted her teeth so Nancy would not hear her whimper of pain. Nancy was saying, "I knitted you a bed jacket; it's in the parcel. Saved a bit of angora since before the war. The air raids have let up a bit lately; a lull, they say. But they've cut the meat ration again. I've been eating so much fish I'm starting to get scales, I think."

After the nurse left and they could look at each other again, Geneva said, "Did they tell you . . ."

"About Ian? Yes." Nancy blinked the tears away again. "I think I knew . . . months ago . . . that he was gone. An empty, lost feeling came over me, you know."

"Yes. I know. But he won't die for us, Nancy—he won't ever leave us. Someday, when it doesn't hurt so much, we'll share our memories of him."

"We'll do that, lass. Yes, we will." Nancy played with a fine gold chain around her neck for a moment, then she said, "I've something else to tell you. I hope you won't be cross, but I've got someone else with me who wants to see you. He's in the waiting room."

"No!" Geneva said, panic-stricken, knowing there was only one person it could be. "No, I can't see him."

"Now listen, Gennie, he was hanging around the Hall and the village for weeks, trying to find out where you were. I took pity on him."

"No, you had no right. I don't want him to see me like this." She began to shake violently and couldn't stop until Nancy wrapped her arms around her. "All right, Gennie, calm down, lass. You don't have to see him if you don't want."

After a while Nancy said, "Gennie, can you tell me how your dad died? I can't stand not knowing . . . was it quick?"

Nancy called on her every day, and a week passed before she confided that Matt had refused to leave and had been camping at the hospital during each of her visits. He refused to leave until Geneva agreed to see him, if only for a minute.

Geneva was feeling particularly tired that evening and frightened by the clarity of the images from her slowly returning memory. "All right, Nancy," she said. "I suppose I must see him."

Ten minutes later Matt was standing at the door. He looked well fed, well dressed, healthily out of place. A stranger from a different world. He crossed the room in three quick strides, bent to place a gentle kiss on her cheek. Something warm and wet splashed on her face.

"I'm sorry, I didn't bring you anything," he said awkwardly. "I had a truckload of flowers that first day, but they took them to the wards. Gennie, oh, God, Gennie—"

"Do you believe in God, Matt?" she asked, seizing upon the subject as though pouncing on prey. "When you were in the lifeboat, did you pray for deliverance? Did you feel you were being called upon to endure, in some test of your faith? Please, it's important to me to know."

There was a moment's silence as Matt searched her face with a worried frown. Then he said, "No. But I guess I did have a mystical experience, in a way." He told her briefly how he thought he heard Specks' voice and was convinced the line he was holding was attached to floating wreckage.

She listened carefully, remembering how she had prayed to a stone-deaf God during the hours she was beaten and tortured and could not remember where she had hidden her poison capsule. Her prayers during those hours had collided with her anguished questions, her search for a plausible explanation to what was happening to her and why. Prayer and thoughts were like an intricate tapestry that had faded and come unraveled, and putting all the threads back was a task she had been too dispirited to attempt.

"Gennie? You were going to tell me something?"

She looked at Matt blankly for a few seconds, trying to remember. Then she said, "Nothing changes. Do you realize that *nothing changes?* It's the most horrifying discovery I've made. Terrible things happen—to people, to places. Wars happen, but they don't change anything. You suffered all those weeks in the middle of the Atlantic. What did your suffering accomplish? What good did it do anyone? What good did it do for my father, and Terry, and Dulcie . . . and Andre—to die? What purpose was served by me? By my—" She broke off, puzzled. "I'm sorry. I've lost the thought. I don't know what I was going to say."

He patted her hand. "Gennie, life isn't that hopeless. Things do change for the better. Listen, I don't know much about what you've been through, but I can guess. I talked to Huw Wakefield in the waiting room. He told me they can arrange a release from the service for you on medical grounds. When you're far away from them, when you're physically strong again, you'll shake off the depression too. Christ, they kicked you when you were down, didn't they? You were still reeling from one bereavement after another.

But nobody's going to hurt you again. I swear it. Like it or not, Gennie, you're stuck with me. You're not going to send me away again."

"Matt, my father . . . my biological father was German. That's why my uncle threw my mother out of the house. But in the end, he—" There it was again, that hole in the continuity. She tried to concentrate. "The endings—they're there, in the beginnings, I believe." She closed her eyes. There was something important she had to tell him. She wished she could remember what it was. It was just out of reach of her groping thoughts. "I was so afraid. I thought I was going to die. It was a shock to discover how cowardly I am."

"You're the bravest woman I know, Gennie. You're stronger than even you realize. You know, when Nancy told me you were in hospital, and Wakefield said you'd been to France, all I could think of was that I should have come and got you out before they did this to you. I guess I had this idea that I'd have come along like the cavalry, charging to your rescue. Only life isn't that accommodating, is it? I didn't even know where you were. I badgered the St. John's Ambulance people in Liverpool, asked everyone in the village. No one knew where you were. I was playing two-bit detective when I should have girded my armor and ridden out to save the damsel. Some hero I'd make, huh?"

She tried to smile, knowing he was attempting to cheer her up with his self-deprecating humor. She could see in his eyes the reflection of her own suffering. "I think I had to do this alone, Matt. I think it was always written in my stars. And now it's over, perhaps there's a lesson to be learned, only I'm too tired at the moment to know what it is. Perhaps it's a symbolic lesson . . . perhaps *I'm* the symbol—of the futility of war. I'm talking nonsense, aren't I? The doctors say . . . the electric shocks . . ."

A tear trickled slowly down his cheek. He didn't wipe it away. "We're going to be together from now on. We're going to make it. Lie back, rest . . . And let me tell you what I've been thinking, feeling. Only one thing matters. Being together. If we can't be together, then nothing else means anything either. You see, Gennie, I had doubts. I worried about transplanting you to a strange country, different customs, people. Who was it who said we were two countries divided by a common language?"

A faint smile hovered. "Shaw, I think."

"I kept asking myself—would it have worked, anyway, even if there hadn't been all of those other obstacles? Would you have settled down, Gennie, in my home? Would you have exchanged your morning kippers for hotcakes and grits? How about Debussey for the blues? Would you have pined for cool English meadows . . . long summer twilights . . . nightingales . . ."

"I'd have had you, Matt." Her voice was a whisper; she wasn't sure if he heard. She struggled to stay awake, wanting to listen to all he had to say. She wanted to reach for him, draw him into her arms, but her body was trapped by the stupefying lethargy that threatened to creep into her mind again. "The other things you're talking about . . . are just adjustments to be made. The main thing—" She broke off, trying to think what the main thing was. His fingers were rubbing gently over her hands, tracing knuckles and nails with a wonderfully healing touch.

"Is that we would have had each other, constant and sure," he finished for her, "in a changing world. Gennie, I looked for some meaning to my life for so long—yet when I found it, I was afraid to fight for it. I guess I wanted you to come to me. Maybe all men fear rejection more than anything else. But these past months I've come to realize that sometimes decisions have to be made alone—even those involving another person. I think I'm telling you that whatever happens, I won't give you up. Because if I do, then nothing has any meaning for me. Damn it, Gennie, I can't concentrate on my work or any other part of my life. Without you, I have no life."

She looked into his eyes and was overwhelmed by the sheer physical impact of meeting his gaze. It was as moving a sensation as the touch of his fingertips. She loved him so much. Why, then, was she so devastated by all he said? She remembered then. The veil was snatched away and harsh memories rushed back. She said in a small voice, "I wrote to you. I *did* write and tell you. I didn't imagine I did? That I can't have any more children. Did you get that letter?"

"Yes. It doesn't matter, Gennie. Did you think I want you only to be a brood mare? I want *you*. I love you. I want to spend my life with you. I never want to be far from your side again, never. I came to ask you again to marry me."

"Do I look terrible? They won't let me have a mirror."

"Nothing permanent, Gennie. Bruises on your face. They said there were burns."

"Yes. You can't see those other scars, can you?"

"Gennie, it's you I love, the essence of you. Nothing they did to you can change that. It will still be there when you're an old lady of ninety."

"I didn't mean what the Gestapo did to me. I meant what Dutton did to me. I think perhaps you mean what you say—now—about it not making any difference to you. You're blinded by emotions that I understand very well, because I feel them too. But eventually you would come to feel you'd been deprived of something important. Then I wouldn't be able to bear it . . . knowing that if I'd just been strong, now—"

"Gennie, I'm not going to take no for an answer. It's out of your hands now. We're going to be together. There won't be any peace for either of us if we aren't."

She leaned back on the stiff hospital pillow. "We can't escape one another, you and I, can we? We each felt the other's presence long before we ever met, and we're never really apart even when distance separates us. I suppose it will always be so. It's an incurable malaise we have."

"A malaise called love, Gennie. Will you marry me, come home with me?"

She asked abruptly, "Don't you want children of your own?"

A stricken, trapped expression claimed his face. He drew a deep breath and seemed afraid to speak for a moment. She watched the different emotions changing his eyes, his mouth, telling of some deep turmoil; then his words came with great difficulty. "I didn't want to tell you this now . . . not until you're feeling stronger. Gennie, I have a son."

She stared at him, too amazed to feel an immediate reaction. "Why didn't you ever tell me?"

"He was born this year."

"*This* year? Then, you were married?"

"No. A brief affair. I never dreamed—"

"But why are you asking *me* to marry you? What about the boy's mother?"

"She died. She was killed in an accident when he was only a couple of weeks old. I adopted him. Gennie, he's Specks' grandson. I have to tell you this, because he's one-fourth Negro. You've never been to America, so it's no use my trying to explain—" He broke off, ran his hand through his hair in a gesture of baffled exasperation. "Not that you'd understand even if you lived there, I guess. There's a mystique to black-white relationships in the South that's beyond the understanding of outsiders."

"I understand perfectly, Matt. You're asking me to marry you and be a mother to your son. You feel this is a tidy solution all around. And I can hardly express outrage—since I myself conceived a child outside of marriage—can I? It's all quite logical. You fell in love with a barren woman and so impregnated another woman. Now you expect the barren woman to be grateful that motherhood is restored to her so that she can marry you without a qualm, because you have your son, your immortality."

"Gennie, no. No, it isn't like that at all."

"Did you meet her, have your affair with her . . . before or after I sent you that letter and you knew I couldn't have children?"

"For God's sake, Gennie!"

"Please go. And don't come back. It's over. Once and for all, Matt, it's over. I feel more betrayed at this moment than ever before in my life."

She turned her face from him.

A chill wind shook the trees, sending the last of the dead leaves swirling about their faces. Nancy's cheeks were pink with the cold, and Matt pushed his hands into his coat pockets. They had stopped beside the gateposts leading to Saxon Hall, where once elegant wrought-iron gates formed a fragile barrier against the world. "Go on in, lad," Nancy urged. "If you don't go now, you'll miss her. The new owners arrive tomorrow and Gennie hasn't told me where she's going to live. She's in there saying good-bye to her home. Go to her."

Matt looked at her helplessly. "How is she feeling? How did she seem to you?"

"Stronger, I think. It's hard to say, she's so delicate looking."

"They warned me at the hospital that she shouldn't have discharged herself yet. They've had a couple of people who escaped after being held by the Gestapo who . . . who . . . just died. I don't want to do anything to hurt her."

"She needs you. She doesn't know it, but she does."

"Why did it have to be today, of all days, that she has to move out?"

"Her birthday? Well, couldn't be helped, I suppose. Most of the furniture's gone already."

"Good-bye, Nancy. Thank you for everything."

Matt began to walk up the drive. The November sky was a pallid noncolor, the air cemetery damp. His shoes crunched the frozen gravel. The date—November 11, 1941—kept dancing in front of his eyes. Geneva's birthday. Could she bear to leave her home today? Oh, God, was there any way to make her smile again?

He reached the house, climbed the steps, passed the twin stone eagles. The front doors were open and he saw Geneva immediately, standing in the hall in front of an empty alcove. Out of her hospital bed she seemed even thinner, more fragile looking. Her dark hair was short, falling in soft waves about her face, emphasizing her pallor. When he spoke her name, she looked at him and her eyes were opalescent gray, luminous with tears. He felt a tremendous wave of both love and compassion.

She spoke as though he had been there with her for some time and they were merely continuing a conversation. "We used to gather here around the grandfather clock, every year on the eleventh day of the eleventh month, to mourn the dead of the First World War. I think of it with capital letters now—because we're in the midst of the Second World War. I suppose your son will fight in the Third World War. Funny, I can almost see the clock . . . a great monstrosity with a huge brass pendulum and two brass weights that looked like shell casings. It had a booming chime. I used to think those eleven chimes would never end. But of course they did. Everything ends."

Matt was silent, feeling her pain, not knowing how to comfort her. Several doors were open, giving glimpses of empty rooms, and her voice rang in hollow echoes. He said, "Perhaps it would help to remember the happy times you spent here." He crossed the marble floor to stand at her side. At least she was not angered by his arrival. She didn't even seem surprised to see him.

She looked past him, through the open front doors. "I would have liked to see the daffodils lining the drive, just once more. Do you know we once had a cook who picked the daffodils, dipped them in lemon juice and egg white, and sprinkled them with powdered sugar? Can you imagine crystalized daffodils? Isn't that absurd?"

"No. I think it's charming."

"I kept one or two pieces of furniture. They're in storage. I do hope they aren't bombed. There's so little left. The thread in the tapestry that was the Saxon family is severed forever. Oh, I forgot, you don't know what I'm talking about—I'm not sure I know myself. I think of it all as a tapestry. Have you ever been in a concert hall, at the very end of the performance, and been aware of the fading echo of a great symphony? That's how I feel about them . . . my adopted family that is no more."

"It's a sad day for you, Gennie. I wish I could help."

"There's still the colliery, of course. But they tell me that as soon as the war's over, the coal mines will be nationalized; it's inevitable." She walked across the hall to the foot of the staircase and ran her hand down the carved newel post. "The new owners of the house have a factory in Liverpool that makes bullets for rifles and machine guns. No children in the family, just a couple and his mother. His wife said she thought the old place was a bit gloomy; she'd have to get all the wood painted, cheer it up." Her forefinger made a small loving circle on the golden patina of the wood. "I'm glad Father didn't hear that."

She turned and looked at Matt. "I knew you'd come, of course. I think perhaps I came back today because I was expecting you."

"I couldn't leave without seeing you again. I've been staying in the village, waiting for you to come back."

"I expect you're anxious to see your son again."

"I want to explain—if I can—how it happened with Leah and me. I'm not trying to throw up a smokescreen. I'm not excusing my affair with her and I'm not asking you to forgive. She came along at a time in my life when I was confused and vulnerable. I wish I could wipe out the entire episode, but I can't, Gennie, so I have to live with it—and the knowledge that I hurt you by it—for the rest of my life. Gennie, it wasn't love. It was a giving-in to human weakness—like eating when we aren't hungry, or shucking responsibility for a mistake, or being amused by someone else's misfortune. We do it, then we feel like hell afterward. I didn't even particularly like her. I couldn't talk to her, except in banalities. She played on my senses and my nerves and I knew, all the time I was with her, that I would regret what I was doing. What I'm trying to tell you is that there was no depth to my relationship with her—not as there is with you."

"But there was a tangible result." Geneva's voice shook. "Your son."

"Gennie, what I told you in the hospital . . . that wasn't

the whole story. I'm not absolutely sure he *is* my son. His mother . . . well, I wasn't her only lover. But he *could* be mine. I probably would have adopted him anyway—not because of her or me and what we were to each other, but because of Specks. It was a way to repay him. To go back to the beginning and try again, avoid all the mistakes of the last time. I guess that's the best any of us can hope for. A fresh start, another try."

Geneva's lips parted, he thought in surprise, but perhaps it was in sudden understanding. He ached to hold her in his arms so much that he had to keep his hands balled into fists inside his coat pockets. She said softly, "After you left the hospital that night, I kept going over it all again and again, in my mind. Trying to reweave the broken threads."

"Yes, I know. I did the same thing. You know, when I was a boy, Specks and I spent a couple of years along the Mississippi—just bumming around, I guess. I remember one day we were fishing and I asked him why he'd taken care of me, given up so much for me. He said, 'Lookit all the trees growing down the riverbank, Matt. How come you suppose they all came to be here? Now some of them was here in the very beginning, sure—but lots more were just seeds that got fetched in by birds and they took root and grew. And some trees dropped their seeds in the river, got carried off, and grew in places where even the bird hadn't been. Now you reckon that bird know he's planting a tree? Heck, no, he don't know. I reckon I thought I was bringing you up 'cause your daddy and me was friends, Matt—but see, there was more to it than that.' Gennie, I didn't really understand, at the time, what he was telling me with his simple wisdom. The analogy of the bird carrying the seed and the current of the river planting the tree in some distant place, unaware. We're here, linking the generations, making sure our species survives, sometimes without even knowing how or why. We're just a part of the grand design. We've got to keep it going along on a current of faith. I guess it's a way to perceive destiny. Gennie, Specks was trying to tell me that we're all each other's children and father and mother to every generation."

He held his breath, watching her, not knowing if she understood. Her lips were compressed slightly, as though she were afraid to speak. After an eternal minute she said, "I remember once my father had a painting cleaned and we discovered the artist had painted one picture over another—

the same scene, but shown in a subtly different way, a more careful blending of light and shade. I kept remembering that picture . . . while I tormented myself with thoughts of you in the arms of another woman, and I wasn't sure of the significance of the image until now. You see, I wanted there to be hope. Not only for us, but for humanity. Matt . . . you just gave it to me."

His hands came slowly out of his pockets. "Gennie . . . Gennie, are you telling me what I hope to God you're telling me?"

She took the single step that closed the distance between them, and he enfolded her in his arms, feeling a long shuddering sigh slip away from them, not knowing if it came from her or from himself. He kissed her eyelids where the tears dampened her lashes and her cheek where the last of her bruises was fading. "You'll come back with me? Home to America with me? We can be at Greenboughs by Christmas."

"Yes. Yes, we'll spend Christmas in your home," she said clinging to him. "Wonderful Christmas 1941. Tell me what it will be like to leave the war behind. Tell me what it will be like to live in a country at peace."

They arrived in America just under a month later, on December 7, 1941, the day Pearl Harbor was bombed and the United States entered the war.